複製・替換・零失誤的
英文E-mail
實用性、正確度最高！

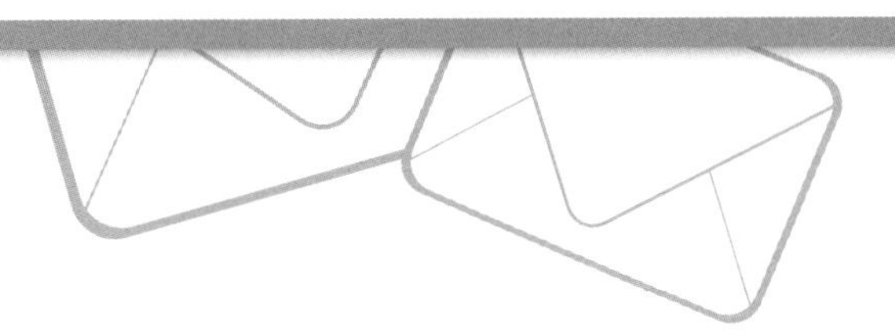
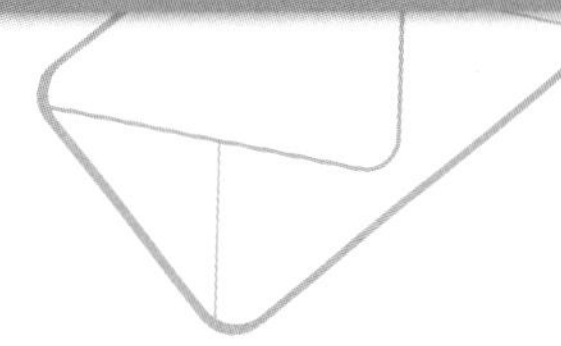

本書

作者介紹

Hello readers!
In this book I will introduce correct English phrases that I would love to use.
各位讀者大家好。
本書收錄的都是正確的英語說法，我自己也經常使用喔！

中川萬里

共同撰寫本書的工作伙伴日語不好，所以託他們的福（！？），我的英語溝通能力持續提升。但是，當他們要求我使用正確的英語時，我的聲音就會越來越小…。

Patrick

大阪腔日語說得非常流利的紐西蘭人，經常有人認為「他其實是在大阪出生的吧？」

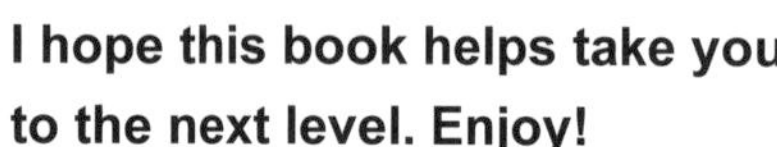

I hope this book helps take you to the next level. Enjoy!
希望本書能提升你的英語能力。請用愉快的心情好好學習吧！

Janet

喜歡說冷笑話的美國人，個性和冷靜的外表完全不搭。雖然從事英語旁白錄製工作，私底下最常用的語言還是日語。

I hope you all enjoy using this book as much as we enjoyed writing it!
我們編寫這本書的時候非常開心，所以希望各位讀者也能開開心心地善用書中的內容。

前言

「英語？多多少少會講一些啊。我喜歡出國旅行，有時候工作上也會用到英語。」

但是，你們是否一直在使用不正確的英語呢？

我們有時會用中文的邏輯來使用英文，外國人聽了卻會感到一頭霧水。因為，中文裡有許多慣用語並不能用英文直接翻譯，例如，「你給我過來」這句話不能翻譯成 “You give me come”，「讓我看看」也不是 “Let me see see”。

像這樣的英文，就被稱為「中式英文」。我們學了這麼久的英語，當然要學最道地最正確的英文，怎麼能夠放任自己使用「台灣人可以理解，但外國人聽不懂」的英文呢？

所以，這次我和幾位以英語為母語的老師們，一起彙整了這本「絕對不會讓外國人偷偷笑你的英語不道地」的英語寫作書。

本書提供工作上或日常生活裡各種情境的字彙和例句，讀者可以配合自己的需求自行替換字彙，自由運用。以英語為母語的老師們也在書中提出許多建議，請大家務必善加利用，努力擺脫隨口說出錯誤英語的壞習慣。

本書使用說明

本書附25個常用商業主題，包括詢價、請託、談判、訂購、緊急事件與約定會面等，讀者只要找到自己需要的主題、選擇想要的詞彙，就能輕鬆寫出一封完美的英文E-mail。

25個常用商業主題

E-mail範例

為了讓讀者了解如何將本書句型實際應用於E-mail寫作，常用的商業書信主題會附上全文範例以及中文翻譯。

※因為每個人的個人資料都不同，範例內的收件人稱謂、寄件人姓名、信末結尾語（例如Regards）與署名等，這些部分在中文翻譯裡會省略。

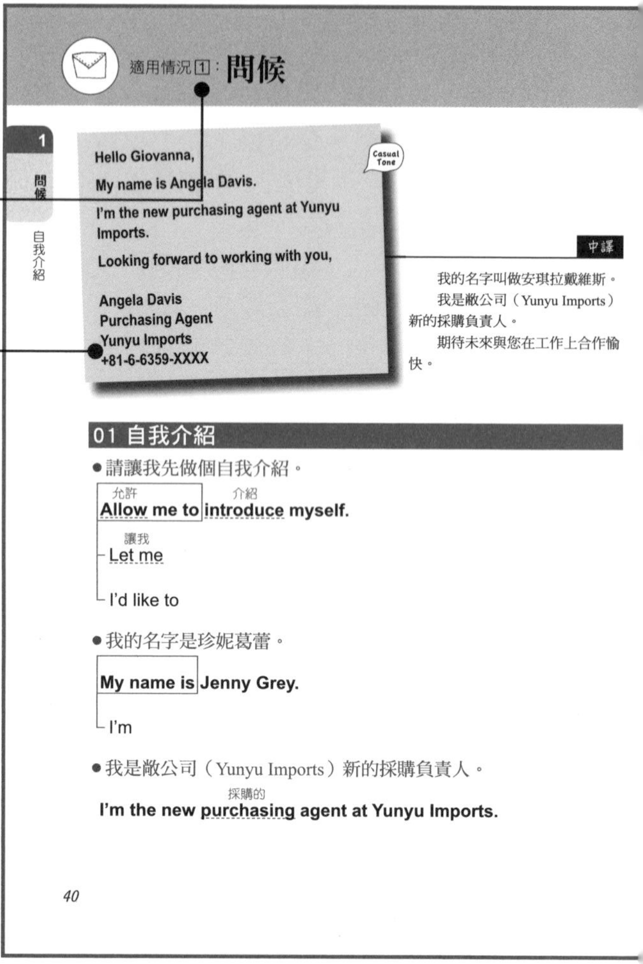

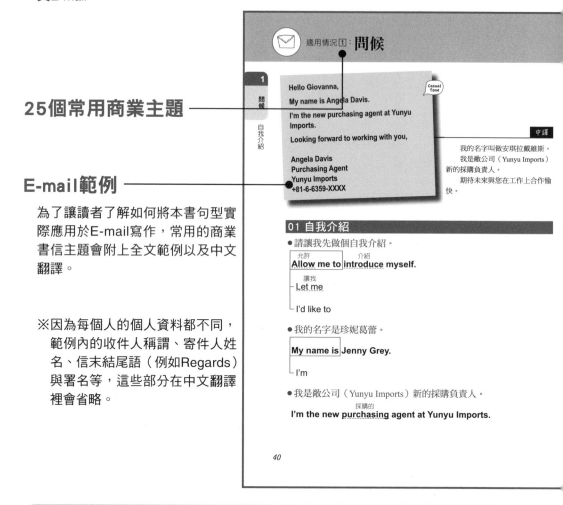

適用情況1：問候

1 問候

自我介紹

Casual Tone

Hello Giovanna,

My name is Angela Davis.

I'm the new purchasing agent at Yunyu Imports.

Looking forward to working with you,

Angela Davis
Purchasing Agent
Yunyu Imports
+81-6-6359-XXXX

中譯

我的名字叫做安琪拉戴維斯。

我是敝公司（Yunyu Imports）新的採購負責人。

期待未來與您在工作上合作愉快。

01 自我介紹

● 請讓我先做個自我介紹。

Allow me to（允許） **introduce**（介紹） **myself.**

Let me（讓我）

I'd like to

● 我的名字是珍妮葛蕾。

My name is Jenny Grey.

I'm

● 我是敝公司（Yunyu Imports）新的採購負責人。

I'm the new purchasing（採購的） **agent at Yunyu Imports.**

40

小試身手！

針對想擺脫中式英文的人，我們以台灣人常犯的英語錯誤為基礎，編寫了二選一的測驗題。解答就在下一頁的最下方（請把書翻轉過來看），方便讀者立刻對答案。請務必挑戰看看！

小試身手
空格裡的正確答案是哪一個呢？
The cat is eating ______ dinner.
❶ it's
❷ its
解答就在下一頁

Formal Tone
Casual Tone

較口語且不拘小節的語氣標示為"Casual Tone"，較正式的語氣標示為"Formal Tone"，請根據你的收信對象來選擇適當的字彙。

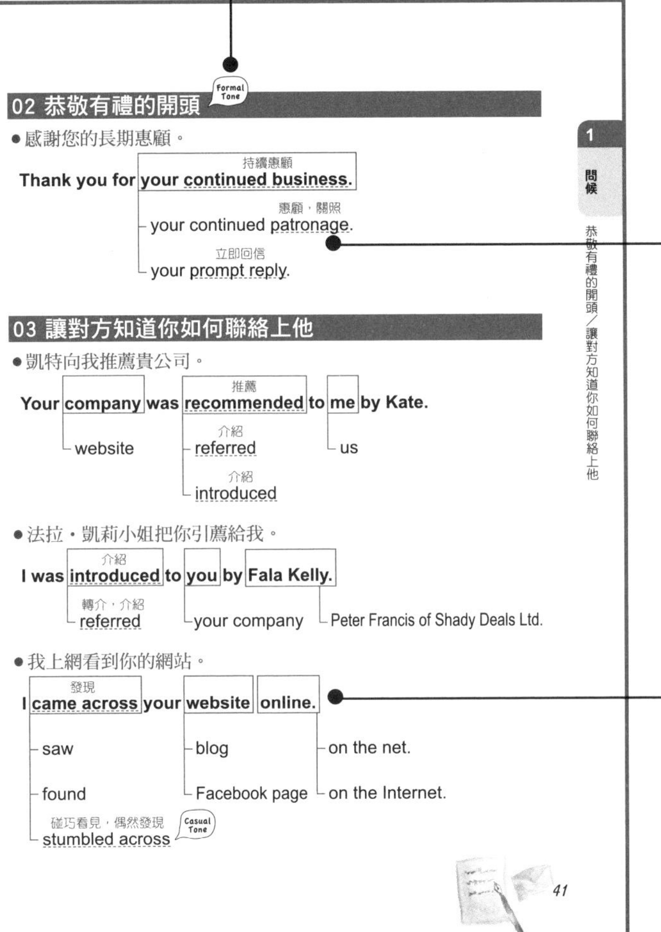
02 恭敬有禮的開頭
Formal Tone
●感謝您的長期惠顧。
持續惠顧
Thank you for your continued business.
惠顧，關照
your continued patronage.
立即回信
your prompt reply.
03 讓對方知道你如何聯絡上他
●凱特向我推薦貴公司。
推薦
Your company was recommended to me by Kate.
website
介紹
referred
us
介紹
introduced
●法拉・凱莉小姐把你引薦給我。
介紹
I was introduced to you by Fala Kelly.
轉介，介紹
referred
your company
Peter Francis of Shady Deals Ltd.
●我上網看到你的網站。
發現
I came across your website online.
saw
blog
on the net.
found
Facebook page
on the Internet.
碰巧看見，偶然發現
stumbled across
Casual Tone
1
問候
恭敬有禮的開頭／讓對方知道你如何聯絡上他
41

不必查字典！

較困難的單字上方都附有中文解釋，不需另外查字典就能立刻讀懂整個句子。

隨選隨用的「替換式字彙」！

以粗體字標示出主要句型，並提供多組關鍵字替換，方便讀者自行重組、靈活運用。全書包括650個句型，共有9900種變化！

使用範例

"**I came across your website online.**" 為主要句型。
"came across" 可替換 "saw / found / stumbled across"
"website" 可替換成 "blog / Facebook page"
"online"可替換成 "on the net / on the internet"
自行選擇重組後，可寫成 "I found your blog on the net." / "I stumbled across your Facebook page on the Internet." 等36個不同的句子！

Contents

適用情況 3

請託
Requests

適用情況 4

交涉・說服
Negotiations

適用情況 5

同意・支持
Agreements

適用情況 6

訂單
Orders

Contents

Contents

Contents

Business E-mail Tips

附錄　英語萬用句典

一起努力
寫出一封
「簡潔零錯誤」的
E-mail吧！

第 1 章
別讓老外
偷偷笑你的英文不道地

!?
I'm exciting to write in English!

咦？我的英語很可笑嗎？

正在閱讀本書的各位讀者們，你們知道的英語單字和文法可能比我還多，一般的英語會話也沒什麼問題。但是，你的英語真的「正確」嗎？

當我們聽到外國人講中文的時候，常常也會覺得有些地方怪怪的，那是因為不同國家的人在發音、文法、文化以及習慣上都有所不同，所以他們說中文的時候，當然會出現一些獨特的錯誤。因此，無論英文程度多好，台灣人也會不自覺地使用中式英文（Chinese English），這是很自然的事情。

話雖如此，當我們在課堂上練習英文或是與朋友互動時，即使犯點錯也沒什麼好丟臉的；但是在工作場合中，或是有許多聽眾的大庭廣眾之下，為避免出糗，我們還是會想使用「正確的英語」。

1
試試看用英語說，
「我很喜歡狗！」
2
I like dog!!
咚！
3
4
I like a dog...?
咦？
5
I like dogs!!
汪！

可數名詞在這種情況下要用複數形才正確，但是因為中文裡沒有單複數的差別，我常常忘記要用複數形。一旦有人說這樣不對，我就會失去信心，開始在名詞前面亂加“a”或“the”，然後聲音越來越小…。大家也有過同樣的經驗嗎？

台灣人是個「重禮數」的民族，因此中文裡有許多客套話與慣用句。這些用語，如果直接翻成英文，聽在外國人耳裡就會覺得很奇怪。

例如台灣人打招呼時最常問的「吃飽沒？」，與人道別時常用的「改天讓我請你吃飯吧」，提起某人時可能會提到的「我跟他不熟耶！」，跟上司套交情時會說的「以後就請您多照顧了」，請人幫忙事情時會用的「這件事情就麻煩你了…」諸如此類的慣用句，在英文中只有意義相近的用法，而不能將這些句子逐字翻譯成英語使用。

使用英語時，請好好思考「我應該說些什麼才對」，然後用正確的英語表達出來，你的英語遣詞用字才會更加優雅得體。

1
Sorry for keeping you waiting!
2
咦？
我沒有久等啊？
她不是很準時嗎？
笑容滿面
3

與人相約見面時，有人習慣見面就跟對方說「不好意思，讓您久等了！」即使自己並沒有遲到。這是中文裡的客套話，我們聽起來並不覺得有什麼不妥。但如果你與外國人相約見面，對他說了 “Sorry for keep you waiting!”，對方就會覺得很奇怪，會想著：「你也是準時到啊，為什麼要這麼說呢？」

你有自信嗎!?
中式英文指數測驗

如果用說中文的習慣來說英文，

就很容易說出「中式英文」。

現在就來測試一下你的中式英文指數吧。

不管是對自己英文能力超有自信的人，

還是沒什麼自信的人，

都請你測試看看，

可以讓你更了解自己的英語弱點在哪裡！

測驗1 找出「錯誤的句子」，並在方框內打勾。

- □ I'm going to Canada next week. I'm so exciting!
- □ Please call me until 5:30pm.
- □ When are you going in Hawaii?
- □ I play skiing every winter.
- □ Do I need to bring both of books?
- □ Almost Japanese drink green tea everyday.
- □ Did you cut your hair?
- □ I weigh 50 kgs.
- □ We had a trouble at work.
- □ Do you drink Blandy?
- □ A: I love you. B: Me, too. / So do I.
- □ I was tried to travel in Thailand by myself.
- □ He is white hair.
- □ Did you reform your room?
- □ I want to image change.
- □ I'm going to yoga class now.
- □ I tripped to Hawaii.
- □ My boyfriend proposed me.
- □ I ate peanuts butter toast.
- □ A: I made a few mistakes on the job. B: Don't mind!

測驗2 找出錯誤的句子，並在錯誤的部分下方劃線。
請注意，以下也有完全正確的句子。

- Most Japanese can use chopsticks.
- He weights 68 kgs.
- I'm going to N.Y. 3 days later.
- Where are you come from?
- There were a little people.
- Satomi is a designer.
- I'm watching the TV.
- A: Who did you go with? B: Only one.
- Did you see the general elections by TV?
- Tiramisu is still famous in Japan.
- Do you like flied shrimp?
- I very enjoyed the party.
- What is this mean?
- I'll be back by the time you will arrive.
- I like listening music.
- I'm going to hair-make.
- Ali Baba said, "Open the Sesame!"
- What is happen?
- The cock at that restaurant was magnificent.
- It's relieved.

測驗3 哪一個中文翻譯是正確的呢？請從以下A、B、C三個選項中選出正確答案。

- **You can count on me.**

A：請交給我來處理。 B：可以算我一份喔。
C：請別小看我。

- **We're making good time.**

A：和我們在一起可以過得很開心。 B：我們的日子過得很快樂。
C：我們進展得比預期更快。

- **I'm not up to it.**

A：我不是上司。 B：我並不適任。
C：我不喜歡那個。

- **That's out of the question.**

A：那是不可能的。 B：請不要迴避問題。
C：這種事不需要問。

- **I got carried away.**

A：我去了很遠的地方。 B：我得意忘形了。
C：這是遠方寄來的東西。

- **I go camping once in a blue moon.**

A：天氣晴朗的時候，我會去露營。 B：我為了賞月而去露營。
C：我很少去露營。

- **Drop me a line when you get to L.A.**

A：抵達L.A.之後，要跟我聯絡喔。 B：抵達L.A.之後，我要下車喔。
C：你抵達L.A.的時候，我已經誤入歧途。

- **I was supposed to go to dinner with her, but she stood me up.**

A：我原本想和她去吃晚餐，但是她讓我等太久了。
B：我原本想和她去吃晚餐，但是她把我給惹火了。
C：我原本想和她去吃晚餐，但是她放我鴿子啊。

答案揭曉 你有自信嗎!?中式英文指數測驗

測驗1 找出「錯誤的句子」,並在方框內打勾。

☑ I'm going to Canada next week. I'm so exciting!
正確用法是 I'm going to Canada next week. I'm so excited.

☑ Please call me until 5:30pm. 正確用法是 Please call me by 5:30pm.

☑ When are you going in Hawaii? 正確用法是 When are you going to Hawaii?

☑ I play skiing every winter. 正確用法是 I go skiing every winter.

☑ Do I need to bring both of books? 正確用法是 Do I need to bring both_books?

☑ Almost Japanese drink green tea everyday.
正確用法是 Most Japanese drink green tea everyday.

☐ Did you cut your hair?

☐ I weigh 50 kgs.

☑ We had a trouble at work. 正確用法是 We had_trouble at work.

☑ Do you drink Blandy? 正確用法是 Do you drink Brandy?

☑ A: I love you. B: Me, too. / So do I. 正確用法是 I love you, too.

☑ I was tried to travel in Thailand by myself.
正確用法是 I travelled to Thailand by myself.

☑ He is white hair. 正確用法是 He has white / gray hair.

☑ Did you reform your room? 正確用法是 Did you rearrange / redo / remodel your room?

☑ I want to image change. 正確用法是 I want to change my image.

☐ I'm going to yoga class now.

☑ I tripped to Hawaii. 正確用法是 I took a trip to Hawaii.

☑ My boyfriend proposed me. 正確用法是 My boyfriend proposed to me.

☑ I ate peanuts butter toast. 正確用法是 I ate toast with peanut butter.

☑ A: I made a few mistakes on the job. B: Don't mind!
正確用法是 Don't worry about it.

測驗2 找出錯誤的句子，並在錯誤的部分下方劃線。
請注意，以下也有完全正確的句子。

- Most Japanese can use chopsticks.
- **He weights 68 kgs.** 正確用法是 He weighs 68 kgs.
- **I'm going to N.Y. 3 days later.** 正確用法是 I'm going to N.Y. in 3 days.
- **Where are you come from?** 正確用法是 Where do you come from?
- **There were a little people.** 正確用法是 There were a few people.
- Satomi is a designer.
- **I'm watching the TV.** 正確用法是 I'm watching_TV.
- **A: Who did you go with? B: Only one.** 正確用法是 I went alone. / I went by myself.
- **Did you see the general elections by TV?**
  正確用法是 Did you see the general elections on TV?
- **Tiramisu is still famous in Japan.** 正確用法是 Tiramisu is still popular in Japan.
- **Do you like flied shrimp?** 正確用法是 Do you like fried shrimp?
- **I very enjoyed the party.** 正確用法是 I really enjoyed the party.
- **What is this mean?** 正確用法是 What does this mean?
- **I'll be back by the time you will arrive.**
  正確用法是 I'll be back by the time you_arrive.
- **I like listening music.** 正確用法是 I like listening to music.
- **I'm going to hair-make.** 正確用法是 I'm going to get my hair done.
- **Ali Baba said, "Open the Sesame!"** 正確用法是 Ali Baba said, "Open_Sesame!"
- **What is happen?** 正確用法是 What_happened?
- **The cock at that restaurant was magnificent.**
  正確用法是 The cook at that restaurant was magnificent.
- **It's relieved.** 正確用法是 It's a relief. / I'm relieved. / What a relief!

測驗3　哪一個中譯是正確的呢？請從以下A、B、C三個選項中選出正確答案。

- **You can count on me.**

A：請交給我來處理。

- **We're making good time.**

C：我們進展得比預期更快。

- **I'm not up to it.**

B：我並不適任。

- **That's out of the question.**

A：那是不可能的。

- **I got carried away.**

B：我得意忘形了。

- **I go camping once in a blue moon.**

C：我很少去露營。

- **Drop me a line when you get to L.A.**

A：抵達L.A.之後，要跟我聯絡喔。

- **I was supposed to go to dinner with her, but she stood me up.**

C：我原本想和她去吃晚餐，但是她放我鴿子啊。

中式英文指數測驗的結果如何？

「雖然覺得自己英文還不錯，但還是會不經意地犯錯…」你是不是也有這種不甘心的感覺呢？

文法或拼字稍有錯誤（或者發音有點不準），這都算是枝微末節，就算出現在對話當中，通常也不會對溝通造成影響。但是這些錯誤如果化為文字，白紙黑字就顯得有些丟臉。所以，要注意避免把說中文的習慣套用在英文裡，努力降低你的中式英文指數吧。

從下一頁開始，我們要來探討，台灣人常誤用的「中式英文」究竟是怎麼一回事。

出現中式英文的原因

字典裡查不到的微妙差異

台灣人在寫英文時，經常犯的錯誤就是將中文直接逐字翻譯成英語使用。

舉例來說，「羨慕的」如果查字典就會找到 “envious” 這個單字，但是其實 “envious” 多半用來意指「眼紅」和「艷羨」，與我們在中文應答中常用的「好好喔～」、「好羨慕喔～」的語感不一樣，不能直接替換使用。“envious” 這個字通常用在 “He became a millionaire.” → “I am truly envious.” 這種無法輕易實現的事物上，或者在 “I envy Jay Chou’s talent.” 這類艷羨別人才華的情況下使用。

I went to Hawaii on vacation!
Oh, I envy you!!
...
1
2
3

用更自然的英語說出「好好喔～」、「好羨慕喔～」
Oh man!
Lucky you!
I'm so jealous!

再來看看另外一個例子。要形容一道菜「好吃的」，查字典的話就會找到 “delicious” 這個單字，這和 “envious” 的情況相同，並不是單字的意義不對，而是使用在日常生活中會讓人感到很誇張。“delicious” 是在吃非常特別的餐點，或者發現完全合乎自己口味的食物時使用的單字。

之所以會出現這些問題，是因為大家「太依賴字典」或者「太相信逐字翻譯」的結果。翻閱字典的時候，除了查看單字本身的意思，也必須同時閱讀例句，看看這個字的語感是否適合用來表達自己的情況。

It's delicious♡

用更隨性的英語，說說看「這個好好吃！」
This tastes good!
This is good!
Yum!

用英文寫E-mail的訣竅

第一次寫E-mail給對方時，只需要在第一封信的開頭自我介紹，並寫些簡單的問候語讓收信人認識你，接下來的書信往返就可以就事論事，直接切入重點。不過，習慣用中文寫E-mail的人，在信的開頭和結尾若不加上一些問候語，總覺得有些沒禮貌，會有這種顧慮的人想必不少吧。因此，以下列舉一些雖然沒有必要，但是寫了人家也不會覺得奇怪的英文句子。

恭敬有禮的E-mail開頭

1「承蒙您的照顧」

可以替換成…

Thank you for your E-mail.
感謝您的來信。

Thank you for your payment.
已收到您支付的費用，謝謝您。

Thank you for shopping with us.
感謝您購買我們的商品。

Thank you for sending the information.
謝謝您把資料寄給我。

Thank you for your interest in our products.
謝謝您對我們的商品感興趣。

Thank you for your inquiry regarding....
感謝您詢問與…相關的問題。

恭敬有禮的E-mail結尾

2「請您多多指教」

可以替換成…

I look forward to hearing from you.
期待您的回信。

I look forward to seeing you.
期待與您相聚。

I look forward to meeting you in person.
期待與您見面。

I wish you continued success.
祝您事業成功，更上層樓。

I wish you all the best.
祝您一切順利。

I hope you like our products.
希望您會喜歡我們的產品。

I hope you enjoy our products.
希望您滿意我們的產品。

Let me know if you have any more questions.
假如您還有任何疑問，請與我聯絡。

Please don't hesitate to contact us with any questions.
如果您有任何疑問，不必客氣，請與我們聯絡。

小心喔！口語和寫作用語不可混用

口語上，把 “I am going to...” 省略成 “I’m gonna...” 是沒問題的，但在寫作的時候，還是寫成 “I am going to...” 或者 “I’m going to...” 比較好。當然，跟熟悉親友間的書信往來使用簡略的句子也無傷大雅，不過對初學者來說，還是先從最正確完整的句子開始練習，打好英文寫作的基礎吧。

以英語為母語的人也搞不清楚！日期的陷阱

舉例來說，2012年3月7日這個日期，在台灣會簡寫為2012/3/7。那麼，英語系國家的人會怎麼寫呢？美式英文寫作March 7, 2012，或者3/7/2012。英式英文則會寫作7 March 2012，或者7/3/2012。

更容易令人混淆的是，2000年的「20」也常常被省略，如此一來，哪一個數字代表月、哪一個代表日，真是讓人摸不著頭緒。

英語圈的人在自己的國家裡會各自使用自己的標示法，當然可以只用數字標記日期，但是，假如你有機會和世界各國的人用英文交流，為了保險起見，最好還是寫成March 7, 2012或者7 March 2012，如此一來，即使順序錯誤，對方還是看得懂。尤其是在寫英文商業書信時，盡量不要省略年份和月份比較好。

! 日期的書寫方式

英國式 → 日／月／年

4/8/1971

4/8/71

4th August 1971

4 August 1971

※月份和年份之間不需要加逗號。

美國式 → 月／日／年

8/4/1971

8/4/71

August 4th, 1971

August 4, 1971

※如果只需標示月份而不必精確地寫出哪一天，就不必在日期與年份之間加逗號。

Ex: The contest was held in December 2009.

第 2 章
開始用英語寫作之前的重點提醒

擺脫中式英文！

英文寫作的基礎在於
「簡潔扼要」

在開始動筆用英文寫作之前，有幾個重點必須注意。

跟英語系國家的人不同，同一件事情或概念，台灣人習慣以委婉的文字敘述做說明，外國人則力求清楚明瞭，務必要讓對方了解自己的意思。因此，若以書寫中文的習慣寫英文信，內容往往會變得拐彎抹角，想表達的重點也會顯得曖昧不清。這或許是因為台灣人習慣說「客套話」了，連帶影響了寫作時的遣詞用字。

用英文寫作的時候，不必擔心「如果直接切入重點，對方會不會覺得我很冷淡？」或者「文字敘述太簡單，是否會顯得我文筆不好？」反而要將「簡潔扼要」的原則牢記在心。

只要注意文法和拼字不要出錯，文字敘述盡量言簡意賅，務必要讓收信人一目了然，相信你很快就能掌握英文寫作的要領了。

擺脫中式英文！

如何寫出文法通順且自然的英文E-mail

1 簡潔扼要

首先要注意的是，不必每次一開頭都加一句「你好嗎？」或「感謝您的來信」。

只有在第一次寫信給對方時，才需要在信的開頭簡單自我介紹，或者附加幾句問候語，其後信件往返的重點則要盡量簡潔扼要，用詞遣字時注意禮貌就行了。必要時，善用條列方式清楚表達自己的想法，避免長篇大論。

2 標題

英文E-mail的標題避免使用「Your Order」、「Information」、「Thanks for your cooperation」之類語焉不詳的一般詞彙，以免被誤認為垃圾郵件。盡量在標題中提及自家公司名稱以及寄信目的，最好讓收件人一看到標題，就能大概猜到信件內容為何。

3 收件人稱謂

如果你是客戶，寫信向提供服務或商品的窗口聯絡時，開頭可以用輕鬆的筆調向對方打招呼，例如「Hi Giovanna,...」。而寫信給客戶時，就要稍微恭敬謹慎一些，改以「Dear Andrew,...」之類的用語開頭。

一般的書信往來，不必在收信人名字前方附加Mr.或Ms.等稱謂。

4 條列說明

有很多事要說的時候，例如提出許多疑問或者說明採購項目時，請務必以條列的方式分項說明。此外，若對方以條列方式來信詢問各項事宜，也要以條列方式回信。

5 署名

署名以簡單最佳，不要附註複雜的標記。電子郵件只需點選回信按鍵，就能自動回覆，因此只要附上自己的姓名、公司名稱（單位或部門名稱）以及電話就足夠了。

使句子更流暢！外國人都在用的英語接續詞

obviously 顯然地

• Obviously, we cannot accomplish that (task) overnight.
顯然地，我們無法只用一個晚上就完成那項工作。

apparently 看起來，似乎

• Apparently, we misunderstood.
看來我們是誤會了。

evidently 明顯地，顯然

• Evidently, he has mistaken me for you.
他顯然是把我當成你了吧。

in addition 除此之外

• In addition, we believe that economy should go hand in hand with ecology.
除此之外，我們相信經濟和環保必須相輔相成。

類似用法
furthermore 此外，再者／besides 而且（用於肯定句時）
moreover 除此之外，再加上

consequently 因此，結果

• Consequently, your order will be three weeks late.
因此，貴公司的訂單將會延遲三週交貨。

類似用法 as a result 結果／for this reason 因此

while 做某事的這段時間，（趁著）做某事的時候

• While I was waiting for Mr. Chen, I ate lunch.
等待陳先生的那段時間，我去吃了午餐。

generally 一般而言，整體而言

• Generally, we don't allow pets in the building, but we'll make an exception in this case.
我們通常不允許寵物進入館內，但是這次我們可以特別通融。

類似用法 as a rule 原則上／ordinarily 通常地／for the most part 大多數情況下

for example 舉例來說

• For example, if you buy two, we'll give you one free.
舉例來說，如果你買兩個，我們會再免費贈送一個給你。

類似用法 for instance 例如／in this case 在這種情況下

for one thing 首先，其一

• For one thing, he drinks.
首先，他會喝酒。（例如想列舉某人的缺點時，可以用這種方式表達）

above all = above all things 最重要，尤其，首先

• In order to write English well, you must, above all things, read as much as you can.
如果想用英文寫出通順自然的文章，首先你必須盡可能地大量閱讀。

apart from 另當別論，除…之外

• Apart from the news, I don't watch TV at all.
除了新聞之外，我完全不看電視。。

類似用法 besides 另當別論，…除外（用於否定句時）／other than …以外
aside from 另當別論，將…排除在外／except …除外

in essence 本質上，從本質來看

• In essence, it simply can't be done.
基本上，那是不可能的任務。

類似用法 in other words 用另外一種說法，換言之／in short 簡而言之，一言以蔽之

on one hand 一方面

- On one hand, we like the design.
  一方面是我們喜歡這個設計。

類似用法 on the other hand 另一方面／on the contrary 恰恰相反
however 但是，然而／still 話雖如此，不過

first / firstly 首先

- First, we'll have a representative call you.
  首先，我們會請業務代表致電給你。

類似用法 secondly 第二，其次／then 然後／next 接著／lastly 最後

at first 一開始，最初

- At first, we were planning to do the translation in-house.
  一開始我們計畫請公司內部的人執行那件翻譯工作。

類似用法 to begin with 首先，起初／for now 現在／for the time being 當下，目前
in the meantime 在此期間／meanwhile 在這段時間裡，同時

one more thing 最後再提一件事

- One more thing, keep in mind that there will be a price increase next month.
  最後提醒一件事，請記得下個月價格就要上漲。

類似用法 one last thing 最後再提一件事／lastly 最後

by the way 順帶一提

- By the way, we have finished the new catalogue if you'd like a copy.
  順帶一提，我們已經做好新的目錄了，你想要一本嗎？

類似用法 incidentally 順帶一提，附帶一提／one another note 岔個題，改變一下話題
on a personal note 補充一下個人意見

later on 隨後，以後

- Later on, we'll talk about price.
  我們隨後再談談價格的問題。

類似用法 afterward 之後，以後／with this (problem) in mind 將這件事放在心上

in conclusion 結論，總而言之，最後

- In conclusion, we'd like to thank each and every one of you for purchasing this book.
  最後，我們想向每一位購買本書的人表達謝意。

類似用法 finally 最後，在結束之前，終於，最終，決定性的
in the long run 從長遠來看，最後
after all 畢竟，終究，歸根究底／in brief 簡單來說，簡而言之

in spite of 雖然

- In spite of the rain, we thoroughly enjoyed our time.
  雖然下雨了，但是我們玩得非常盡興。

類似用法 despite 雖然／even though 雖然如此，即便如此
although 雖然／though 雖然

because of 由於

- Because of the excellent response, we would like to order ten more cases.
  由於反應非常熱烈，我們想再加訂十箱。

類似用法 due to 因為，…的結果／on account of 因為，由於／owing to 因為…

拉近彼此的距離！外國人常用的英語縮略語

下表列出的語句都不能使用於正式的商務書信，但卻都是外國人看一眼就能明瞭的英語縮略語。這些用法都非常口語，通常會出現在簡訊或MSN的對話裡，請先將這些省略的簡寫當作參考，即使看到外國人的來信中使用這類縮略語，你也能迅速明白對方的意思。

但在能寫出正確流暢的英文書信前，請先不要貿然使用這些語句。尤其特別注意標示★號的部分，除了與很熟的親友互動之外，要盡量避免使用。

簡寫	原本的單字	使用範例	原本的英語表達方式	意義
2	to, too, two	Andy's goin 2nite 2.	Andy's going tonight, too.	安迪今晚也會去喔。
4	for, four	Ths is 4 u!	This is for you!	這個給你！
8	ate	A: U eat my choc? B: Yep, I 8 it!	A: Did you eat my chocolate? B: Yes, I ate it!	A：你吃了我的巧克力嗎？ B：嗯，吃掉了！
@	at	Janet'll b thr @ 8am.	Janet will be there at 8:00am.	珍妮特早上八點會到。
~ng, ~in, 'ing, in'	~ing	im hvng a prty 2nite. wanna come?	I'm having a party tonight. Do you want to come?	今天晚上我要開派對。你想來嗎？
2nite, 2nght, tnght tonite	tonight	c u 2nite.	See you tonight.	晚上見。
2U2, 2u2	to you, too	Congrts 2u2!	Congratulations to you, too!	也恭喜你！
4 u	for you	Yep! I cn do tht 4 u.	Yes, I can do that for you.	啊，我可以幫你。
abt	about	B thr abt 7pm.	I'll be there about 7pm.	我大概晚上七點到喔。
aftr	after	plz call me aftr 7.	Please call me after 7:00.	七點以後打電話給我。
anywy	anyway	We shld go anywy.	We should go anyway.	不管怎樣我們都該去啦。
arr	arrive	Wht tme u arr 2day?	What time do you arrive today?	你今天幾點會到呢？
awy	away	I'll b awy frm 2nite til da wknd.	I'll be away from tonight till the weekend.	我今晚開始一直到週末都不在。
b	be	I'll b hme @ 10 2nite.	I'll be home at 10pm tonight.	今晚十點的時候我會在家。
b4	before	Call b4 u come!	Call before you come!	你來之前要打個電話給我喔！
babe, babes*	baby	Hey babe, r u ok? ★	Hey baby, are you okay? ★	寶貝，你還好嗎？
bday	birthday	Hppy Bday!!!	Happy Birthday!	生日快樂！
bro	brother, mate, pal	Hey bro! hru?	Hey brother/mate friend! How are you?	嘿！小子，你混得好嗎！？（用於男性之間）
bt	but	I'm goin 2nite bt I'll b a bit lte.	I'm going tonight, but I'll be a bit late.	我今晚會去，但是會遲到一下。

簡寫	原本的單字	使用範例	原本的英語表達方式	意義
btw	by the way	btw, I'll b cming wt my gf.	By the way, I'll be coming with my girlfriend.	對了，我會帶我女朋友一起去喔。
bf	boyfriend	Whts ur bfs nme?	What's your boyfriend's name?	你男朋友叫什麼名字？
c	see	k. c u @ hme thn.	Okay. See you at home then.	好。那家裡見。
c u	See you	c u 2nite!	See you tonight!	晚上見！
coz, bcoz	because	Mari cnt mke it coz of wrk.	Mari can't make it because of work.	麻里要工作所以沒辦法啦。
cud; cudnt	could; couldn't	Sry i cudnt mke it lst nite. wz bsy.	Sorry I couldn't make it last night. I was busy.	抱歉，我昨晚沒辦法去。我在忙。
cme, comin, comng	come, came	Can u cme 2 Hankyu dptmt str?	Can you come to Hankyu department store?	你可以到阪急百貨來嗎？
cuz	cousin	Tlk 2u l8r, cuz!	Talk to you later, cousin!	待會再跟你說，表哥（堂／表兄弟）！
da, d	the	I'm gona sty @ da Ritz in Tky.	I'm going to stay at the Ritz (Carlton) in Tokyo.	我會住在東京麗池卡登飯店。
dad	dad, father	Pls say hi 2 ur dad frm us!	Please say hi to your dad from us!	請代我向你爸問好。
dep, dprt, dpt, dprts	depart	my flgt dpts @ 11 am.	My flight departs at 11:00 am.	我的班機早上十一點出發。
dnt	don't	I dnt smk @ hme coz my gf hates it.	I don't smoke at home because my girlfriend hates it.	我不在家裡抽菸，因為我女朋友不喜歡。
dring, dar'ln*	darling	C u l8r d'ng.*	See you later darling.*	親愛的，待會見。（主要用於男朋友或丈夫。）
eg, ex	for example	For ex...	For example...	舉例來說…
eve, evng	evening	I'll tlk 2u ths evng.	I'll talk to you this evening.	今晚我想和你談談。
f2f	face to face, flesh to flesh	Y dnt we mt f2f?	Why don't we meet face to face?	何不見個面談一談？
frwd, fwrd, 4wrd	forward	I lk fwrd 2 c'ing* 2mrw.	I look forward to seeing you tomorrow.	我很期待明天與你見面。
fw	few	Brng a fw beers whn u come ovr.	Bring a few beers when you come over.	你過來的時候帶幾瓶啤酒來。
fyi	for your information	fyi, my flgt dprts @ 7:30 tmrw mrng.	For your information, my flight departs at 7:30 tomorrow morning.	我的班機明天早上七點半出發，供您參考。
Gd	Good	Gd 2 hear frm u.	Good to hear from you.	很高興收到你的消息。
Gday	Good day, Hello	Gday mate!	Good day / Hello mate.	嗨／哈囉／你好。
gf	girlfriend	Do u hv mre than 1 gf? ...yes.	Do you have more than 1 girlfriend? ...Yes.	你的女朋友不只一個啊？…嗯。
goin	going	Hwzit goin?	How is it going?	最近如何？／過得好嗎？
gona~	going to~	r u gona b @ da salsa prty 2nite?	Are you going to be at the salsa party tonight?	你今晚要去薩爾薩舞會嗎？
grt, gr8	great	Thts grt nws abt ur job prmtn!	That's great news about your job promotion!	聽說你升官啦，真是太棒了！

簡寫	原本的單字	使用範例	原本的英語表達方式	意義
gt	get, got	i gt sum frnds in NZ.	I've got some friends in New Zealand.	我在紐西蘭交了幾個新朋友喔。
hldys, hols	holidays	Whn do ur hldys strt?	When do your holidays start?	什麼時候開始休假呢？
hon, hons*	honey	C u l8r hons.*	See you later, honey.*	再見，甜心。
Howzit goin?	How's everything going (with you)?	Howzit goin @ work?	How's everything going at work?	工作還順利嗎？
hr	hour	Sry! B thr in 1hr!	Sorry! I'll be there in an/one hour!	抱歉！我會在一小時之內趕到！
hv, hs, hvnt; hving	have, has, haven't,: having	Hvnt u gt any mny?	Haven't you got any money?	你一毛錢都還沒收到嗎？
Hw, H	How	Hru? Hw ws ur bday?	How are you? How was your birthday?	你好嗎？生日那天過得如何？
luv	love	I luv ya!	I love you!	我愛你喔！
jst	just	Jst gt ur msg.	I just got your message.	我剛收到你的訊息。
k	okay	A: Tlk 2 u 2mrw? B: k. l8r.	A: I'll talk to you tomorrow, ok? B: Okay, see you later.	A：我明天再跟你說好嗎？ B：好，明天見。
lol	laughing out loud	N my pnts fell dwn n frnt of evryne! lol!	And my pants fell down in front of everyone! Hahaha! (lol)	然後，我的長褲就在大家面前從我腿上滑下來了啦。哈哈哈！
lst	last	I saw ur sis lst nite.	I saw your sister last night.	我昨晚有看到你姊姊。
l8	late	did u gt hme l8?	Did you get home late?	你回家的時候很晚了嗎？
ltr, l8r	later	c u l8r!	See you later!	待會見！
min	minute	Hld on a min.	Hold on a minute.	等我一下。
mnth	month	r u wrking ths mnth?	Are you working this month?	你這個月要工作嗎？
mom, mum	mother	Say hi 2 ur mom frm me!	Say hi to your mother from me!	請代我向你媽媽問聲好！
mrng, morn	morning	Gd mrng!	Good morning!	早安！
msg	message	Thnx 4 ur msg.	Thanks for your message.	感謝你的來信。
mt	meet	Hi! im gona mt Pat 2nite.	Hi! I'm going to meet Pat tonight.	嗨。我今晚要和派特見面喔。
n	and	my bro n sis r cming 2nite 2.	My brother and sister are coming tonight, too.	今晚我的兄弟姐妹也會來喔。
n frnt	in front	mt u n frnt of Hnky dpt bldg.	I'll meet you in front of Hankyu department building.	我們在阪急百貨前面碰面吧。
nite	night	r u gona b hme al nite?	Are you going to be home all night?	你今天整個晚上都會在家嗎？
nvr	never	I nvr drnk n drve!	I never drink and drive!	我從來不酒後駕車！

第3章

來吧！
嘗試用英文寫作吧！

Hello Giovanna,
My name is Ai Fujiwara.
I'm the new purchasing
agent at Yunyu Imports.

Casual Tone

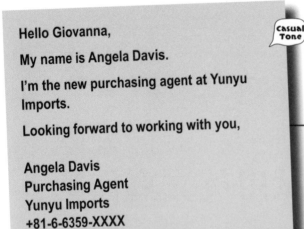

Hello Giovanna,

My name is Angela Davis.

I'm the new purchasing agent at Yunyu Imports.

Looking forward to working with you,

Angela Davis
Purchasing Agent
Yunyu Imports
+81-6-6359-XXXX

中譯

我的名字叫做安琪拉戴維斯。

我是敝公司（Yunyu Imports）新的採購負責人。

期待未來與您在工作上合作愉快。

01 自我介紹

● 請讓我先做個自我介紹。

Allow me to introduce myself.（允許：Allow me to；介紹：introduce）

- Let me（讓我）
- I'd like to

● 我的名字是珍妮葛蕾。

My name is Jenny Grey.

- I'm

● 我是敝公司（Yunyu Imports）新的採購負責人。

I'm the new purchasing agent at Yunyu Imports.（採購的：purchasing）

02 恭敬有禮的開頭

Formal
Tone

● 感謝您的長期惠顧。

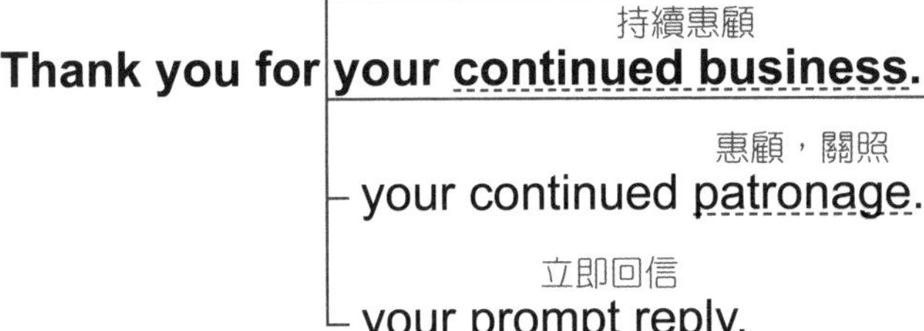
持續惠顧
Thank you for your continued business.
惠顧，關照
your continued patronage.
立即回信
your prompt reply.

03 讓對方知道你如何聯絡上他

● 凱特向我推薦貴公司。

推薦
Your company was recommended to me by Kate.
website
介紹
referred
介紹
introduced
us

● 法拉・凱莉小姐把你引薦給我。

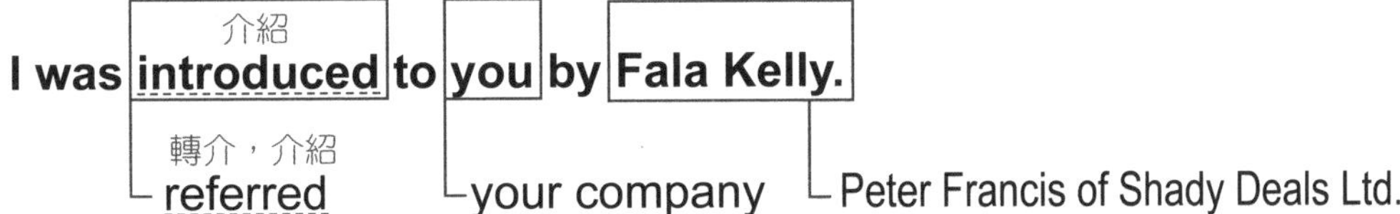
介紹
I was introduced to you by Fala Kelly.
轉介，介紹
referred
your company
Peter Francis of Shady Deals Ltd.

● 我上網看到你的網站。

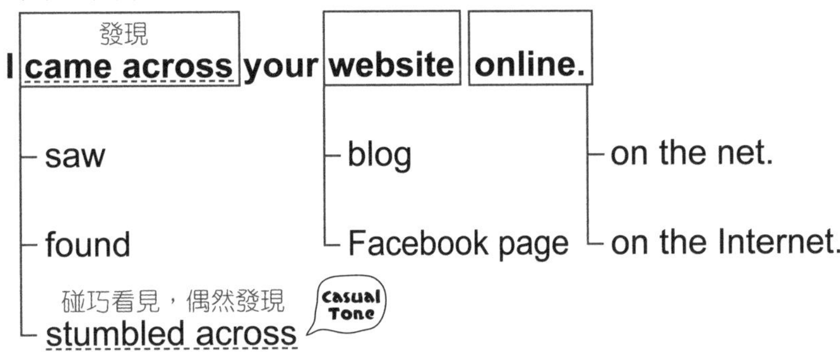
發現
I came across your website online.
saw
found
碰巧看見，偶然發現
stumbled across
Casual
Tone
blog
Facebook page
on the net.
on the Internet.

Dear John,

Thank you for your continued business. My name is Kenny Anderson.

I'm writing to let you know that I'm the new manager of the European sales division.

Please let me know if you have any questions or concerns.

Best regards,

Kenny Anderson
European Sales Manager
Yushutsu Exports
www.yushutsuexports.com
+81-XXX-XXX-XXXX

中譯

感謝您的長期惠顧。我的名字叫做肯尼安德森。

寫信給您的原因是要通知您我剛接任歐洲業務部的部長。

假如您有任何問題或疑慮，請與我聯絡。

● 我們曾在會議上打過照面。

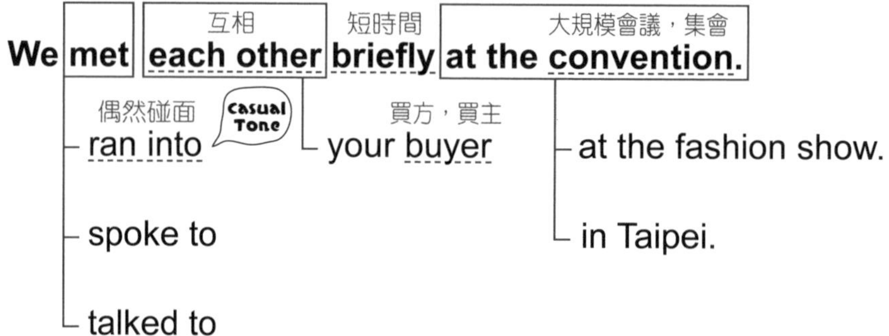
互相
短時間
大規模會議，集會
We met each other briefly at the convention.
偶然碰面
ran into
Casual Tone
買方，買主
your buyer
at the fashion show.
spoke to
in Taipei.
talked to

● 我在《今日美國》上看到你的廣告。

廣告
I read your ad in *USA Today*.

聽過
- heard about your company from a friend.

得知
- was given your address by Dr. Hopkins.

04 告訴對方你與他聯絡的理由

● 我第一次與您聯絡。

I am writing to you for the first time.
- in hopes we can assist（支持） each other（互相）.
- to apply（應徵） for the mortician's（葬儀社） job.

● 我從五月開始將接任王小姐的工作。

I will be taking over（接任） from Ms. Wang from May.
- visiting your offices.
- sending a full report.

● 您可能已經知道這個消息，我將於十月調職到上海。

- You are probably already aware（察覺的） that
- You probably already know that
- Due to（由於） personnel changes（人事異動）,
- **You have probably（也許） already heard that**

I am being transferred（調職） to Shanghai in October.
- moved
- sent

● 寫信給您的原因是要通知您我剛接任部長。

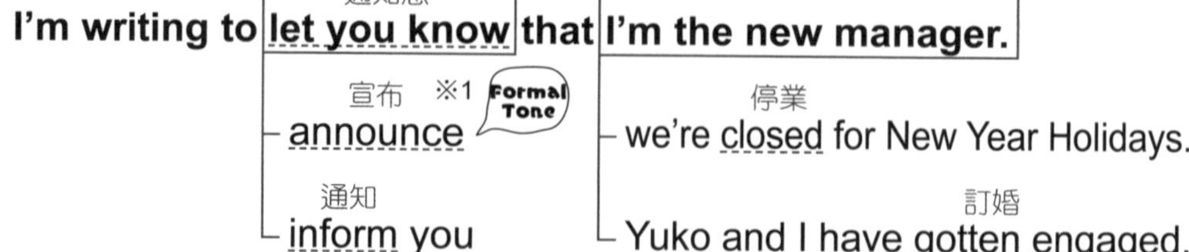
I'm writing to let you know (通知您) that I'm the new manager.
announce (宣布) ※1 Formal Tone
inform you (通知)
we're closed (停業) for New Year Holidays.
Yuko and I have gotten engaged (訂婚).

※1 "announce" 是比 "Let you know" 更正式的說法，有「公佈，發表」的意思，通常在正式的信件裡才會使用。

● 張先生告訴我，你正在找水管工人。

Mr. Chang told me you were looking for a plumber (水管工).

- volunteers (義工).
- a way (方法) to cut costs (降低成本).
- an alternative (替代方法) to chemical fertilizers (化學肥料).

● 我關注你的研究好幾年了。

I've been following (注目，追蹤) your research for years.

● 我希望我們能拋開歧見，回到工作崗位上。

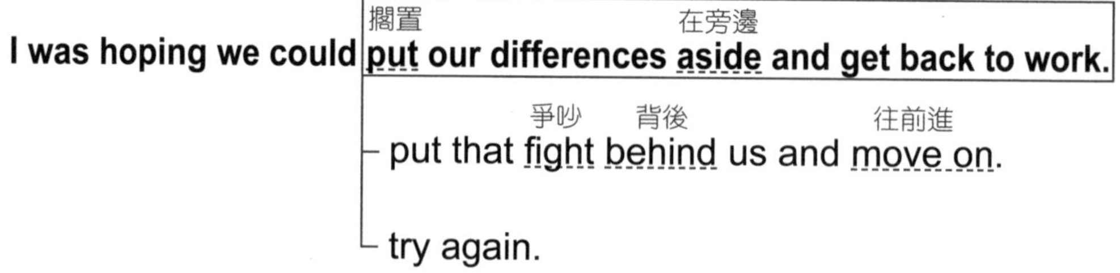
I was hoping we could put (擱置) our differences aside (在旁邊) and get back to work.
put that fight (爭吵) behind (背後) us and move on (往前進).
try again.

小試身手 空格裡的正確答案是哪一個呢？

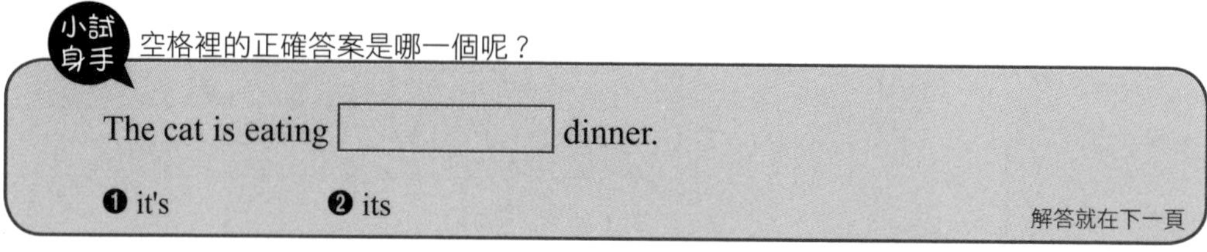
The cat is eating [ ] dinner.
❶ it's ❷ its
解答就在下一頁

● 我即將前往度假。

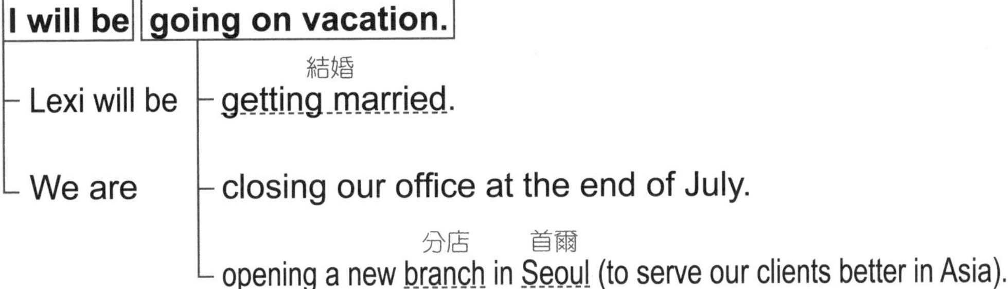
I will be
going on vacation.
Lexi will be
結婚
getting married.
We are
closing our office at the end of July.
分店 首爾
opening a new branch in Seoul (to serve our clients better in Asia).

● 我偶然在市中心碰到你的朋友。

I
偶然碰面 ※1
bumped into
a friend of yours
in town.
Casual Tone
突然碰到※1
ran into
業務員，營業員
your sales rep.
in Shanghai.
spoke with
in the elevator.

※1 “run into...” 和 “bump into...” 都有 ①與…偶然相會 ②與…相撞 的意思。

● 我們必須聚一聚。

We must
get together.
抽出時間
make time for a round of golf.
arrange a meeting.

● 我是你的超級粉絲。

I'm your biggest fan.

● 你的小說我全部都讀過。

I've read all of your novels.

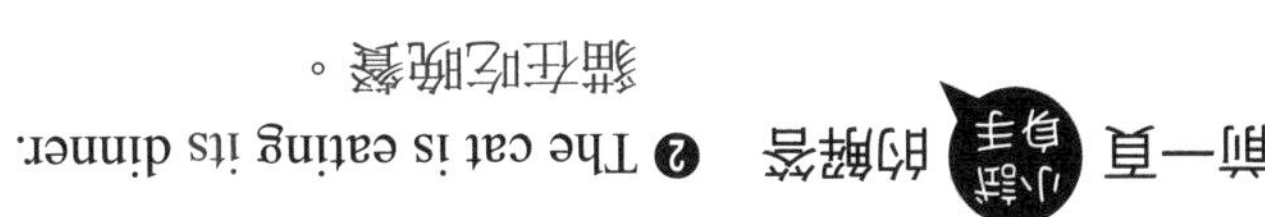
前一頁
小試身手
的解答
❷ The cat is eating its dinner.
貓在吃晚餐。

● 你的CD我全部都有。

I have all your CDs.

05 寫信給很久沒聯絡的對象

● 從上次見面之後，我們很久沒聯絡了呢。

It's been too long since we met. （too long：很長一段時間）
- we communicated.
- we touched base. （touched base：聯絡）

● 好久沒有你的消息了。（你好嗎？）

I haven't heard from you in forever. （heard from：收到某人的消息）Casual Tone
- seen you in too long.
- had a spare moment to write in ages. （a spare moment：片刻；in ages：長久以來）

● 真不敢相信距離上次見面已經過了一年。

I can't believe it's been a year since we met.
- it's you. It's been so long. （It's been so long：好久不見了呢）

No Chinese English!

當別人為自己做了某件事之後，我們基於禮貌，常常會跟對方説「辛苦你了！」但在英文裡可沒有這樣的説法喔！如果看到有人直譯為“You must be tired.”，這可就是最典型的「中式英文」了。

06 告訴對方你的聯絡方式

● 以下是我新的聯絡方式。（手機號碼、E-mail…等）

Here is my new contact information:

090-xxxx-xxxx

satoh@coldmail.com

● 你可以透過我的個人電子信箱或行動電話090-XXX-XXXX與我聯絡。

Please contact me

I can be reached

You can reach me at my personal E-mail address or at my personal cell phone number 090-xxx-xxxx.

（reach：聯絡）

告別中式英文

14P

Business E-mail Tips

The safest approach is to take cues from the people you are doing business with.

最安全的方法就是照著對方的用詞來寫信。

即使是商務書信往來
輕鬆的語氣＝◎ 正式的語氣＝○

寫E-mail給客戶時，雖然不必像書寫公文一樣寫些恭敬的客套話，例如「某某鈞鑒，祈願貴公司業務日益繁盛…」，但是一般還是會以「感謝惠顧」之類的寒暄話語開頭，「請多多指教」之類的客氣字眼結尾吧。那麼，寫英文E-mail的時候呢？這些客套話還有必要嗎？

本書第2章有提到過，在英語系國家，E-mail講求的是言簡意賅，用字遣詞通常比一般書信來得隨性。當然，如果信中使用太多俗語或簡寫會顯得有些失禮，但一般而言，用詞無須刻意修飾，自然就好。剛開始與人書信往返的時候，用字方面可盡量恭敬有禮，之後再配合對方回信的語感，慢慢調整你的筆調。

07 以「期待未來某件事」做結尾

● 期待你的回信。

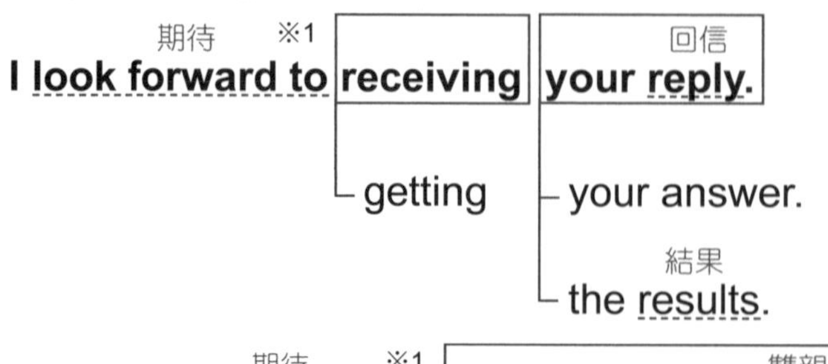
期待
※1
回信
I look forward to receiving your reply.
getting
your answer.
結果
the results.

期待 ※1 雙親

I'm looking forward to meeting your parents.

更進一步認識你

- getting to know you.
- seeing you at the trade show.
- the party.
- the movie.

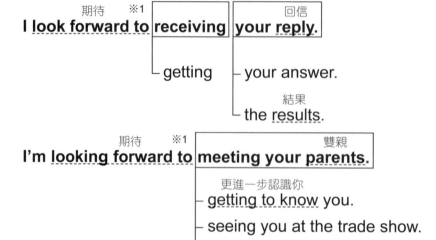

※1 在寫作的時候，"I look forward to..." 和 "I'm looking forward to..." 兩者意思幾乎相同。但是，在對話時兩者的語感則略有差異，"I look forward to..." 指的是未來即將發生的事，是兩人在當下這一刻才決定的事，而 "I'm looking forward to..." 則是指說這句話之前就決定的事件。

「期待未來某件事」的不同用法
I look forward to / I'm looking forward to working with you.
meeting you.
playing a round of golf.
最新的
receiving your latest catalogue.
發展
親密的
關係
developing a close relationship.
the trade show.
dinner.
our lunch meeting.
為您提供服務
serving you.

● 我等不及要跟你見面了！

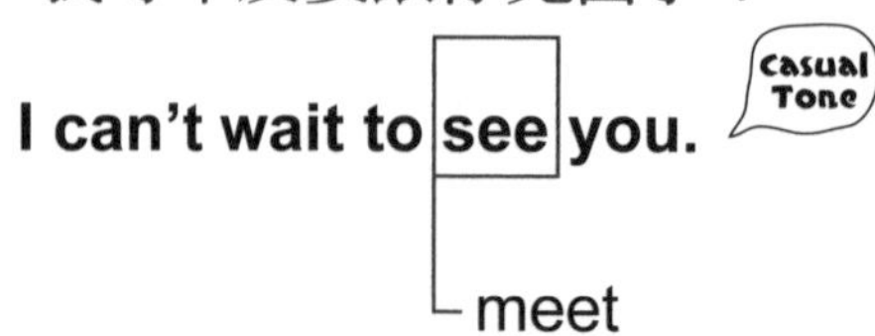
Casual Tone
I can't wait to see you.
meet

08 信件收尾的方式

● 假如您有任何問題或疑慮，請與我聯絡。

Please let me know (讓我知道) if you have any questions or concerns (不安，疑慮).

- Please let me know / contact me / E-mail me
- if you have any questions or concerns. / need anything (有任何需要). / would like to get together (聚會；合作). / would like to talk on Skype (在Skype上討論).

適合用來表示「敬意」的結尾語 (Formal Tone)

Best regards,	Sincerely,	Yours truly,
Kind regards,	Sincerely yours,	

帶有「謝謝」、「改天見」、「祝福」意義的結尾語

Thanks,	Many thanks,	Regards,
Thanks again,	Best wishes,	Yours,
Thanks in advance,	All the best,	Your friend,

Thank you again for all your help,

類似「改天見」的結尾語 (Casual Tone)

Talk to you soon,	See you tomorrow,
Have a nice day,	Cheers,

其他結尾語

非常抱歉 Many apologie,	真令人難過（我與你感同身受） My thoughts are with you,
你的同事 Your colleague,	保持聯絡 Keep in touch,
想念你 Thinking of you,	保持聯絡 Let's stay in touch,

Dear Andrew,

I received the catalogue. Thank you.

I have a number of questions:

1) Do you ship to Japan?
2) Do you offer discounts for large orders?
3) If so, what is the minimum order to receive a discount?
4) Does the price include shipping?
5) Is it possible for you to send samples of the following:
0002-4754 metallic green
0003-8832 orange splash
0006-0004 sunny yellow

Regards,
Angela

中譯

我已經收到商品目錄。謝謝。

我有以下幾個疑問：

1) 是否能夠運送到日本？
2) 大量購買是否有提供折扣？
3) 如果有提供的話，最少要訂購多少才能得到折扣？
4) 售價是否包含運費？
5) 能否請貴公司將下列樣品寄給我們參考？

01 告知對方你的疑問

● 我有幾個問題（想請教）。

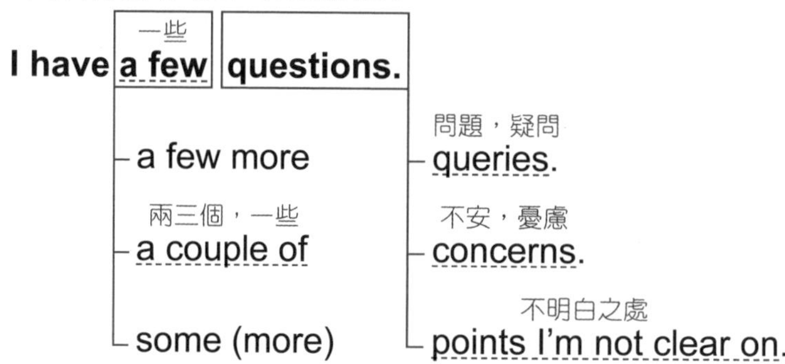
I have a few questions.
一些
a few more
兩三個，一些
a couple of
some (more)
問題，疑問
queries.
不安，憂慮
concerns.
不明白之處
points I'm not clear on.

小試身手
空格裡的正確答案是哪一個呢？

[　　　] he gets caught, he'll make a lot of money.

❶ Unless　　❷ If

解答就在下一頁

02 關於服務與內容

● 我想詢問關於你的翻譯服務。

I'd like to ask about your translation services.
翻譯
探詢，詢問
enquire
know
了解，明白
find out more
諮詢
consulting
法律，法務
legal

● 我想詢問關於下週活動的相關事宜。

I'd like to ask you about the event next week.
探詢，詢問
enquire
了解，明白
find out more
薩爾薩舞蹈課
salsa classes.
有機農業
organic farming.
投資
股票
investing in penny stocks.

● 你在台灣有賣產品給其他人嗎？

Do you sell to anyone else in Taiwan?

● 是否能夠運送到台灣？

Do you ship to Taiwan ?
Can
大量，大批
in bulk?
空運
by air?

前一頁

小試身手

的解答 ❶ Unless he gets caught, he'll make a lot of money.

除非被逮捕，否則他就能賺進大把鈔票。

● 請問貴公司的玩具狗是在哪裡製造的呢？

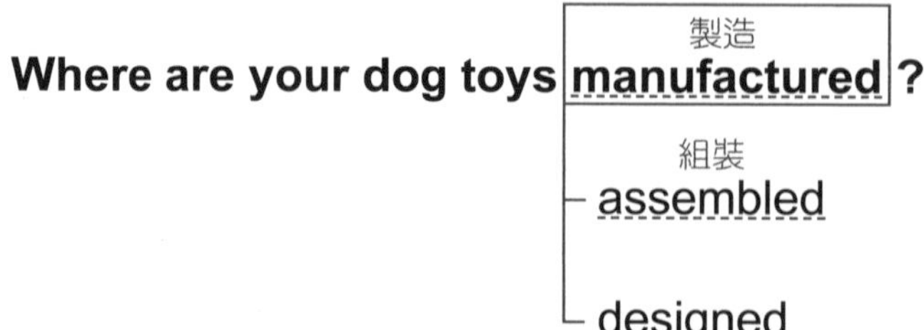
Where are your dog toys manufactured ?
製造
組裝
assembled
designed

03 關於存貨

● 請問商品編號117有現貨嗎？

Do you currently have item number 117 ?
現在，目前
still
有庫存
stock
make
外銷
export
product number 1221
type 2012

● 假如XYZ自行車（仍然）有存貨，麻煩您通知我好嗎？

Could you let me know if you (still) stock XYZ wheels ?
通知我
Could you tell me
※1
Please tell me
Y字形彈弓
改善，升級
your slingshots have been upgraded
組裝
書架
you have any problems assembling the bookcases

※1 以 “Please tell me” 開頭的句子，句末不需要加問號。

● ＃9317這一款還有其他顏色嗎？

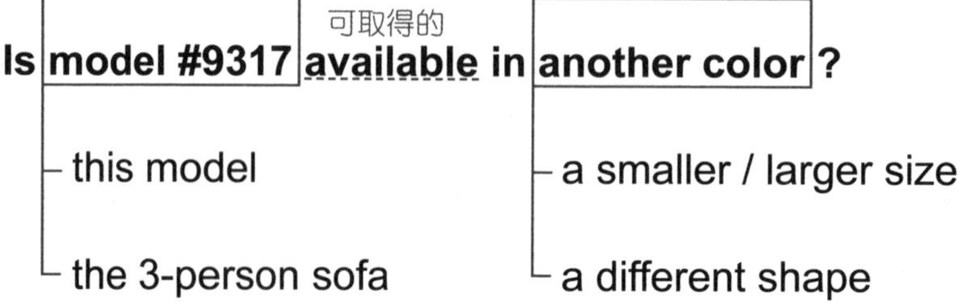
Is model #9317 available in another color ?
可取得的
this model
the 3-person sofa
a smaller / larger size
a different shape

04 關於時間

● 工廠巡視需要花費多少時間呢？

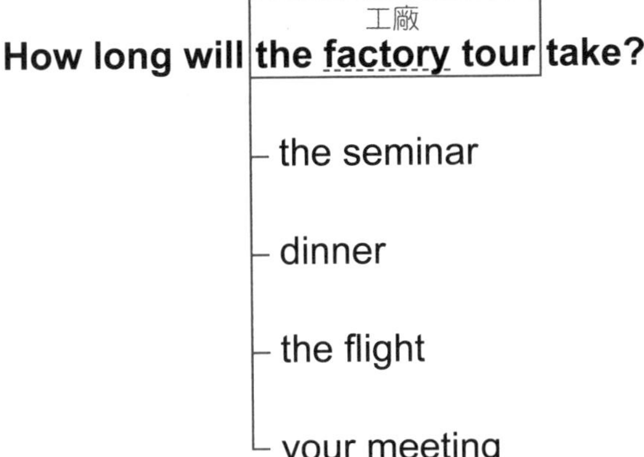
工廠
How long will the factory tour take?
the seminar
dinner
the flight
your meeting

● 我們應該預留多少時間組裝呢？

預期 組裝

How much time should we expect it to take for assembly?

05 關於費用

● 售價是否包含運費？

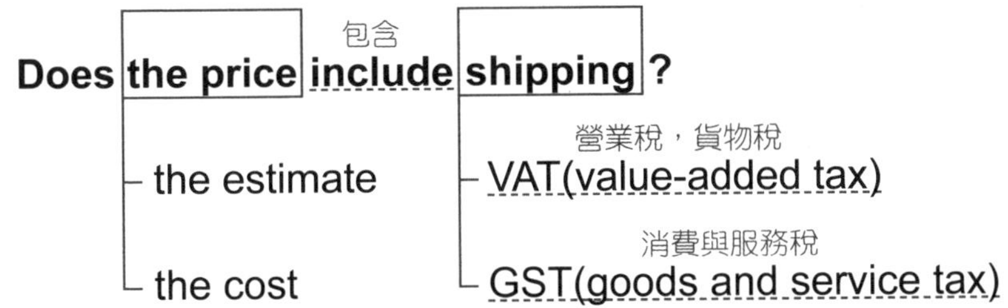
包含
Does the price include shipping ?
the estimate
the cost
營業稅，貨物稅
VAT(value-added tax)
消費與服務稅
GST(goods and service tax)

06 提出要求

● 請問可以讓商品333防水嗎？

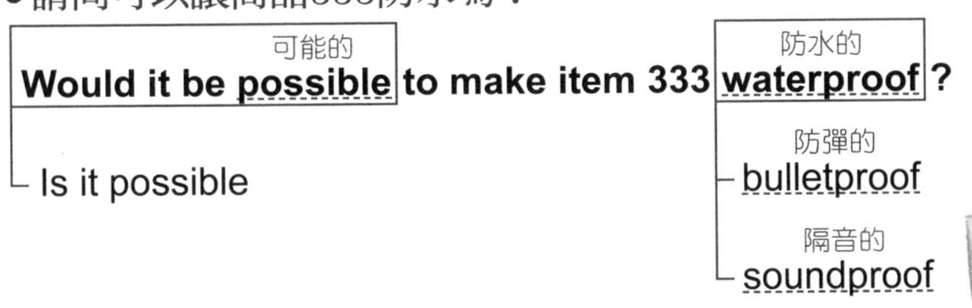
可能的
Would it be possible to make item 333 waterproof ?
防水的
Is it possible
防彈的
bulletproof
隔音的
soundproof

● 貴公司是否接受客製化訂單？

Do you accept custom orders?（accept：接受）

● 我想索取一些關於旅行團的相關資訊。

I'd like to request some information regarding tours.（regarding：關於）

room rates.

● 是否可以讓我與貴公司的社長會面？

Will it be possible for me to meet your president ?
可能的
社長
O.K.
access the internet
借用
borrow a projector
rent a car
雙方的
visit both offices

● 你可以使用新的板材嗎？

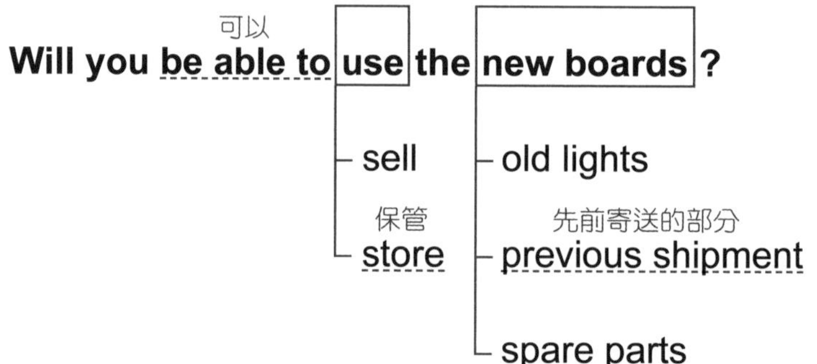
可以
Will you be able to use the new boards ?
sell
保管
store
old lights
先前寄送的部分
previous shipment
spare parts

07 關於機能

● 這項商品的基本功能有哪些？

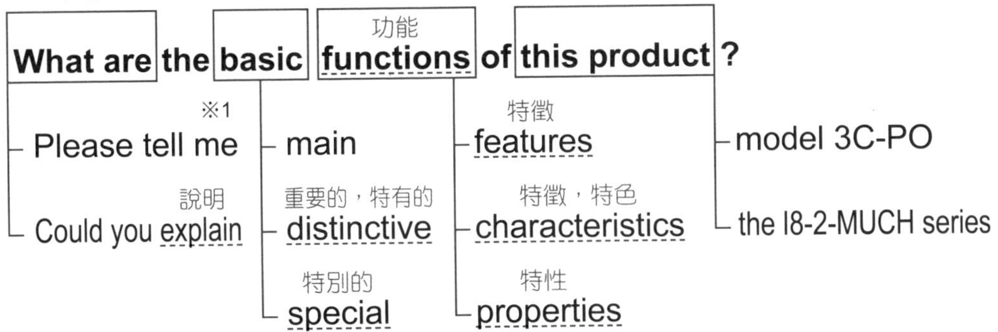

What are the basic functions of this product ?
功能
※1
Please tell me
說明
Could you explain
main
重要的，特有的
distinctive
特別的
special
特徵
features
特徵，特色
characteristics
特性
properties
model 3C-PO
the I8-2-MUCH series

※1 以 "Please tell me" 開頭的句子，句末不需要加問號。

08 關於運送

● 你們是否提供海外運送服務？

提供
Do you offer international shipping ?
do
快捷服務
expedited services
tours
discounts
training

● 商品寄送到台北需要多久？

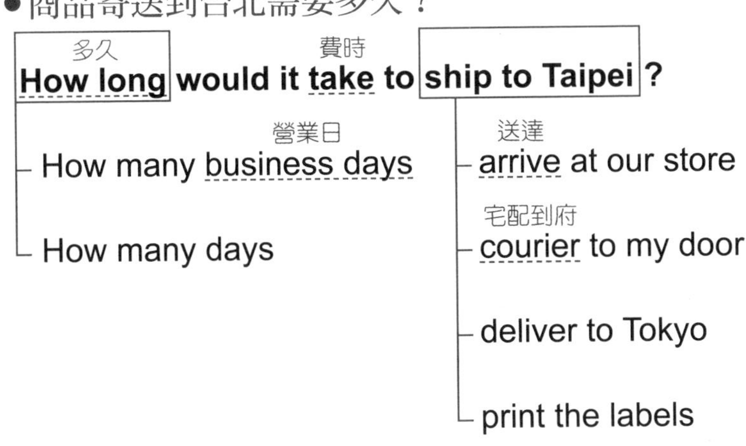

多久
費時
How long would it take to ship to Taipei ?
營業日
How many business days
How many days
送達
arrive at our store
宅配到府
courier to my door
deliver to Tokyo
print the labels

● 你們需要多久時間才能寄出商品？

寄送
How much time can you ship the items ?
運送
What's the fastest way
freight
products
宅配到府
What's the earliest
courier
container
How soon
send

09 關於售後服務

● 貴公司的商品附有哪些售後保證？

種類的
保證
What sort of warranty do your products come with?
保證
guarantee
保證，保險
assurance

● 貴公司的商品是否附有退費保證？

退費 保證

Do your products come with a money-back guarantee?

● 該項產品會和使用說明DVD一起寄到嗎？

使用說明書
Does the unit come with DVD instructions?
product
English
淺顯易懂
item
easy-to-follow
機械
machinery

● 在維修方面有什麼特殊要求嗎？

維修，保養 注意事項

Are there any special maintenance requirements?

清潔指南
- cleaning instructions

操作注意事項
- handling requirements

保管注意事項
- storage requirements

● 你或許有中文的使用說明書？

或許，可能 使用說明書

Do you by any chance have instruction manuals in Chinese?

● 組裝時需要哪些工具？

工具 組裝

What tools are required for assembly?

- parts

告別中式英文

14P

Business E-mail Tips

People are busy. They don't have time to read E-mail that goes on and on.

大家都很忙。他們沒有時間閱讀長篇大論的E-mail。

寫信記得要 "K.I.S.S."！

英語 E-mail 裡有 "K.I.S.S." 這個用語，代表 "Keep it short and simple"（簡潔扼要），也有人會說 "Keep it simple, stupid!"（講重點啊，笨蛋！）

收信的人很忙，人家對你的廢話連篇、一堆藉口和各式各樣的理由不會有什麼興趣。請用最簡潔明瞭的方式明白地向對方表達「你想要什麼？」以及「為什麼想要？」從今天開始，盡量精簡信件的內容，與那些語焉不詳的冗長郵件說再見吧。

10 關於安全性和性能

● 包裝是否能避免小朋友開啟？

防止兒童開啟
Is the packaging childproof ?
密封的
airtight
防水的
waterproof
防火的
fire-resistant
不可燃的，防火的
fireproof

● 這些碳粉是否對人體或動物有害？

有毒的
Are the toners toxic to humans or animals ?
plants
染料
tints
有害的
harmful to skin
可食用
edible
持久的
permanent

● 是否有任何有害的副作用？

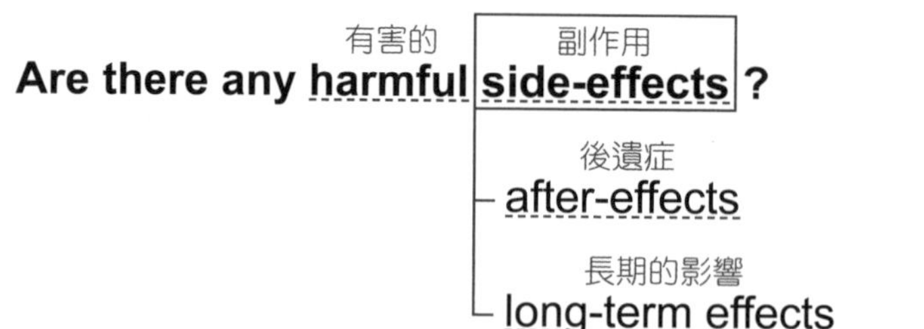

有害的
副作用
Are there any harmful side-effects ?
後遺症
after-effects
長期的影響
long-term effects

2 詢問 關於安全性和性能

- （貴公司的）商品是否具有可燃性？

Are your products flammable?（可燃的）

- water-soluble（可溶於水的）
- heat-resistant（耐熱的）
- moth-resistant（防蟲的）

- 這對小朋友來說是安全的嗎？

Is it safe for children?

- animals

- 在陽光直射下也安全無虞嗎？

Is it safe in sunlight?

11 關於原料和素材

- （貴公司的商品）是否經過有機認證？

Are your products certified organic?（經過認證 有機的）

- GMO ※1
- preservative-free（防腐劑 不使用）
- additive-free（添加物）
- heavy-metal-free（重金屬）
- sodium-free（鈉）

※1 "GMO" 是Genetically Modified Organism（基因改造生物）的縮寫。

●這些木材是來自可永續經營的森林嗎？

Is the wood from a sustainable forest ?
可永續經營的
森林
木材
timber
可再生的
產地
renewable source

●你們的水果是否栽培於噴灑過殺蟲劑的環境？

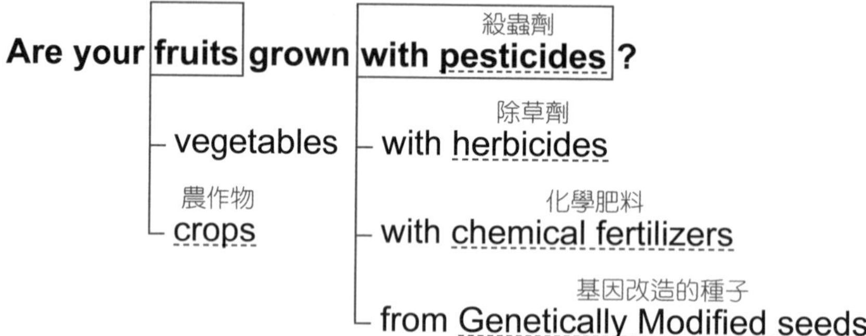
Are your fruits grown with pesticides ?
殺蟲劑
vegetables
農作物
crops
除草劑
with herbicides
化學肥料
with chemical fertilizers
基因改造的種子
from Genetically Modified seeds

●這種商品可以使用在木頭上嗎？

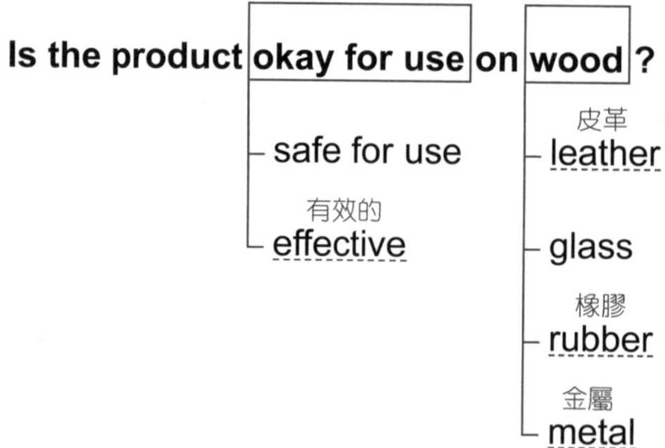
Is the product okay for use on wood ?
safe for use
有效的
effective
皮革
leather
glass
橡膠
rubber
金屬
metal

12 詢問對方是否有疑問

●關於這份契約，您還有任何疑問嗎？

Do you have any questions regarding the contract ?
關於
契約
the catalogue

●你需要其他相關資訊嗎？

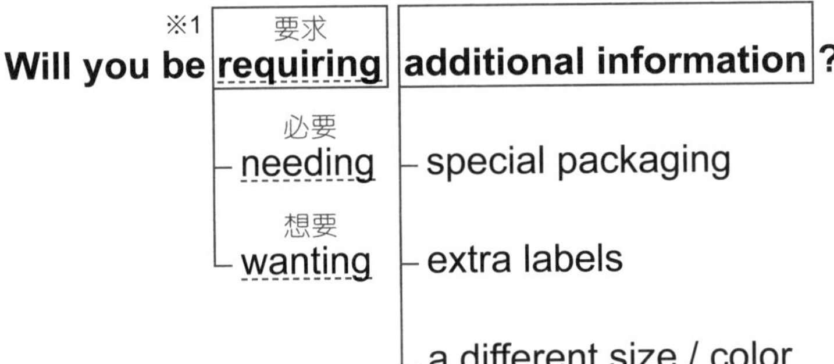

※1
要求
Will you be requiring additional information?
必要
needing
想要
wanting
special packaging
extra labels
a different size / color

※1 "Will you be requiring" 和 "Do you require" 兩者意思幾乎相同，只是前者的語氣比較恭敬。

●請問在技術支援方面還有任何疑問嗎？

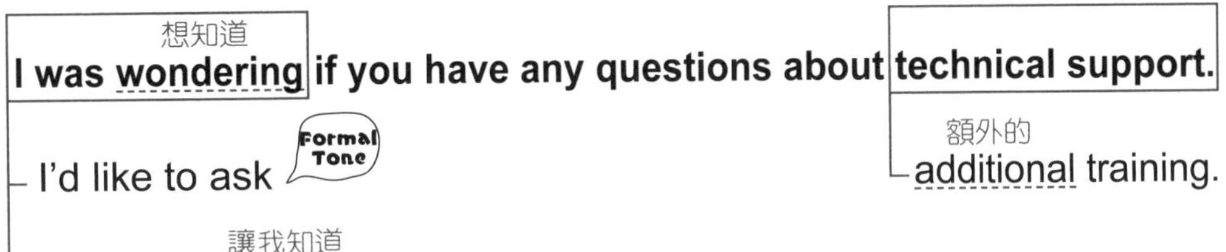

想知道
I was wondering if you have any questions about technical support.
I'd like to ask
Formal Tone
讓我知道
Please let me know
額外的
additional training.

No Chinese English!

基本上，中文裡有許多無法直接翻譯成英文的說法，例如：「不好意思，我先失陪了。」不能直譯成 "I'm sorry, I have to leave before you!" 這樣的句子從文法看起來當然沒有錯，但英語母語人士聽了，一定會感到一頭霧水。

01 請求提供資訊

● 能否請你告訴我營業時間？

Could you tell me your operating hours ?
營業時間
通知我
inform me of
let me know
holiday schedule
時薪
hourly rate
方針
產假
policy on maternity leave

● 我希望你能盡快通知我貨品運送的時間表。

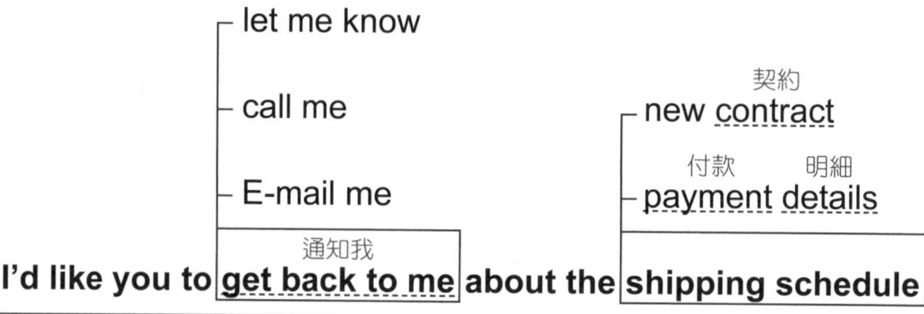
let me know
call me
E-mail me
通知我
I'd like you to get back to me about the shipping schedule
契約
new contract
付款
明細
payment details

盡快
as soon as possible.

之前
by 3:00 pm today.

盡快
as soon as you can.

在您方便的時候請盡快
at your earliest convenience.

● 可否讓我知道您暑休的時間？

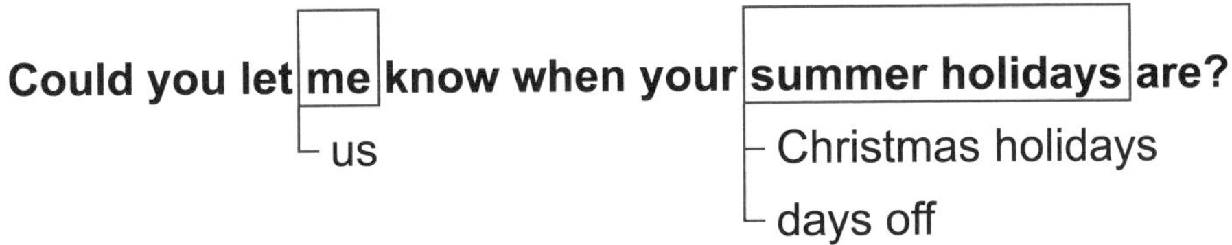
Could you let me know when your summer holidays are?
us
Christmas holidays
days off

● 我是否能再多了解一些關於這個新產品線的資訊？

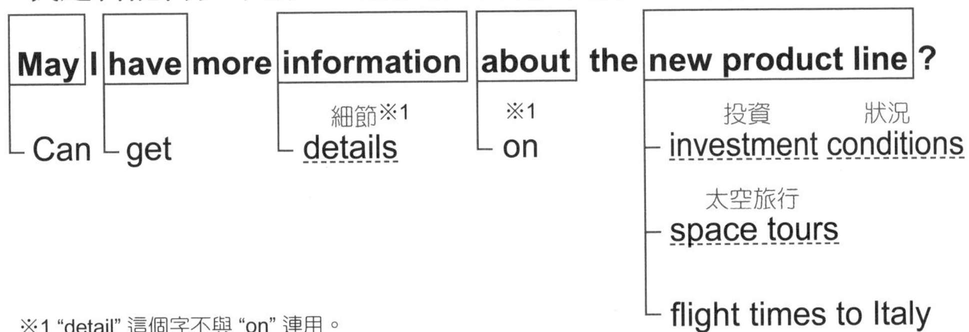
May I have more information about the new product line?
Can
get
細節※1
details
※1
on
投資 狀況
investment conditions
太空旅行
space tours
flight times to Italy

※1 "detail" 這個字不與 "on" 連用。

● 請您將1,000公斤的估價單寄給我。

寄送
估價單
I'd like you to send me an estimate for 1,000 kg.
Please
mail
fax
us
個；單位
a price for 5,000 units.
總價
the total amount.
運費
the shipping costs.

● 關於這個狀況，能否請你再做更詳盡的說明呢？

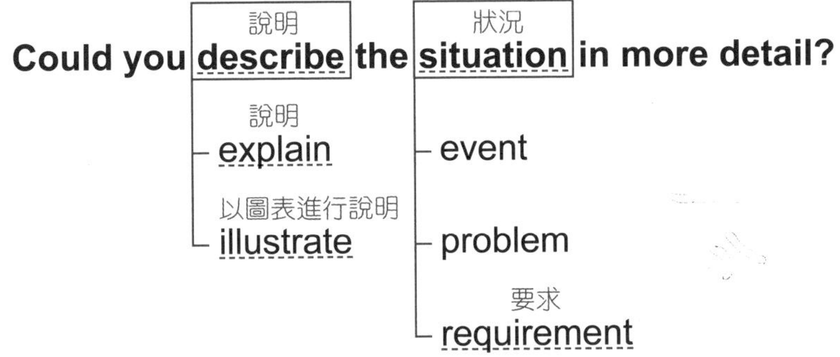
說明
狀況
Could you describe the situation in more detail?
說明
explain
以圖表進行說明
illustrate
event
problem
要求
requirement

● 在您方便的時候請盡快將最新的商品目錄寄來。

寄送
最新的
在您方便的時候請盡快
Please send me your latest catalogue at your earliest convenience.
※1
Could you
the summer product list
the samples
the photos from the party

※1 以 "Could you..." 開頭的句子比用 "Please" 更恭敬。因為是問句，所以句末要加問號。

02 要求確認

● 可否請你再次確認價格（是否正確）？

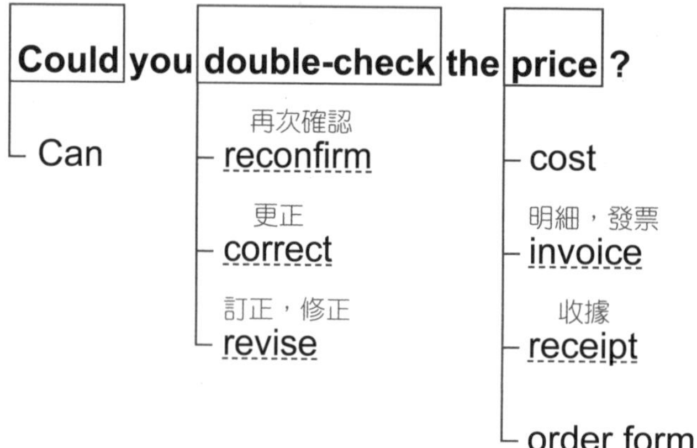
Could you double-check the price ?
Can
再次確認
reconfirm
更正
correct
訂正，修正
revise
cost
明細，發票
invoice
收據
receipt
order form

● 寄出貨品之前請先檢查。

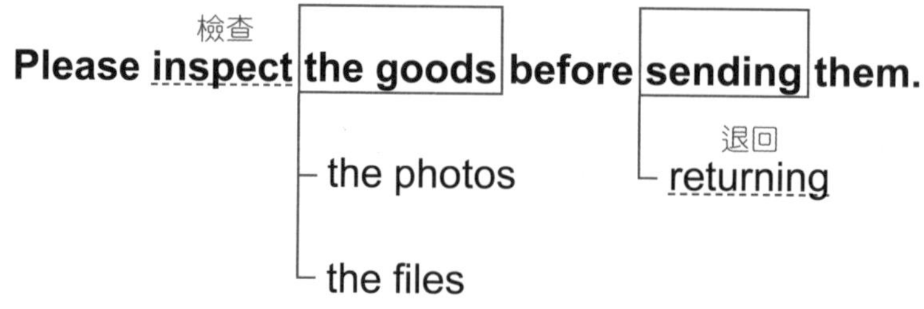
檢查
Please inspect the goods before sending them.
the photos
the files
退回
returning

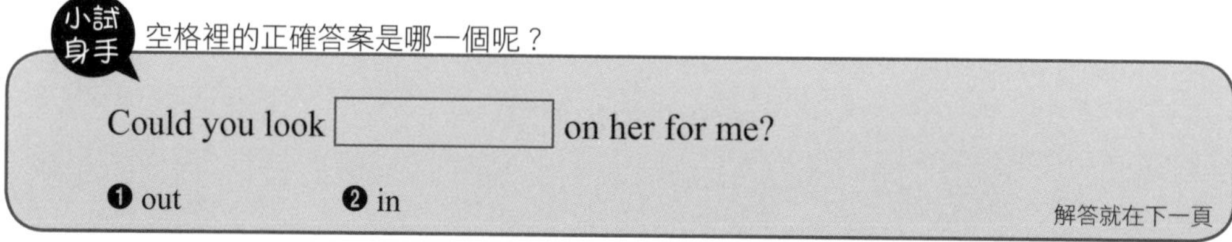
小試身手
空格裡的正確答案是哪一個呢？
Could you look [ ] on her for me?
❶ out
❷ in
解答就在下一頁

● 離開前請確認螺絲已旋緊。

螺絲，固定用零件
弄牢，鎖緊
Make sure the fasteners are secured before leaving.
鎖
locks
閂閂
latches
bolts
操作
operating.
closing.
無人照應
leaving unattended.

● 第一個月請檢視你的使用方法。

檢視，監視　用法
Please monitor your usage for the first month.

記錄　每
- record the data and send it to us each week.

記錄，追蹤　比率　消費
- keep track of the rate of consumption.

再次檢討，再次調查　確保　有效
- review your past records to ensure effective ordering.

03 請對方做某件事

● 可否請你將下列樣品寄過來呢？

可能的
以下的
Is it possible for you to send samples of the following:
receive
額外的
get additional

前一頁 小試身手 的解答 ❷ Could you look in on her for me?
能否請你順道幫我探望她一下呢？

● 這個週末能否請您協助我油漆房間呢？

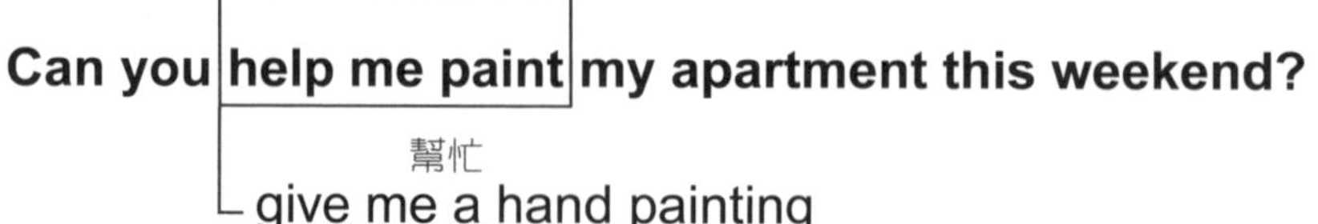
Can you help me paint my apartment this weekend?
幫忙
give me a hand painting

● 請填寫線上申請表。

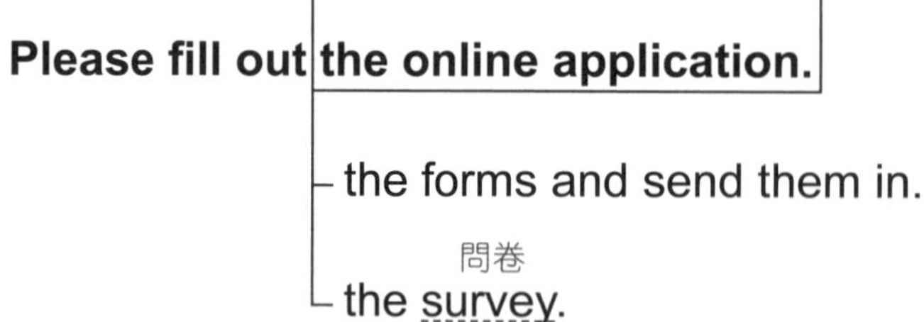
Please fill out the online application.
the forms and send them in.
問卷
the survey.

● 如果你可以在星期五之前把它交給我的話就太棒了。

Casual Tone
如果你可以
把東西交給我、寄給我
It would be great if you could get that to me by Friday.
有幫助
It would be helpful
感謝
I'd appreciate it
打電話給我
call me
回覆
reply
處理那件事
see to that

● 麻煩您將毀損的零件退回。

I'd like to ask you to return the broken parts.

● 請不要吸煙。

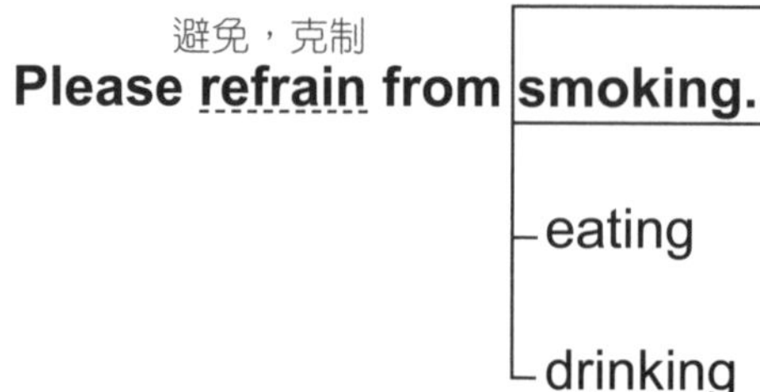
避免，克制
Please refrain from smoking.

eating

drinking

● 可以請你撥冗審閱一下簡報的內容嗎？

審閱
Can you make time to go over the presentation ?

- 會議
  meet before the conference
- check the new design with me
- 契約
  show me the contracts

● 能否請你將那些東西分裝成小包裝呢？

可能的　包裝
Would it be possible for you to package them in smaller lots ?

- 結合，聯合
  combine the orders
- come to my office on Saturday
- 用視訊會議的方式
  talk by video conference

● 等一下可以請你提醒我打電話給理察嗎？

提醒　等一下
Could you remind me to call Richard later ?

- ※1
  Please don't let me forget

- 拿出去　垃圾
  take out the garbage
- 寄出　附件，附屬品
  send those attatchments
- buy some more milk

※1 以 "Please don't let me forget" 開頭的句子，句末不需要加問號。

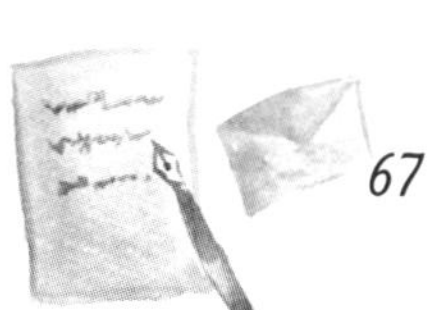

● 假如今晚你能上台說幾句話，我會很感謝你。

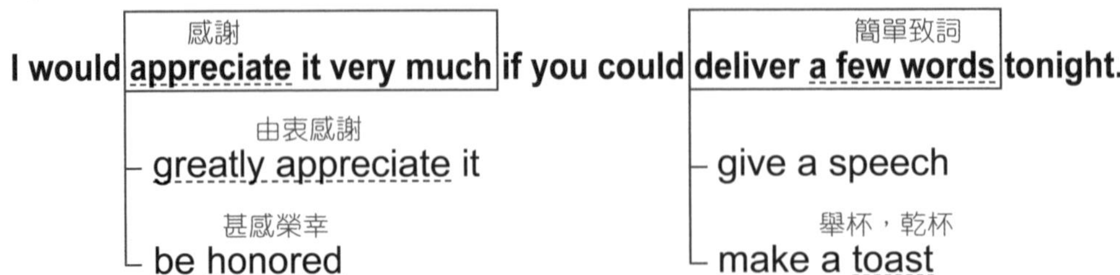
感謝
I would appreciate it very much if you could deliver a few words tonight.
簡單致詞
由衷感謝
greatly appreciate it
甚感榮幸
be honored
give a speech
舉杯，乾杯
make a toast

● 可否請你代表我們在會議上發言？

代表
Can you represent us at the conference ?
會議
代表我們發言
speak on our behalf
談判，協商
negotiation
meeting
集會，大會
rally

● 能否請你說服黛安出席公會的會議？

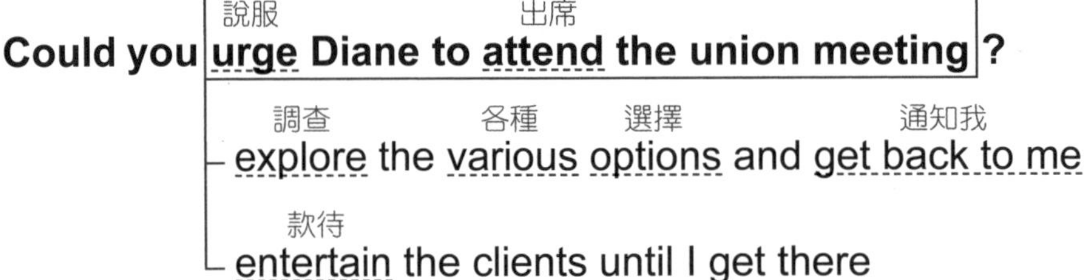
說服
出席
Could you urge Diane to attend the union meeting ?
調查
各種
選擇
通知我
explore the various options and get back to me
款待
entertain the clients until I get there

● 我們要求所有參加者都要準備好自己的用品。

參加者
We are asking all participants to prepare their own kit.
出席者
attendees
volunteers
減少
浪費
reduce waste.
用具
bring their own materials.
準備
三餐
arrange their own meals.

04 委託工作

● 我希望你能在會議中擔任我的口譯。

I'd like you to **interpret** (口譯) **for me at** **the conference.** (會議)

- Could you ※1
- translate (翻譯)
- do the translating (翻譯)
- do the interpreting (口譯)
- tomorrow's meeting.
- the Ambassador's (大使的) farewell party (歡送會).
- Alex and Yoko's wedding.

※1 以 "Could you..." 開頭的句子，句末要加問號。

● 能否請你幫我們將這本手冊翻譯成中文？

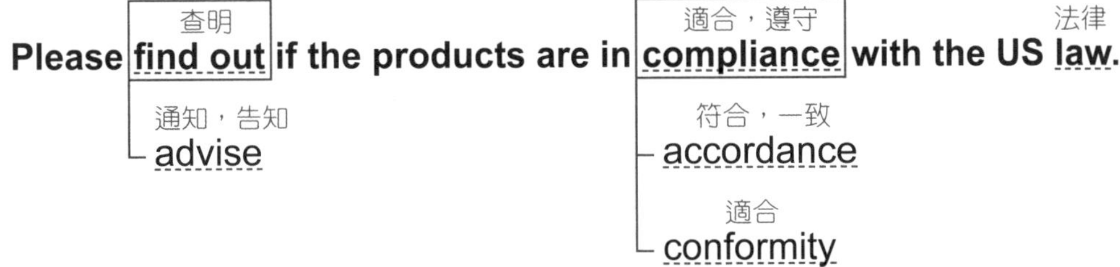

Could we ask you to **translate** (翻譯) **the manual into Chinese** **?**

- copy the instruction booklet (使用說明書)
- add English subtitles to the DVD

● 請查明這些商品是否符合美國的法律規範。

Please **find out** (查明) **if the products are in** **compliance** (適合，遵守) **with the US law** (法律)**.**

- advise (通知，告知)
- accordance (符合，一致)
- conformity (適合)

05 請求許可

● 請把我們也算進去。

Please **include** (包括) **us in.**

- count (將…計算在內)

Casual Tone

●可否再給我一些時間重新考慮？

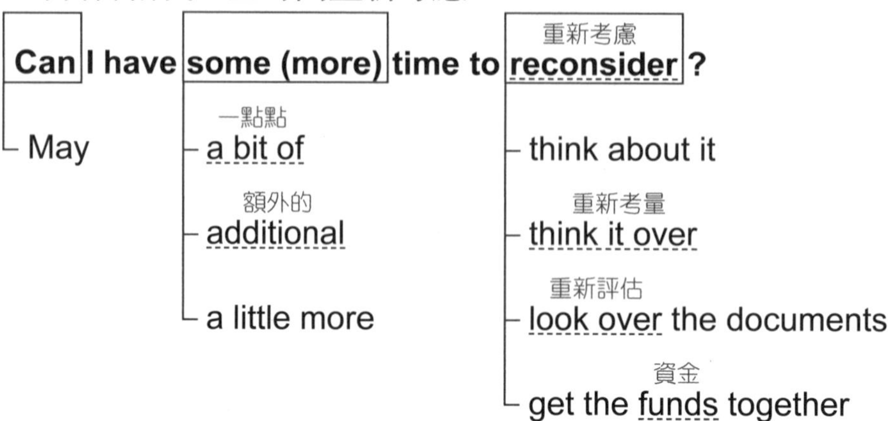
重新考慮
Can I have some (more) time to reconsider ?
May
一點點
a bit of
額外的
additional
a little more
think about it
重新考量
think it over
重新評估
look over the documents
資金
get the funds together

●您介意早一點來參加會議嗎？

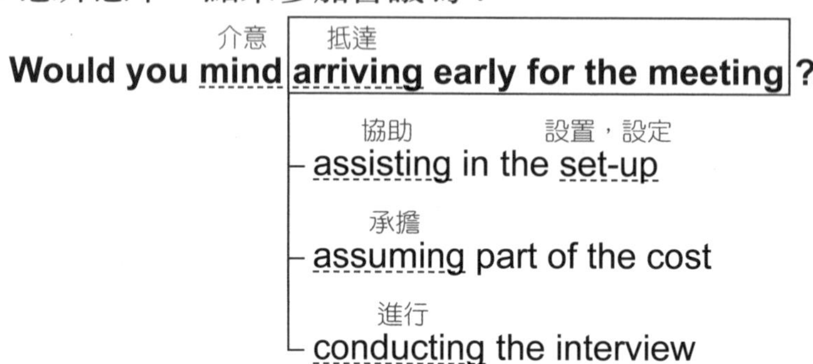
介意
抵達
Would you mind arriving early for the meeting ?
協助
設置，設定
assisting in the set-up
承擔
assuming part of the cost
進行
conducting the interview

●是不是能夠請你幫忙給個方便，安排我與社長見面洽談？

Is there any way you could facilitate a meeting for me with the president ?

給個方便

護送

escort me back to the hotel after the meeting?

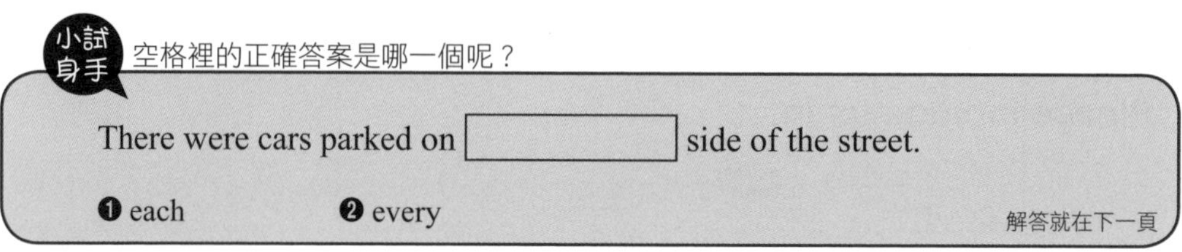
小試身手
空格裡的正確答案是哪一個呢？
There were cars parked on [ ] side of the street.
❶ each
❷ every

解答就在下一頁

● 請給我們一個機會展現我們能夠如何為您服務。

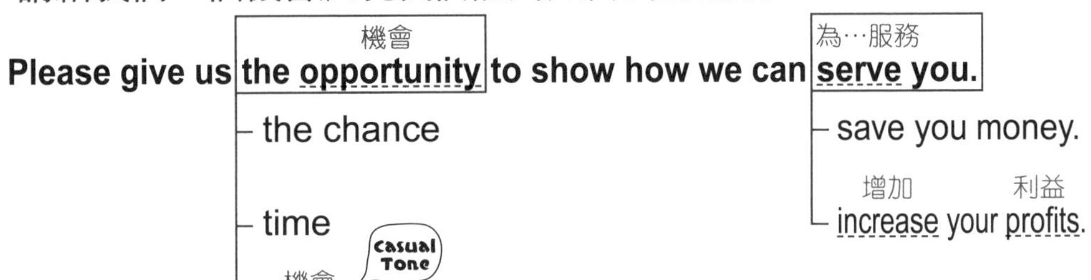

Please give us the opportunity to show how we can serve you.
機會
為…服務
the chance
time
a shot
機會
Casual Tone
save you money.
increase your profits.
增加
利益

06 請求告知結論

● 星期五之前請告訴我你的決定。

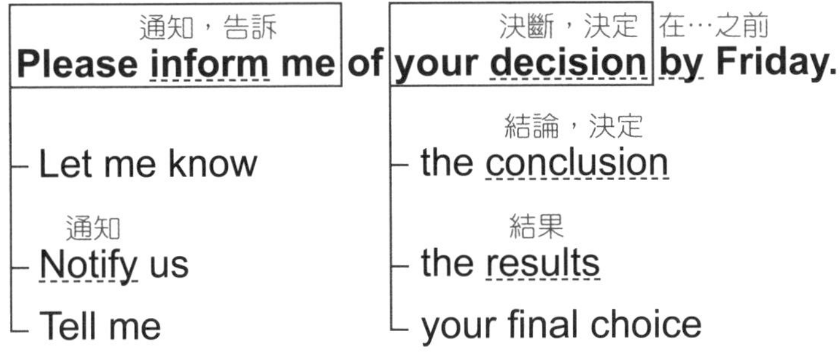

Please inform me of your decision by Friday.
通知，告訴
決斷，決定
在…之前
Let me know
Notify us
通知
Tell me
the conclusion
結論，決定
the results
結果
your final choice

如何提出請求

有沒有機會（可能性）…？
Is there any chance...?

有沒有可能…？
Is it possible to...?

我希望你可以…。
I was hoping you could...

能否請你…？
Could you...?

不知道你是否願意…。
I was wondering if you could...

你可不可以…？
Would you...?

我是否能懇請你幫忙…？ (Formal Tone)
Can I entreat you to...?

你想要…嗎？
Do you want to...?

請你…也沒問題嗎？
Would it be alright if...?

你何不…？
Why don't you...?

假如…你介意嗎？
Do you mind if...?

你覺得…如何？
How about... V-ing?

前一頁小試身手的解答 ❶ There were cars parked on each side of the street.
道路兩旁都停有車輛。

01 價格交涉

● 大量訂貨有提供折扣嗎？

提供
折扣
大量訂貨
Do you offer discounts for large orders?
免運費
free shipping

● 對於訂購500個以上的訂單，我們提供折扣。

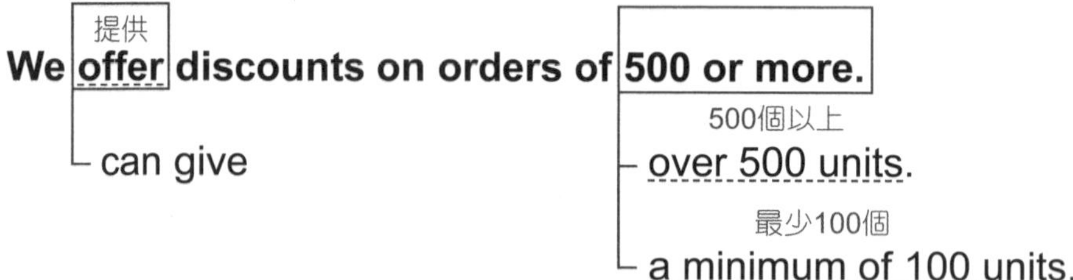
提供
We offer discounts on orders of 500 or more.
can give
500個以上
over 500 units.
最少100個
a minimum of 100 units.

● 如果你們未來持續大量訂貨，我們願意調降商品價格。

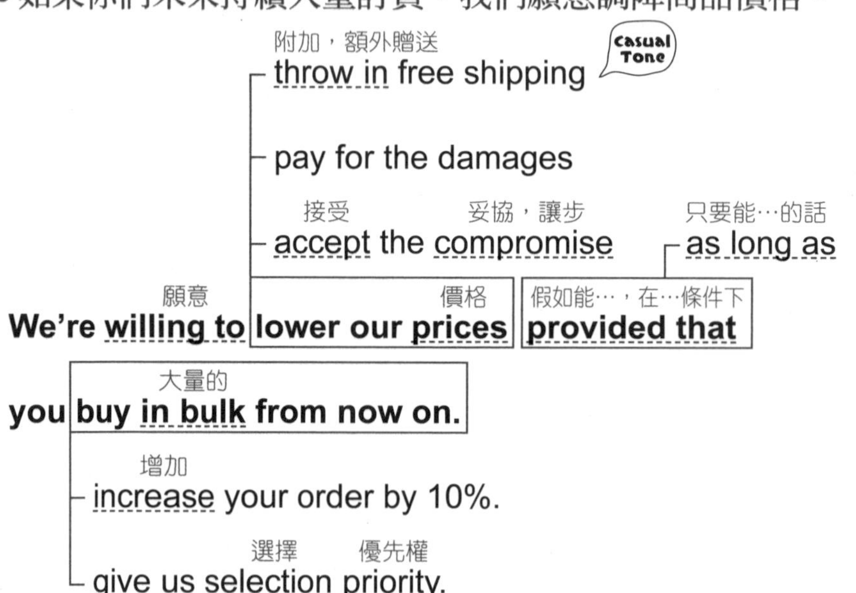
附加，額外贈送
throw in free shipping
Casual Tone
pay for the damages
接受
妥協，讓步
accept the compromise
只要能…的話
as long as
願意
價格
假如能…，在…條件下
We're willing to lower our prices provided that
大量的
you buy in bulk from now on.
增加
increase your order by 10%.
選擇
優先權
give us selection priority.

● 假如你們能增加訂購數量，我們就願意調降價格。

願意 / 調降 / 增加

We are willing to go down on the price if you increase your order.

- knock 10% off the price (減價百分之十) Casual Tone
- pay the shipping costs

● 我們無法支付運費，但是也許能夠提供您一些折扣。

We cannot pay for shipping, but we may be able to offer you a discount.

- reduce the price (降低) ※1
- upgrade the product.

※1 "reduce the price" 和 "offer you a discount" 不會同時使用。

● 在下訂單之前，我想確認我是否能拿到折扣。

確認 / 折扣

I'd like to make sure I can get the discount before I order.

- the goods will arrive by 12/16 (送達… 在…之前)
- you have the correct address (正確的)

● 如果你今天簽約，我可以將報價降低一成。

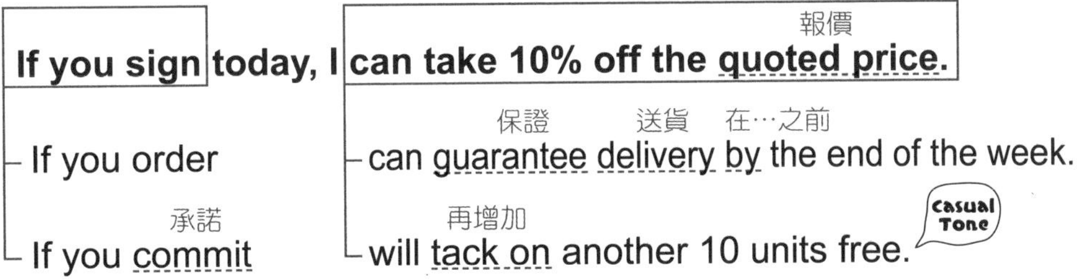

報價

If you sign today, I can take 10% off the quoted price.

- If you order
- If you commit (承諾)

- can guarantee delivery by the end of the week. (保證 送貨 在…之前)
- will tack on another 10 units free. (再增加) Casual Tone

02 條件

● 假如我們把訂貨數量增加50%，你們能開出更好的條件嗎？

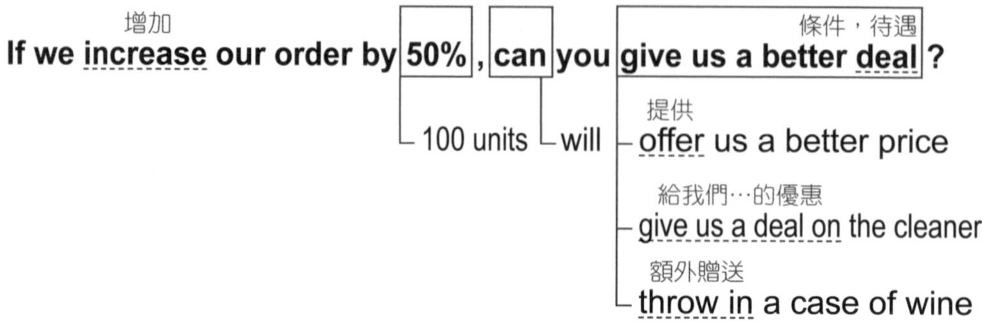
增加
If we increase our order by 50% , can you give us a better deal ?
條件，待遇
100 units
will
提供
offer us a better price
給我們…的優惠
give us a deal on the cleaner
額外贈送
throw in a case of wine

● 如果你們能接受那個條件，我們今天就簽約。

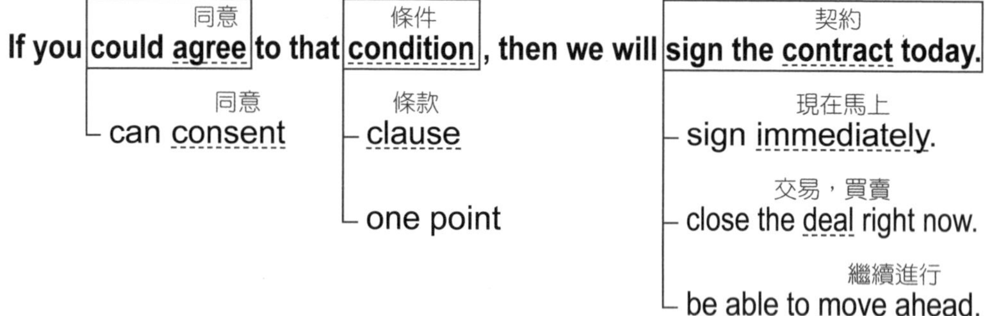
同意
If you could agree to that condition, then we will sign the contract today.
條件
契約
同意
can consent
條款
clause
one point
現在馬上
sign immediately.
交易，買賣
close the deal right now.
繼續進行
be able to move ahead.

● 假如你們給我們獨家銷售權，我們就追加一萬個。

同意
agree to pay for shipping
打85折
take 15% off the sofas
獨家的
權利
If you give us exclusive rights,
增加
we will increase our order by 10,000 units.
order 50 more tables.

● 如果你能保證房間都看得到海景，我們就加訂30個房間。

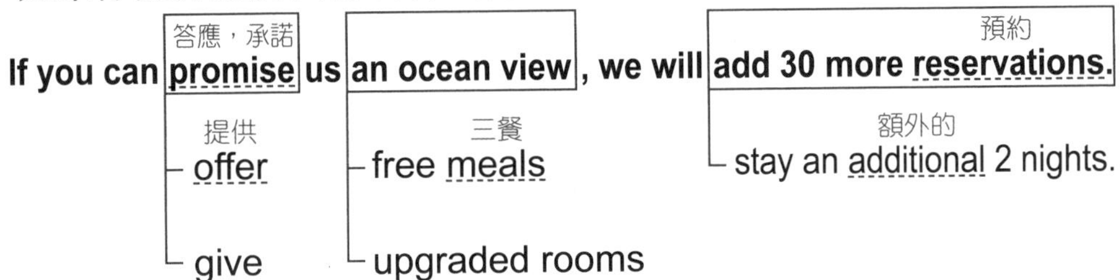

If you can promise us an ocean view, we will add 30 more reservations.
答應，承諾
預約
提供
offer
give
三餐
free meals
upgraded rooms
額外的
stay an additional 2 nights.

03 強調優惠

● 我們的價格比其他同業便宜，而且還提供一年免費維修。

We will beat their price and give you free maintenance for 1 year.
比其他競爭對手便宜
降價百分之十
take 10% off
add 10 units
Casual Tone
提供
現場實習
provide on-site training.
增加
保固期
increase the warranty by 2 years.

● 如果你與我們簽約，我們願意翻譯所有的使用說明書。

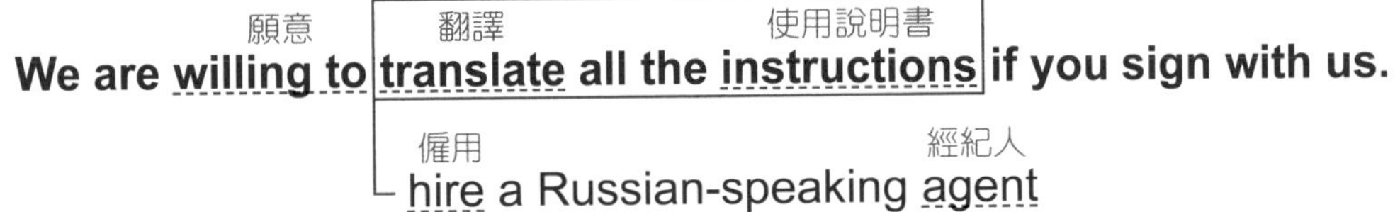

We are willing to translate all the instructions if you sign with us.
願意
翻譯
使用說明書
僱用
經紀人
hire a Russian-speaking agent

04 強調滿意度

● 我有自信我們可以準時交貨。

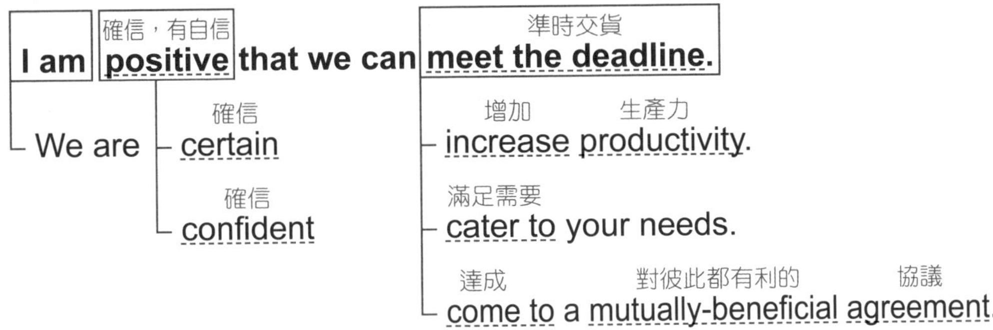

I am positive that we can meet the deadline.
確信，有自信
準時交貨
We are
確信
certain
確信
confident
增加
生產力
increase productivity.
滿足需要
cater to your needs.
達成
對彼此都有利的
協議
come to a mutually-beneficial agreement.

● 我們有信心可以在期限內完成。

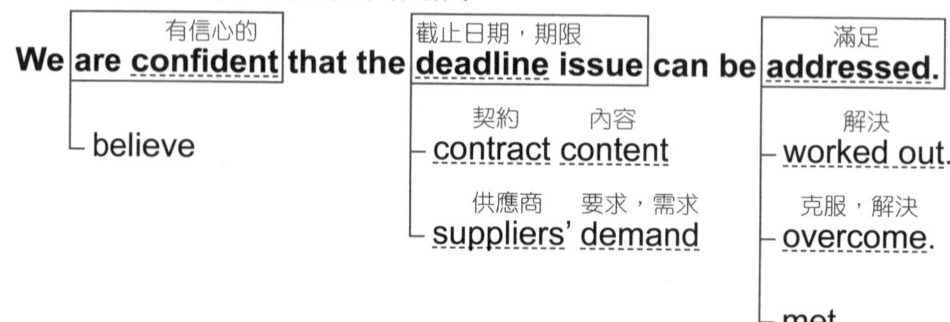
We are confident that the deadline issue can be addressed.
有信心的
截止日期，期限
滿足
believe
契約 內容
contract content
供應商 要求，需求
suppliers' demand
解決
worked out.
克服，解決
overcome.
met.

● 我深信那件事是可以辦到的。

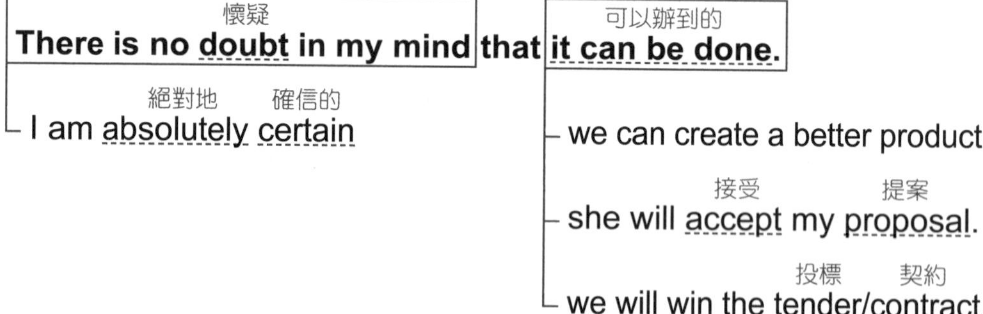
There is no doubt in my mind that it can be done.
懷疑
可以辦到的
絕對地 確信的
I am absolutely certain
we can create a better product.
接受 提案
she will accept my proposal.
投標 契約
we will win the tender/contract.

● 假如您選擇Crystal Sky，我保證我們將為滿足您的需求而全力以赴。

If you choose Crystal Sky, you have my personal guarantee (保證)

that we will do everything in our power to meet your needs. (滿足您的需求)

05 對問題的因應之道

● 我們深切盼望能找出一個折衷的方法。

We are eager to find a compromise.
渴望的，急切的
妥協方案，折衷辦法
堅定的
committed to find
動機強烈的 達成
motivated to achieve
解決方案
solution.
決議，共識
settlement.

● 這個問題顯然必須處理。

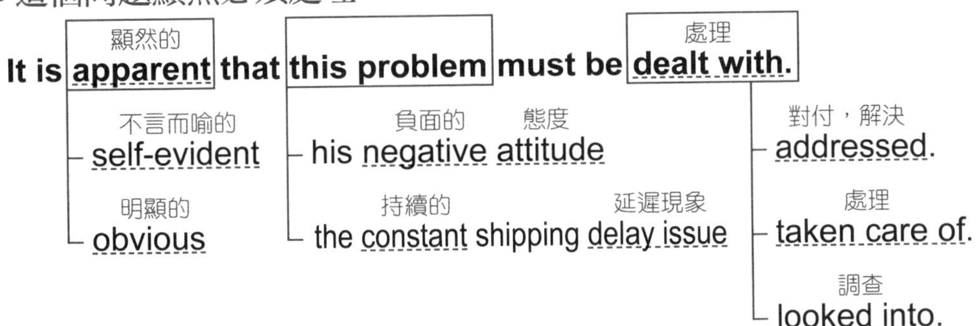

顯然的
處理
It is apparent that this problem must be dealt with.
不言而喻的
self-evident
負面的 態度
his negative attitude
對付，解決
addressed.
明顯的
obvious
持續的 延遲現象
the constant shipping delay issue
處理
taken care of.
調查
looked into.

● 除非你們也多少做些讓步，否則我們不會接受這些條件。

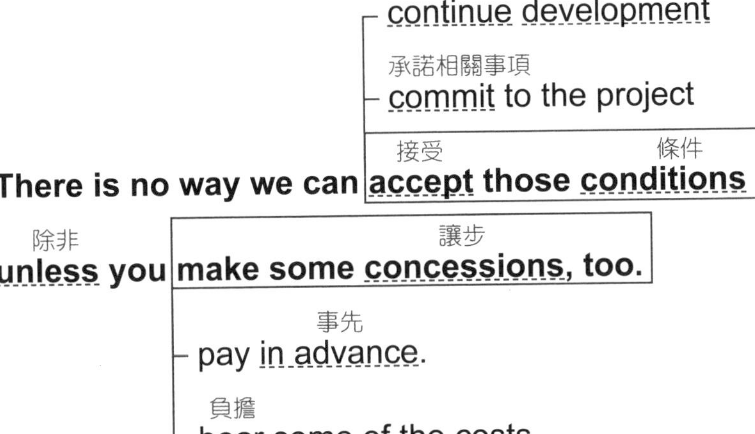

繼續 開發
continue development
承諾相關事項
commit to the project
接受 條件
There is no way we can accept those conditions
除非 讓步
unless you make some concessions, too.
事先
pay in advance.
負擔
bear some of the costs.

● 要我考慮繼續跟你們合作，你們必須免費更換訂單編號444的全部商品。

考慮
For me to even consider staying with you, you would have to

更換 全部的
replace the entire lot from order 444 free of charge.

● 要怎麼做你才願意簽名呢？

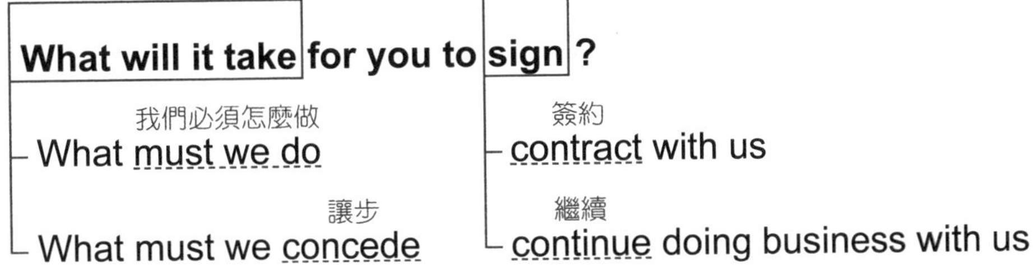

What will it take for you to sign ?
我們必須怎麼做
What must we do
簽約
contract with us
讓步
What must we concede
繼續
continue doing business with us

●讓我們繼續這樁生意的唯一方法，就是你們降低成本。

The only way we can continue doing business is you lower the cost price.

- we will achieve success（達成／成功）
- we can re-up with you（再次簽約）Casual Tone
- we will consider it（考慮）
- **we can continue doing business**（繼續）

- **lower the cost price.**
- shoulder a portion of the costs.（負擔／一部分）
- provide a longer warranty.（提供／保固期）

14P

Business E-mail Tips

告別中式英文

When you write in all capital letters, it reads AS THOUGH YOU ARE SHOUTING.

當你用全部大寫的英文字來寫文章時，別人讀起來的感覺就像你在對他吼叫。

英文字全部大寫，不好嗎？

用英文填寫表格等個人資料時，有時候會要求全部以大寫英文字填寫。這是因為大寫英文字母的辨識度比較高，避免因為字跡過於潦草而被誤讀重要的資訊。但是在撰寫英文書信時，若把全部的英文字母都大寫的話，就會讓人覺得你在大呼小叫；相對的，如果整篇都用小寫字母書寫，則顯得有些孩子氣，會給人不專業的印象。所以在撰寫商業書信時，務必記得要正確區分大小寫。

01 100%同意

● 你說的我100%贊成。

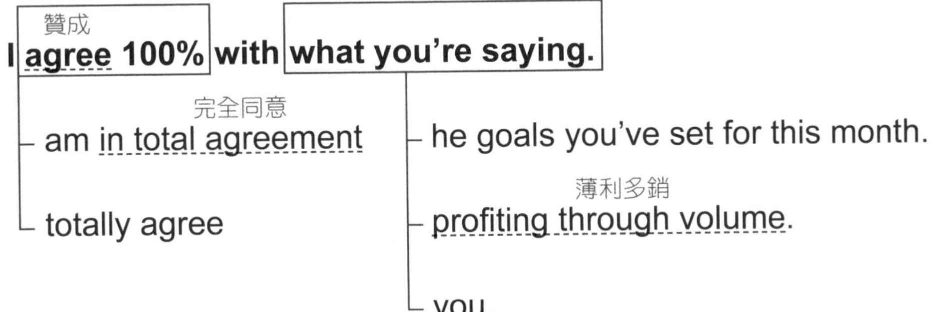
贊成
I agree 100% with what you're saying.
完全同意
am in total agreement
totally agree
he goals you've set for this month.
薄利多銷
profiting through volume.
you.

● 我們全面支持你變更廣告公司的決定。

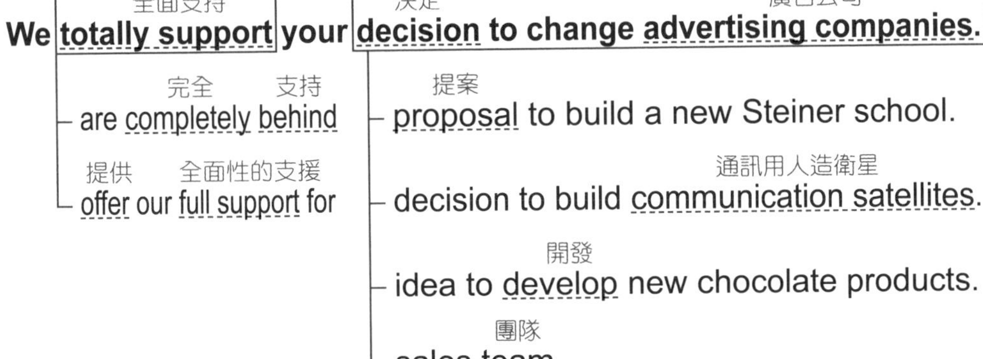
全面支持
決定
廣告公司
We totally support your decision to change advertising companies.
完全
支持
are completely behind
提供
全面性的支援
offer our full support for
提案
proposal to build a new Steiner school.
通訊用人造衛星
decision to build communication satellites.
開發
idea to develop new chocolate products.
團隊
sales team.

● 關於這件事，你有我全面且無條件的支持。

無條件的
這件事
You have my total and unconditional support on this matter.
our
total support

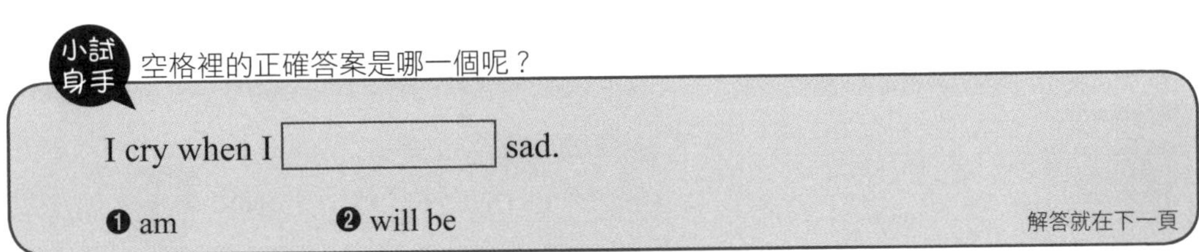
小試身手
空格裡的正確答案是哪一個呢？
I cry when I [ ] sad.
❶ am
❷ will be
解答就在下一頁

5 同意・支持 100%同意

● 我上司和我都一致認為我們應該繼續開發。

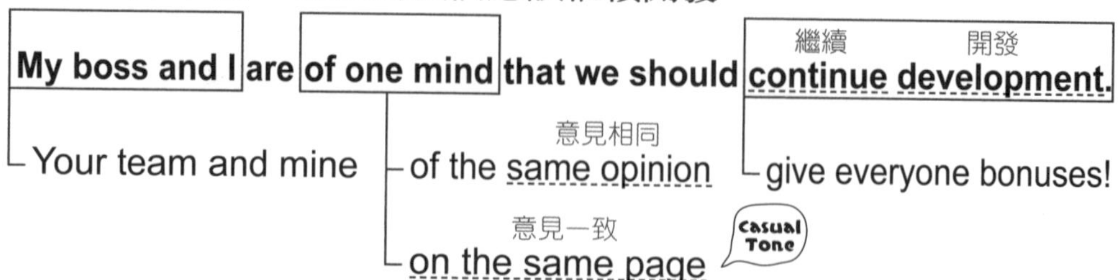

My boss and I are of one mind that we should continue development.
繼續 開發
Your team and mine
意見相同
of the same opinion
意見一致
on the same page
Casual Tone
give everyone bonuses!

● 我贊成提前幾天出發到古巴的計劃。

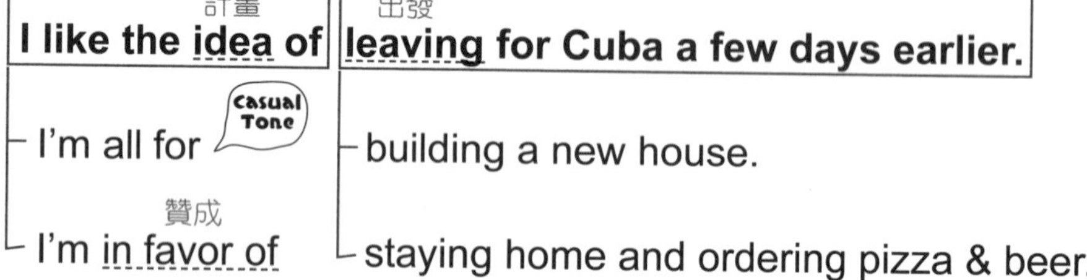

計畫
I like the idea of
出發
leaving for Cuba a few days earlier.
I'm all for
Casual Tone
贊成
I'm in favor of
building a new house.
staying home and ordering pizza & beer.

02 大致贊成

● 我們之間也許存在一些歧異，但是我傾向認同你的意見。

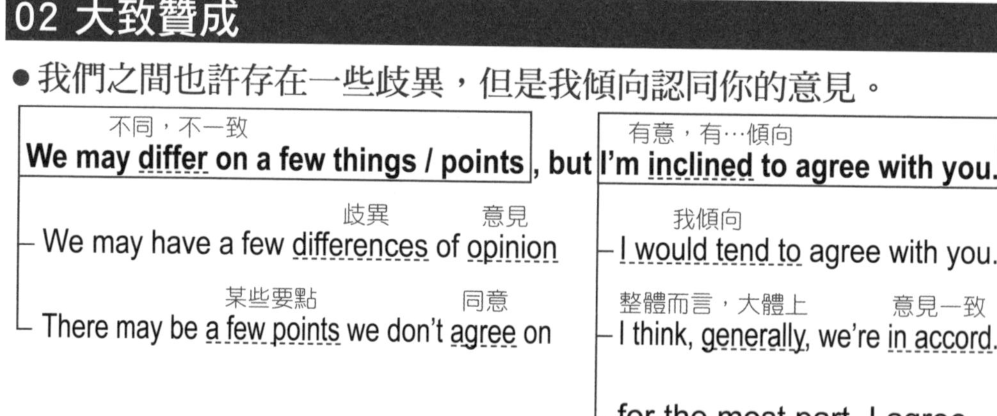

不同，不一致
We may differ on a few things / points, but
有意，有…傾向
I'm inclined to agree with you.
歧異 意見
We may have a few differences of opinion
某些要點 同意
There may be a few points we don't agree on
我傾向
I would tend to agree with you.
整體而言，大體上 意見一致
I think, generally, we're in accord.
for the most part, I agree.

前一頁 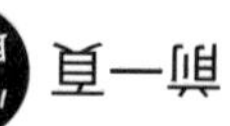 的解答 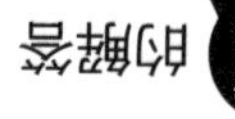 I cry when I am sad.
我在悲傷的時候哭泣。

● 我基本上支持李先生變更設計的想法。

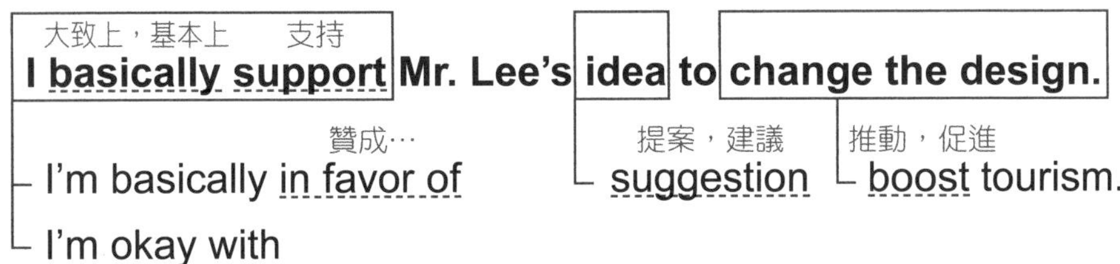
大致上，基本上 支持
I basically support Mr. Lee's idea to change the design.
贊成…
I'm basically in favor of
I'm okay with
提案，建議
suggestion
推動，促進
boost tourism.

03 詢問是否同意

● 你同意我們重新包裝嗎？

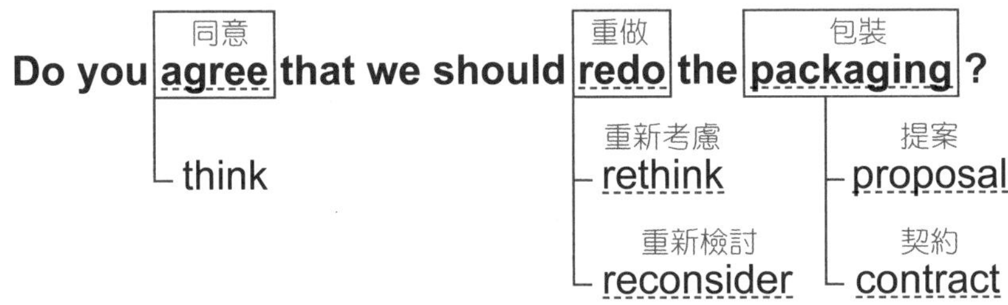
同意 重做 包裝
Do you agree that we should redo the packaging?
think
重新考慮
rethink
重新檢討
reconsider
提案
proposal
契約
contract

04 表示批准・同意

● 他從他的上司那裡得到販售土地的書面同意書。

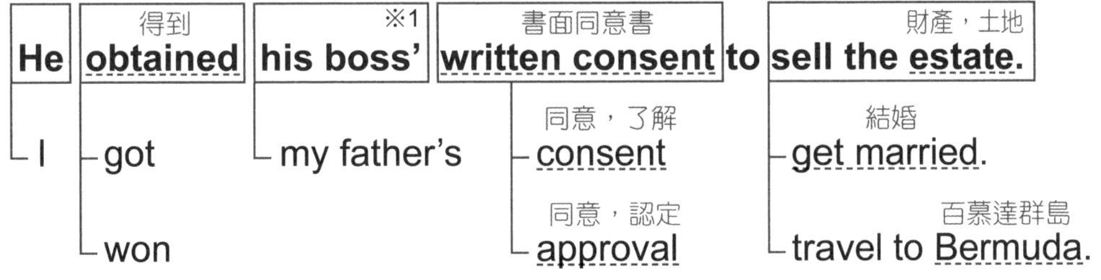
得到 ※1 書面同意書 財產，土地
He obtained his boss' written consent to sell the estate.
I
got
won
my father's
同意，了解
consent
同意，認定
approval
結婚
get married.
百慕達群島
travel to Bermuda.

※1 以 "s" 結尾的名詞，其所有格標示方法為在 "s" 後面加一撇。

● 我的上司同意退費以彌補你的損失。

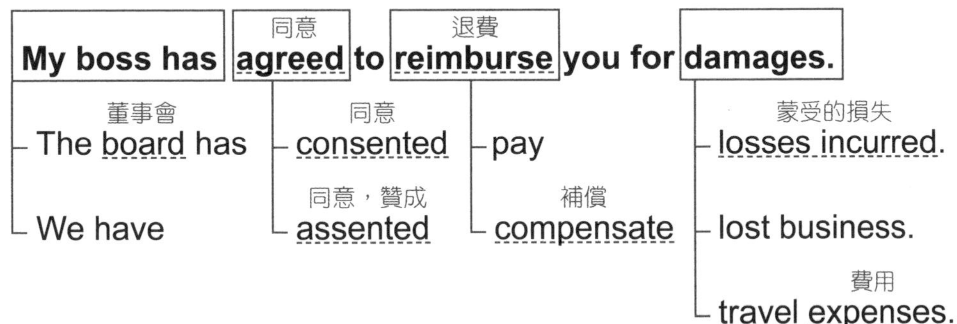
同意 退費
My boss has agreed to reimburse you for damages.
董事會
The board has
We have
同意
consented
同意，贊成
assented
pay
補償
compensate
蒙受的損失
losses incurred.
lost business.
費用
travel expenses.

5 同意・支持

詢問是否同意／表示批准・同意

● 我收到巫術研究學校寄來的入學許可。

I received a letter of acceptance (許可通知書) from the School of Shamanic Studies.

05 有條件的同意

● 我並不反對變更這本書的格式。

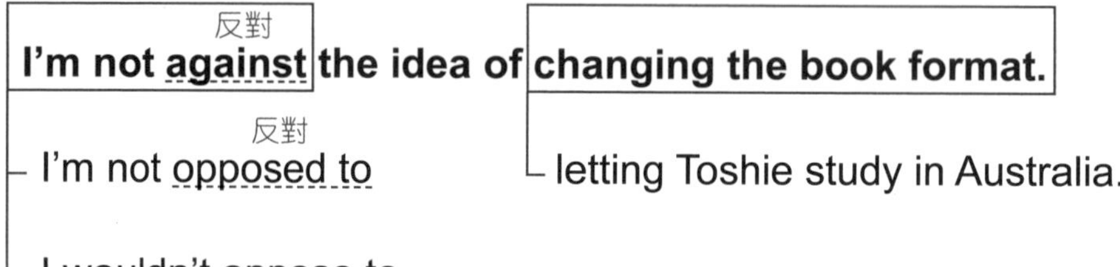

I'm not against (反對) the idea of changing the book format.
I'm not opposed to (反對)
I wouldn't oppose to
letting Toshie study in Australia.

● 我並不完全認同你的意見，但是你確實提出一個很好的論點。

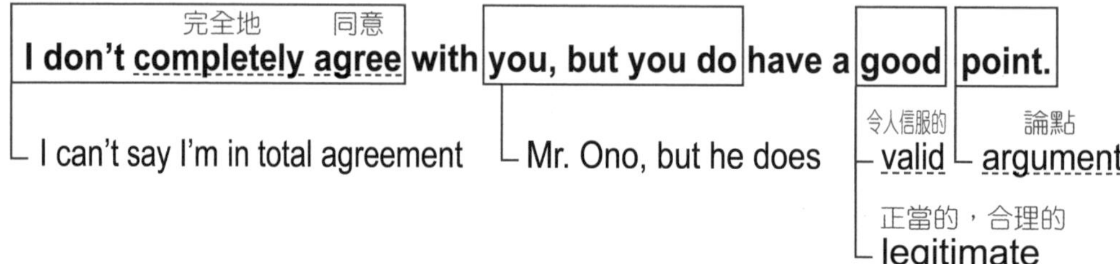

I don't completely (完全地) agree (同意) with you, but you do have a good point.
I can't say I'm in total agreement
Mr. Ono, but he does
valid (令人信服的)
legitimate (正當的，合理的)
argument (論點)

06 表示反對

● 我認為你重新評估系統的提議不太可行。

I think that your idea to review (重新評估) the system just isn't feasible (可實行的).
feel
plan
suggestion (提案，建議)
ship everything by air (空運)
move the factory to Laos
wouldn't work.
isn't practical (實際的).
isn't viable (可實行的).

● 很抱歉，但是我完全無法認同你的做法。

完全的
不一致
做法
I'm sorry, but I am in total disagreement with your approach.
totally disagree
don't agree
can't agree
意見
opinion.
idea.
方法
methods.
解決方案
solution.

● 關於如何提升成本效益，恐怕我無法贊同你的意見。

意見相同
提升，改善
成本效益
I can't say that I share your idea on how to improve cost-effectiveness.
I'm afraid I do not
看法
view
見解
perspective
觀點
viewpoint
意見，觀點
sentiments
提升性能
how to enhance performance.
what to do about the bug.
上市
the best way to market it.

No Chinese English!

跟中文含蓄客氣的語感比起來，英語是一種「有話直說」的語言。不過以下這些句子，在英語也有相對應的說法，而且十分常用喔！

ex.1「不好意思，可以請你…嗎？」

→ Excuse me, but could you...?

ex.2「非常感謝您，但是…」

→ Thanks anyway, but...

Thank you for the kind offer, but...

Dear Giovanna,

Thank you for the samples.
The response to the Mango Tea was very positive. In fact, many of our customers expressed that they would like to buy the tea loose rather than in individual bags.
I would like to talk to you about this. For now, I would like to place an order for the following:
1966-0921 3 cases
1966-0317 2 cases
1967-0102 3 cases

Also, could you let me know when your summer holidays are?
We have a week off from Aug 11-18.

Regards,
Angela

中譯

謝謝你寄來的樣品。
芒果茶的反應非常好。事實上，跟個別包裝的茶包比起來，我們許多顧客都表示比較想買茶葉。所以，我希望能和你討論這件事。
目前，我要訂購的貨品如下。

（中略）

另外，能否請你告訴我，你們的暑休是哪幾天呢？
敝公司從8月11日到18日休息一週。

01 關於訂貨的方法

● 可以打電話訂購嗎？

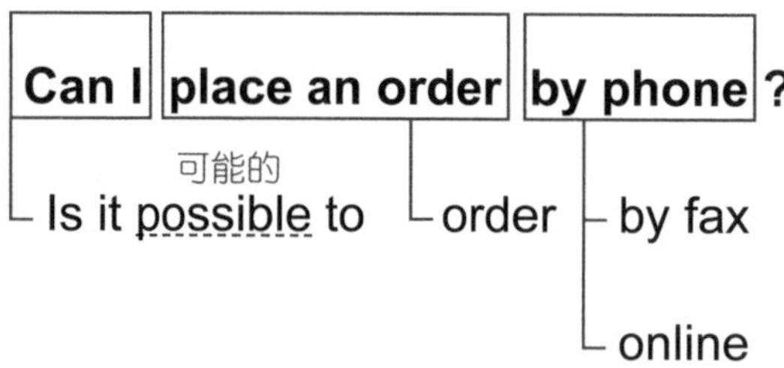
Can I
place an order
by phone ?
可能的
Is it possible to
order
by fax
online

● 另一個選擇是在網路上訂購。

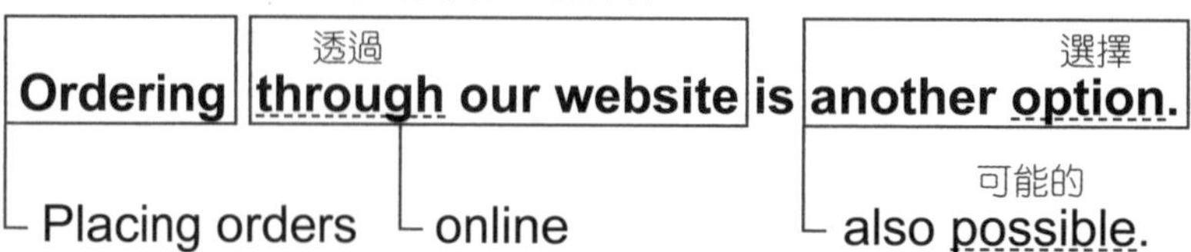
Ordering
透過
through our website
is
選擇
another option.
Placing orders
online
可能的
also possible.

02 訂貨

● 我考慮這星期訂購三張桌子。

I'm thinking of ordering 3 tables this week.

- purchasing 購買
- getting

● 我想預購最新一集的Mary Notter。

I'd like to pre-order the latest Mary Notter book.

- I'd like to reserve a copy of（reserve 預約）
- the forthcoming（forthcoming 即將發行的）（latest 最新的）
- Star Odyssey DVD.

● 我的訂單如附件。

I wish to place the attached order.（attached 附加的）

- I want
- I'd like
- following 如下的，以下的※1

※1 使用 "following" 這個字的時候，在 "order" 的後面通常會使用冒號 ":"。

● 我會在星期五之前寄給您最終的訂單。

I will send you my final order by Friday.

- decision 決定，結論
- request

●我已在你的網站上下訂單。

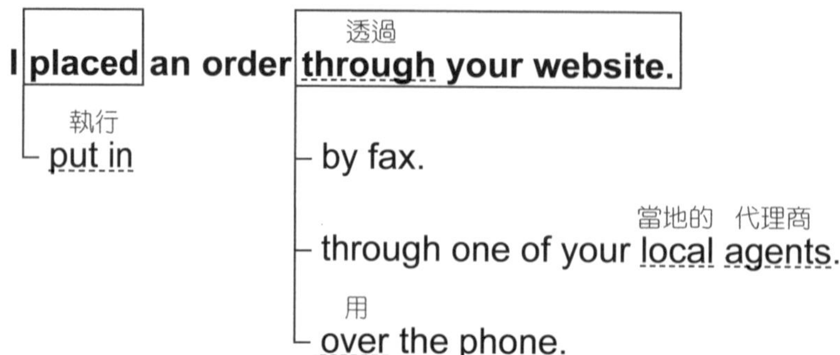
I placed an order through your website.
透過
執行
put in
by fax.
through one of your local agents.
當地的
代理商
用
over the phone.

03 接受訂單

●我們已經接到你訂購三箱荷荷芭油的訂單。

We have received your order for 3 cases of jojoba oil.

└ would like to confirm（確認）

Thank you for your interest.

Here are the answers to your questions:

1) We do ship to Australia.
2) We offer discounts on orders of 500 or more (I will send the schedule of discounts to you in a follow-up mail).
3) All of the products in the catalogue I sent you are in compliance with Australian law.
4) The prices do not include shipping.
5) For an additional price, we can bottle and custom label the product before shipping.
6) I will courier the samples to you tomorrow.

Please mail me with any further questions you may have and let me know how the samples work out.

Kenny

中譯

很高興您對本公司的產品感興趣。

關於您的疑問，我們的解答如下：

1) 我們提供送貨到澳洲的服務。
2) 訂貨數量超過500以上可享有折扣優惠。（我們會在下一封郵件中附上完整的折扣方案表）。
3) 之前寄送給您的商品目錄中，所有商品都符合澳洲的法律規定。
4) 商品費用並不包含運費。
5) 出貨之前，我們提供裝瓶和客製化標籤的服務，這項服務必須額外收費。
6) 我明天就會將樣品宅配到貴公司。

假如您還有進一步的疑問，請寄信與我聯絡。此外，也請您與我分享試用樣品之後的感想。

● 我們已經收到您的訂單。

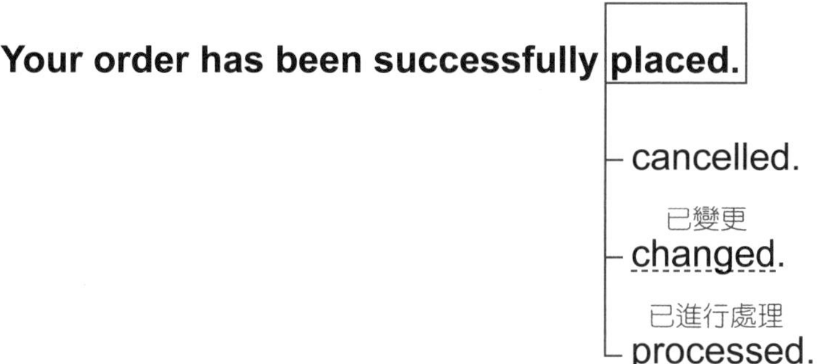
Your order has been successfully placed.
cancelled.
已變更
changed.
已進行處理
processed.

● 訂購數量至少要100個以上。

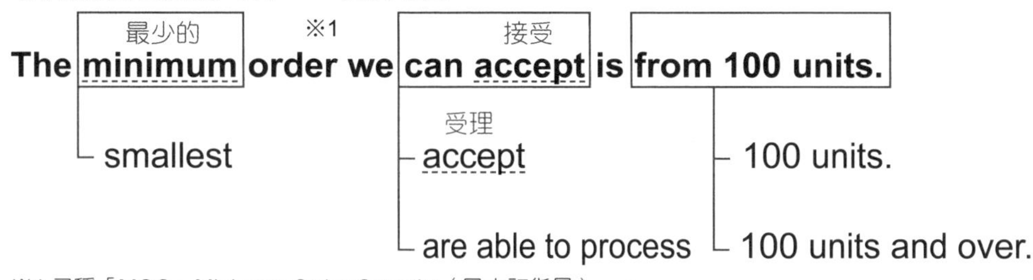
最少的
※1
接受
The minimum order we can accept is from 100 units.
smallest
受理
accept
are able to process
100 units.
100 units and over.

※1 又稱「MOQ＝Minimum Order Quantity（最小訂貨量）」。

04 確認訂單

● 你將在24小時內收到訂單確認通知。

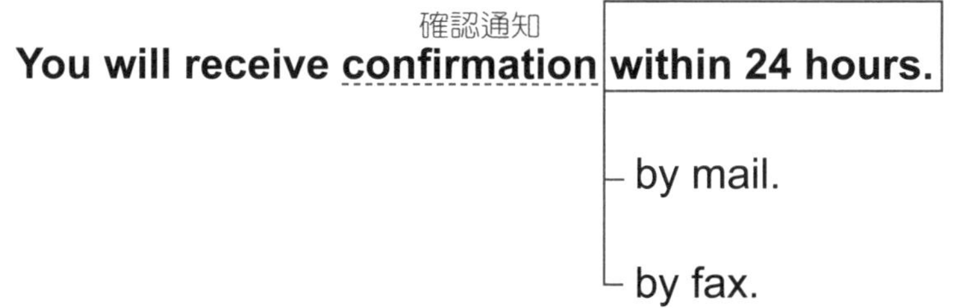
確認通知
You will receive confirmation within 24 hours.
by mail.
by fax.

● 感謝您訂購我們的商品。能否請您再次確認（訂購內容）呢？

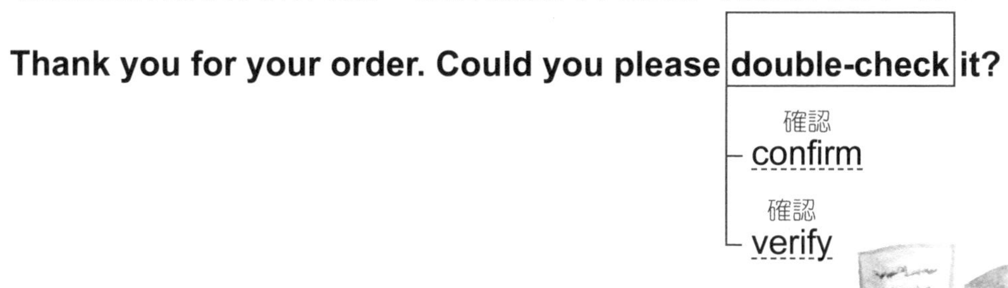
Thank you for your order. Could you please double-check it?
確認
confirm
確認
verify

John,

Thanks for your order. I need clarification on one point.
You have ordered 2 dozens of the model number 1841-01 twice.
Did you want 4 cases or is one of the orders an error?

Please get back to me as soon as possible.
The deadline for the next shipment is 6/15.
I'll hold the order until I get confirmation.

Also, I'll be taking a vacation from July 1 – July 10.
My assistant, Chris, will be taking care of my accounts during my absence.

Kenny

中譯

感謝您的訂購。有一件事想進一步向您確認。

您訂購了兩打產品型號1841-01的商品兩次。

請問您是需要四箱產品，還是因為訂購失誤呢？

希望您盡早回覆。我們下一次出貨的截止時間是6月15日。在我得到確認之前，將暫停處理您的訂單。

另外，我將於7月1日到10日休假。

我的助理克里斯在我休假的這段時間將代理我的相關業務。

● 可否請您確認訂單上的總金額呢？

Could you please verify (確認) the total amount on your order form?

- Could you please → May we ask you to / Please ※1
- verify → confirm (確認) / check

※1 以 "Please" 開頭的句子，句末不需要加問號。

● 我寫信的目的是想確認訂單C-22的處理狀況。

I am writing to check on the status (狀況) of order C-22.

- status → progress (發展，進展)

● 在我得到確認之前，將暫停處理您的訂單。

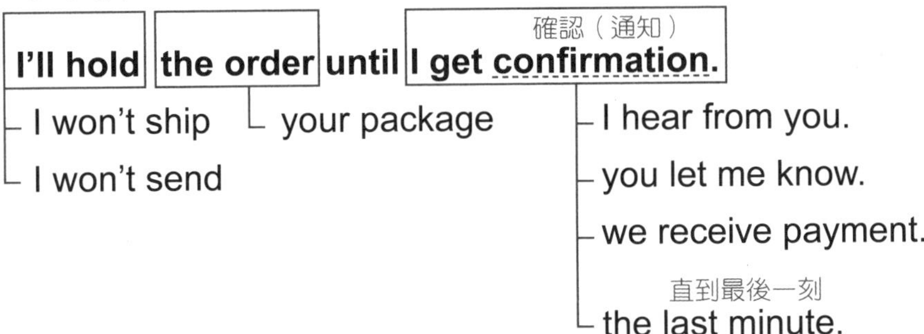
I'll hold the order until I get confirmation.
確認（通知）
I won't ship
I won't send
your package
I hear from you.
you let me know.
we receive payment.
the last minute.
直到最後一刻

● 可否請您確認訂單內容後回覆我？

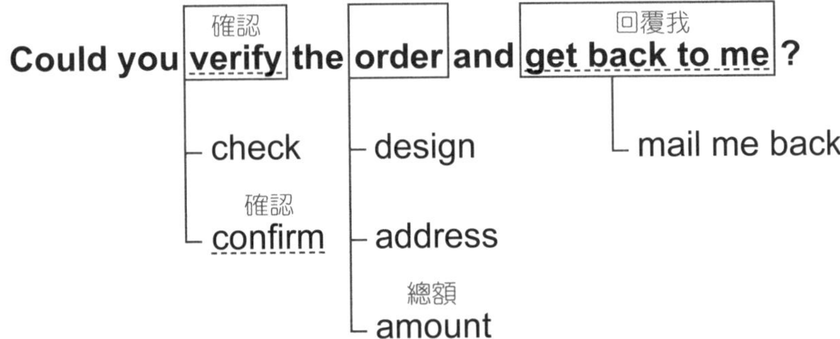
Could you verify the order and get back to me?
確認
回覆我
check
confirm
確認
design
address
amount
總額
mail me back

05 要求

● 我想與代理商談過之後再下訂單。

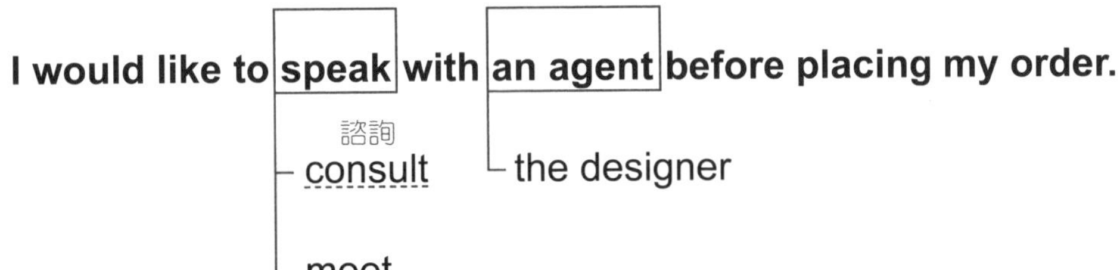
I would like to speak with an agent before placing my order.
consult
諮詢
meet
the designer

● 如果你能保證持續供貨，我們就向你下訂單。

If you can guarantee a constant supply, we'd like to order from you.
保證
持續的
供應
promise
承諾
contract with
簽約

● 我們計畫每個月訂購500箱，但是你們必須保證能夠穩定供應這個數量而不出錯。

We plan to order 500 cases per month, but need your assurance that you can supply that amount without fail.

- assurance（約定，保證）→ guarantee（保證）
- supply（供給）that amount → meet that demand（滿足需求）

● 在下訂單之前，我必須看一下物質安全資料表。

I will need the MSDS before I can place my order.

- the MSDS（物質安全資料表）→ the specs（規格）
- → the full list of colors（所有顏色列表）

06 追加訂單

● 我想在上次的訂單中，另外追加30箱滾珠軸承。

I would like to add an additional（追加的） 30 cases of ball bearings（滾珠軸承） to my last order.

- my last order → the order I placed yesterday.

● 假如訂單編號679的貨品尚未寄出，請再追加6個。

If order 679 has not been shipped yet, please add another 6 units.

- add another 6 units → replace（交換，更換） the red shirts with the yellow shirts.
- → cancel the eye patches（（保護傷口用的）眼罩）.

07 取消訂單

● 我想取消上一筆訂單。

I'd like to cancel my last order.

my order for the 25 silver pendants.

● 現在取消訂單編號8854是不是太遲了？

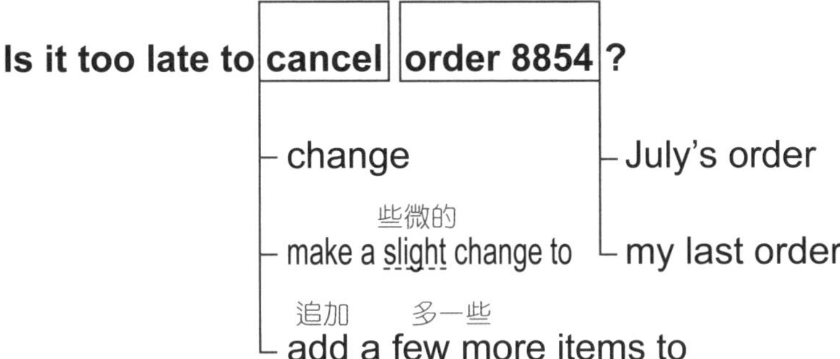

Is it too late to cancel order 8854 ?
change
些微的
make a slight change to
追加 多一些
add a few more items to
July's order
my last order

08 發生問題

● 因為存貨不多，您的訂單將會比預定日期稍微延後交貨。

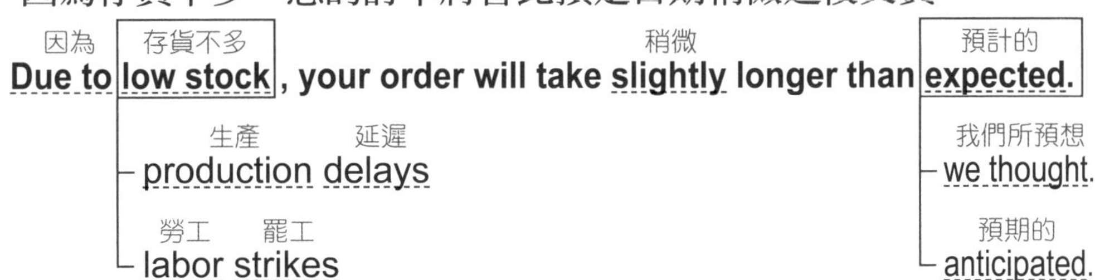

因為 存貨不多 稍微 預計的
Due to low stock, your order will take slightly longer than expected.
生產 延遲
production delays
勞工 罷工
labor strikes
我們所預想
we thought.
預期的
anticipated.

● 很抱歉，我可能不慎將同一筆訂單重複訂了兩次。

不慎地，非故意地

I'm afraid I may have inadvertently placed the same order twice.

cancelled my order.

給你 錯誤的

given you the wrong address.

選取了

selected the wrong item.

● 我嘗試透過你們的網站訂購一些商品，但是一直沒收到確認信。

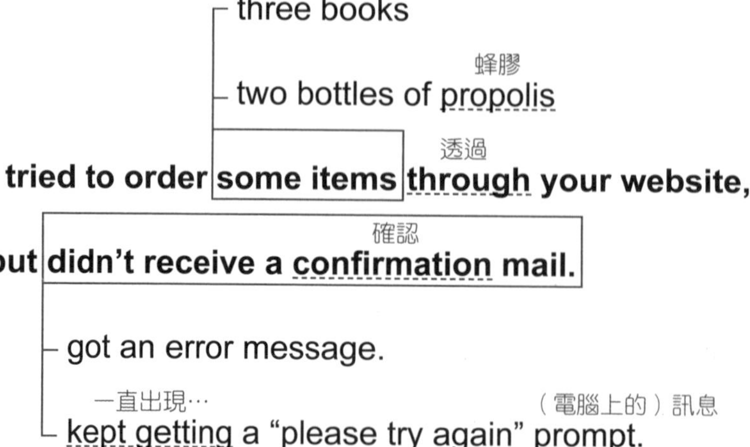
three books
蜂膠
two bottles of propolis
透過
I tried to order some items through your website,
確認
but didn't receive a confirmation mail.
got an error message.
一直出現…
(電腦上的)訊息
kept getting a "please try again" prompt.

● 我檢視過我們的記錄，但是似乎還沒收到你的訂單。

I checked our records, but we don't appear to have received your order.（似乎：appear）

- it seems we haven't（似乎：seems）

09 特別優惠

● 如果你再加訂50個，我們可以提供15%的折扣。

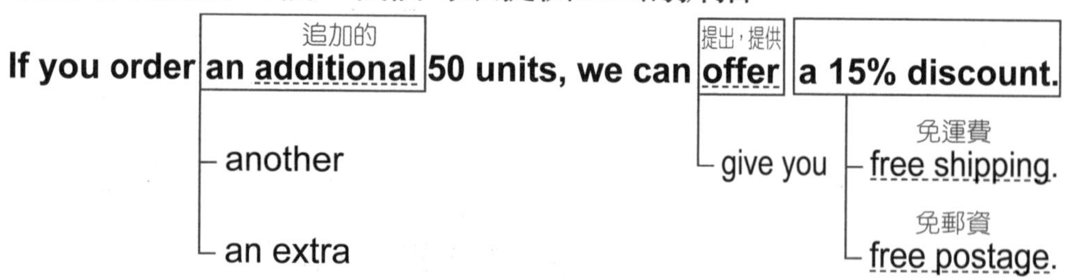
追加的
If you order an additional 50 units, we can offer a 15% discount.
提出，提供
another
an extra
give you
免運費
free shipping.
免郵資
free postage.

● 再加訂兩箱的話就免運費。

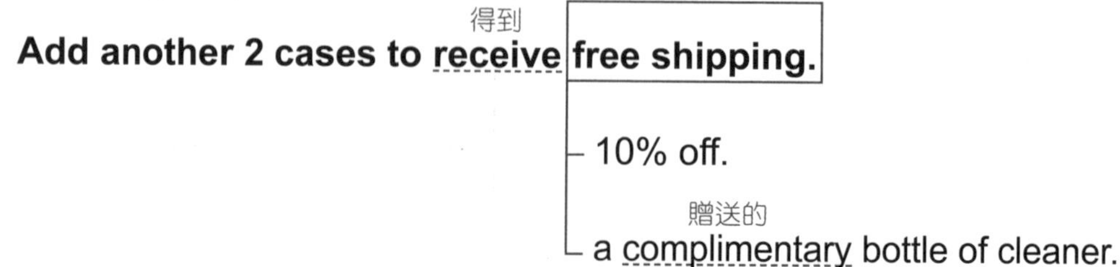
得到
Add another 2 cases to receive free shipping.
10% off.
贈送的
a complimentary bottle of cleaner.

01 傳達時間緊迫的狀況

● 我沒什麼時間，所以請不要遲到。

I don't have a lot of time so please don't be late.

- I don't have a lot of time → I only have an hour
- don't be late. → come prepared.（做好準備再來）
- don't be late. → be on time.（準時）

● 很抱歉造成你的壓力，但是我們必須嚴格遵守進度。

Sorry to pressure you, but we must stick to the schedule.（stick to：堅持，信守，貫徹到底）

- Sorry to pressure you → We apologize（apologize：道歉）
- must stick to the schedule. → need the manuscript by Monday.（manuscript：原稿）
- must stick to the schedule. → have to push the deadline up two days.（push the deadline up：將截止日期提前 ※1）

※1 也可以用 "push the deadline forward"；「將截止日期延後」則是 "push the deadline back"。

● 這筆訂單很趕，所以請用空運寄送。

This is a rush order. Please freight by air.（freight：運送）

- rush order → priority customer（優先服務的顧客）

● 為了提供你最好的交易條件，我們需要您盡快回覆。

We really need an answer as soon as possible in order to get you the best deal.（in order to：為了…；the best deal：條件最佳的買賣）

- an answer → a commitment（承諾，保證）
- possible → you can

● 可否請您立刻與我聯絡？

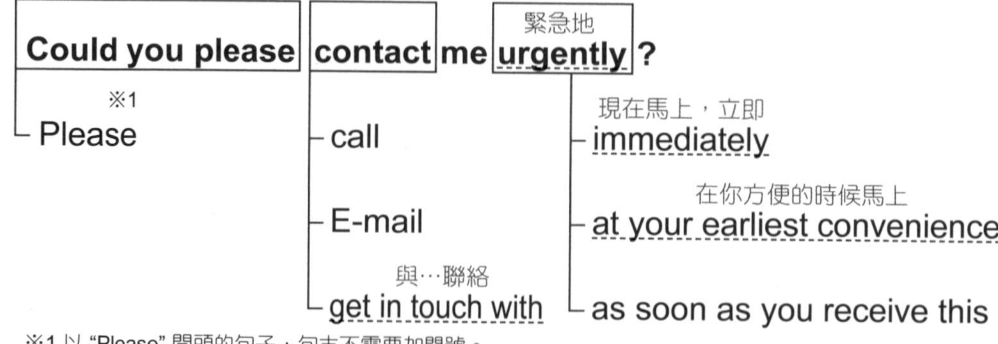
Could you please contact me urgently ?
緊急地
※1
Please
call
E-mail
與…聯絡
get in touch with
現在馬上，立即
immediately
在你方便的時候馬上
at your earliest convenience
as soon as you receive this

※1 以 “Please” 開頭的句子，句末不需要加問號。

02 催促對方立即回覆與因應

● 時間是最重要的關鍵；請在今天之內回覆。

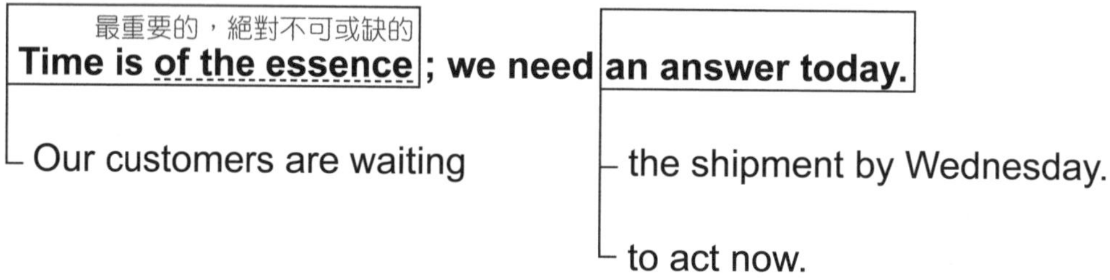
最重要的，絕對不可或缺的
Time is of the essence ; we need an answer today.
Our customers are waiting
the shipment by Wednesday.
to act now.

● 請現在立刻與我聯絡。我有非常重要的事情要通知你。

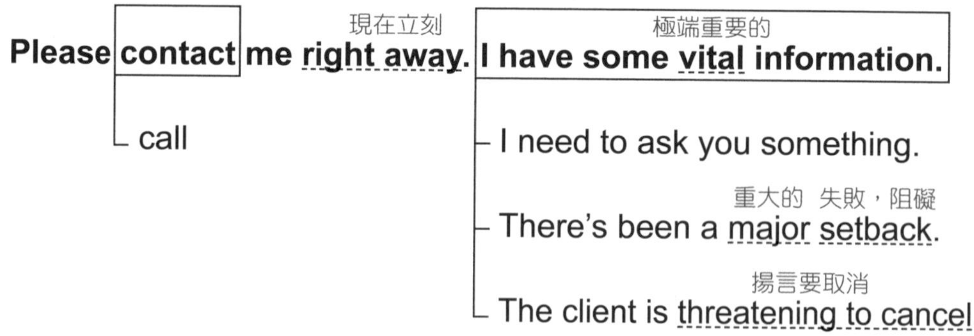
現在立刻
Please contact me right away.
call
極端重要的
I have some vital information.
I need to ask you something.
重大的 失敗，阻礙
There's been a major setback.
揚言要取消
The client is threatening to cancel.

● 我沒辦法再繼續等下去；這是你最後一次機會。 Casual Tone

繼續，一直
I can't wait for you any longer ; it's now or never.
最後一次機會
永遠
forever
最後一搏的，孤注一擲的
do-or-die time.

● 如果我們今天沒有得到答覆，我們就會另覓他途。

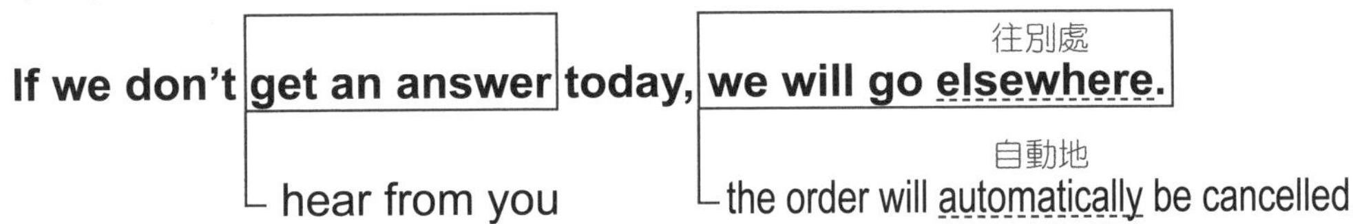
If we don't get an answer today, we will go elsewhere.
往別處
hear from you
自動地
the order will automatically be cancelled.

● 你是否能設法把出發日提前呢？

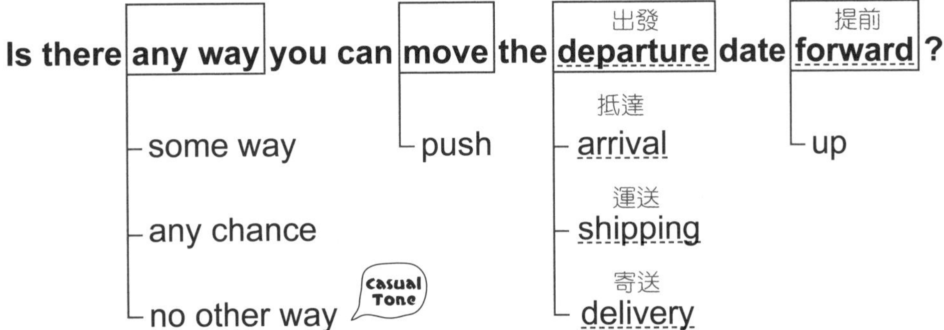
Is there any way you can move the departure date forward?
出發
提前
some way
any chance
no other way
Casual Tone
push
抵達
arrival
運送
shipping
寄送
delivery
up

● 請盡一切努力將貨品準時送達。

Please do everything you can to get the order here on time.
抵達
準時
必要的
take the necessary steps
確保
測試
ensure we finish the trials today.

● 客戶會開始另覓他途，這是早晚的事。

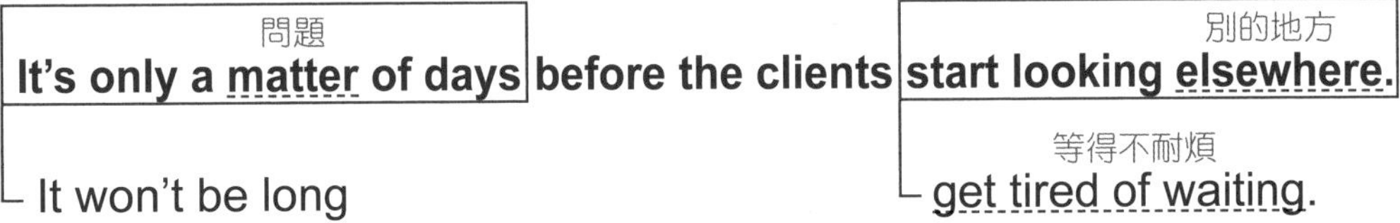
It's only a matter of days before the clients start looking elsewhere.
問題
別的地方
It won't be long
等得不耐煩
get tired of waiting.

● 契約明天就到期，所以我們今天一定要達成共識才行。

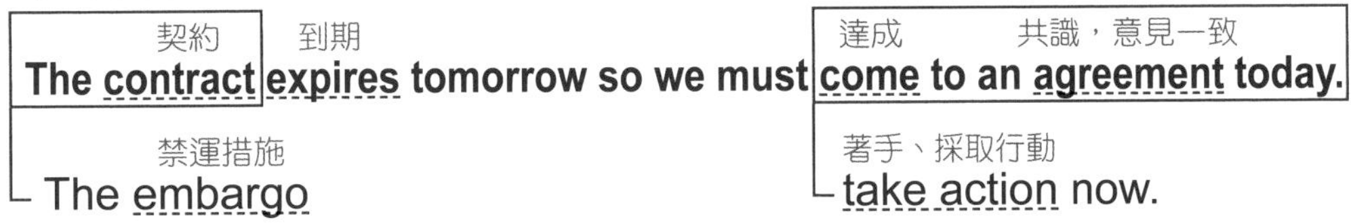
The contract expires tomorrow so we must come to an agreement today.
契約
到期
達成
共識，意見一致
禁運措施
The embargo
著手、採取行動
take action now.

● 機器如果不修理的話，隨時都有可能會故障。

If the machines are not serviced (修理), they could break down (壞掉，故障) any day (隨時).

● 我們可以整理環境的時間越來越少。

We are running out of (將…用完) time to clean up (打掃，整理) the environment (環境).

- We are running out of / We have very little
- clean up the environment. / fix the situation (狀況). / act. / save (挽救) the contract (契約).

● 假如我們在星期二之前無法完成資金調度，這筆交易就會失敗。

If we can't get the funds (資金) together by Tuesday, the deal (交易) will fall through (失敗，成為泡影).

- get the funds together / come to a decision (決定) / persuade (說服) the board (董事會) / find a replacement (代替品，候補)
- deal will fall through. / offer will expire (過期). / sale will be voided (失效). / show will not go on (繼續).

03 因應截止日期

● 我們必須設法提升產量。

We must find a way to step up production (增加生產、產量).

- We must find / There must be / I know
- step up production. / finish in time (在期限內). / get there by Saturday.

● 截止期限迫在眉睫。我們必須趕緊完工。

截止期限 / 迫在眉睫 / 促成，完成

The deadline is looming. We must push through to the end.

- tomorrow
- 頑強地堅持下去 soldier on. (Casual Tone)
- not stop now.
- 加快動作 pick up the pace.

● 如果我們早點開工，午餐時間也加緊趕工，我想我們就可以完成。

某段時間持續某動作

If we come in early and work through lunch, I think we'll make it.

- 外包，委外 outsource part of the work
- 分神，分心 / 失敗，挫折 don't get distracted by these setbacks
- 保持，維持 we can stay on schedule.

● 要在星期五之前完成的話，就必須動員更多工作人員。

帶進，導入 / 在…之前

We'll have to bring in more staff to finish by Friday.

- We need to
- 冒著無法完成的風險 / 及時 or we risk not finishing in time.

● 這個週末先趕工，早點提交吧。

某段時間持續某動作 / 提交（某物）

Let's work through the weekend and hand it in early.

- keep working through the night
- 僱用 / 臨時的 hire some temporary help
- 回到 / 預定計畫 get back on schedule.

小試身手

空格裡的正確答案是哪一個呢？

Weather [　　　] this makes me happy.

❶ as　　❷ like

解答就在下一頁

● 我們一定要在下週三之前拿到零件。

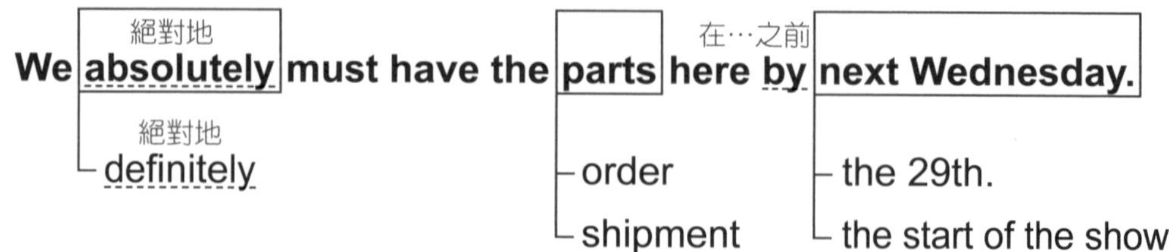
絕對地
We absolutely must have the parts here by next Wednesday.
在…之前
絕對地
definitely
order
shipment
the 29th.
the start of the show.

04 即刻因應

● 假如我們不盡快修理漏水的問題，地板就會受損。

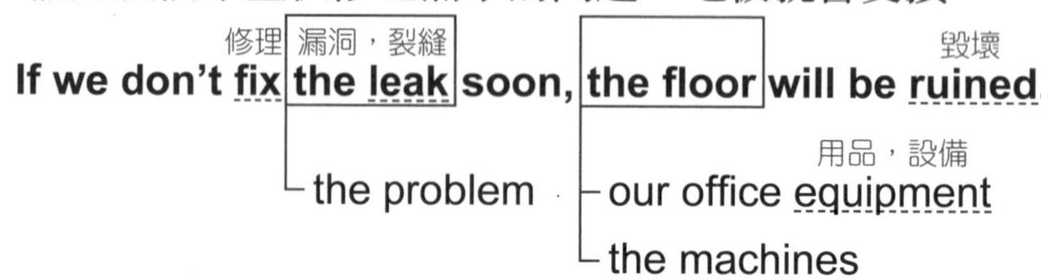
修理
漏洞，裂縫
毀壞
If we don't fix the leak soon, the floor will be ruined.
the problem
用品，設備
our office equipment
the machines

● 我必須立刻與他談談。生產線已經停擺了。

立刻，馬上
生產線
I need to talk to him immediately. The production line has shut down.
see
重大的
We are having major problems.
緊急狀況
This is an emergency.
倉庫
非法闖入
The warehouse was broken into.

05 限時優惠

● 現在就立刻行動以享受這個絕佳優惠！

利用，善用　　出價，優惠

Act now to take advantage of this fantastic offer!

前一頁 小試身手 的解答 ❷ Weather like this makes me happy.
這種天氣讓我覺得很開心。

●您越早決定，我們就能越早因應。

越早 / 決定，下定決心

The sooner you make up your mind, the sooner we can act.

- 負起責任 take responsibility
- ※1 start exercising

- I can help you.
- ※1 you'll lose weight.

※1 這裡的 “start exercising” 只和 “you'll lose weight” 搭配成一句。

06 強調我方可以快速處理需求

●我們將會盡全力加速處理您的訂單。

盡全力 / 迅速處理，加速處理

We will do everything in our power to expedite your order.

- 無論如何 whatever it takes
- all we can

●我將會提前處理您的訂單。

提前

I will have your order bumped to the front of the line. Casual Tone

- I have had

- put on the top of the list.
- 最高 優先順位 given the highest priority.

●我會立刻處理。

安排，處理 / 立刻

I will see to it at once.

- 親自 I will personally

- 及時 that the package arrives in time.
- 火速處理好 that your order is fast tracked.

適用情況 8：寄送・收發

01 索取資料

● 能否請你寄更多相關資訊給我呢？

Could you please send me more information?
E-mail
轉寄
forward
郵寄
post
us
最新的
your latest catalogs
a price list for your cosmetics
工廠
photos of your factory

● 請以電子郵件告知我們貨品追蹤碼。

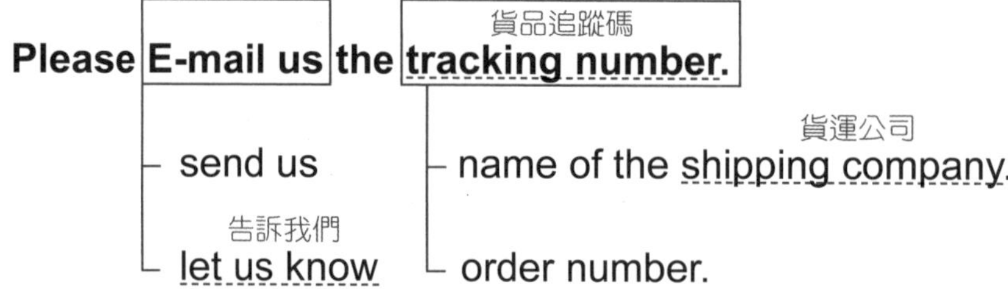
Please E-mail us the tracking number.
貨品追蹤碼
send us
告訴我們
let us know
貨運公司
name of the shipping company.
order number.

● 請將資料寄給我們，以證實你投訴的事項。

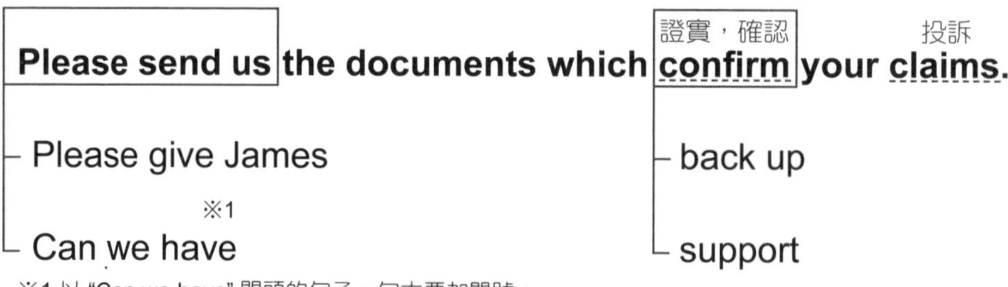
Please send us the documents which confirm your claims.
證實，確認
投訴
Please give James
※1
Can we have
back up
support

※1 以 "Can we have" 開頭的句子，句末要加問號。

02 寄送信件或其他物品的通知

● 請確認信件中附上的最新手冊以及價目表。

Please find enclosed our latest brochure and price list.
（附件的 enclosed；最新的 latest；小冊子，宣傳品 brochure）

● 我正要把我們網站的連結寄給你。

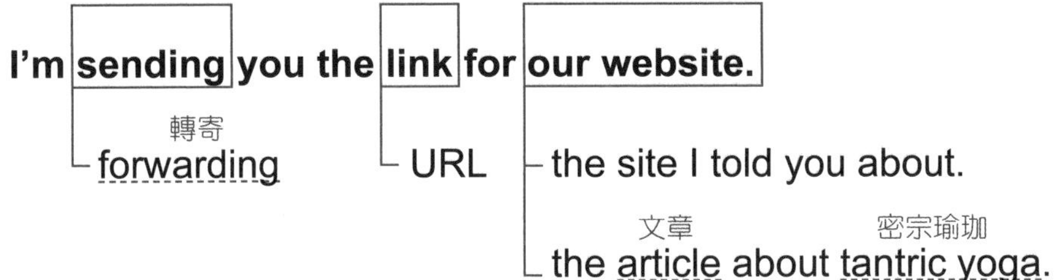
I'm sending you the link for our website.
轉寄
forwarding
URL
the site I told you about.
文章
密宗瑜珈
the article about tantric yoga.

● 我會從我們開發中的新系列產品裡，寄幾個樣品給你。

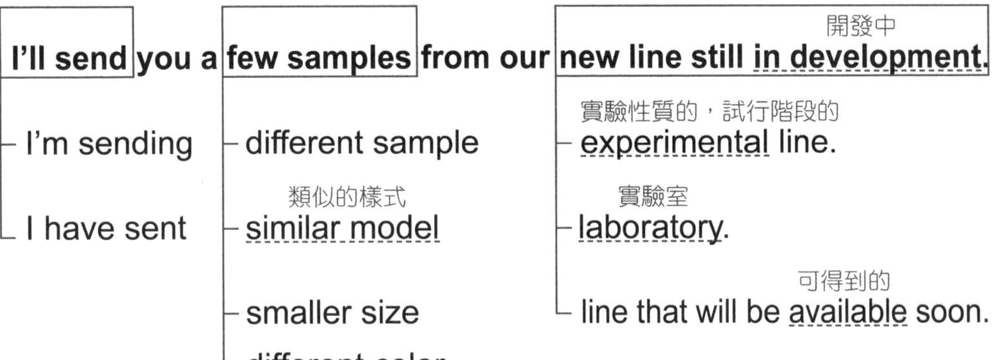
I'll send you a few samples from our new line still in development.
開發中
I'm sending
I have sent
different sample
類似的樣式
similar model
smaller size
different color
實驗性質的，試行階段的
experimental line.
實驗室
laboratory.
可得到的
line that will be available soon.

● 我會將商品規格以PDF格式的檔案寄給你。

I'm sending you a file of the product specs by PDF.
規格
附加
I've attached
加入，附上
I have included
轉寄
I'm forwarding you
修訂過的
our revised price list.
行程表
檢查，調查
the itinerary for the site inspection.
櫻花下的野餐
the photos from our picnic under the cherry blossoms.

● 我想確認你是否已經收到行程表。

I'd like to check if you've received the itinerary.
收到
行程表
know
贊成，同意
if you approve of
how you like
catalogue.
order.

03 關於寄送方法

● 我們會將最初的那一半的商品以空運寄出，接著把剩下的另一半以船運寄出。

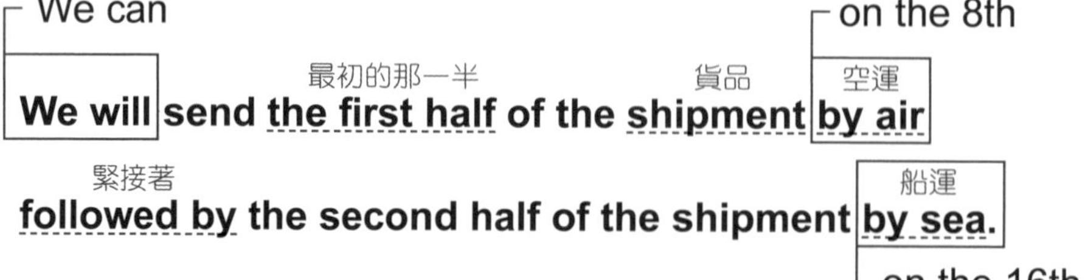

We can
We will send the first half of the shipment by air
最初的那一半
貨品
空運
on the 8th

緊接著
followed by the second half of the shipment by sea.
船運
on the 16th.

04 指定日期與時間

● 我們必須在15號之前收到貨品。

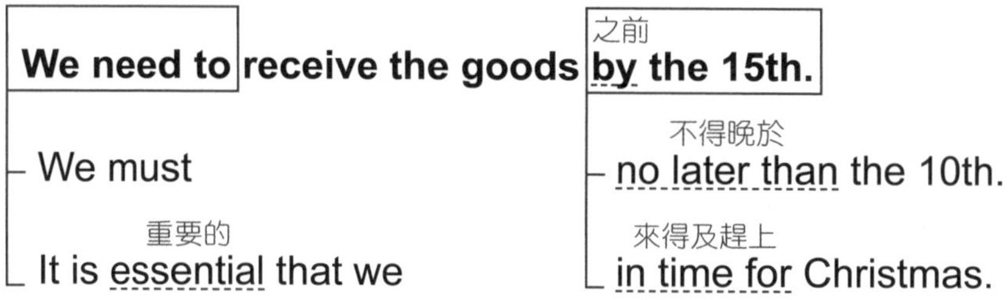

We need to receive the goods by the 15th.
之前
We must
It is essential that we
重要的
不得晚於
no later than the 10th.
來得及趕上
in time for Christmas.

● 請問預計哪一天我們可以收到寄送的物品呢？

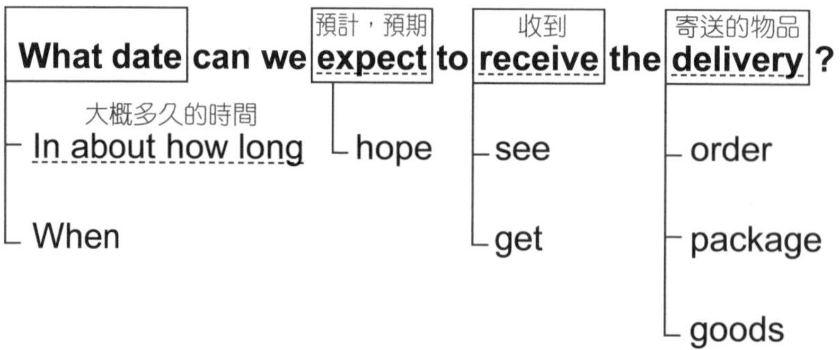

What date can we expect to receive the delivery ?
預計，預期
收到
寄送的物品
大概多久的時間
In about how long
When
hope
see
get
order
package
goods

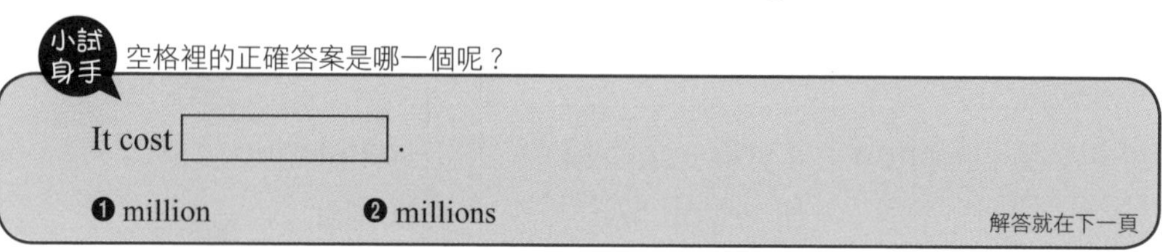

小試身手
空格裡的正確答案是哪一個呢？
It cost ______.
❶ million
❷ millions
解答就在下一頁

● 你希望我們哪一天將貨品寄出呢？

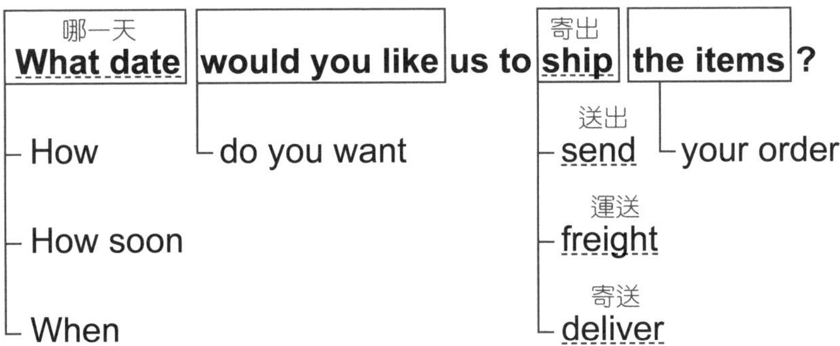
哪一天
What date
would you like
us to
寄出
ship
the items
?
How
How soon
When
do you want
送出
send
運送
freight
寄送
deliver
your order

● 如果17號之前你的貨物還沒抵達的話，請立刻通知我們。

抵達　在…之前　通知我們　立刻地

If your order does not arrive by the 17th, please let us know immediately.

包含　錯誤

contains any errors

遭受

incurs any damage

● 我們可以在15號將你的貨品寄出，到貨日期大約會在30號前後。

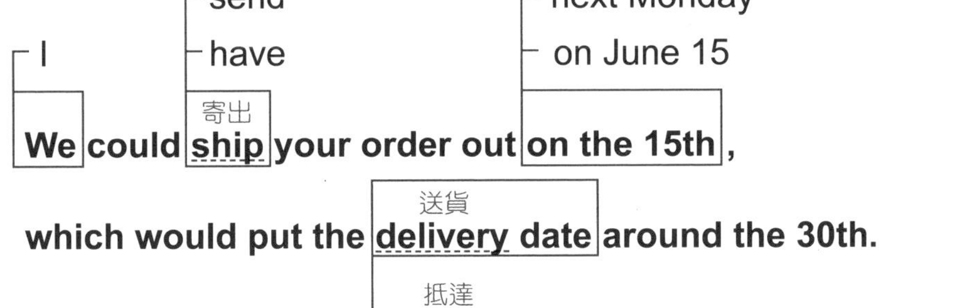
I
send
have
next Monday
on June 15
We
could
寄出
ship
your order out
on the 15th
,
which would put the
送貨
delivery date
around the 30th.
抵達
arrival date

● 可否請你確認貨品會在週五寄到？

確認
Can you confirm
寄送的貨物
that the shipment
抵達
will arrive
on
Friday
?
確定的
Are you certain
arrived
was sent
February 7th

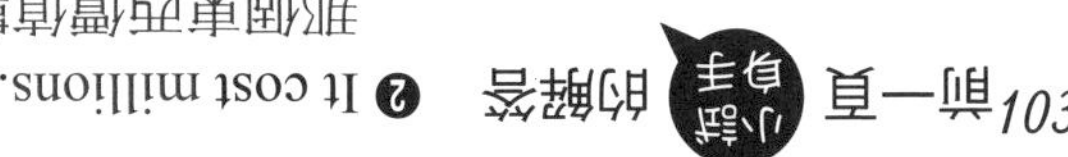
與一直心話自主的解答
❷ It cost millions.
那個東西價值數百萬。

05 運送狀況

● 你訂的貨品今天早上已經從工廠出貨了。

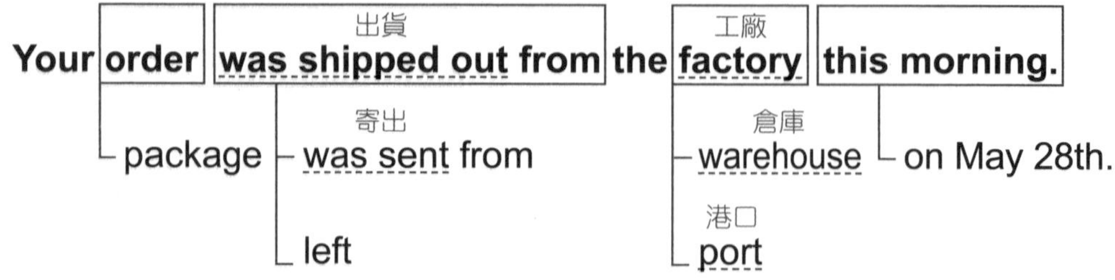
Your order was shipped out from the factory this morning.
出貨
工廠
package
寄出
was sent from
left
倉庫
warehouse
港口
port
on May 28th.

● 你寄送的物品三天前就離開了我們的倉庫。

Your shipment left our warehouse 3 days ago.
寄送的物品
倉庫
package
order
工廠
our factory
港口
Yokohama Port
this morning.

● 你的包裹應該明天會寄達。

Your package should arrive tomorrow.
應該※1
寄達
寄送的貨品
shipment
order
container
※2
will
※3
might
※3
may
get there
reach there
be there
on the 30th.
現在隨時
anytime now.
未來幾天之內
in the next few days.

※1 "should" 在這裡是「應該會…」的意思，為非確定的語氣。

※2 "will" 是一種確定的說法，使用時要注意。

※3 "might" 和 "may" 都是「說不定…」的意思，在不確定的情況下使用。助動詞的語氣由弱到強依序為 could＜might＜may＜can＜should＜ought to＜would＜will＜must。

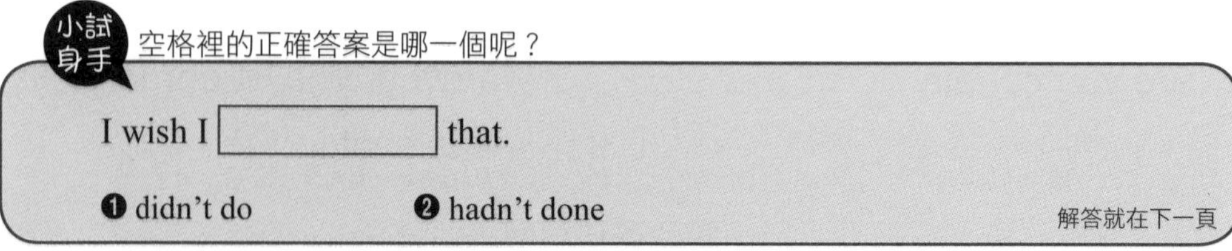
小試身手
空格裡的正確答案是哪一個呢？
I wish I [ ] that.
❶ didn't do
❷ hadn't done
解答就在下一頁

● 請將每一筆訂單間隔一週出貨。

間隔，錯開 每一個
Please stagger the shipping of each order by one week.

● 如果一切順利的話，你的包裹應該會在兩週內抵達。

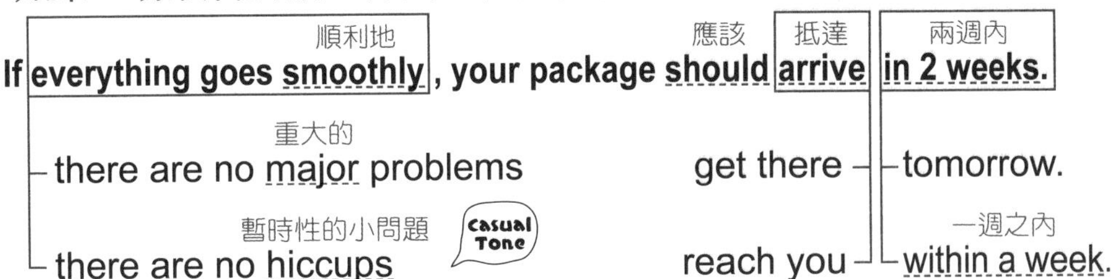
順利地
應該
抵達
兩週內
If everything goes smoothly, your package should arrive in 2 weeks.
重大的
there are no major problems
get there
tomorrow.
暫時性的小問題
Casual Tone
there are no hiccups
reach you
一週之內
within a week.

● 目錄現在應該已經寄到了才對。

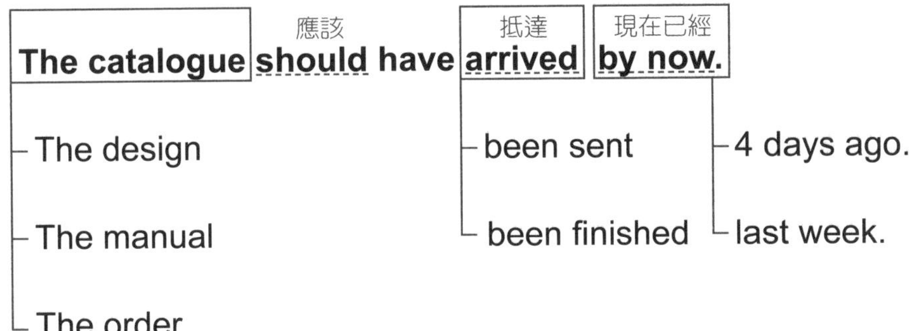
應該
抵達
現在已經
The catalogue should have arrived by now.
The design
been sent
4 days ago.
The manual
been finished
last week.
The order

● 我想知道我們訂的商品是否已經寄出。

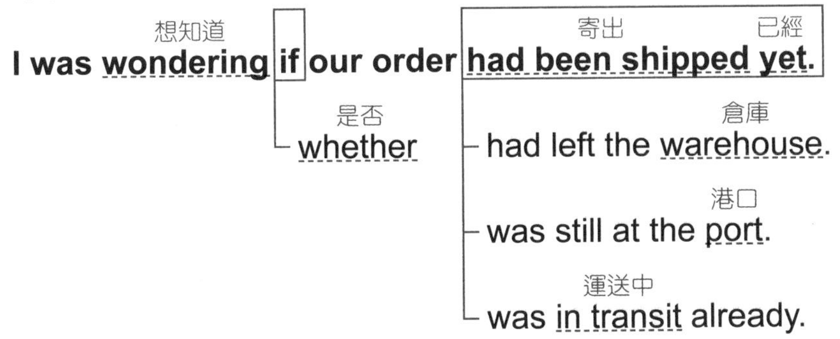
想知道
寄出
已經
I was wondering if our order had been shipped yet.
是否
whether
倉庫
had left the warehouse.
港口
was still at the port.
運送中
was in transit already.

前一頁 小試身手 的解答 ❷ I wish I hadn't done that.
我真希望我沒做過那件事。

06 寄達通知

● 我很高興得知貨物準時抵達。

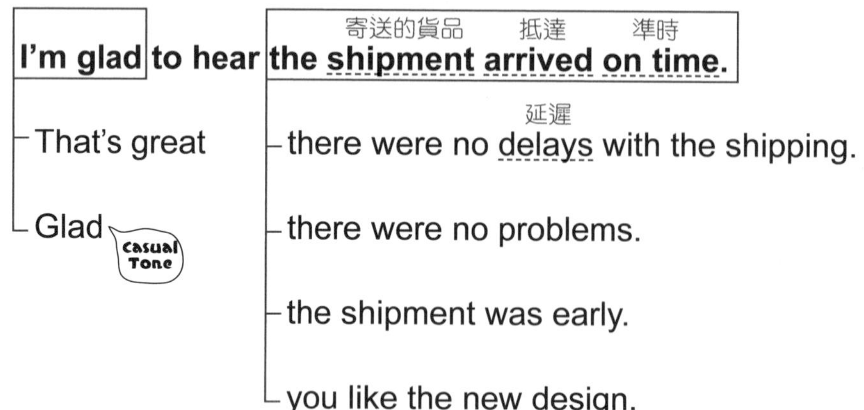

I'm glad to hear the shipment arrived on time.
寄送的貨品
抵達
準時
That's great
Glad
Casual Tone
there were no delays with the shipping.
延遲
there were no problems.
the shipment was early.
you like the new design.

● 感謝你努力確保我們訂購的商品如期寄達。

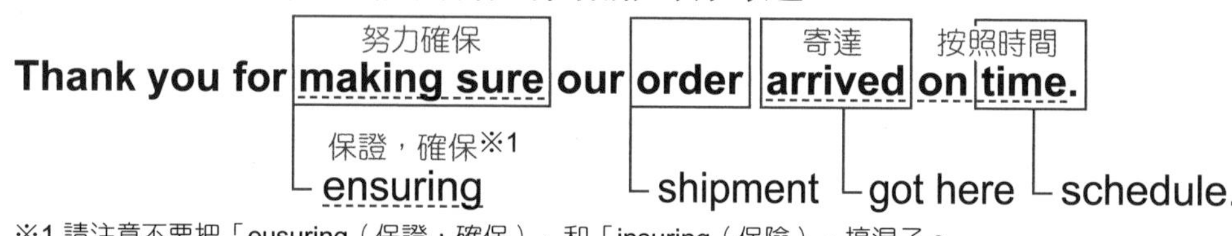

Thank you for making sure our order arrived on time.
努力確保
寄達
按照時間
保證，確保※1
ensuring
shipment
got here
schedule.

※1 請注意不要把「eusuring（保證，確保）」和「insuring（保險）」搞混了。

● 我們訂購的商品正確無誤地送達了。

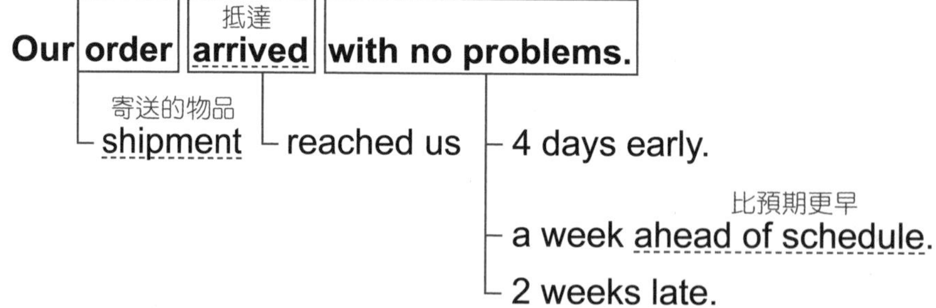

Our order arrived with no problems.
抵達
寄送的物品
shipment
reached us
4 days early.
比預期更早
a week ahead of schedule.
2 weeks late.

07 運送延遲

● 我訂購的商品尚未寄達。

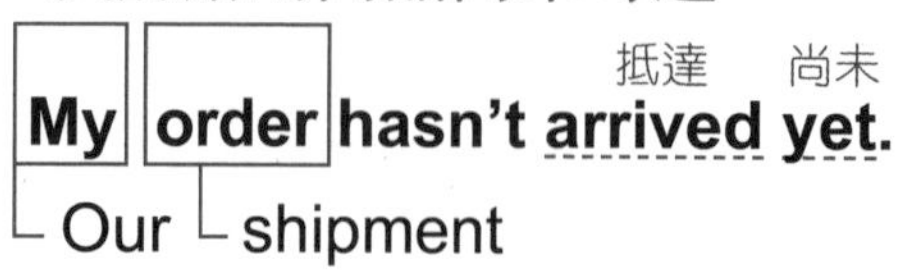

My order hasn't arrived yet.
抵達
尚未
Our
shipment

8 寄送・收發

寄達通知／運送延遲

● 看樣子，貨物延遲是因為碼頭的罷工。

Apparently (似乎，看樣子), **the delay** (延遲) **was due to** (因為) **a strike** (罷工) **at the docks** (碼頭)**.**

- It seems (好像，似乎)
- bad weather.
- a mix-up (混亂) at our warehouse (倉庫).

● 關於頻繁發生的寄送延遲問題，請與你們的貨運業者商討。

Please talk to your shipping company (貨運業者) **about the frequent** (經常發生) **delays** (延遲)**.**

- Please ask
- the excessive (過度的，嚴重的) damage.
- delivery before noon.

08 發生問題時的說明

● 由於經常發生貨物破損的情況，我們希望你們使用更堅固的包裝。

Due to the (因為) **frequent damage** (經常發生的), **we would like you to use sturdier packaging** (更堅固的)**.**

- the numerous (很多的) problems
- the lengthy delays (長時間延遲) ※1
- waterproof (防水的) packaging.
- a different shipping agent. ※1

※1 "the lengthy delays" 只能和 "a different shipping agent" 搭配成一句。

● 我們公司的倉庫裝不下這一整批貨。

Our warehouse (倉庫) **cannot accommodate** (對應，收容) **the entire** (全部的) **lot.**

● 已經有人向我們保證，這個問題正在處理中。

We have been assured (向…保證) **the problem has been dealt with** (已經處理)**.**

01 大受好評

● 無論顏色或設計我們都（一樣）喜歡。

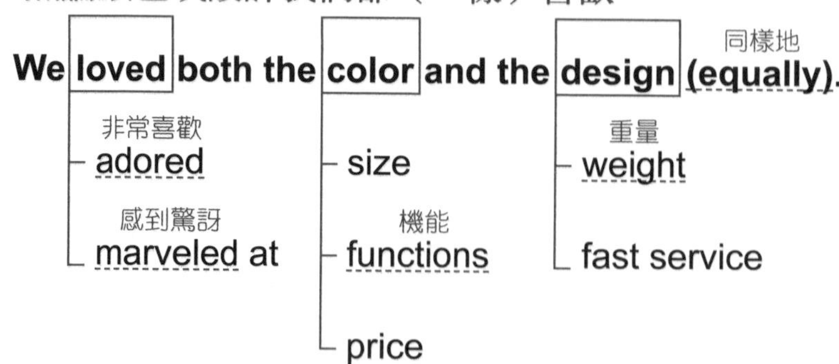
We loved both the color and the design (equally).
同樣地
非常喜歡
adored
感到驚訝
marveled at
size
機能
functions
price
重量
weight
fast service

● 我們的顧客把貴公司的商品評價為他們使用過最好的商品。

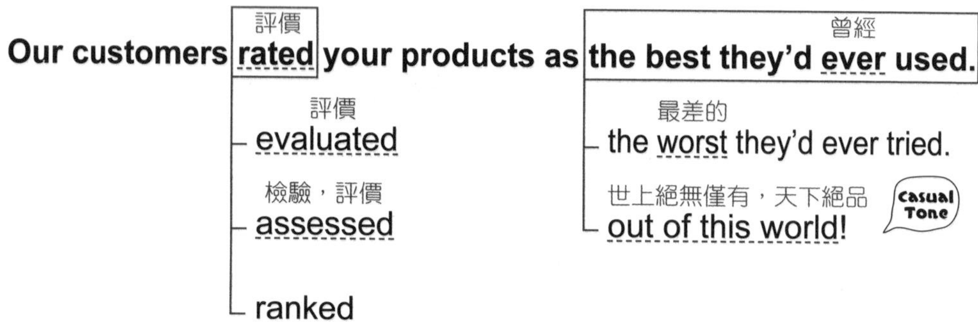
Our customers rated your products as the best they'd ever used.
評價
曾經
評價
evaluated
檢驗，評價
assessed
ranked
最差的
the worst they'd ever tried.
世上絕無僅有，天下絕品
out of this world!
Casual Tone

● 顧客對芒果茶的反應非常好。

The response to the Mango Tea was very positive.

● 你的簡報非常精采。大家都覺得很感動。 Casual Tone

Your presentation was fantastic. Everyone was blown away.
感動，受到衝擊
Your speech
提案
Your proposal
具啟發性
enlightening
令人大開眼界
eye-opening
聯絡
We will be in touch.
Our directors want to go with you.

● 貴公司的服務品質令人印象非常深刻。

We are very impressed with the quality of your service.
印象非常深刻
充分地 感謝
duly appreciative of
感到驚喜
pleasantly surprised at
Formal Tone
speed of your deliveries.
誠意
sincerity of your staff.
創造性，獨創性
creativity of your designs.
手工藝，技術
craftsmanship of your products.

● 我覺得你的表現有非常大的進步！

I think that you have made some huge progress!
非常大的
成長，進步
believe
feel
your designs have
your company has
great
wonderful
太棒了，令人無法置信的
incredible
改善，提升
improvements
進步
steps forward

● 我深信你有能力邁向成功！

I honestly believe you have the ability to go far!
真的
※1
能力
成功
確信
I am convinced
I really think
潛力，可能性
potential
獻身，有心想做某事
dedication
耐力，毅力
patience
Casual Tone
head / skill
go all the way to the top
be a leader
make management
大規模的 成長，進步
make massive progress

※1 其後還可以連接「that with a little more experience（再多累積一些經驗）」、「that if you apply yourself（如果你能專心的話）」或者「that with a little more effort（再更努力一些）」。

● 說實在話，我之前並不怎麼看好你，但是你的進步真的很驚人！

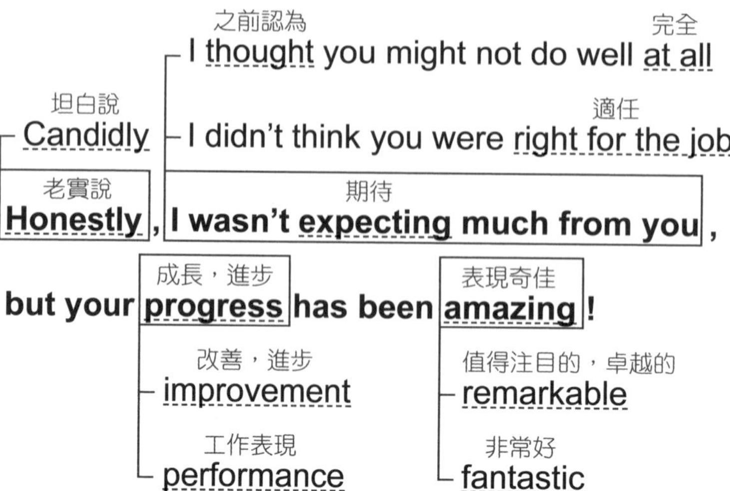
坦白說 Candidly
老實說 Honestly,
之前認為 I thought you might not do well at all 完全
I didn't think you were right for the job 適任
I wasn't expecting much from you, 期待
but your progress has been amazing!
成長，進步 progress
改善，進步 improvement
工作表現 performance
表現奇佳 amazing
值得注目的，卓越的 remarkable
非常好 fantastic

● 對於你在新工作上的（非凡）表現，我非常有信心。

Casual Tone

I am totally convinced（確信）

I have every confidence（自信） that

you will do (exceptionally)（非常地，特殊地） well in your new job.

staying on with us（繼續（簽約）） is your best move（最棒的選擇）.

You will not regret（後悔） choosing us.

02 指出問題

● 我們很喜歡這裡的氣氛，但是不太滿意這裡的服務。

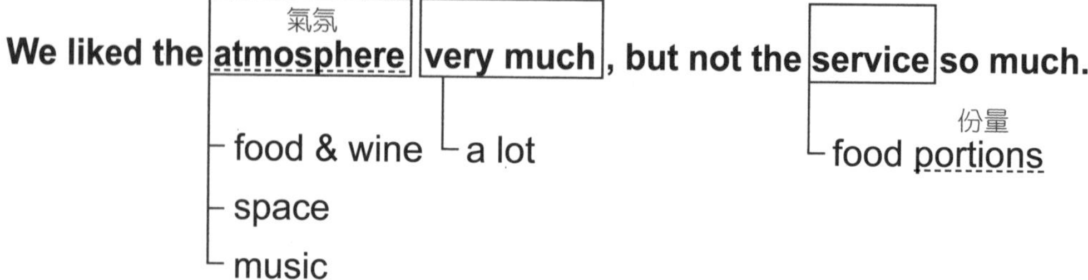
We liked the atmosphere very much, but not the service so much.
氣氛 atmosphere
food & wine
space
music
a lot
份量 food portions

● 我們非常喜歡這個產品的設計，但是不太能接受它的價格。

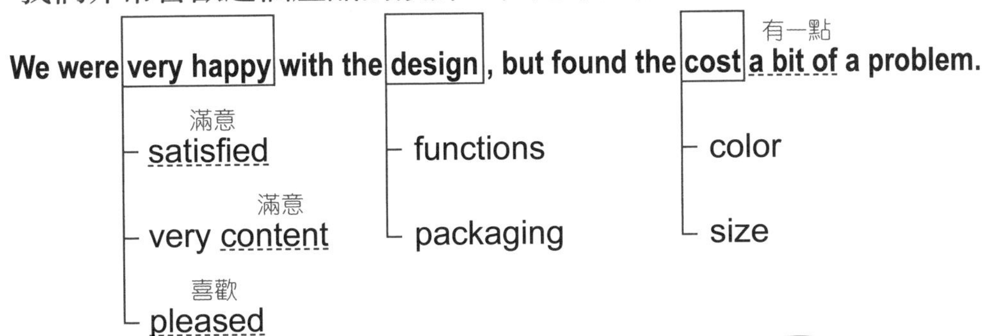

We were very happy with the design, but found the cost a bit of a problem.
有一點
滿意
satisfied
滿意
very content
喜歡
pleased
functions
packaging
color
size

● 這個表演很精采，但是服務讓人覺得有點不滿。

Casual Tone
The show was fantastic, but the service left a bit to be desired.
盼望
氣氛
atmosphere
speaker
絕佳的
excellent
有趣的
interesting
company
food
location

● 你曾提及問題出在顏色上。

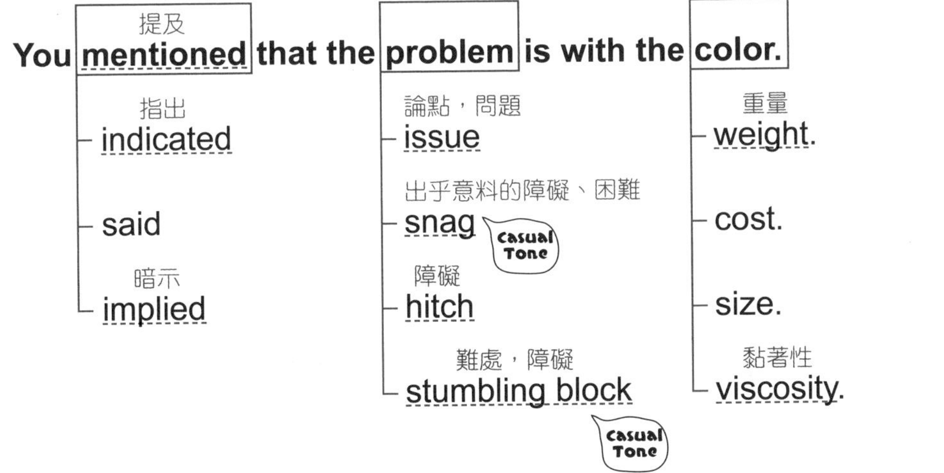

You mentioned that the problem is with the color.
提及
指出
indicated
said
暗示
implied
論點，問題
issue
出乎意料的障礙、困難
snag
Casual Tone
障礙
hitch
難處，障礙
stumbling block
Casual Tone
重量
weight.
cost.
size.
黏著性
viscosity.

03 建議

● 我們的顧客認為你應該少用一些鹽。

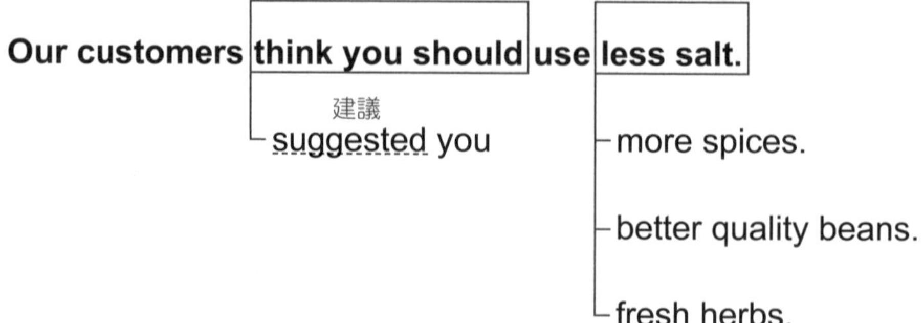

Our customers think you should use less salt.
建議
suggested you
more spices.
better quality beans.
fresh herbs.

● 我認為如果份量大一點顧客會比較喜歡。

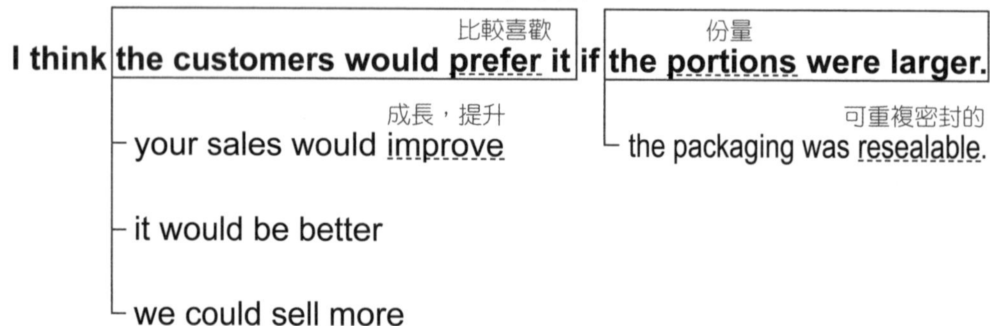

比較喜歡
份量
I think the customers would prefer it if the portions were larger.
成長，提升
your sales would improve
可重複密封的
the packaging was resealable.
it would be better
we could sell more

● 跟個別包裝的茶包比起來，有些顧客表示他們比較想買茶葉。

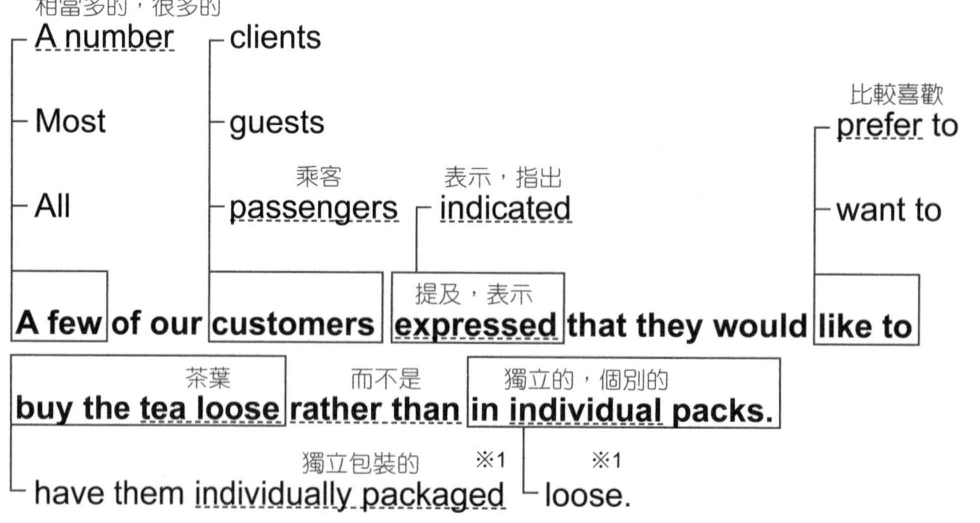

相當多的，很多的
A number
clients
Most
guests
比較喜歡
prefer to
All
乘客
passengers
表示，指出
indicated
want to
提及，表示
A few of our customers expressed that they would like to
茶葉
而不是
獨立的，個別的
buy the tea loose rather than in individual packs.
獨立包裝的
※1
※1
have them individually packaged
loose.

※1 "have them individually packaged" 只能和 "loose" 連接成一句。

04 負面評價

● 這項商品未能滿足我們的期待。

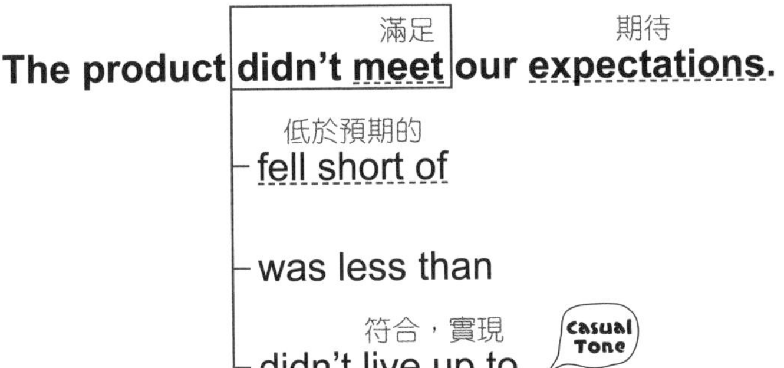

滿足
期待
The product didn't meet our expectations.
低於預期的
fell short of
was less than
符合，實現
didn't live up to
Casual Tone

● 很可惜，這項商品與我們的喜好不符。

遺憾地，可惜
喜好，嗜好
Unfortunately, we didn't find the products to our liking.
很遺憾，很糟糕
It's a shame, but
useful.
抱歉地，遺憾地
Regrettably,
相同的效果
聲稱過的
as effective as you claimed.

● 這項商品的品質完全令人無法接受。

無法接受的
We found the product quality totally unacceptable.
延遲
shipping delays
packaging
完全
completely
不滿意的
unsatisfactory.
令人失望的
disappointing.

● 坦白說，我原本期待你會有更好的工作表現。

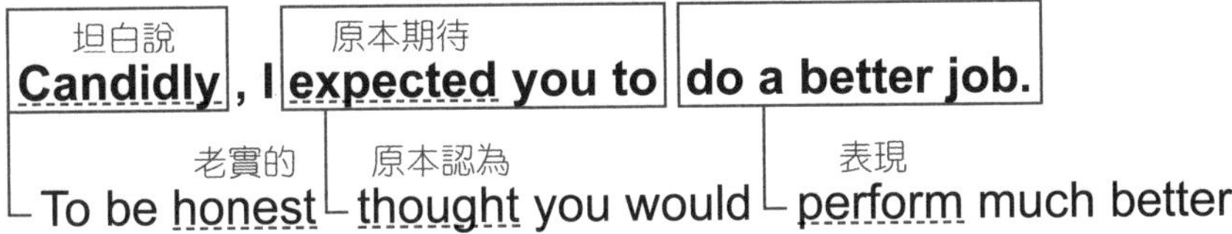

坦白說
原本期待
Candidly, I expected you to do a better job.
老實的
To be honest
原本認為
thought you would
表現
perform much better.

● 說實在的，你的工作表現（充其量）只能說是平庸。

說實在的 Frankly,	工作表現、能力 your performance has been	平庸的 mediocre 充其量 (at best).
老實說 Honestly,		普通的 average 充其量 at best.
我不想這麼說，但是 I hate to say this, but (Casual Tone)		a little 令人失望的 disappointing.
		slower than 原先的期待 expected.
		持續下滑 declining 最近 recently.

Business E-mail Tips

告別中式英文

One of the nice things about E-mail is that it is okay to abbreviate some things.

寫E-mail的好處之一是：可以使用縮寫。

到底能不能用縮寫？

E-mail和正式的商業信件相較之下，遣詞用字可以比較不拘小節。商業信件和E-mail之間有一個很大的不同，那就是寫E-mail的時候可以使用簡寫。舉例來說，商業信件中必須寫成 "I am writing..." 的時候，在E-mail裡，把 "I am" 縮寫成 "I'm" 也沒關係。

但是，你當然不能像和朋友在網路上聊天一樣，使用 "c u 2nite" 之類的口語縮略語。假如收信對象不是很熟的朋友，除了 "etc."、"inc."、"FYI (For Your Information)" 和 "ASAP (As Soon As Possible)" 等常見的簡寫之外，最好不要使用太過於通俗的口語用法。

適用情況10：金錢

01 支付方法

● 你可以用銀行轉帳的方式支付費用。

支付費用
銀行轉帳
You can make payment by bank transfer.
pay
credit card.
郵局轉帳
post office transfer.
貨到付款
POD (pay on delivery).
信用狀
L/C (Letter of Credit).

● 請與我們聯絡以討論付費方式。

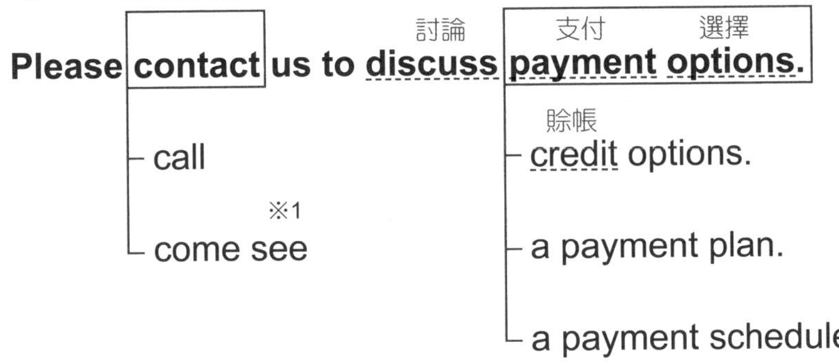
討論
支付
選擇
Please contact us to discuss payment options.
call
※1
come see
賒帳
credit options.
a payment plan.
a payment schedule.

※1 也可以用 “come and see”。

● 若支付帳款時遭遇困難，請打電話給我。

遭遇
困難
支付帳款
If you are experiencing difficulty making payment, please call me.
having problems
遇到
encountering problems
在期限之內
paying by the due date
符合
截止日期，期限
meeting the deadline
contact

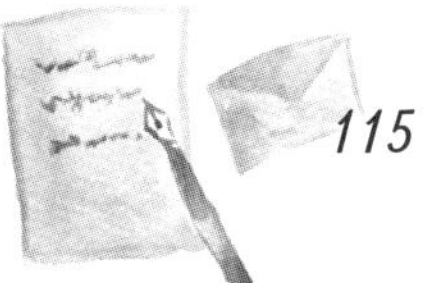

● 費用請以美金支付，並轉入以下帳號：

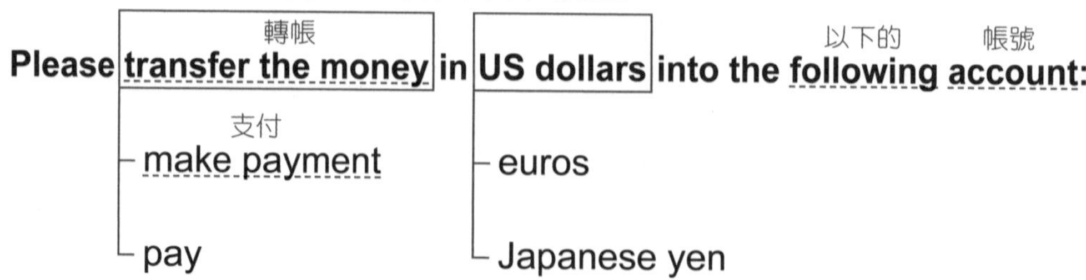
轉帳
以下的
帳號
Please transfer the money in US dollars into the following account:
支付
make payment
euros
pay
Japanese yen

02 款項單據

● 請將請款單以PDF的檔案格式寄過來。

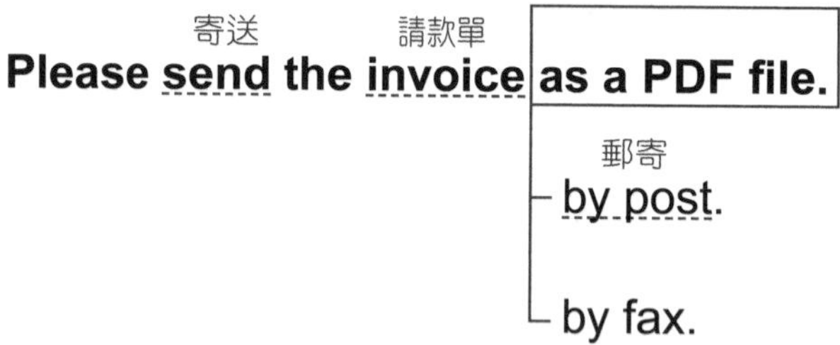
寄送
請款單
Please send the invoice as a PDF file.
郵寄
by post.
by fax.

● 請附上收據讓我們能夠詳細調查這件事。

附加
收據
詳細調查
這件事
Please attach the receipts so we can investigate the matter.
We need
※1
Could you send us
(載明支付狀況的)單據
dockets
請款單，帳單
invoice
photos
確認
投訴
confirm the claim.
check the claim.

※1 以 "Could you" 開頭的句子最後要加問號。

● 隨信附上你要求的請款單。

把…封入
請款單，帳單
I've enclosed the invoice as you requested.
附上
attached
sent
帳號相關細節
our bank details
收據
the receipt

●我們很滿意你寄過來的報價。

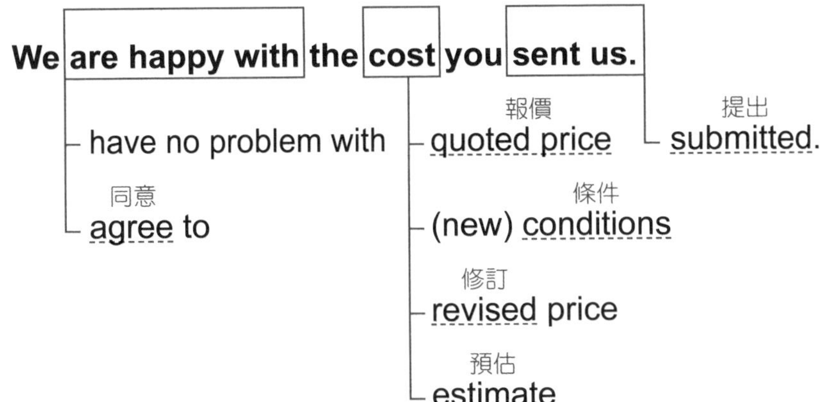
We are happy with the cost you sent us.
have no problem with
同意
agree to
報價
quoted price
條件
(new) conditions
修訂
revised price
預估
estimate
提出
submitted.

●很遺憾地通知您，我們之前寄給您的帳單有誤。

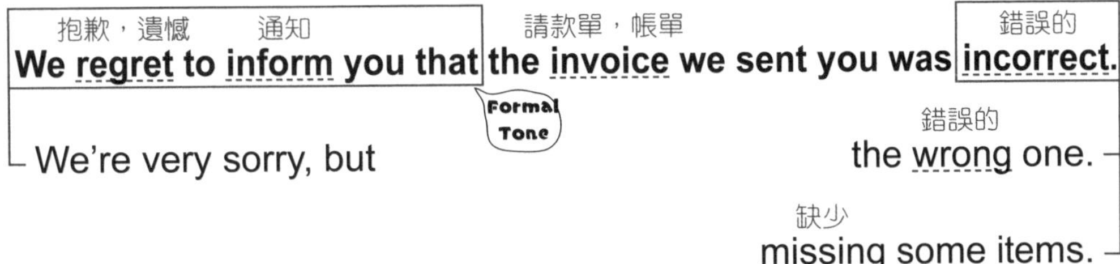
抱歉，遺憾 通知
We regret to inform you that
請款單，帳單
the invoice we sent you was
錯誤的
incorrect.
Formal Tone
We're very sorry, but
錯誤的
the wrong one.
缺少
missing some items.

●請您確認是否在收據上蓋了章？

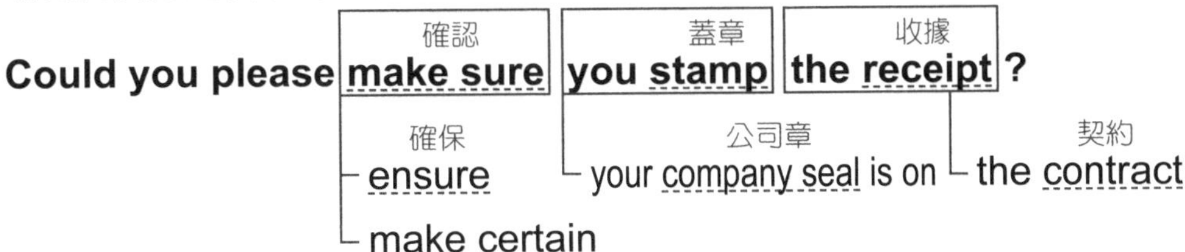
Could you please
確認
make sure
蓋章
you stamp
收據
the receipt ?
確保
ensure
make certain
公司章
your company seal is on
契約
the contract

●我已經附上T-0203系列產品的估價單。

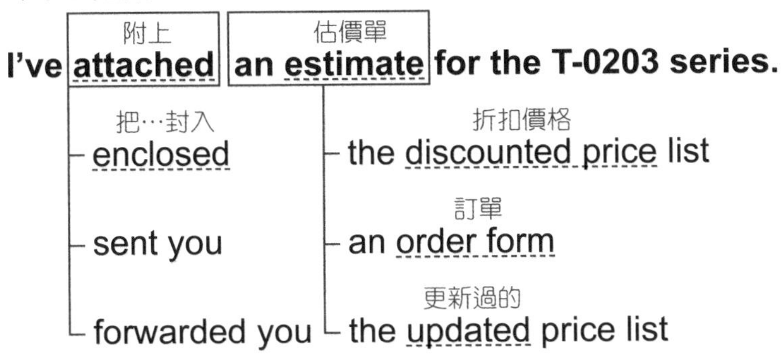
I've
附上
attached
估價單
an estimate
for the T-0203 series.
把…封入
enclosed
sent you
forwarded you
折扣價格
the discounted price list
訂單
an order form
更新過的
the updated price list

10 金錢 款項單據

●可否請你確認在我們公司登錄的帳號號碼是否正確呢？

Can you confirm (確認) that the account numbers (帳號號碼) we have are correct (正確)?

└ payment details (付款明細)

●我寄給你的款項總額包含運費。

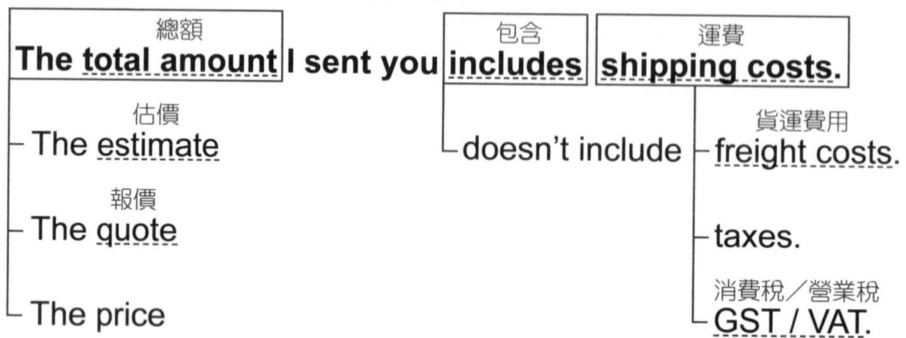

總額
The total amount I sent you
包含
includes
運費
shipping costs.
估價
The estimate
報價
The quote
The price
doesn't include
貨運費用
freight costs.
taxes.
消費稅／營業稅
GST / VAT.

●（以今天的匯率計算）總價為911,000美金。

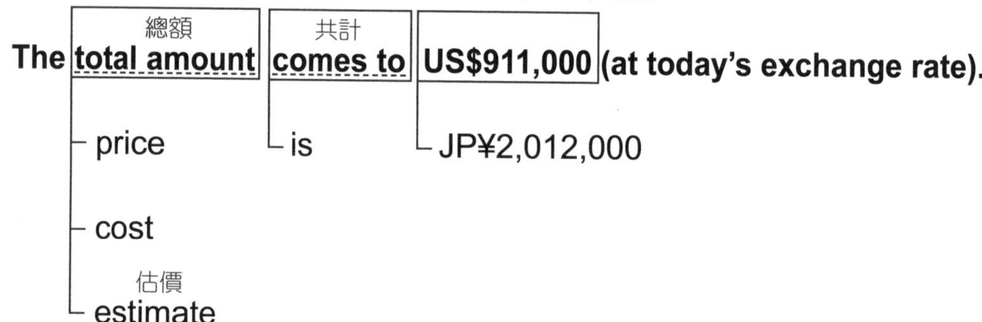

The
總額
total amount
共計
comes to
US$911,000
(at today's exchange rate).
price
cost
估價
estimate
is
JP¥2,012,000

03 確認支付狀況

●收到支付款項後請你通知我們。

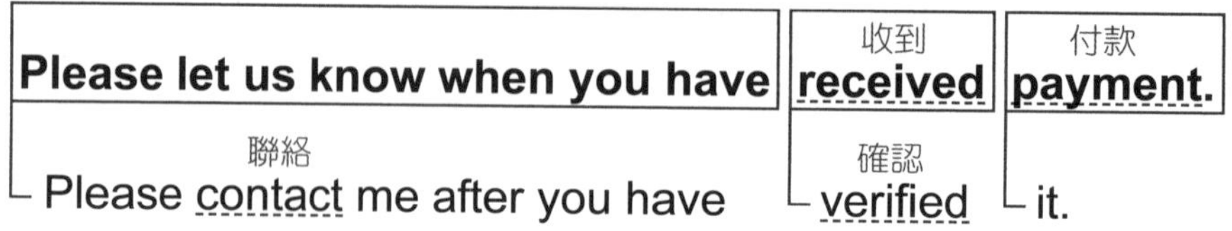

Please let us know when you have
收到
received
付款
payment.
聯絡
Please contact me after you have
確認
verified
it.

●我已經附上電匯付款的證明。

附上
證明書
電匯付款
I have attached proof of payment by wire transfer.
sent
our payment of June 14.
以宅配寄送
couriered

●假如你已經完成付款動作，請不必理會本通知。

不予理會　通知

If you have already **sent** payment, please disregard this notice.

已匯款 remitted

已轉帳 transferred

made

04 支付日期與期限

●我們將會立刻付清帳款。

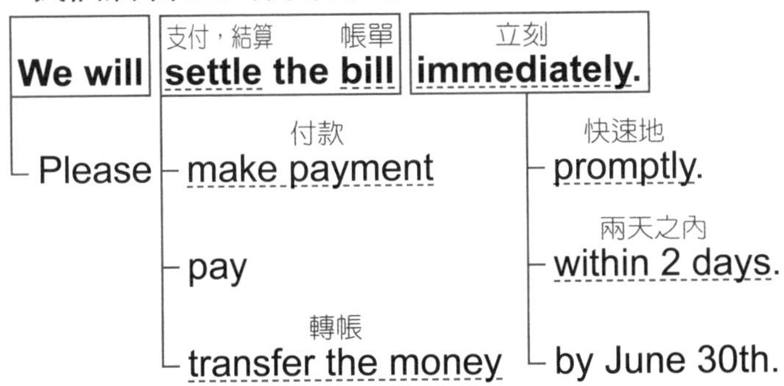
支付，結算
帳單
立刻
We will
settle the bill
immediately.
Please
付款
make payment
快速地
promptly.
pay
兩天之內
within 2 days.
轉帳
transfer the money
by June 30th.

●我們已經收到請款單，並且將會在30號付款。

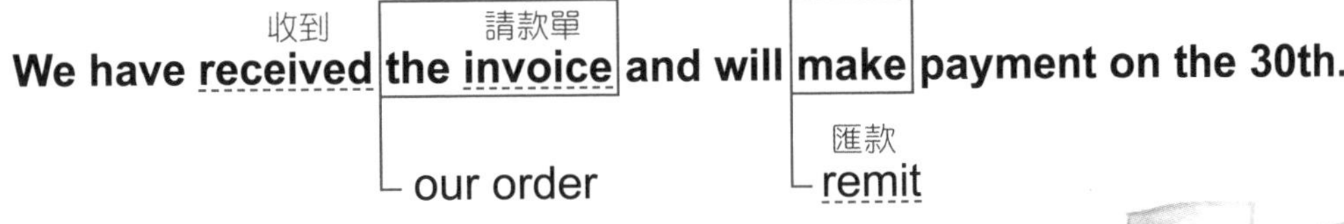
收到
請款單
We have received the invoice and will make payment on the 30th.
匯款
our order
remit

● 你預訂的商品已經寄出。請在收到商品後30天之內完成匯款。

sent.
已處理
processed.
已寄出

Your order has been **shipped.**

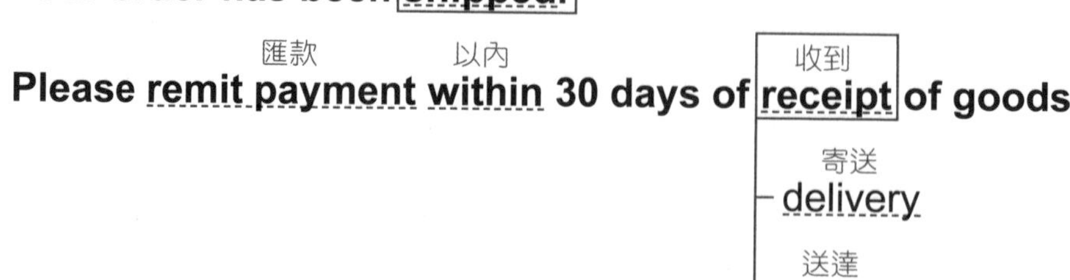
匯款
以內
收到
Please remit payment within 30 days of receipt of goods.
寄送
delivery
送達
arrival

05 支付報告

● 我們已經用轉帳的方式付清差額了。

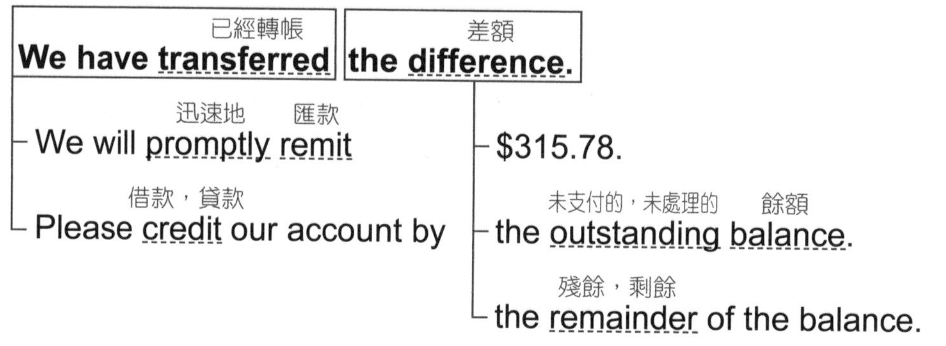
已經轉帳
We have transferred
差額
the difference.
迅速地
匯款
We will promptly remit
借款，貸款
Please credit our account by
$315.78.
未支付的，未處理的
餘額
the outstanding balance.
殘餘，剩餘
the remainder of the balance.

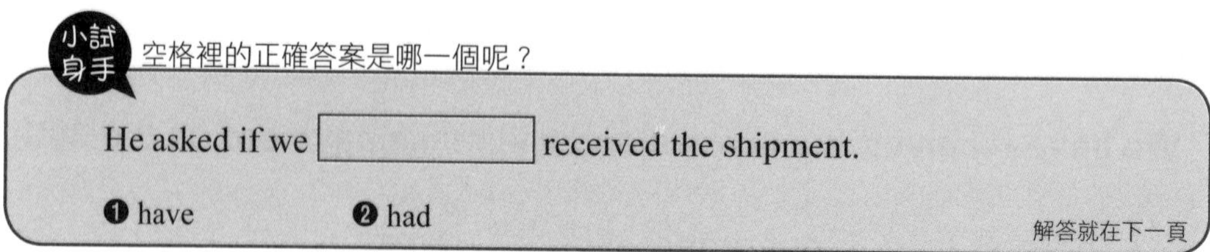
小試身手
空格裡的正確答案是哪一個呢？
He asked if we ______ received the shipment.
❶ have
❷ had
解答就在下一頁

● 我已經附上我們在7月2日已付款的證明副本。

附上
付款
I have attached a copy of the payment we made July 2.
sent
yesterday.

06 付款出錯：溢繳或金額不足

● 根據我們的紀錄，您溢繳了361美金。

根據
紀錄
溢繳
According to our records, you overpaid by $361.00.
繳款不足
Our records show that
underpaid

● 敝公司的會計部門發現總金額有誤。

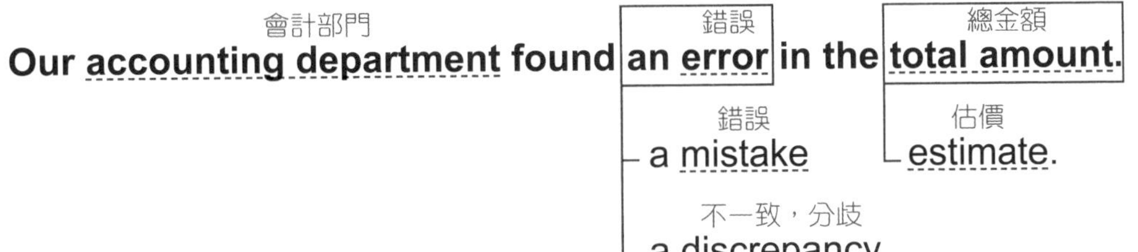

會計部門
錯誤
總金額
Our accounting department found an error in the total amount.
錯誤
a mistake
估價
estimate.
不一致，分歧
a discrepancy

● 能否請你修正710號請款單的錯誤之後，再寄過來一次？

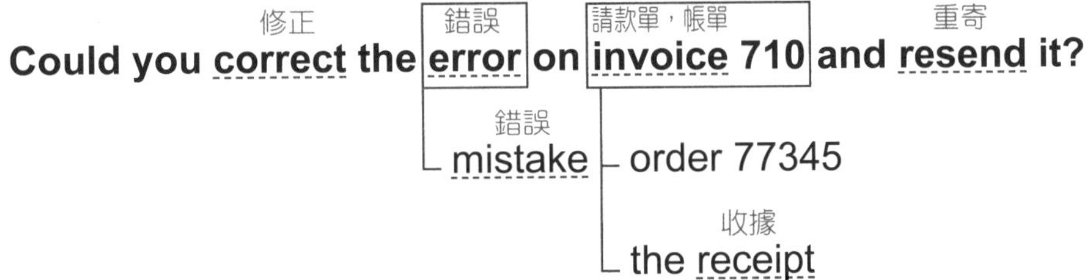

修正
錯誤
請款單，帳單
重寄
Could you correct the error on invoice 710 and resend it?
錯誤
mistake
order 77345
收據
the receipt

※1 以 "Could you" 開頭的句子，句末要加問號。

前一頁 小試身手 的解答 ❷ He asked if we had received the shipment.
他詢問我們是否已經收到貨物。

● 請立即支付差額。

電匯，支付
差額
迅速地，立即地
Please remit the difference promptly.
※1
轉帳
立刻
Could you transfer
immediately.
退款
在您方便的時候盡快
return
at your earliest convenience.

● 我對此疏忽感到非常抱歉，但我們寄出的金額似乎有誤。

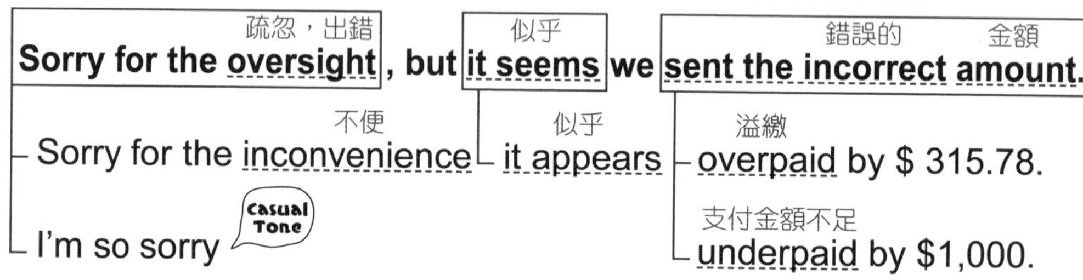
疏忽，出錯
似乎
錯誤的
金額
Sorry for the oversight, but it seems we sent the incorrect amount.
不便
似乎
溢繳
Sorry for the inconvenience
it appears
overpaid by $ 315.78.
Casual Tone
支付金額不足
I'm so sorry
underpaid by $1,000.

● 要不要我們將差額退還至你的帳戶呢？

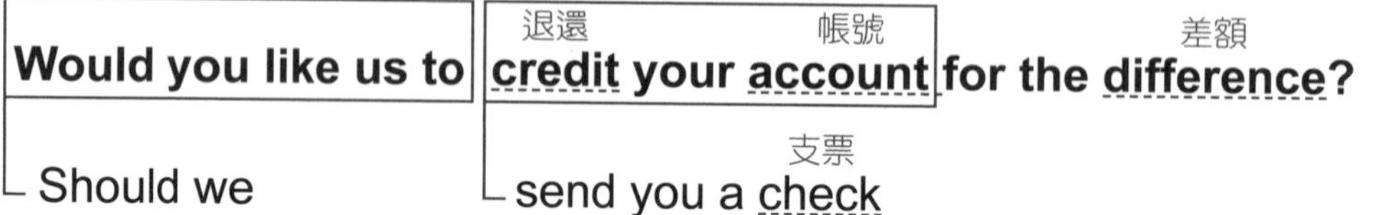
退還
帳號
差額
Would you like us to credit your account for the difference?
支票
Should we
send you a check

07 延遲付款

● 由於發生意料之外的狀況，我們將延遲付款。

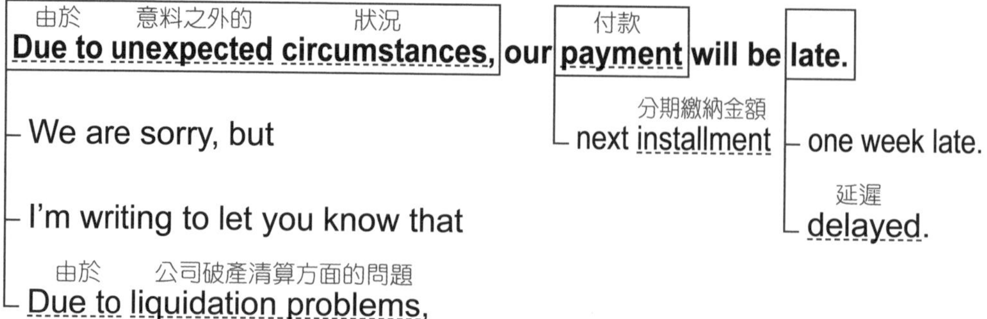
由於
意料之外的
狀況
付款
Due to unexpected circumstances, our payment will be late.
分期繳納金額
We are sorry, but
next installment
one week late.
延遲
I'm writing to let you know that
delayed.
由於
公司破產清算方面的問題
Due to liquidation problems,

● 我們對於延遲感到萬分抱歉。

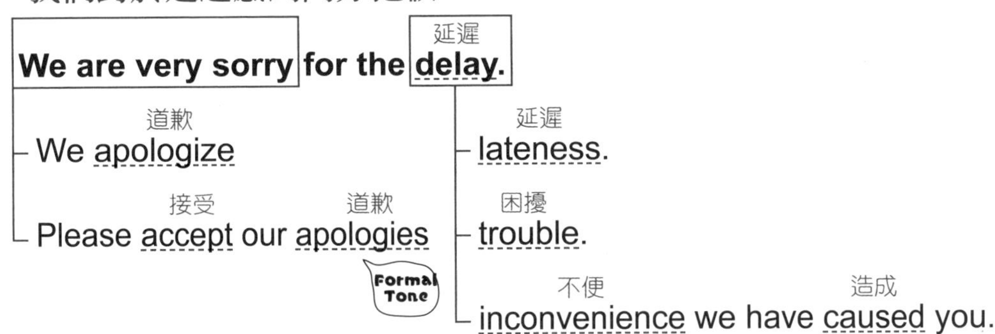
延遲
We are very sorry for the delay.
道歉
We apologize
接受 道歉
Please accept our apologies
Formal Tone
延遲
lateness.
困擾
trouble.
不便 造成
inconvenience we have caused you.

● 由於敝公司的電腦系統故障，有可能會延遲付款。

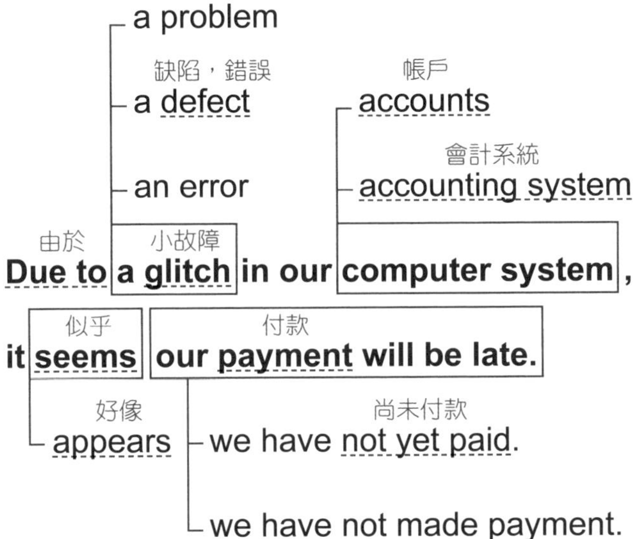
a problem
缺陷，錯誤
a defect
an error
帳戶
accounts
會計系統
accounting system
由於 小故障
Due to a glitch in our computer system,
似乎 付款
it seems our payment will be late.
好像
appears
尚未付款
we have not yet paid.
we have not made payment.

08 催收

● 789號訂單已經過了支付期限。

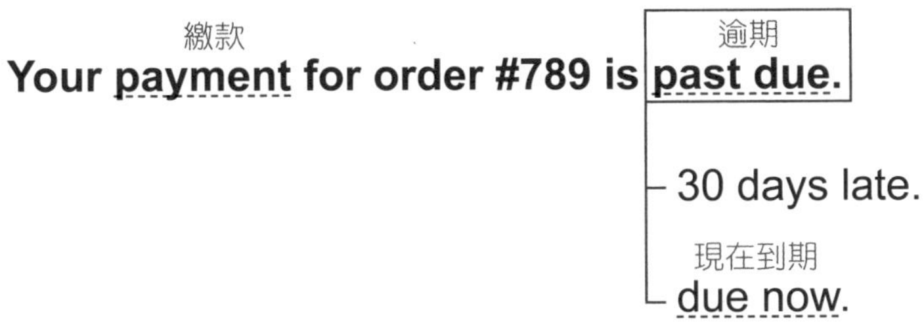
繳款 逾期
Your payment for order #789 is past due.
30 days late.
現在到期
due now.

10 金錢 催收

● 3939號請款單尚未收到支付款項。

We have not received payment for invoice 3939. (收到 received；支付款項 payment；請款單 invoice)

- the invoice for order 7651. (請款單 invoice)
- the estimate for our order. (估價單 estimate)
- the receipt. (收據 receipt)

● 請支付8181號請款單所列之款項，否則我們將不會寄出71號訂單的貨物。

Please submit payment for invoice 8181 or we will not ship order 71. (支付款項 submit payment；請款單，帳單 invoice)

- can not send
- will hold (留置 hold)

● 請在9月11日之前支付帳單，以避免服務中斷。

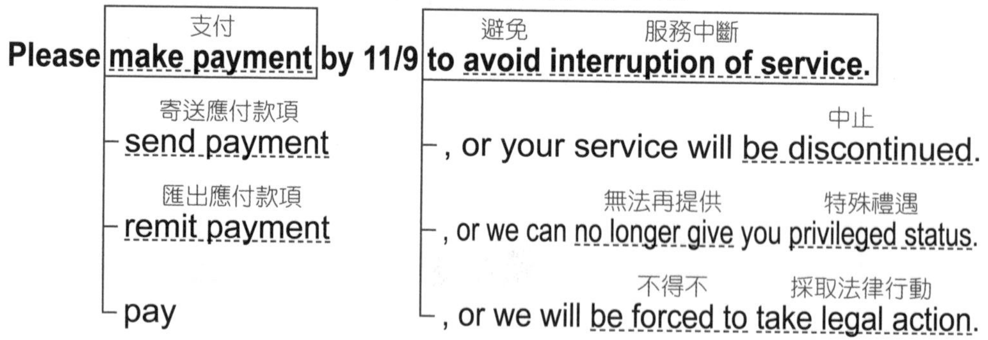

支付
避免
服務中斷
Please make payment by 11/9 to avoid interruption of service.
寄送應付款項
send payment
中止
, or your service will be discontinued.
匯出應付款項
remit payment
無法再提供
特殊禮遇
, or we can no longer give you privileged status.
pay
不得不
採取法律行動
, or we will be forced to take legal action.

● 我們尚未收到789號訂單的請款單。

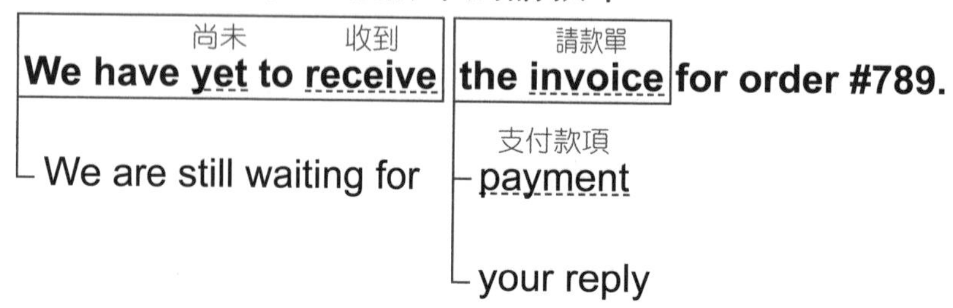

尚未
收到
請款單
We have yet to receive the invoice for order #789.
We are still waiting for
支付款項
payment
your reply

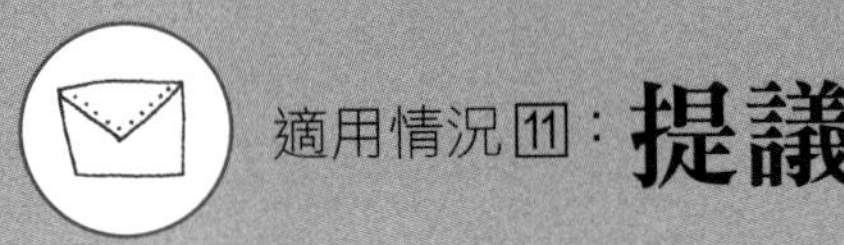

適用情況 11：提議

01 提議寄送

● 我可以將測試的數據寄給你。

I can send you data from the tests.

- 結果 the results of
- 統計資料 the statistics from
- 數值 the figures from

● 如果你希望，我可以將行程表寄給你沒有問題。

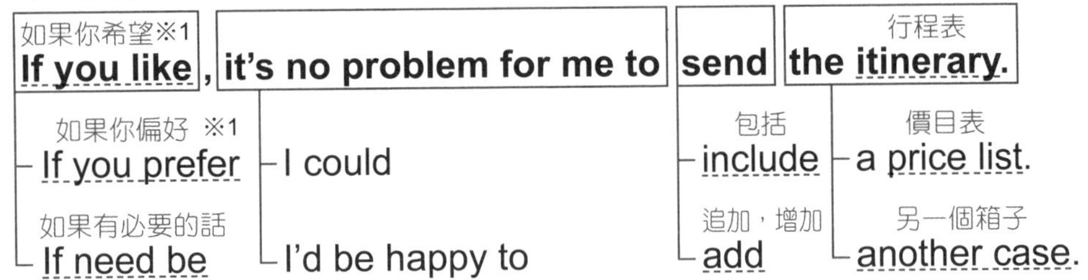
如果你希望※1
If you like
, it's no problem for me to
send
行程表
the itinerary.
如果你偏好 ※1
If you prefer
I could
如果有必要的話
If need be
I'd be happy to
包括
include
追加，增加
add
價目表
a price list.
另一個箱子
another case.

※1 "If you like" 和 "If you prefer" 兩者之間存在著微妙的差異，但是如上述例句用在句首時，兩者意思相同。

02 提議額外服務

● 關於有哪些彈性支付方案的選擇，請與我們聯絡。

Contact us about our flexible payment options.
（彈性的，可變通的 flexible；選擇 options）

- 特別訂製的，客製化的 customized designs.
- 個人化的 personalized services.

● 我們提供裝瓶和客製化標籤的服務，這項服務必須額外付費。

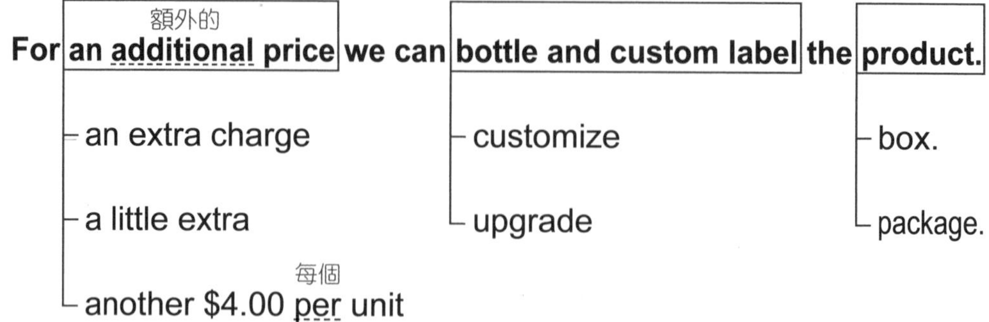
For an additional price we can bottle and custom label the product.
額外的
an extra charge
a little extra
another $4.00 per unit
每個
customize
upgrade
box.
package.

03 業務服務

● 請讓我們協助你做出正確的決定。

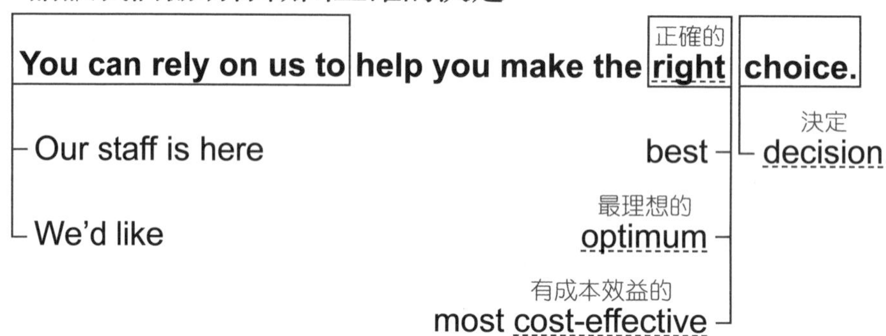
You can rely on us to help you make the right choice.
正確的
Our staff is here
We'd like
best
optimum
最理想的
most cost-effective
有成本效益的
decision.
決定

● 請告訴我們如何協助你的事業更上層樓。

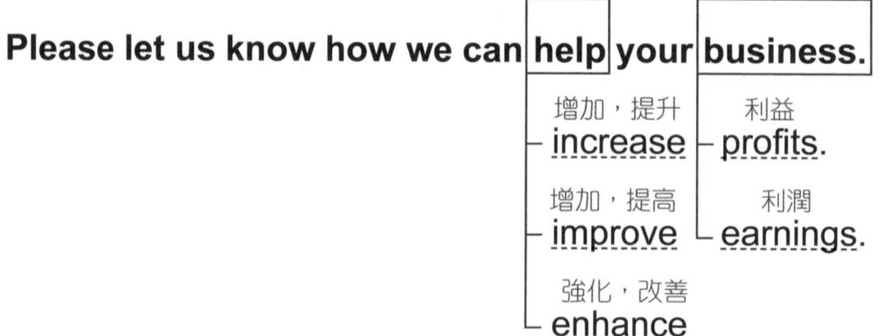
Please let us know how we can help your business.
increase
增加，提升
improve
增加，提高
enhance
強化，改善
profits.
利益
earnings.
利潤

04 推銷服務

● 我們能夠幫你處理所有的關稅表格。

We can take care of all the customs forms for you.

- getting reservations (預約) for you.
- your translation (翻譯) requirements (要求).
- arranging (安排) financing (融資).

● 我們可以量身打造你需要的旅遊行程。

We can tailor (量身打造) the tour to your needs.

- tour → seminar / program
- your needs → meet your requirements (符合你的要求). / serve your company's best interests (最佳利益). / your desired (想要的) length (長度).

● 如果你找到喜歡的商品，我會加快處理程序。

If you find one that is to your liking (喜好，喜歡), I'll have it fast-tracked (加快處理).

- one → anything
- to your liking → suitable (合適的) / better / more appropriate (適當的) / more effective (有效的)
- I'll have it → I'll see that it's
- fast-tracked → given priority (優先) status. / given the highest priority (優先). / pushed to the front.

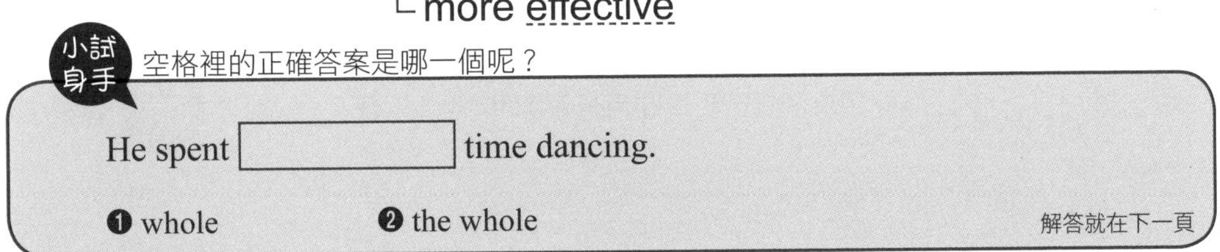

小試身手 空格裡的正確答案是哪一個呢？

He spent ______ time dancing.

❶ whole ❷ the whole

解答就在下一頁

● 根據你的設計，我們已經備妥生產包裝和標籤的設備。

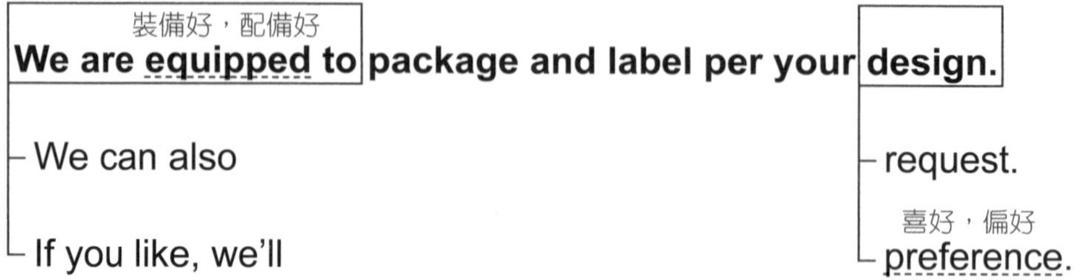
裝備好，配備好
We are equipped to package and label per your design.
We can also
If you like, we'll
request.
喜好，偏好
preference.

● 如果你希望的話，我很樂意為你安排貨運相關事宜。

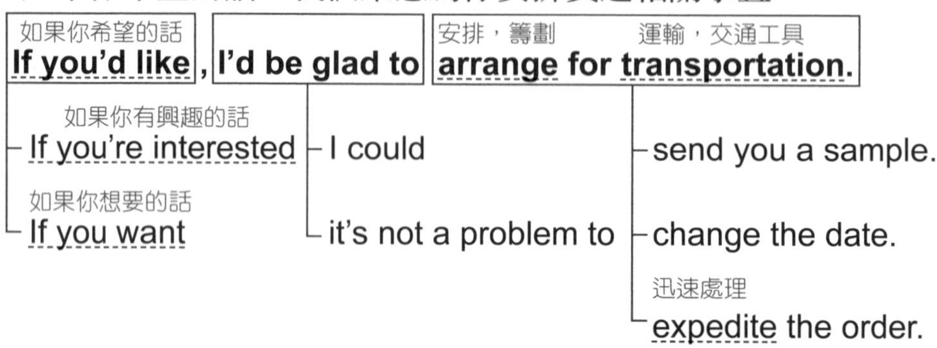
如果你希望的話
If you'd like, I'd be glad to
安排，籌劃 運輸，交通工具
arrange for transportation.
如果你有興趣的話
If you're interested
如果你想要的話
If you want
I could
it's not a problem to
send you a sample.
change the date.
迅速處理
expedite the order.

● 我剛想到一個關於商品型錄的好點子！

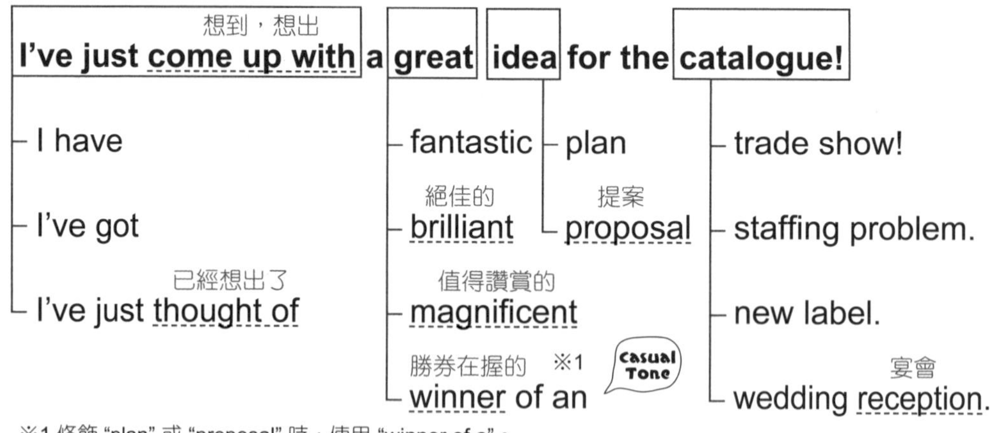
想到，想出
I've just come up with a great idea for the catalogue!
I have
I've got
已經想出了
I've just thought of
fantastic
絕佳的
brilliant
值得讚賞的
magnificent
勝券在握的 ※1
winner of an
Casual Tone
plan
提案
proposal
trade show!
staffing problem.
new label.
宴會
wedding reception.

※1 修飾 "plan" 或 "proposal" 時，使用 "winner of a"。

前一頁 
小試身手
的解答 ❷ He spent the whole time dancing.
他把那段時間全都用來跳舞。

05 徵詢對方情況

● 請告訴我您方便的日期。

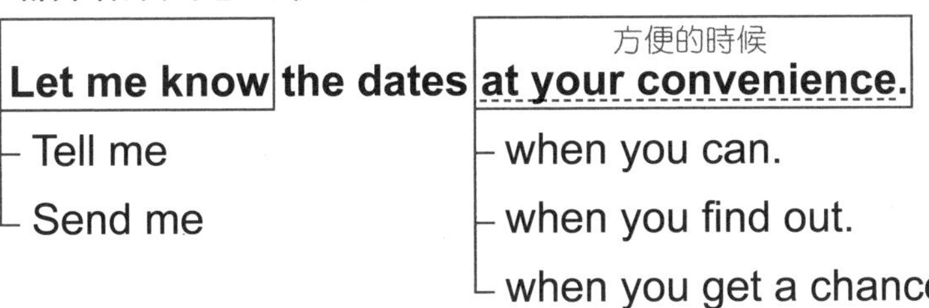
方便的時候
Let me know the dates at your convenience.
Tell me
Send me
when you can.
when you find out.
when you get a chance.

● 如果你希望的話，我可以讓你在車站／機場下車。

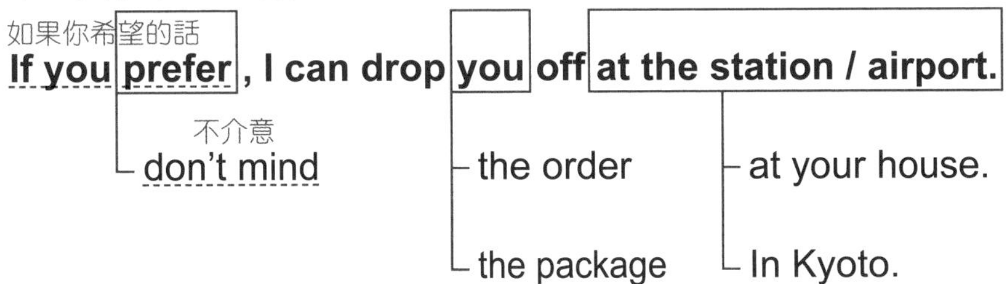
如果你希望的話
If you prefer, I can drop you off at the station / airport.
不介意
don't mind
the order
the package
at your house.
In Kyoto.

● 如果你想要的話，我可以在上班途中過來接你。

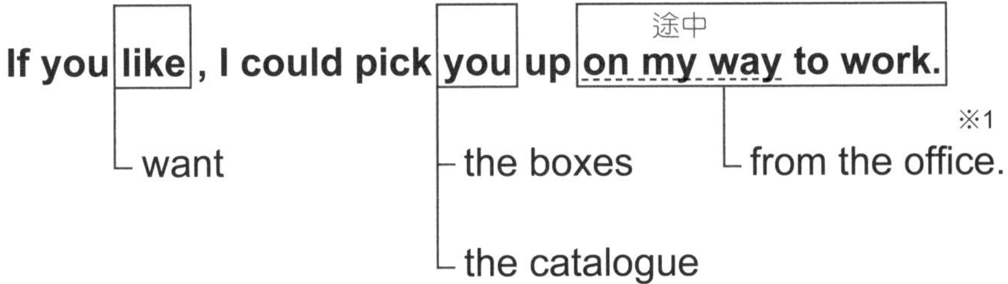
途中
If you like, I could pick you up on my way to work.
want
the boxes
the catalogue
※1
from the office.

※1 也可以用 "at the office"。

06 徵詢意見

● 如果有任何問題，請與我們聯絡，不要客氣。

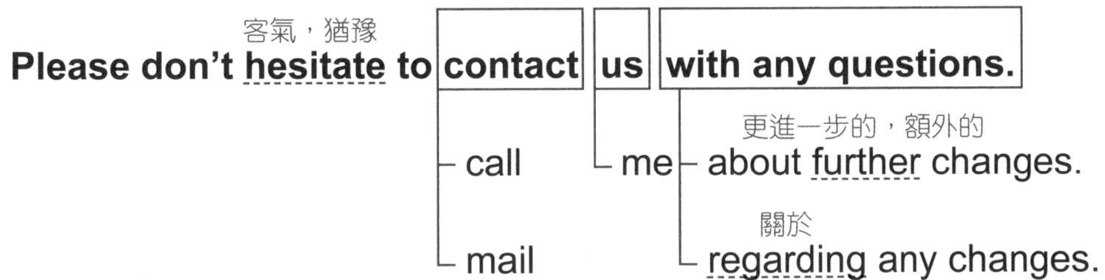
客氣，猶豫
Please don't hesitate to contact us with any questions.
call
mail
me
更進一步的，額外的
about further changes.
關於
regarding any changes.

●如果你有任何問題或疑慮，請告訴我。

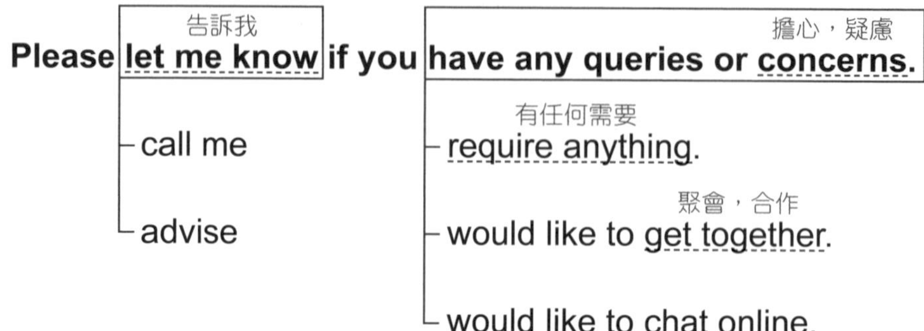
Please let me know if you have any queries or concerns.
告訴我
擔心，疑慮
call me
advise
有任何需要
require anything.
聚會，合作
would like to get together.
would like to chat online.

●你對這些商品滿意嗎？

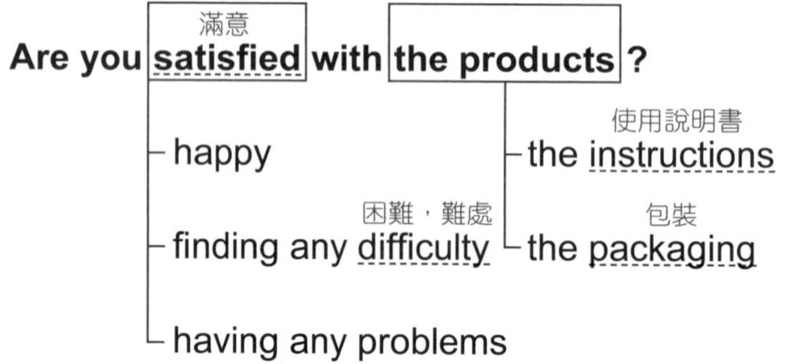
Are you satisfied with the products ?
滿意
happy
困難，難處
finding any difficulty
having any problems
使用說明書
the instructions
包裝
the packaging

●如果你有任何問題，請立刻與我們聯絡。

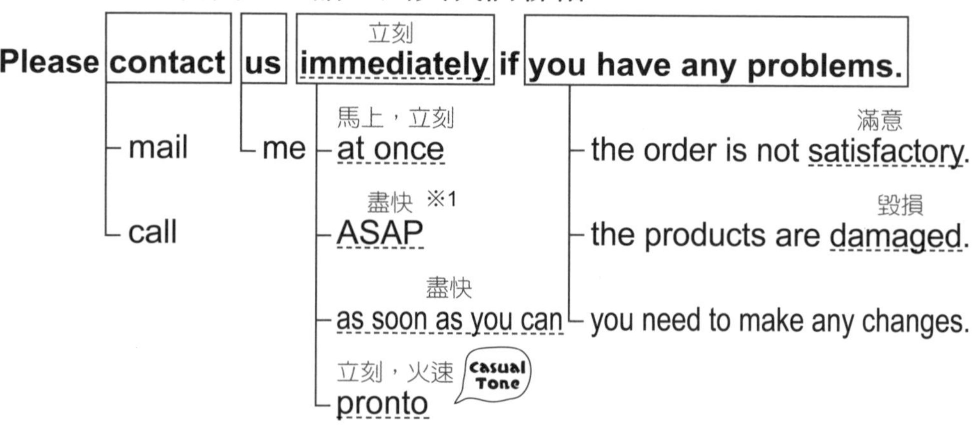
Please contact us immediately if you have any problems.
立刻
mail
call
me
馬上，立刻
at once
盡快 ※1
ASAP
盡快
as soon as you can
立刻，火速
pronto
Casual Tone
滿意
the order is not satisfactory.
毀損
the products are damaged.
you need to make any changes.

※1 "ASAP" 是 "as soon as possible（盡快）" 的簡寫，在商業書信中也經常使用。

● 我們歡迎你提出建議。

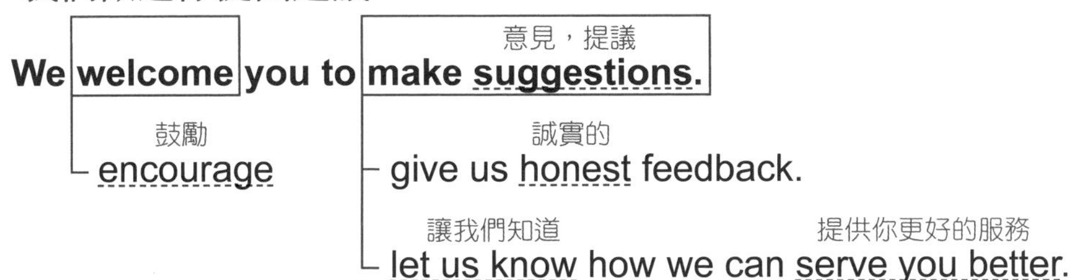
We welcome you to make suggestions.
意見，提議
鼓勵
encourage
誠實的
give us honest feedback.
讓我們知道
提供你更好的服務
let us know how we can serve you better.

● 如果你有任何特殊要求，請與我聯絡。

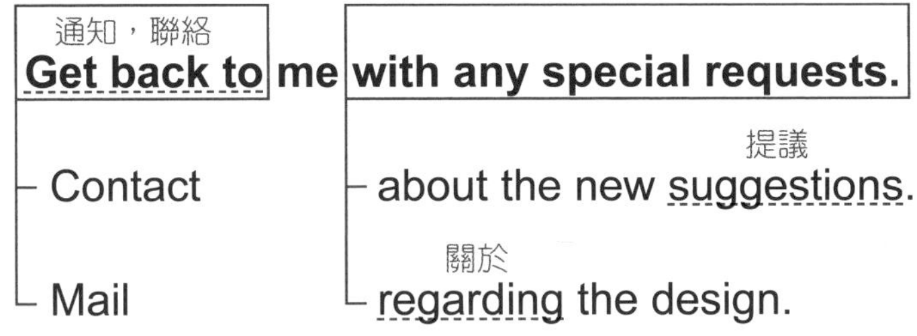
通知，聯絡
Get back to me with any special requests.
Contact
提議
about the new suggestions.
Mail
關於
regarding the design.

● 無論你有任何疑問，請與我們聯絡。

無論
If you have any questions at all, please contact us.
疑問
queries
擔心，疑慮
concerns
不管怎麼樣
whatsoever
請…不必客氣
feel free to call us.
let us know.

告別中式英文

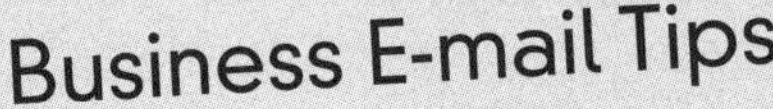

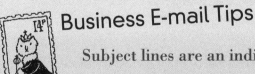

Business E-mail Tips

Subject lines are an indispensable part of E-mail.

信件標題是電子郵件不可缺少的部分。

不讓信件跑到垃圾郵件匣的訣竅

寫電子郵件時，每封信都務必要寫上適合的標題。因為標題為 “Thank you for the information” 或 “Your Order” 之類、甚至是空白不寫的郵件，很可能會被系統自動歸類為垃圾信件。如果能在郵件標題主旨欄簡要地說明信件內容，不但可以讓收件人一眼就看出來信的目的為何，也有助於對方在他的信箱裡搜尋你的郵件。

01 條件談不攏

● 在這樣的條件下，我們無法與貴公司簽約。

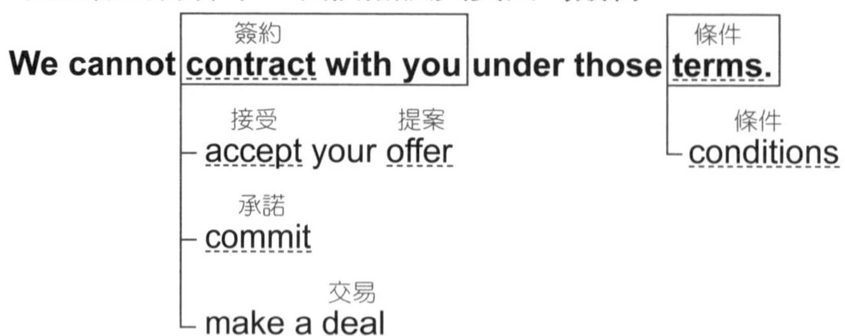

簽約
We cannot contract with you under those terms.
條件
接受 提案
accept your offer
條件
conditions
承諾
commit
交易
make a deal

● 我們無法配合你提出的條件。

條件
給予，提供
The terms you are offering will not work for us.
契約書
of the contract
限制的，束縛的
are too restrictive.
可實行的
are not feasible.
調整，修正
need adjustment.

● 很遺憾，我們無法認同你的見解，我不認為這些條件對我們雙方的公司都有利。

很遺憾 / 分享，共有 / 條件 / 適用，有利

I'm afraid we do not share your view that these terms serve both our companies.

小試身手
空格裡的正確答案是哪一個呢？
The trip did me a lot of ______.
❶ good
❷ well
解答就在下一頁

● 我很遺憾我必須婉拒，但我們誤以為你們的蔬菜是有機的。

婉拒，謝絕 / 誤解的，錯誤的 / 印象 / 有機的

I'm very sorry to decline, but we were under the mistaken impression that your vegetables were organic.

- under the mistaken impression →
  - led to believe
  - told
- your vegetables were organic. →
  - your materials were recyclable.（材料 / 可回收再利用的）
  - your goods were all handmade.（手工的）
  - you could do custom orders.
  - you were a discount broker.（仲介業者，經紀人）

02 拒絕承接業務

● 如果你需要更快速的服務，我們建議你找另一家供應商。

需要 / 提議 / 尋求 / 供應商

If you require faster service, we suggest you look for another supplier.

- faster service →
  - further discount（更多的）
  - custom designs
- suggest you look for another supplier. →
  - recommend you contact Speedy Tailors Ltd.（推薦）

● 由於客戶的高需求量，我們現在無法服務新的客戶。

由於 / 高需求量 / 接受

Due to high demand, we are not accepting new clients.

- Due to high demand →
  - As we are running at full capacity（運轉，進行 / 生產力）
- new clients. →
  - additional orders.

前一頁  的解答 ❶ The trip did me a lot of good.

這趟旅程對我很有幫助。

● 很抱歉，但是我們現在不提供海外寄送服務。

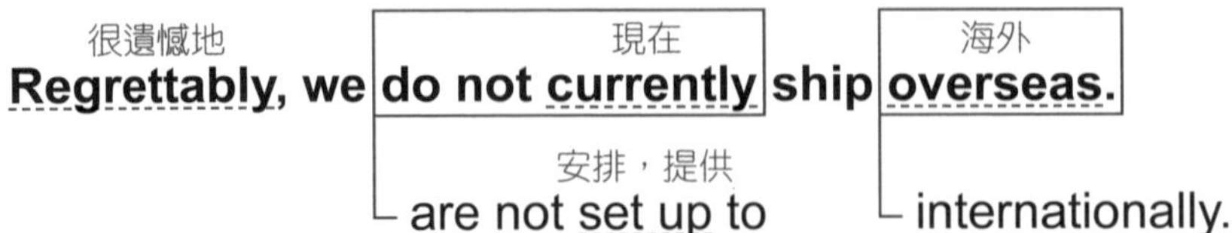
很遺憾地
現在
海外
Regrettably, we do not currently ship overseas.
安排，提供
are not set up to
internationally.

● 我們工廠的生產力無法滿足這種訂單。

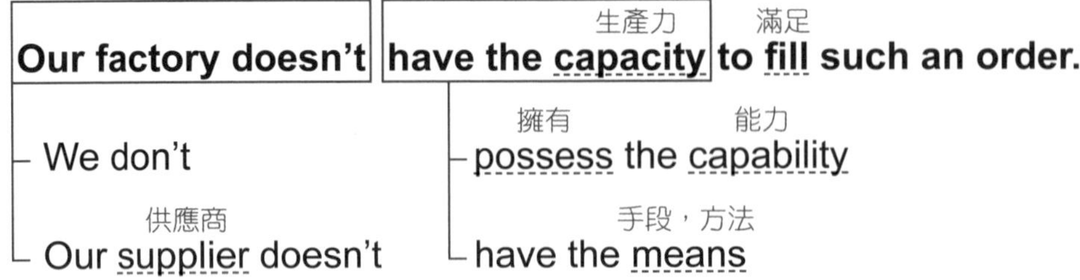
生產力
滿足
Our factory doesn't have the capacity to fill such an order.
擁有
能力
We don't
possess the capability
供應商
手段，方法
Our supplier doesn't
have the means

● 我們只能保證每個月最多生產1萬個。

保證
最多
每個月
We can only guarantee up to 10,000 units per month.
生產
produce
3 shipments
可獲得的，能提供的
make available

● 我們現在不生產那種尺寸的機器。

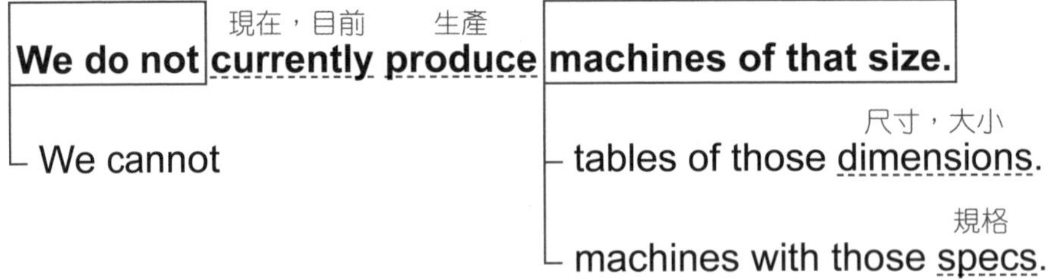
現在，目前
生產
We do not currently produce machines of that size.
We cannot
尺寸，大小
tables of those dimensions.
規格
machines with those specs.

● 在這個時間點上，我們必須婉拒你的提議。

婉拒
提議
在這個時間點上
We must decline your offer at this time.
拒絕，放棄
We will have to pass up on
確保
資金周轉
until we secure financing.

● 由於現在的經濟狀況，我們必須拒絕你的提案。

In light of the 考量到
trend
political upheaval 政治動盪
decline 婉拒
refuse 拒絕

Due to the current economic conditions, we must turn down your offer.

由於 現在的 經濟狀況 拒絕 提案

● 在這個時間點上，依我們的立場無法和你們做生意。

We are not in a position to do business with you at this time.

立場

able
prepared
accept your offer. 接受 提案
offer any additional discount. 額外的
offer any additional concessions. 讓步；優惠

● 雖然我們必須婉拒你的提案，但是我們歡迎你未來參與投標。

Although we cannot accept 雖然

Though we must decline your offer,

雖然 婉拒 提案

we welcome you to submit bids in the future.

投標 未來

invite
encourage 推動，鼓勵，希望
keep us in mind for future work. 將我們列入考量
bring projects to us at another time.

03 解除與變更契約

● 由於價格變動，我們決定中止那條生產線。

With the change in price, we have decided to discontinue that line.
（決定 decided；中止，停止 discontinue；生產線 line）

- With the change in price → Due to the increase in cost（由於 Due to；增加，上升 increase）
- discontinue that line. → seek another supplier.（尋求 seek；供應商 supplier）
- discontinue that line. → do the work in-house.（在公司內部 in-house）

● 如果你無法接受我們最新的條件，我們就不得不與其他公司接洽了。

※1 **If you are unable to accept our latest terms, we will be forced to take our business elsewhere.**
（接受 accept；最新的 latest；條件 terms；不得不 be forced to；其他地方 elsewhere）

- terms → offer（提案）
- terms → conditions（情況，條件）
- be forced to take our business elsewhere. → look for another supplier.（尋求 look for；供應商 supplier）

※1 這種說法態度非常強硬，所以請注意使用的時機。

04 拒絕對方的提案

● 很感謝你的提案，但恐怕我們必須婉拒。

Thank you for your offer, but I'm afraid we must decline.
（提案 offer；婉拒 decline）

- offer → proposal（提案，提議）
- offer → suggestion（提議）
- must decline. → must refuse.（拒絕 refuse）
- must decline. → cannot accept those terms.（接受 accept；條件 terms）
- must decline. → forgo the opportunity.（放棄 forgo；機會，時機 opportunity）

小試身手　空格裡的正確答案是哪一個呢？

The soup was [　　　] hot that I couldn't eat it.

❶ so　❷ too

解答就在下一頁

● 經過審慎的考量，我們認為我們必須否決你的提案。

仔細思量，認真考慮
After due consideration, we feel we must reject your proposal.
駁回，否決
提案，建議
a long discussion
徹底的
重新調查
a thorough review
接受
提案
we cannot accept your proposal.
條件
反映
方針
the terms do not reflect our company policy.

● 雖然你的提議很合理，但是我們沒有足夠的資本採納這項提案。

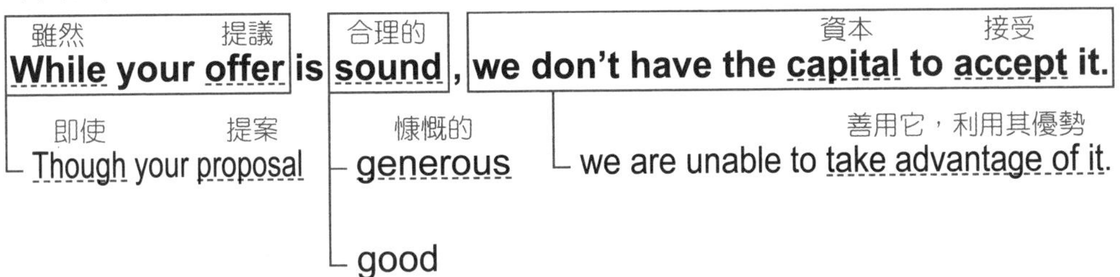
雖然
提議
While your offer is sound, we don't have the capital to accept it.
合理的
資本
接受
即使
提案
Though your proposal
慷慨的
generous
good
善用它，利用其優勢
we are unable to take advantage of it.

● 很抱歉，但是我們目前並不需要貨運公司的服務。

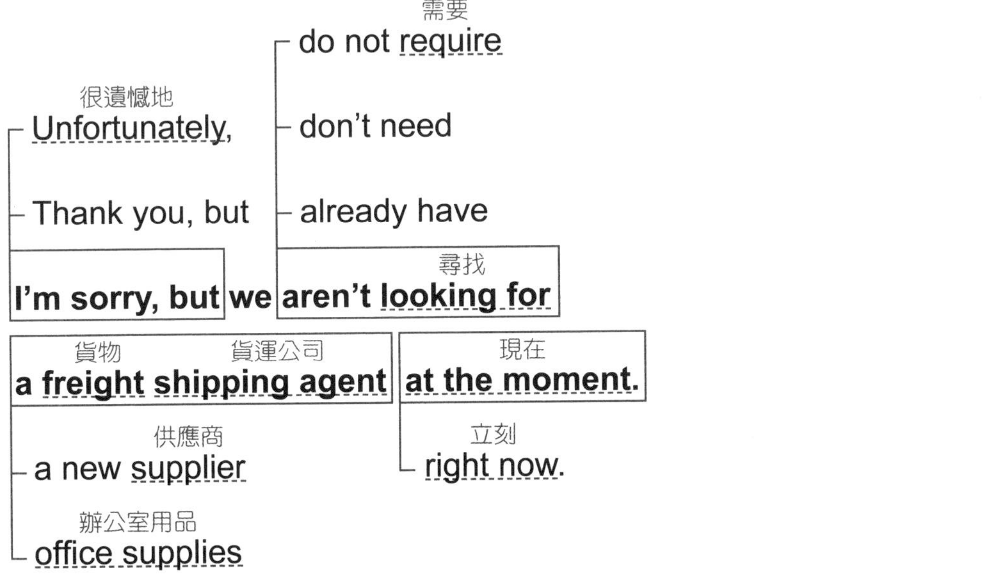
很遺憾地
Unfortunately,
Thank you, but
I'm sorry, but we aren't looking for
需要
do not require
don't need
already have
尋找
貨物
貨運公司
a freight shipping agent
供應商
a new supplier
辦公室用品
office supplies
現在
at the moment.
立刻
right now.

前一頁 小試身手 的解答 ❶ The soup was so hot that I couldn't eat it.
那碗湯太燙了，我根本沒辦法喝。

●很遺憾地通知您，我無法參加派對。

Formal Tone

I regret to inform you that I won't be able to make it to the party.
(為…遺憾 regret；告知 inform；完成某事 make it)

- I'm really sorry, but
- Regrettably,（很遺憾地）

Casual Tone

- can't make it
- will be unable to make it

●很遺憾地，我們無法在這個時間點處理你的要求。

Unfortunately we cannot process your request at this time.
(很遺憾地 Unfortunately；處理 process；要求，請求 request；現在這個時間點 at this time)

- I am unable to
- until the end of the month.
- until our machines have been repaired.

Business E-mail Tips

告別中式英文

How short is too short?

多簡短才是太過於簡短？

書信內容太精簡也不行？

我們曾在前面提到過，E-mail要「簡潔扼要」（Keep It Short and Simple）。如果你已經和對方熟識到某種程度（彼此互相通過幾次E-mail之後），對方也許就會希望你以更簡潔的用詞傳達訊息。舉例來說，若是要告訴對方貨物已寄達，只要一句 "Order 117 arrived, thank you." 就足以充分傳達主旨。有時收到國外客戶寄來的E-mail，內容只寫著 "Yes" 或 "No"，雖然多多少少會覺得對方有些冷淡，但不必太介意也不需要擔心，因為有些人經常在外奔波，常常以iPhone之類的智慧型手機或PDA當作生意上聯絡的工具，他們覺得用大拇指打一堆文字很浪費時間，所以發送極簡短的E-mail以即時傳達重要訊息，這對他們來說是很平常的事情。

Giovanna,

The latest shipment has arrived.

Unfortunately, one of the cases was damaged.
Should we take this up directly with the shipping company, or is it better to take care of it at your end?
We still need another case. Could you send one more case of Coconut Oil? Can I assume there will be no charge since the original shipment was damaged?

Thanks,

Angela

中譯

最新的貨品已經寄達。

很遺憾地，其中有一箱貨品毀損。

我們應該直接與貨運公司聯繫，還是由貴公司自行解決比較好呢？

我們仍需要另一箱貨品。能否請你們再寄一箱椰子油過來？既然寄來的貨品原本就有毀損，我想這次應該不必支付費用吧？

01 未寄達與貨品缺損

● 不好意思，我們還沒收到貨品。

I'm afraid we haven't received our shipment yet.

- I'm afraid → Unfortunately,（很遺憾地）
- our shipment → our order / the products

● 我們訂購的零件尚未到貨。

The parts we ordered still[※1] haven't arrived（寄達）.

- parts → products / used cars

※1 "still" 用來強調貨品「尚未」寄達的情況。

● 你曾經保證我們三天內就會收到商品，但是到現在都還沒寄達。

told
承諾過 promised
保證過 assured

You guaranteed (保證過) us that we would receive (get) the delivery (order) in 3 days, but we haven't.

● 我們仍未收到替代品。

We haven't received the replacement order. (更換，替代品)

acknowledgement of our complaint. （信件已收到的）回音 / 申訴，投訴

● 很遺憾地，其中有一箱貨品毀損。

Unfortunately, one of the cases was damaged. (很遺憾地)

02 指出錯誤

● 我們訂的是貨號394-ZIP的產品，但是你寄給我們錯誤的產品。

We ordered stock number 394-ZIP, but you sent us the wrong item.

model / a different product.

● 訂單816810的出貨明細有問題。

There is a problem with the invoice for order 816810. (請款單，出貨明細)

● 我們（只）訂購了5個商品編號394-zip的產品，但是你（只）寄給我們4個，而不是5個。

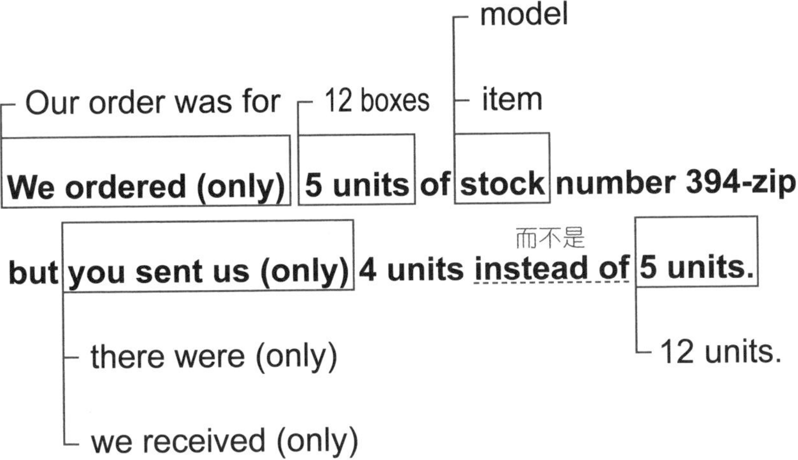

model
Our order was for
12 boxes
item
We ordered (only)
5 units
of
stock
number 394-zip,
而不是
but
you sent us (only)
4 units instead of
5 units.
there were (only)
12 units.
we received (only)

● 我們發現總金額有誤。

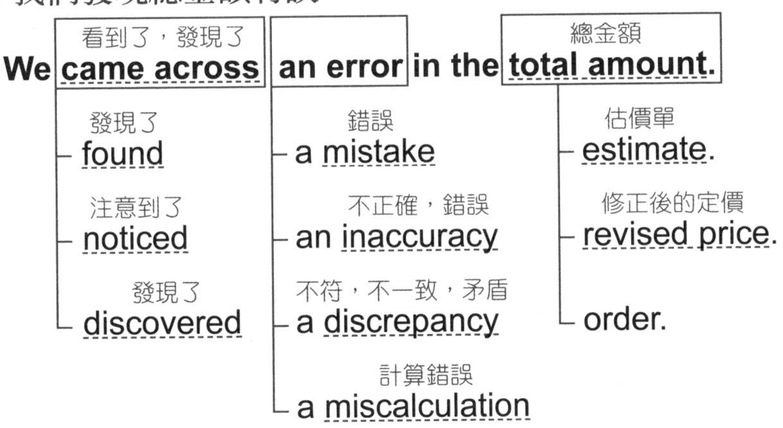

看到了，發現了
總金額
We
came across
an error
in the
total amount.
發現了
found
錯誤
a mistake
估價單
estimate.
注意到了
noticed
不正確，錯誤
an inaccuracy
修正後的定價
revised price.
發現了
discovered
不符，不一致，矛盾
a discrepancy
order.
計算錯誤
a miscalculation

● 我們訂購了一個陶製的阿多尼斯小雕像，但是請款單上卻標示為三個。

Our order included（包含了）

We ordered **one ceramic（陶製的） Adonis figurine,**

but the invoice（請款單，發票） shows an order for 3.

total doesn't include（包含） the price of the figurine.

● 你寄來的翻譯完稿錯誤連篇。

The finished translation you delivered was full of mistakes.
完成的
翻譯
寄送的
錯誤連篇
最後的
final
copy
完成的
completed
打字錯誤
full of typos.
full of errors.
少了，欠缺
missing a page.

● 收據上（又）有錯誤。請修正之後再寄過來。

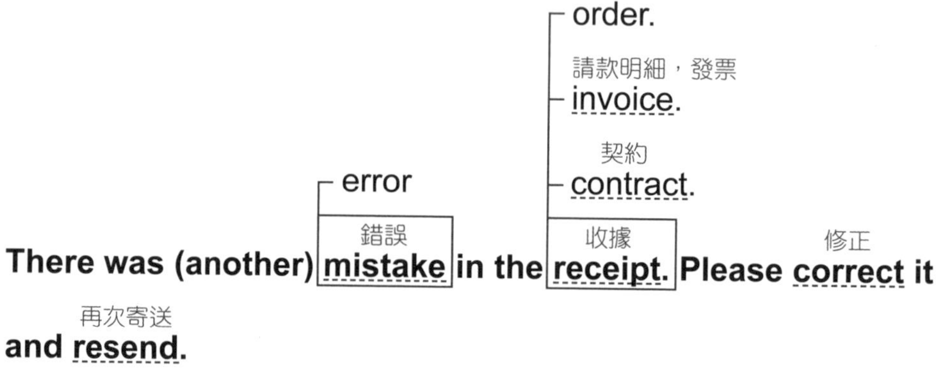
There was (another) mistake in the receipt. Please correct it and resend.
錯誤
收據
修正
再次寄送
error
order.
請款明細，發票
invoice.
契約
contract.

03 請求說明

● 我們仍需要你的解釋。

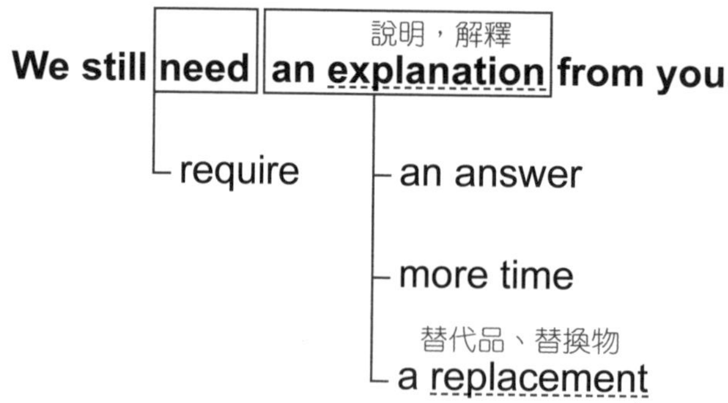
We still need an explanation from you.
說明，解釋
require
an answer
more time
替代品、替換物
a replacement

04 委託調查

● 能否請你盡快詳細調查這件事？

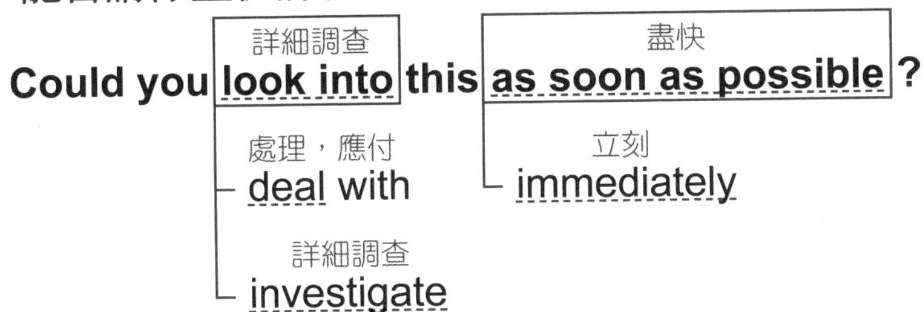

Could you look into this as soon as possible?
詳細調查
盡快
處理，應付
deal with
詳細調查
investigate
立刻
immediately

● 我已經附上我們收到的那一項商品的照片。

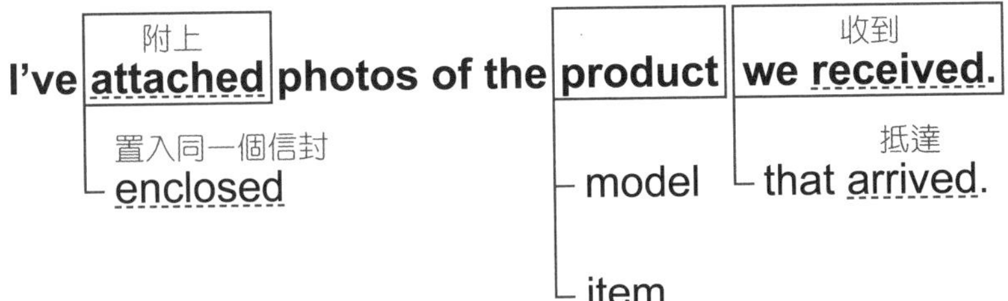

I've attached photos of the product we received.
附上
收到
置入同一個信封
enclosed
model
item
抵達
that arrived.

● 我已經把顯示有貨物毀損狀況的照片寄給你了。

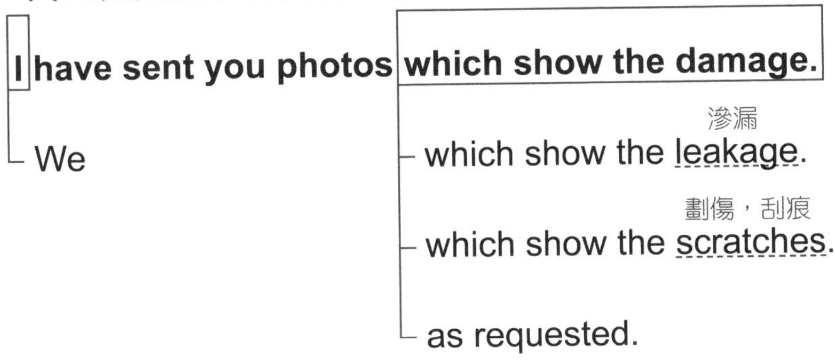

I have sent you photos which show the damage.
We
滲漏
which show the leakage.
劃傷，刮痕
which show the scratches.
as requested.

● 我們希望你立刻對這個問題做出因應。

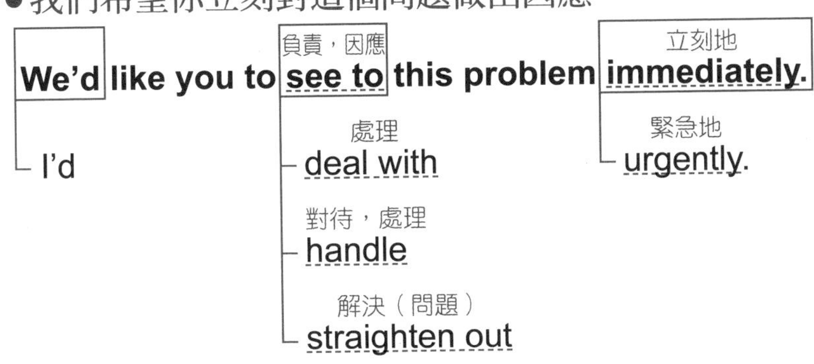

We'd like you to see to this problem immediately.
負責，因應
立刻地
I'd
處理
deal with
對待，處理
handle
解決（問題）
straighten out
緊急地
urgently.

● 我們想知道你打算如何找到解決這個問題的方法。

We would like to know how you plan to find a solution to this problem.

解決辦法 find a solution to
- 解決 solve
- 解決 clear up

05 要求改善

● 我們希望你立刻採取措施以補救這個狀況。

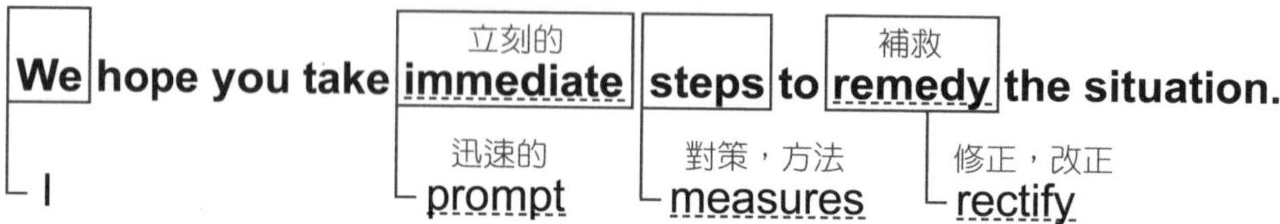
立刻的
補救
We hope you take immediate steps to remedy the situation.
I
迅速的
prompt
對策，方法
measures
修正，改正
rectify

● 請將正確的商品型號再寄給我們一次。

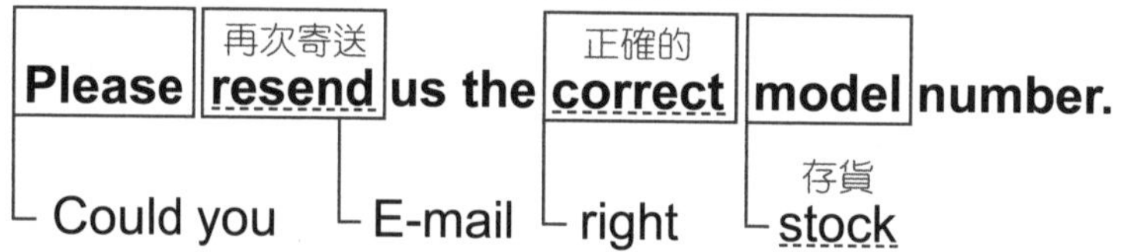
再次寄送
正確的
Please resend us the correct model number.
Could you
E-mail
right
存貨
stock

● 請將你正式提出申訴的內容以PDF的檔案格式寄過來。

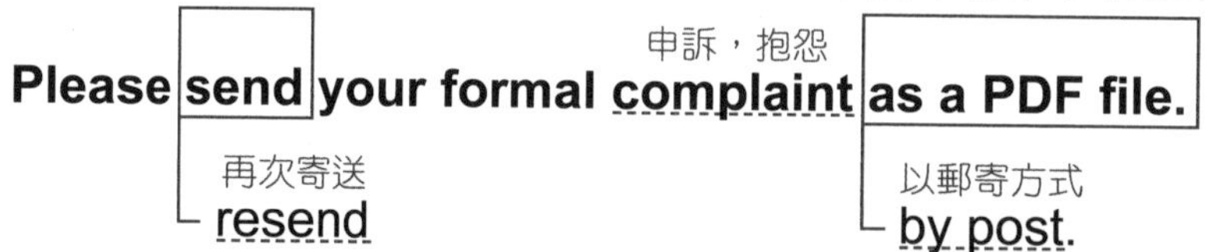
申訴，抱怨
Please send your formal complaint as a PDF file.
再次寄送
resend
以郵寄方式
by post.

● 請確保這樣的事不會再發生。

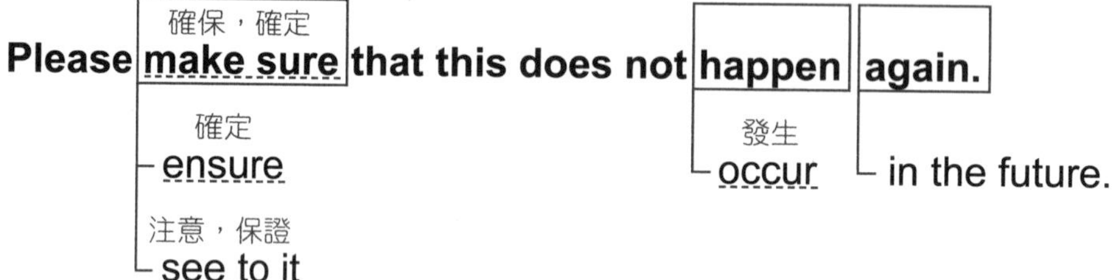
確保，確定
Please make sure that this does not happen again.
確定
ensure
注意，保證
see to it
發生
occur
in the future.

06 來自第三人的抱怨

● 延遲已經導致我們的顧客諸多不滿。

延誤 / 導致 / 多數的 / 投訴，不滿

The delays have resulted in a number of complaints from our customers.

● 我們的顧客抱怨這項商品難以操作。

抱怨 / 難以操作的，麻煩的

Our customers have complained about the units being cumbersome.

組裝 difficult to assemble.

價格過高的 overpriced.

容易故障的 prone to breakage.

07 表達失望

● 我們上次訂購的商品包裝不良。

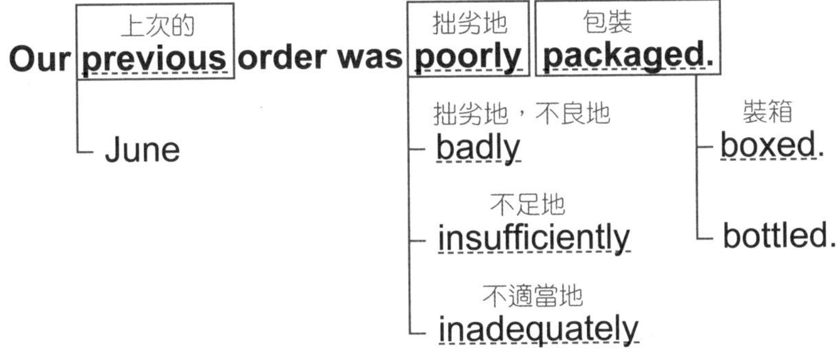

上次的 / 拙劣地 / 包裝

Our previous order was poorly packaged.

- June

拙劣地，不良地 badly

不足地 insufficiently

不適當地 inadequately

裝箱 boxed.

bottled.

● 服務很好，但是餐點很差。

The service was good, but the food was bad.

糟糕 was terrible.

was not fresh.

很爛，糟透了※1 sucked.

casual
Tone

※1 使用時請注意，“sucked” 是非常口語的說法。

● 我們的侍者既沒禮貌又不適任。

侍者 無禮的 無能力的，不適任的

Our server was rude and incompetent.

● 我們等了45分鐘才有人來幫我們點菜。

We waited 45 minutes for our order to be taken.
food.
帳單，結帳
check.
座位
table.

● 音質非常糟糕。

糟糕，極差

The sound quality was terrible.

● 我們的座位完全看不到舞台。

部分

We couldn't see any part of the stage from our seats.

● 我們被那些食物的品質嚇壞了。

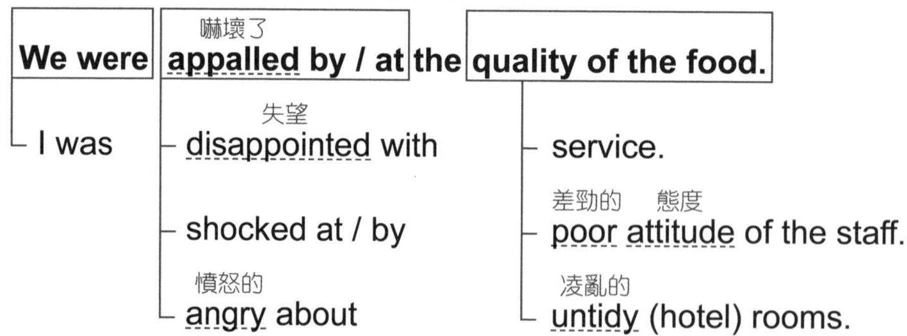
We were
I was
嚇壞了
appalled by / at
失望
disappointed with
shocked at / by
憤怒的
angry about
the
quality of the food.
service.
差勁的 態度
poor attitude of the staff.
凌亂的
untidy (hotel) rooms.

08 說明損害情況

● 由於延遲到貨，我們遭受到巨額損失。

由於
Due to the
抵達
late arrival, we have
遭受到
suffered a
巨大損失
major loss.
Because of
因為
On account of
受損的
damaged goods
延遲
the delay
重大的挫折
serious setback.
財務上的損失
financial loss.

09 要求賠償

● 因為寄來的貨物原本就有毀損，我想應該不必支付費用。

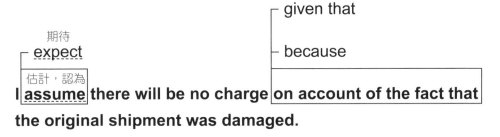

given that

because

期待
expect

估計，認為

I assume there will be no charge on account of the fact that the original shipment was damaged.

● 我們認為要求你們補償毀損的部分是很公平的。

公平的
We feel it is fair to ask you to
補償
compensate us for the damage.
We may require
退還，償還
reimburse
損失
our losses.

10 拒絕接受道歉

● 這種狀況令人無法接受。

無法接受

The situation is unacceptable.

缺失，缺點

high number of defects is

延遲

delays are

● 一直發生未能依照表訂日程到貨的問題，這令人無法接受。

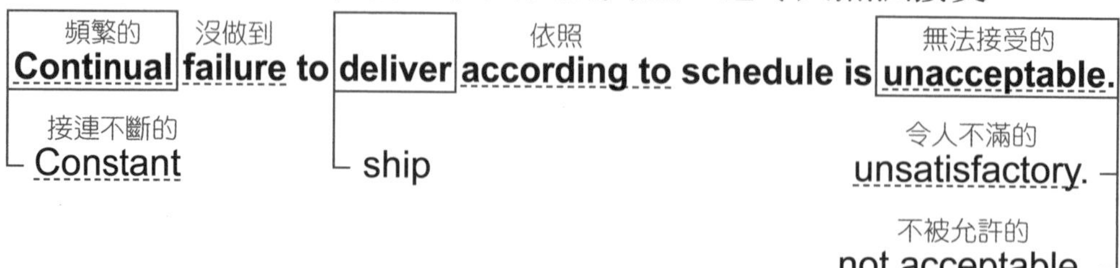
頻繁的
Continual
沒做到
failure to
deliver
依照
according to schedule is
無法接受的
unacceptable.
接連不斷的
Constant
ship
令人不滿的
unsatisfactory.
不被允許的
not acceptable.

11 暗示解約的意圖

● 我們也許會決定取消與你的合約。

We
決定
may decide to
cancel
合約
our contract with you.
have decided to
別無選擇
have no choice but to
宣告無效
annul
取消，廢除
revoke

● 雖然我們很喜歡你的產品，但是如果無法改正這些問題，我們將不得不尋找新的供應商。

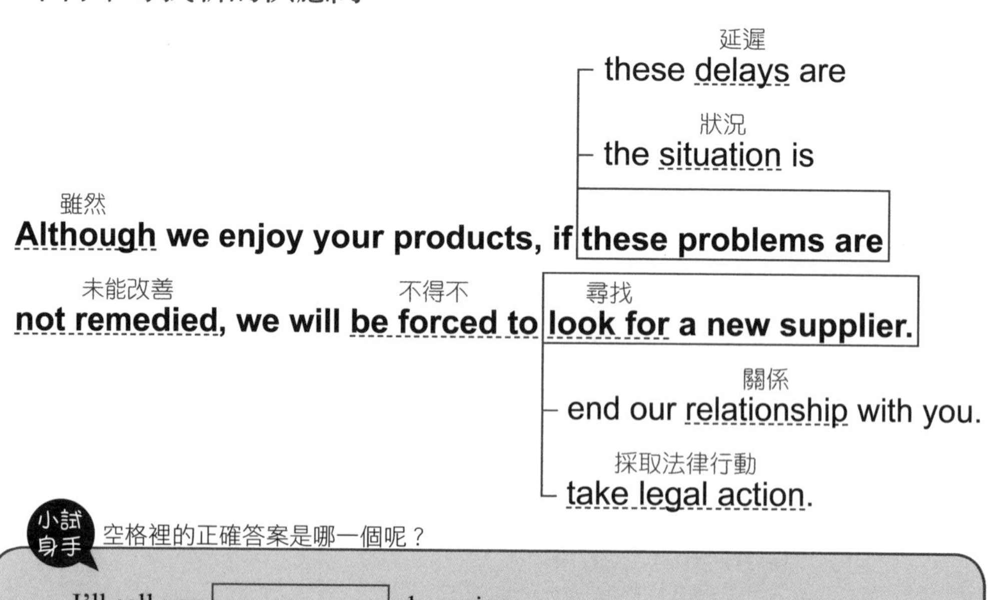
雖然
Although we enjoy your products, if
these problems are
延遲
these delays are
狀況
the situation is
未能改善
not remedied, we will
不得不
be forced to
尋找
look for a new supplier.
關係
end our relationship with you.
採取法律行動
take legal action.

小試身手 空格裡的正確答案是哪一個呢？

I'll call you ______ she arrives.

❶ a moment　❷ the moment

解答就在下一頁

● 雖然我們很想繼續將貴公司視為我們的客戶，但是你們的產品招致的客訴和退貨比例很高，讓我們很難繼續與你們做生意。

Although (雖然) **we would like to continue to count** (視為，看作) **you among our customers, the high rate** (高比例) **of complaints** (投訴，申訴) **and returns** (退貨) **of your products has made it difficult to continue doing business with you.**※1

※ 使用這個例句時請注意，此語氣非常強硬。

● 經過審慎考慮之後，我們決定取消訂單。

After due (應有的) **consideration** (考慮)**, we have decided** (決定) **to cancel our order.**

due → careful (審慎的)

告別中式英文

Business E-mail Tips

Do the hardest and most challenging task first.

最困難且最有挑戰性的事情要先做。

即使會被討厭，還是不得不按下「寄出」鍵…

我們有時不得不寫信向人傳達一些壞消息，例如抱怨或申訴等等，甚至是告知某人已經被炒魷魚了。假如你不得不寫這類信件時，你會怎麼做呢？

《湯姆歷險記》的作者馬克・吐溫曾說過："If you have to eat two frogs, eat the big one first."（假如你必須吃兩隻青蛙的話，先吃大的那一隻）。意思就是說，最困難的事要最先處理，如此一來，就不必整天為那件事傷腦筋了。

前一頁 小試身手 的解答 ② I'll call you the moment she arrives.
她一到，我就會馬上打電話給你。

01 對造成對方的不便致歉

● 造成任何不便之處，我們感到非常抱歉。

We are very sorry for any inconvenience. (不便，困擾)
- I apologize (道歉)
- Please forgive us (原諒)
- the delay. (延遲)

● 對於我們可能對你造成的不便，我們深感抱歉。

We deeply regret any inconvenience we may have caused you. (深深地 覺得遺憾；不便，困擾；導致)
- apologize for (道歉)
- embarrassment we may have caused you and your family. (為難，難為情)
- emotional distress you may have suffered. (精神上的痛苦；遭受)
- setbacks our mistake may have created. (損害，挫折)

02 深表歉意

● 千言萬語也表達不出我真誠的歉意。

Words cannot express how truly sorry I am. (表現；真誠的)

● 請接受我們衷心的歉意。

Please accept our sincere apologies. (衷心的；道歉)
- heartfelt (由衷的)
- deepest (最深厚的)

● 我實在不知道為什麼會發生這種事，但是我願意接受所有的責難。

I honestly don't know how this could have happened, but I accept all the blame.

- honestly 實在 → truly 真誠地
- how this could have happened → what went wrong 弄錯 / what the cause 理由 of the mishap 不幸事故，災難 was
- accept 接受 all the blame 責任，非難 → take full 全部的 responsibility 責任. / will personally 親自 see to it that it is fixed.

● 你是我們很重要的顧客，我們將會採取措施以確保這樣的事不會再發生。

We value 重視，看重 you as a customer and will take steps 採取措施 to ensure 確保 this does not happen again.

- take steps → do whatever 無論如何 it takes / review 再次檢查 our system
- this does not happen again. → we can deliver next time. / you are not inconvenienced 給…造成不便 again.

03 為延誤致歉

● 關於這次延遲付款一事，請接受我的道歉。

Please accept 接受 my apology 道歉 for the late payment 付款.

- Please accept my apology → I'm very sorry
- late payment. → way 方式 I behaved 表現 yesterday. / comment I made.

● 很抱歉我過了這麼久才回信。

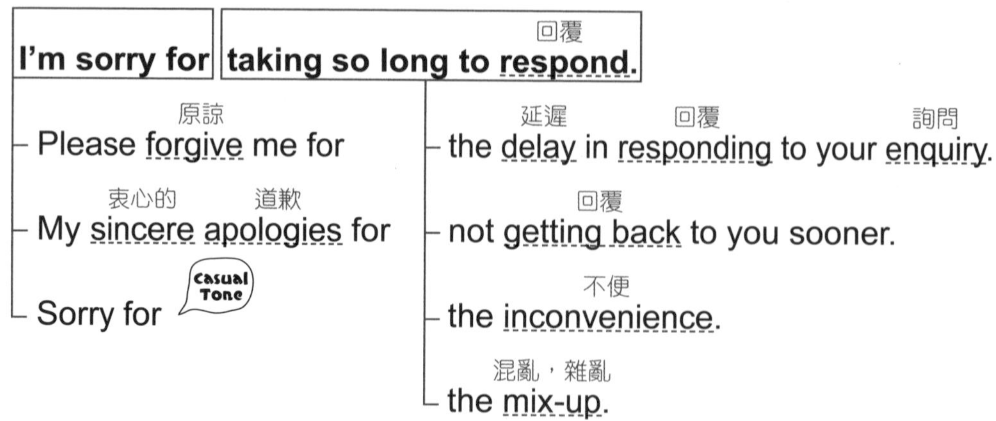

I'm sorry for
taking so long to respond.
回覆
原諒
Please forgive me for
衷心的
道歉
My sincere apologies for
Sorry for
Casual Tone
延遲
回覆
詢問
the delay in responding to your enquiry.
回覆
not getting back to you sooner.
不便
the inconvenience.
混亂，雜亂
the mix-up.

● 我們很抱歉寄送延遲了。

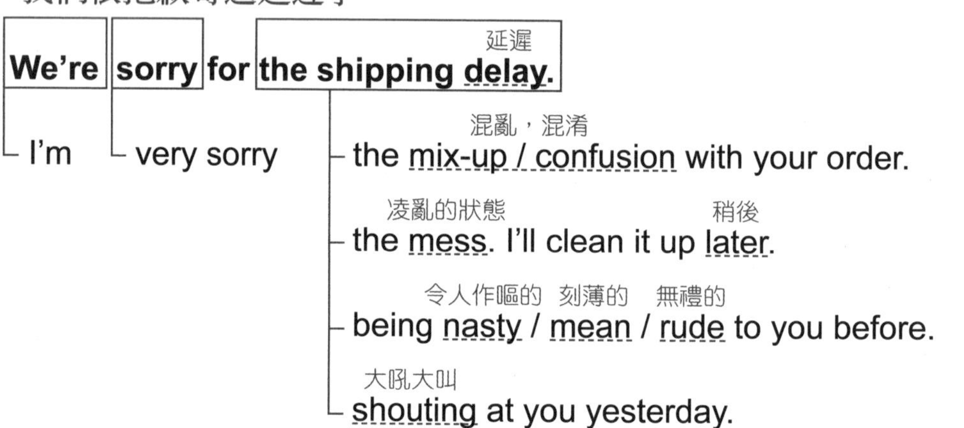

We're
sorry
for
the shipping delay.
延遲
I'm
very sorry
混亂，混淆
the mix-up / confusion with your order.
凌亂的狀態
稍後
the mess. I'll clean it up later.
令人作嘔的
刻薄的
無禮的
being nasty / mean / rude to you before.
大吼大叫
shouting at you yesterday.

● 請原諒我遲到了。

原諒
Please forgive me
for
being late.
致歉
My apologies
弄錯
mixing up your orders.
calling you when I was drunk.
錯過
missing your birthday.

14 致歉 為延誤致歉

04 為無法解決的問題致歉

● 很遺憾地通知您，您所洽詢的產品已經沒有庫存了。

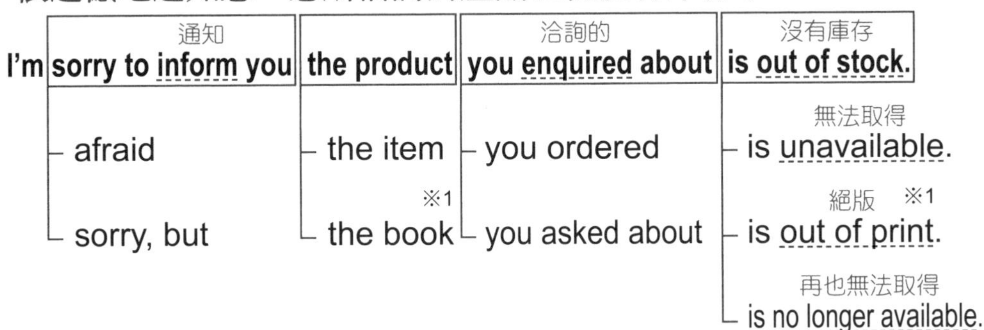

通知
洽詢的
沒有庫存
I'm sorry to inform you the product you enquired about is out of stock.
afraid
sorry, but
the item
※1
the book
you ordered
you asked about
無法取得
is unavailable.
絕版 ※1
is out of print.
再也無法取得
is no longer available.

※1 "out of print" 只能用在書本之類的印刷品。

● 我很不想擔任帶來壞消息的人，但是我們尚未全部備妥你所訂的貨品。

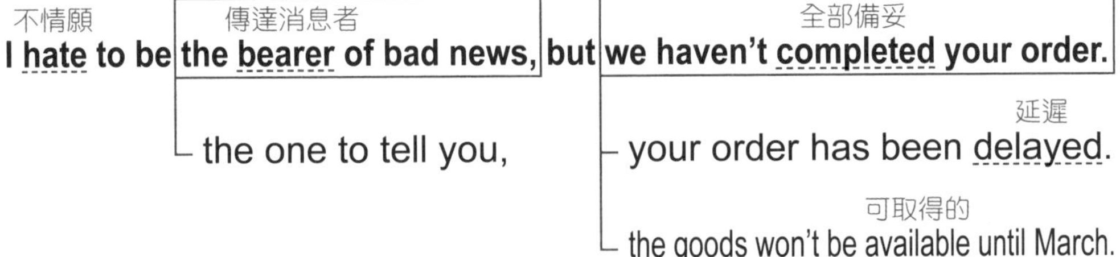

不情願
傳達消息者
全部備妥
I hate to be the bearer of bad news, but we haven't completed your order.
the one to tell you,
延遲
your order has been delayed.
可取得的
the goods won't be available until March.

● 很遺憾地通知您，由於原油價格高漲，我們無法再提供你相同的條件。

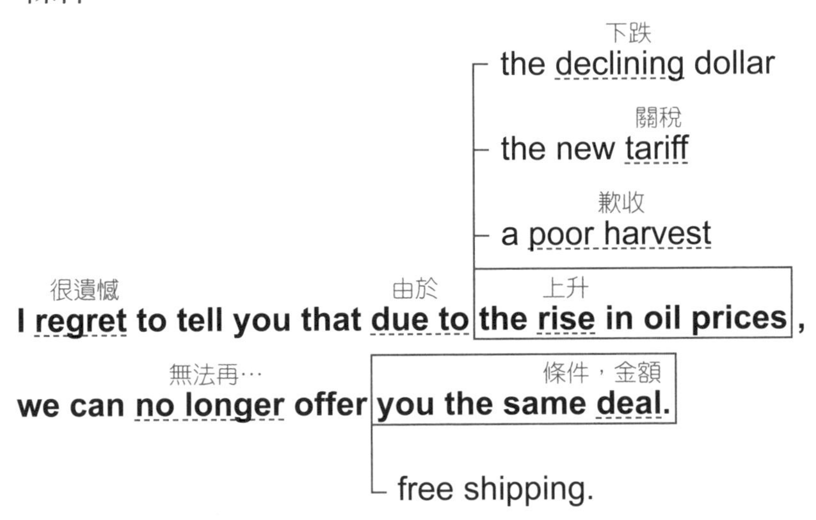

下跌
the declining dollar
關稅
the new tariff
歉收
a poor harvest
很遺憾
由於
上升
I regret to tell you that due to the rise in oil prices,
無法再…
條件，金額
we can no longer offer you the same deal.
free shipping.

● 我們未能在期限內取得原料。

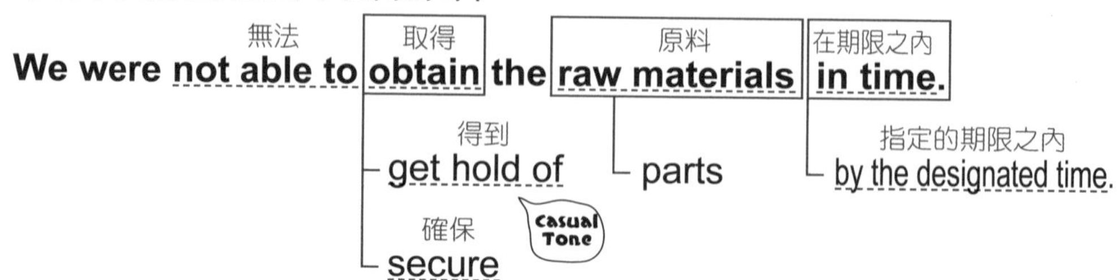

無法
We were not able to
取得
obtain
the
原料
raw materials
在期限之內
in time.
得到
get hold of
確保
secure
Casual Tone
parts
指定的期限之內
by the designated time.

05 為錯誤致歉

● 關於這次會計上的錯誤，請接受我們由衷的道歉。

接受
由衷的
道歉
Please accept our sincere apologies
for the
會計失誤
accounting error.
Sorry
Casual Tone
道歉
Our apologies
error.
疏忽，出錯
oversight.

● 請原諒我未能通知你進度變更一事。

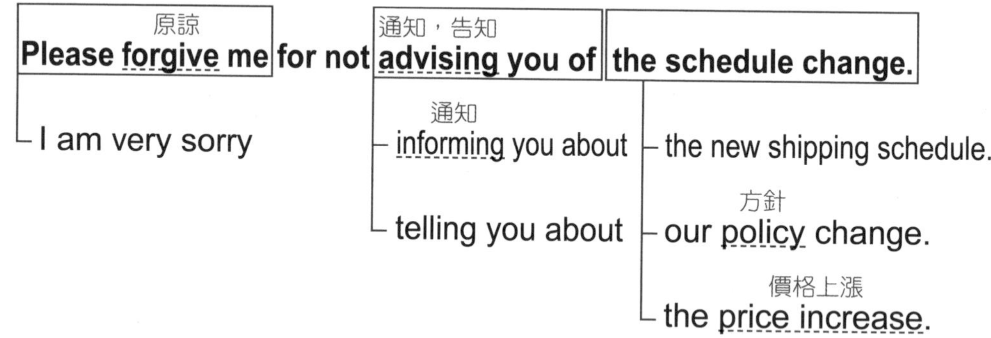

原諒
Please forgive me
for not
通知，告知
advising you of
the schedule change.
I am very sorry
通知
informing you about
telling you about
the new shipping schedule.
方針
our policy change.
價格上漲
the price increase.

● 對不起。我們好像暫時找不到你的訂單。

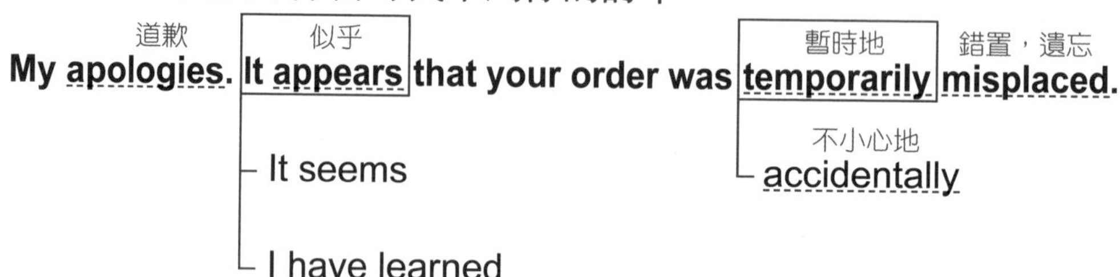

道歉
My apologies.
似乎
It appears
that your order was
暫時地
temporarily
錯置，遺忘
misplaced.
It seems
I have learned
不小心地
accidentally

14 致歉 為錯誤致歉

06 為態度或行為致歉

● 我的提議並不恰當。

My suggestion（提議） was inappropriate（不恰當）.

- comment
- reaction（反應）
- behavior（行為，態度）

- out of line（言行失當）. Casual Tone
- rude（無禮）.

● 關於我們工作人員不專業的態度，我想向大家致歉。

I would like to apologize（致歉） for our staff's unprofessional（不專業的，外行的） behavior（行為，態度）.

- your unfortunate（不幸的） treatment（遭遇，對待） by our staff.
- misplacing your order（訂單出錯）.

● 售貨員的態度令我感到震驚。

I am appalled（驚愕的） by the behavior（行為，態度） of the sales representative（售貨員，販賣員）.

● 引起問題的當事人已經遭到解雇。我將接手負責你的帳戶。

The offending party（引起問題的當事人） has been terminated（免職，解雇）. I will be taking over（接管，繼任） your account.

07 處理問題的對策

● 我對這次的混亂感到很抱歉。下不為例。

I am so sorry for the confusion（混亂）. It won't happen again.

- I am deeply（深深地） sorry
- My apologies（道歉）

● 請告訴我該如何彌補你的損失。

Please tell me **how I can** **make it up to you.** (補償: make it up)

└ Let me know

├ make amends. (賠罪)

└ set things right.

● 為了表示歉意，我會寄一箱免費的洗潔劑給你。

┌ To show our appreciation (感謝: appreciation) ┌ we are

To express my apologies, **I am** (表現: express；歉意: apologies)

sending you a complimentary case of cleanser. (免費的，贈送的: complimentary)

├ giving you 10% off your next order.

└ giving you a 10% discount on your next order.

14P

Business E-mail Tips

告别中式英文

Before hitting the send button, take a minute to reread your E-mail.

按下傳送鍵之前，請再花一分鐘重新閱讀一次你的E-mail。

寄出E-mail之前，請再檢查一次

寄出E-mail之前，請給自己一分鐘的時間，再檢查一下信件的內容：有沒有哪裡寫錯呢？語氣是否正確？拼字都沒有問題嗎？主旨與收件人都沒有錯誤嗎？

業務往來的E-mail中，拼字和文法也非常重要，因為對方很可能會以你的文筆來判斷你的聰明才智。此外，雖然語氣很難拿捏，但仍是很重要的關鍵，注意不要顯得過度強勢，也別讓人覺得你很冷淡無情（除非那就是你想表現的態度）。

別忘了，與國外廠商進行業務往來時，對方通常只能藉由E-mail或電話來評斷你這個人，絕少有機會面對面認識你，所以寫E-mail時千萬不能敷衍了事。

01 說明

● 你訂的貨品應該會在未來幾天之內送達。

Your order should arrive within the next few days.

- Your order（寄出的貨品）→ The shipment
- arrive（抵達）→ be delivered（被運送）
- within：…之內

● 我剛跟貨運公司結束通話。

I just got off the phone with the shipping agent.

- got off the phone with（掛斷電話）→ finished talking to / received an E-mail from（收到）
- shipping agent（貨運公司）→ forwarding agent.（運輸業者）/ customs clearing agent.（報關行）

● 所有產品都符合澳洲法律規定。

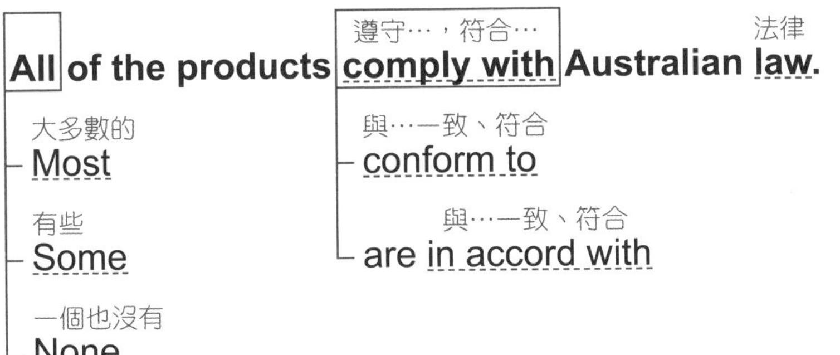

All of the products comply with Australian law.

- All → Most（大多數的）/ Some（有些）/ None（一個也沒有）
- comply with（遵守…，符合…）→ conform to（與…一致、符合）/ are in accord with（與…一致、符合）
- law：法律

02 告知原因

● 我們的電腦故障，所以資料全都消失了。

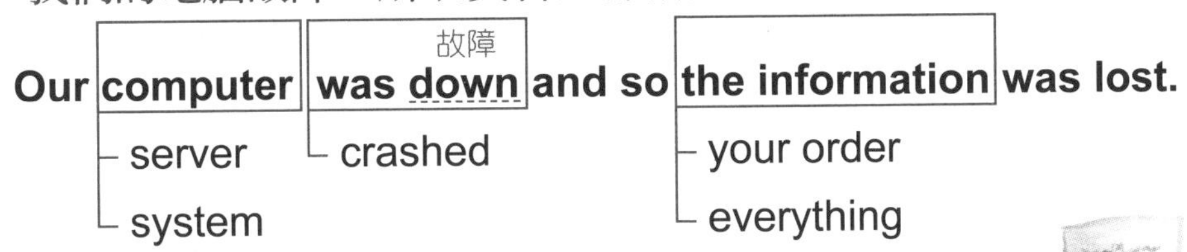

Our computer was down and so the information was lost.

- computer → server / system
- was down（故障）→ crashed
- the information → your order / everything

15

說明原委

請求諒解

●貨物可能在海關被攔截了。

The shipment might have been held up at customs.
貨物，貨品
被攔截
海關
Your
cars
order
package
※1
got
被沒收
impounded by customs.
在運輸途中遺失
lost in transit.
遭竊
stolen.

※1 用 “gotten” 也可以。

●工廠似乎因為罷工而停業了。

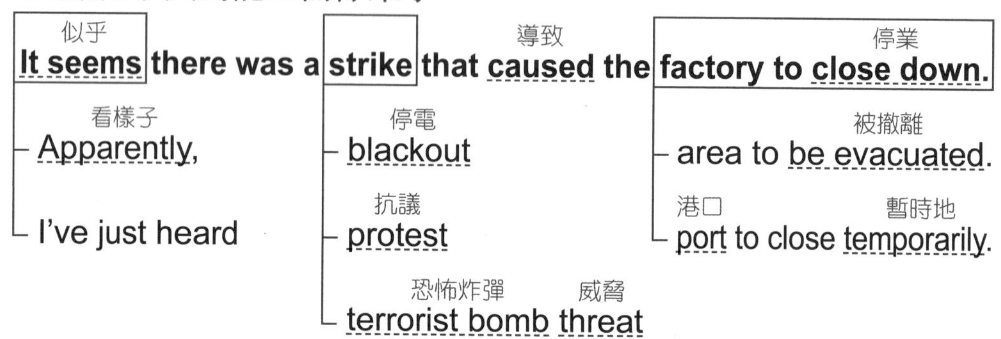

It seems there was a strike that caused the factory to close down.
似乎
導致
停業
看樣子
Apparently,
I've just heard
停電
blackout
抗議
protest
恐怖炸彈
威脅
terrorist bomb threat
被撤離
area to be evacuated.
港口
暫時地
port to close temporarily.

03 請求諒解

●這種情況十分少見，我希望你能了解我們並不是有意的。

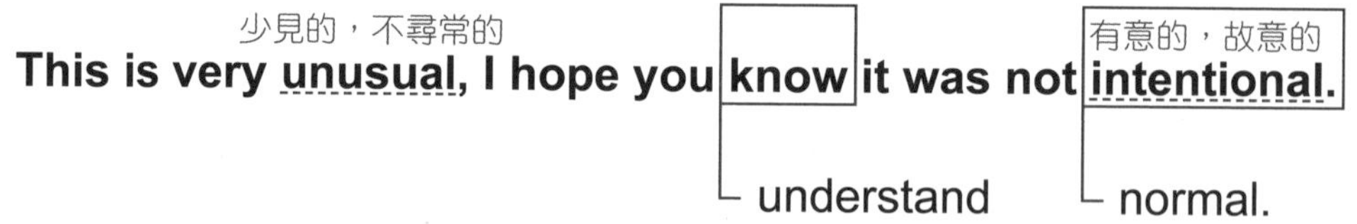

This is very unusual, I hope you know it was not intentional.
少見的，不尋常的
有意的，故意的
understand
normal.

●由於我們無法確認你的訂單，我們必須將其擱置。

As we were not able to confirm your order, we had to put it on hold.
確認
將其擱置、保留
could not
支付的款項
payment
your address
could not ship the goods.
發行，發布
couldn't release the items.

04 調查原因

● 我會親自詳細調查延遲的原因。

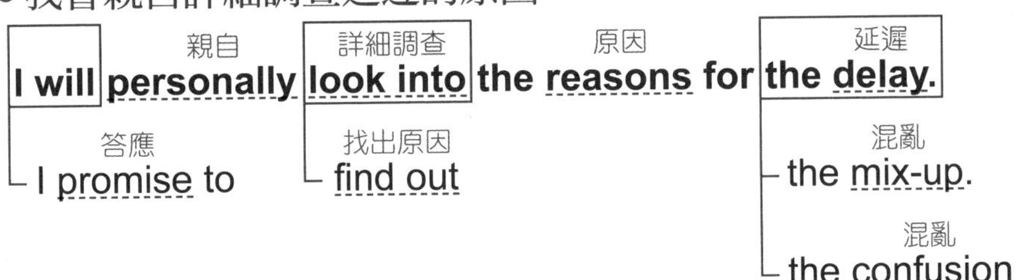
I will personally look into the reasons for the delay.
親自
詳細調查
原因
延遲
I promise to
答應
find out
找出原因
the mix-up.
混亂
the confusion.
混亂

● 詳細調查延遲的情況之後，我再答覆你。

I'll look into the delay and get back to you.
詳細調查
延遲
答覆
investigate
詳細調查
find out about
找出原因
matter
事態，問題
contact you.

● 我正在詳細調查延遲的情況，將會盡快回覆你。

I'm looking into the delay and will get back to you ASAP.
詳細調查
延遲
聯絡
盡快
the missing order
遺失的，缺漏的
the miscommunication
誤解，溝通不良
update you shortly.
近期內
contact you soon.

● 我們仍在與貨運公司調查一些細節。

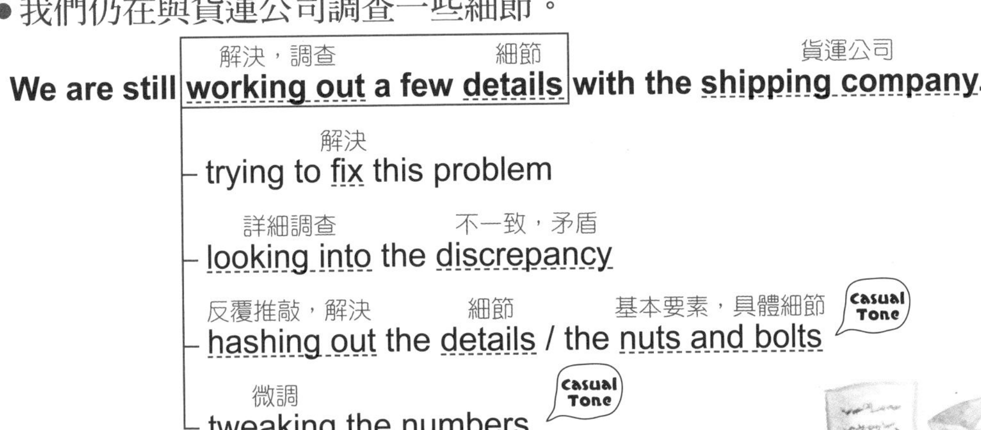
We are still working out a few details with the shipping company.
解決，調查
細節
貨運公司
trying to fix this problem
解決
looking into the discrepancy
詳細調查
不一致，矛盾
hashing out the details / the nuts and bolts
反覆推敲，解決
細節
基本要素，具體細節
Casual Tone
tweaking the numbers
微調
Casual Tone

適用情況16：諮商・建議

01 尋求建議

● 我想跟你談談這件事。

I would like to talk to you about this.
speak to you
in more detail.
細節
hear your opinion
意見
know what you think

● 關於這個問題，可否請您寫信給我一些建議？

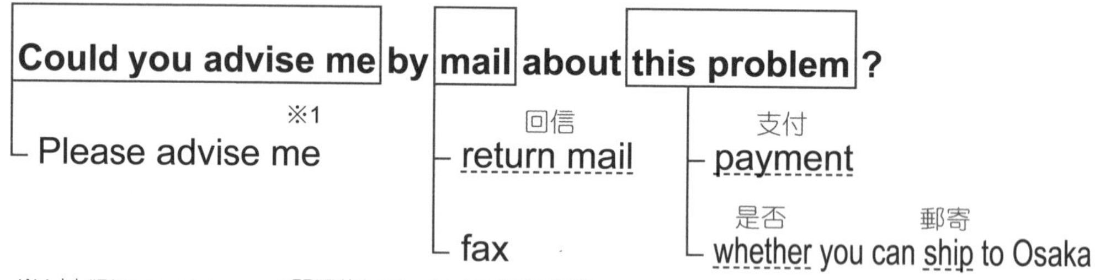

Could you advise me by mail about this problem ?
Please advise me ※1
return mail
回信
fax
payment
支付
whether you can ship to Osaka
是否
郵寄

※1 以 "Please advise me" 開頭的句子，句末不需加問號。

● 你可以試著與經理（上司）聯絡。

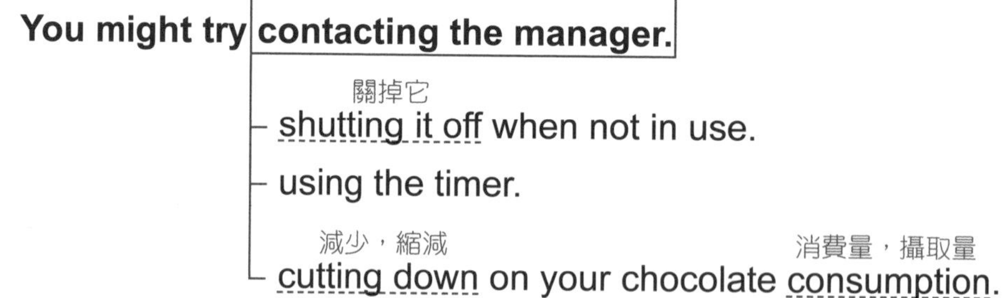

You might try contacting the manager.
shutting it off when not in use.
關掉它
using the timer.
cutting down on your chocolate consumption.
減少，縮減
消費量，攝取量

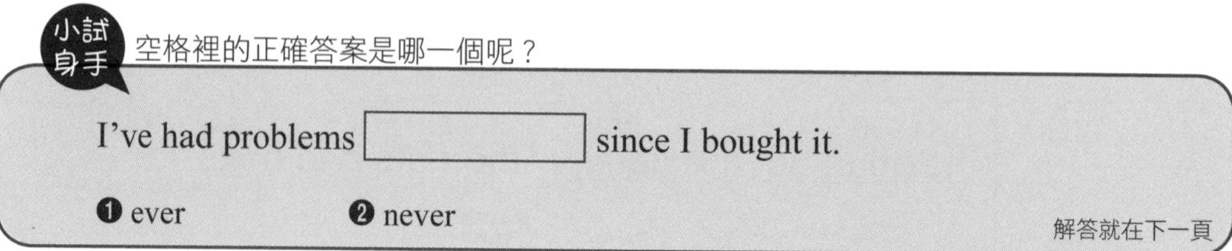

小試身手
空格裡的正確答案是哪一個呢？
I've had problems ______ since I bought it.
❶ ever
❷ never
解答就在下一頁

●我們正在尋找減少浪費的方法，我們想知道貴公司能提供什麼協助。

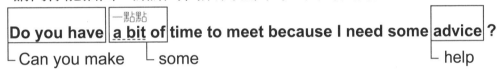

We are looking for ways to **reduce waste** (尋找 looking for；方法 ways；減少 reduce；浪費 waste)
- reward our employees (獎勵 reward；員工 employees)
- improve our bottom line (提升 improve；最終獲利 bottom line)
- improve security (增強 improve；安全性 security)

and we'd like to hear how **your company** can **help.**
- your company → your system
- help. → make a difference.

●請問你能抽出一點點時間跟我碰面嗎？因為我需要一些建議。

Do you have **a bit of** time to meet because I need some **advice**? (一點點 a bit of)
- Do you have → Can you make
- a bit of → some
- advice → help

●我們去跟比較清楚這件事的人談談吧。

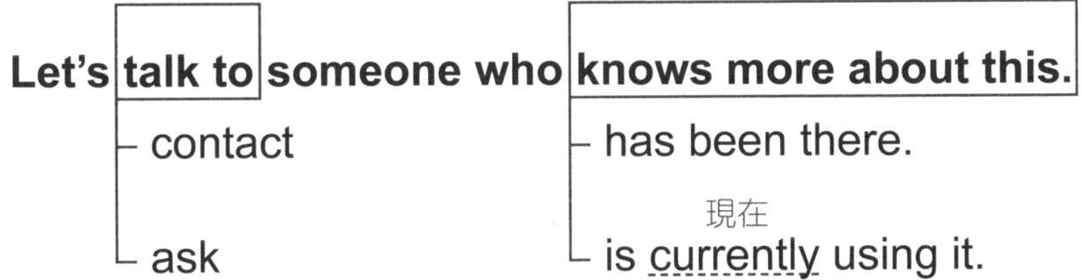
Let's talk to someone who knows more about this.
contact
ask
has been there.
現在
is currently using it.

●假如我要求加薪，你認為他們會同意嗎？

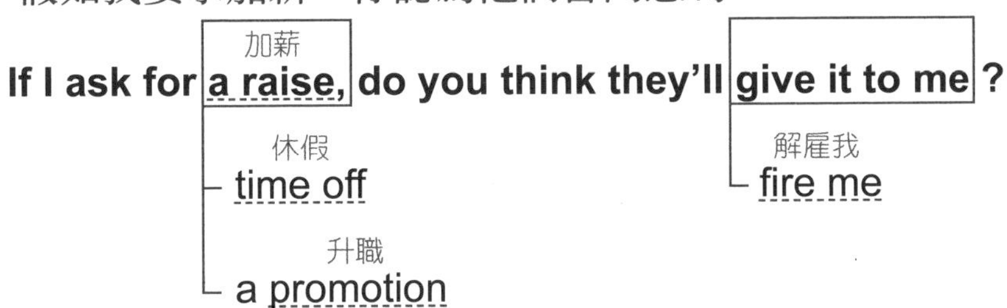
加薪
If I ask for a raise, do you think they'll give it to me?
休假
time off
升職
a promotion
解雇我
fire me

前一頁小試身手的解答 ❶ I've had problems ever since I bought it.
這個產品自我買來之後就一直問題不斷。

● 關於這件事，我可以建議你尋求法律協助嗎？

Could I suggest that you seek legal advice on this matter ?
建議
尋求
法律協助
這件事
May
propose
提議
we concentrate on our core business
專注
主要事業
we focus on R&D (research & development)
專注
研究開發
we cut our losses and move on
繼續努力
Casual Tone

02 討論解決問題的辦法

● 關於員工偷竊一事，我們應該如何處理呢？

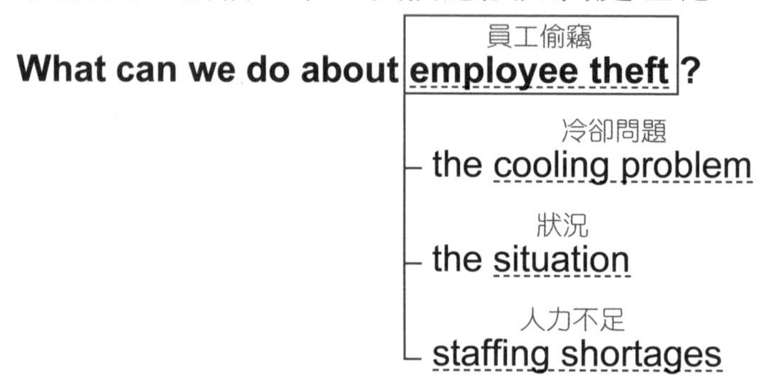
What can we do about employee theft ?
員工偷竊
the cooling problem
冷卻問題
the situation
狀況
staffing shortages
人力不足

● 我想討論一下提高公司效率的方法。

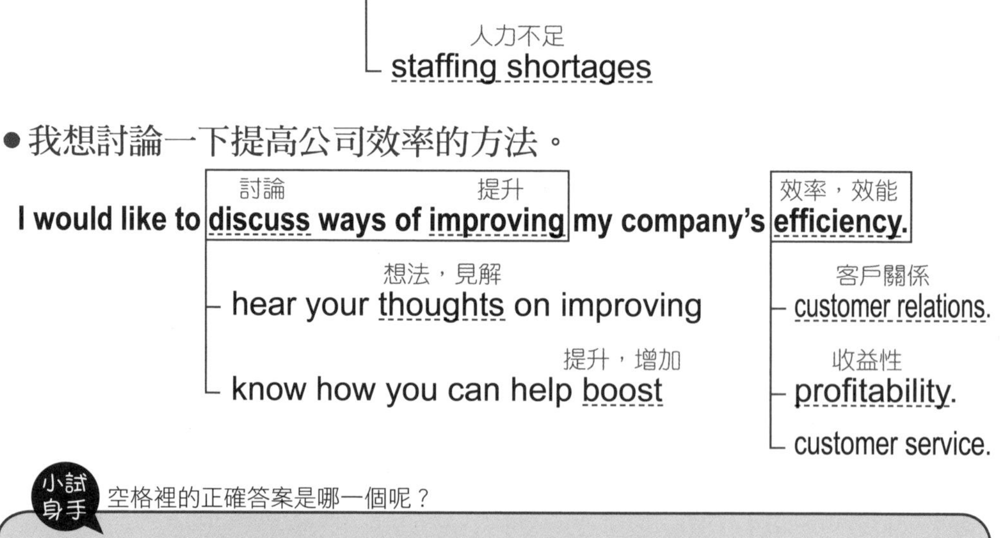
I would like to discuss ways of improving my company's efficiency.
討論
提升
效率，效能
hear your thoughts on improving
想法，見解
know how you can help boost
提升，增加
customer relations.
客戶關係
profitability.
收益性
customer service.

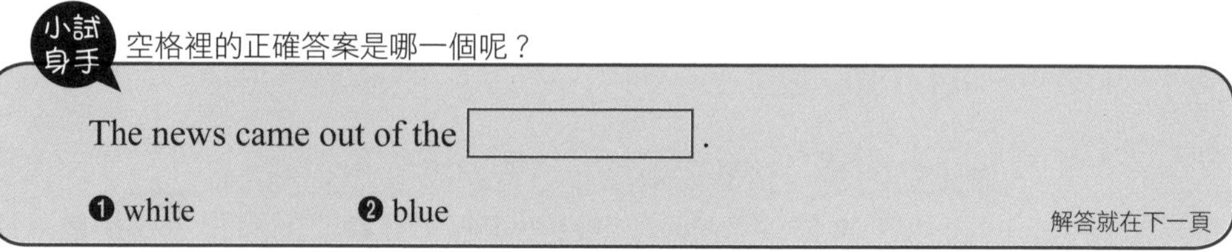
小試身手 空格裡的正確答案是哪一個呢？

The news came out of the ______.

❶ white ❷ blue

解答就在下一頁

● 如何才能使他們接受我們的提議呢？

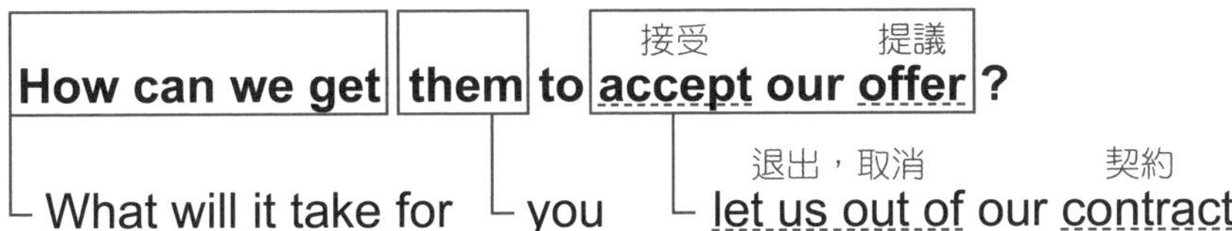
How can we get them to accept our offer ?
接受 提議
What will it take for
you
let us out of our contract
退出，取消 契約

03 提供建議

● 對你來說最好的方法就是聘請律師。

Your best move is to hire a lawyer.
最佳手段
僱用 律師
Your only choice
put it behind you.
別再想那件事、忘卻

● 你應該告訴他們你想要加薪，否則你就要辭職。

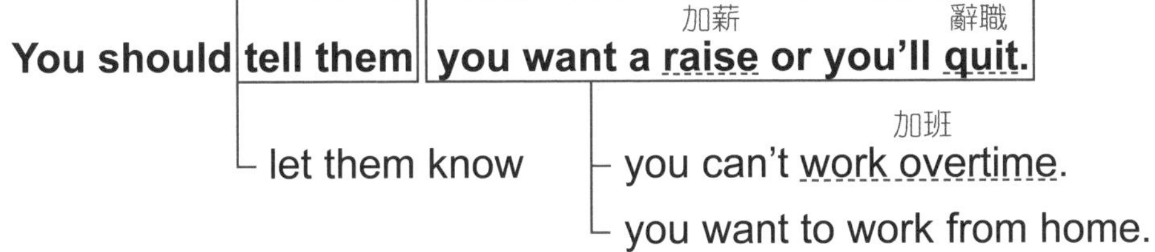
You should tell them you want a raise or you'll quit.
加薪 辭職
let them know
you can't work overtime.
加班
you want to work from home.

● 我認為你應該接受Crystal Sky提供的職位。

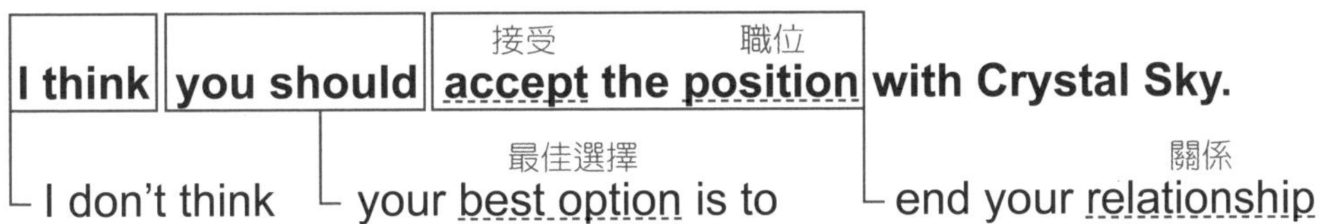
I think you should accept the position with Crystal Sky.
接受 職位
I don't think
your best option is to
最佳選擇
end your relationship
關係

● 關於他的活動，你應該直接問他。

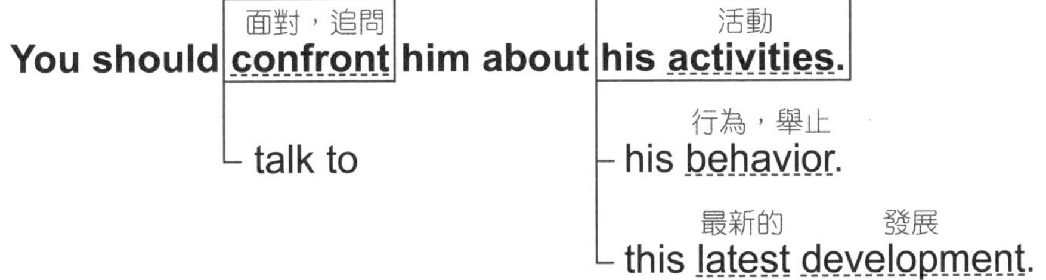
You should confront him about his activities.
面對，追問
活動
talk to
his behavior.
行為，舉止
this latest development.
最新的 發展

● 你能夠採取的最佳行動，就是解除契約。

The best thing you can do is cancel the contract.（contract 契約）

- The best thing for you to do
- What I'd suggest you do（suggest 提議）

- send it by air instead of sea.（by air 空運；instead of 代替）
- talk directly to your boss about it.
- get a quote from another place first.（quote 報價）
- marry that girl!!（marry 與…結婚）

● 你應該休假守喪。

You ought to take some time off to mourn.（ought to 應該；time off 休假；mourn 守喪）

- heal.（治癒）
- recuperate.（恢復，休養）
- have the operation.（operation 手術）

● 假如我是你，我會捨棄掉餐廳，只保留酒吧。

If I were you, I'd get rid of the restaurant and just keep the bar.（get rid of 擺脫，捨棄）

- I would move to a new office with cheaper rent.
- I'd hire someone to take care of your accounts.（hire 僱用；take care of 負責處理；accounts 會計事務）
- I'd hire a student to hand out fliers for your nail salon.（hire 僱用；hand out 發送；fliers 傳單）

● 我認為你除了放手之外無能為力。

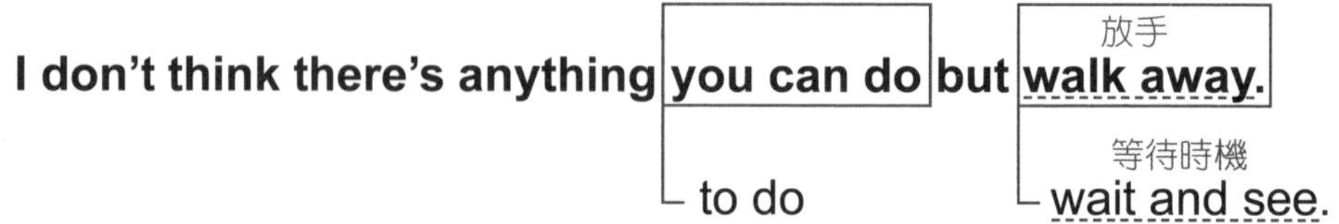

I don't think there's anything you can do but walk away.（walk away 放手）

- to do
- wait and see.（等待時機）

04 告知決定

● 我決定聽從你的建議，不要辭掉工作。

Following your advice (聽從), **I have decided** (決定) **not to quit my job.** (辭去)

- Based on your suggestion (根據 / 提案)
- Because of what you said to me
- to write a book.

● 我決定採納你的建議，重新建置整個網站。

決定
I decided to take your advice and redo our whole website.
重做
整個的
chose
提案
go with your suggestion
聽從
follow your advice
更新
replace all the server computers.
申請
獎學金
apply for the scholarship.
join a gym.

● 我會盡快與董事見面。

※1
I will be meeting with the director as soon as possible.
董事，理事長
盡快
We
Rumi
※1
meeting up
speaking
供應商
the suppliers
運輸業者
the freight company
那些傢伙※2
the gang
Casual Tone

※1 "meet" 的意思包括 ①事先約好見面。②第一次見面。③與認識的人偶然相遇。"meet up" 的意思則包括 ①與認識的人見面。②碰頭；例如在聚餐、宴會或看電影等活動之後，與事先約好的人見面（Ex. I'm going to meet up with Christine for coffee afterwards.）

※2 "the gang" 的意思是「好友或同事」。指的是寄件者與收信人共同認識的人，是一種非正式的用法。

05 對建言表示感謝

● 你要我們下個月發行CD的建議真是太棒了。

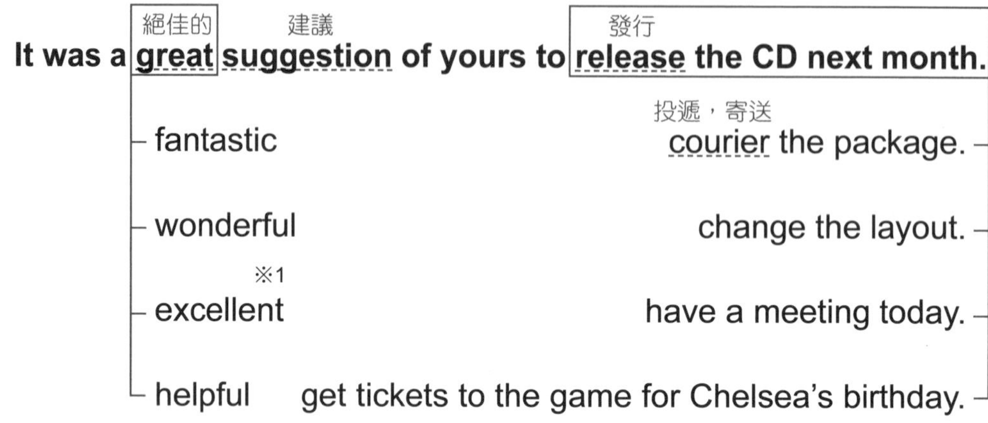

絕佳的 建議 發行
It was a great suggestion of yours to release the CD next month.
fantastic
投遞，寄送
courier the package.
wonderful
change the layout.
※1
excellent
have a meeting today.
helpful
get tickets to the game for Chelsea's birthday.

※1 "excellent" 是母音開頭，所以前面使用 "an" 而不是 "a"。

● 若能得到您關於如何改善口味的建議，我們將會大大地感謝。

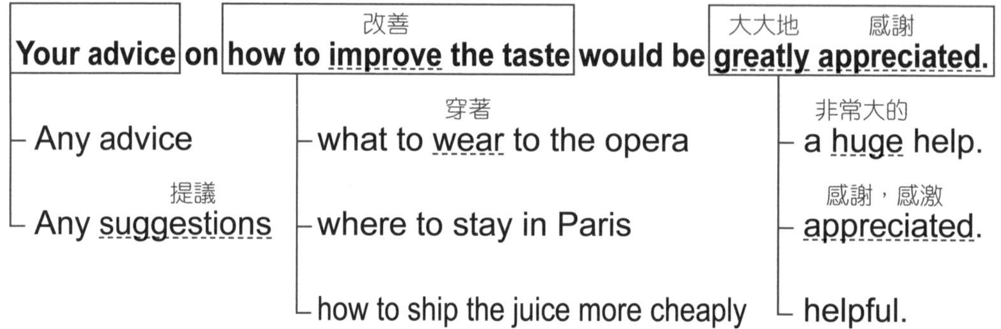

改善 大大地 感謝
Your advice on how to improve the taste would be greatly appreciated.
Any advice
提議
Any suggestions
穿著
what to wear to the opera
where to stay in Paris
how to ship the juice more cheaply
非常大的
a huge help.
感謝，感激
appreciated.
helpful.

No Chinese English!

生活中可見到許多標語，這些標語底下常附有英文翻譯，但這些英文翻譯也有很多「中式英文」喔！例如 "Please shut the fire door." 這個標語，從字面上可以猜到是「請關閉防火門」，但正確的說法其實是 "Please close the fire-proof door." 才對。

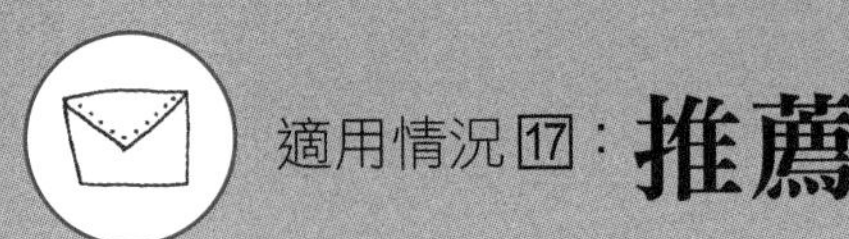

適用情況17：推薦

01 提供意見

- 能否請您聽我的建議，使用塑膠包裝呢？

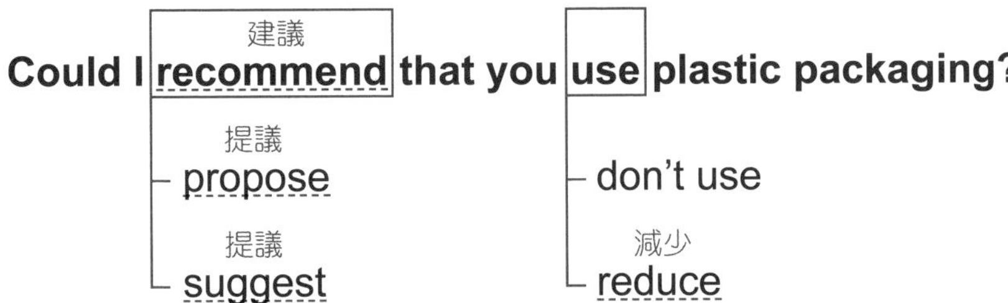
建議
Could I recommend that you use plastic packaging?
提議
propose
提議
suggest
don't use
減少
reduce

- 我想要提議我們在電子展上設置一個攤位。

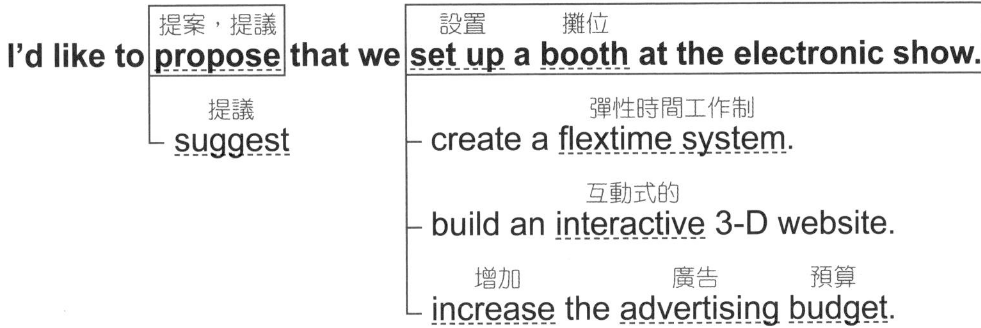
提案，提議
設置
攤位
I'd like to propose that we set up a booth at the electronic show.
提議
suggest
彈性時間工作制
create a flextime system.
互動式的
build an interactive 3-D website.
增加
廣告
預算
increase the advertising budget.

- 你不覺得我們應該試試看嗎？

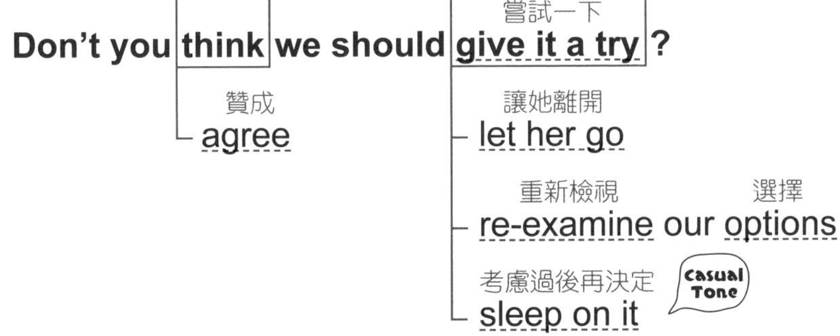
嘗試一下
Don't you think we should give it a try?
贊成
agree
讓她離開
let her go
重新檢視
選擇
re-examine our options
考慮過後再決定
sleep on it
Casual Tone

● 我提議我們建立一個新的伺服器。

提案
My proposal is that we set up a new server.
提議，忠告
suggestion
不賺錢的 事業
sell our unprofitable operations.
投資
invest more money.

● 我認為我們可以藉由支持環保來提升我們的形象。

改善，提升 綠化；支持環保
I think we could improve our image by going green.
關係
customer relations
利益
profits
效率
efficiency

● 我認為我們應該縮小規模以達到節約的目的。

削減，縮小
I think we should downsize to save money.
move our factory
增加，提升 利益
to increase profits.
減少 浪費
reduce waste
太陽能板
install solar panels

02 提議接下來的行動

● 你為何不考慮去算命？

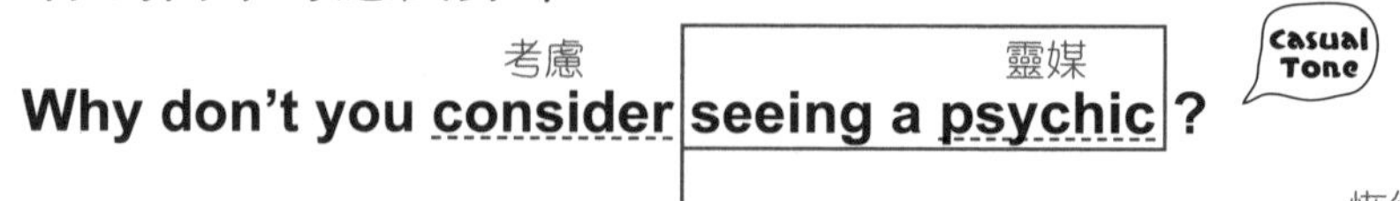
考慮 靈媒
Why don't you consider seeing a psychic ?
Casual Tone
恢復，休養
taking some time off to recuperate

● 你覺得我們出去外面呼吸一下新鮮空氣如何？

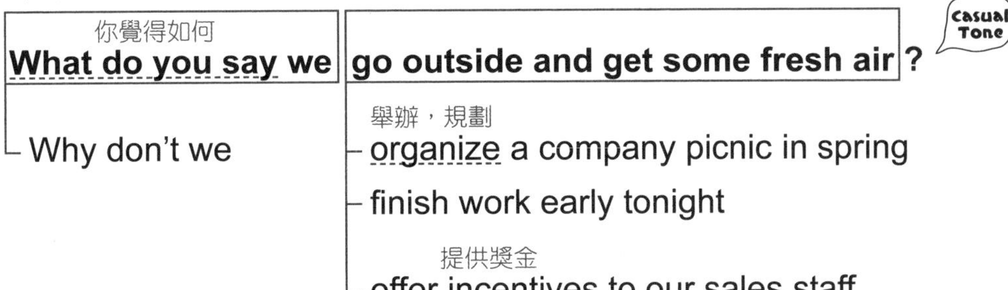
你覺得如何
What do you say we
go outside and get some fresh air ?
Casual Tone
Why don't we
舉辦，規劃
organize a company picnic in spring
finish work early tonight
提供獎金
offer incentives to our sales staff

● 能不能請您再考慮一下我們的提議？

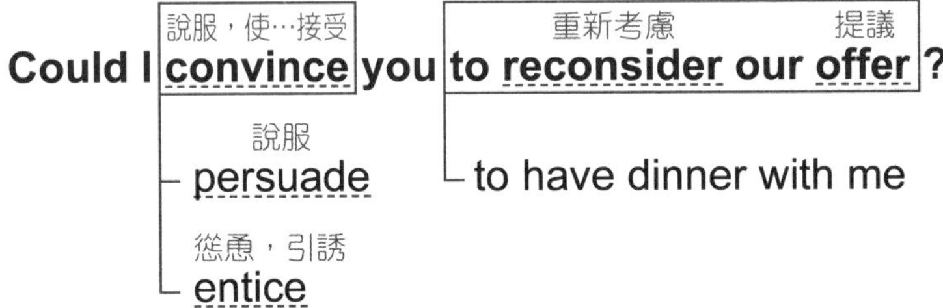
說服，使…接受
Could I convince you
重新考慮 提議
to reconsider our offer ?
說服
persuade
慫恿，引誘
entice
to have dinner with me

03 推薦店家與服務

● 我推薦你到 "Aunt Eulaki" 買東西。

推薦
I would recommend buying from "Aunt Eulaki".
wouldn't
advise
staying at the Templar Inn.
全額保險
fully insuring their order.

● 我建議你至少訂購15,000個，以降低成本。

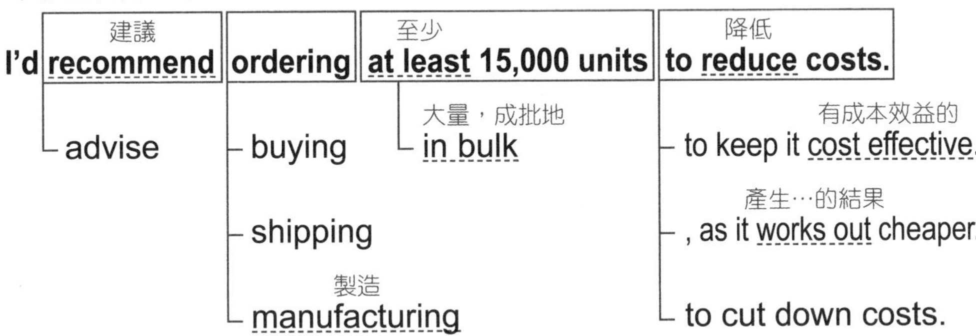
建議
I'd recommend
ordering
至少
at least 15,000 units
降低
to reduce costs.
advise
buying
shipping
製造
manufacturing
大量，成批地
in bulk
有成本效益的
to keep it cost effective.
產生…的結果
, as it works out cheaper.
to cut down costs.

04 提議變更與改善

● 我們應該考慮換另一家供應商。

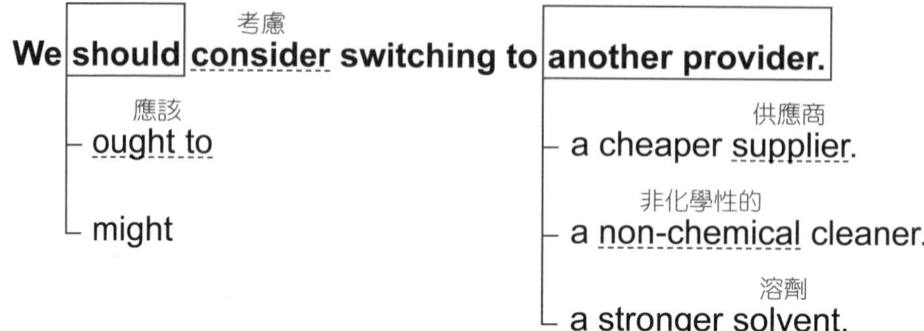
考慮
We should consider switching to another provider.
應該
ought to
might
供應商
a cheaper supplier.
非化學性的
a non-chemical cleaner.
溶劑
a stronger solvent.

● 我可以建議我們找一家新的供應商嗎？

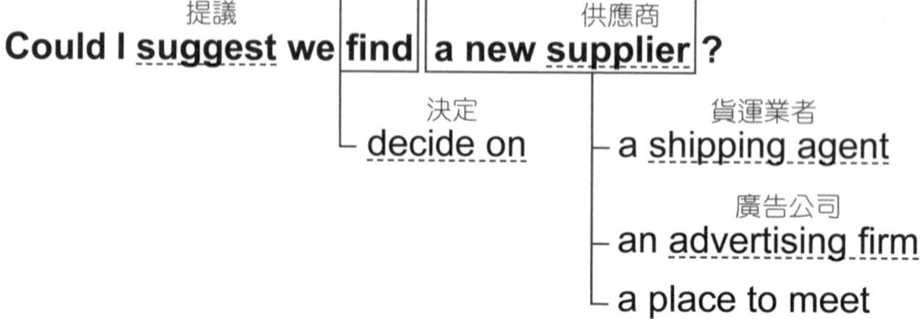
提議
供應商
Could I suggest we find a new supplier ?
決定
decide on
貨運業者
a shipping agent
廣告公司
an advertising firm
a place to meet

● 我堅信我們應該減少不必要的浪費。

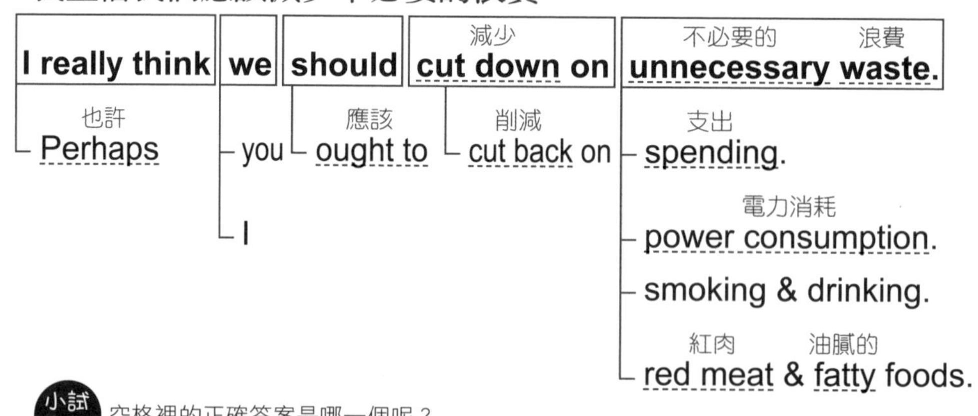
減少
不必要的
浪費
I really think we should cut down on unnecessary waste.
也許
Perhaps
you
I
應該
ought to
削減
cut back on
支出
spending.
電力消耗
power consumption.
smoking & drinking.
紅肉
油膩的
red meat & fatty foods.

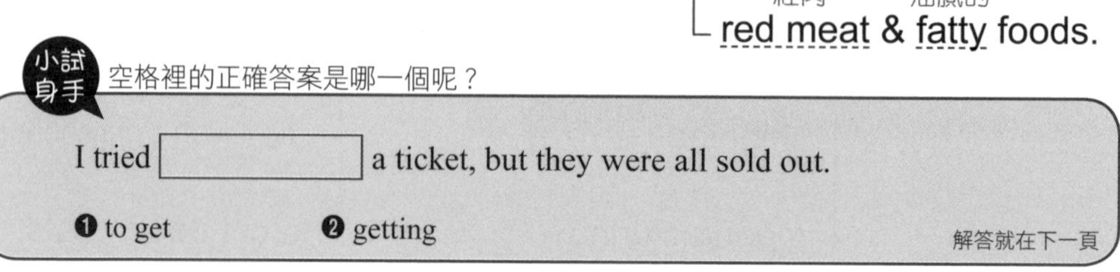
小試身手
空格裡的正確答案是哪一個呢？
I tried [　　　] a ticket, but they were all sold out.
❶ to get
❷ getting
解答就在下一頁

● 我們何不嘗試改變目錄的設計呢？

Why don't (何不) **we try changing the catalogue design?**

- How about (關於…覺得如何？)

- using another color on the packaging
- talking to them
- pushing (力勸) the powder instead (代替) of the cream

● 我強烈建議你重新考慮我們的提議。

I really urge (力勸) **you to reconsider** (重新考慮) **our offer** (提議)**.**

- strongly (強烈地)
- sincerely (由衷地)

- reinstate (使復職) Richard as project manager.
- cease (中斷) operations (運作，運轉).
- make it right (妥善因應) with the injured (受傷的) parties.

05 提醒注意

● 確認你已經做好萬全準備之後再向前邁進。

Make sure (確認) **you have all your bases covered** (萬無一失，做好萬全準備) (Casual Tone) **before moving ahead** (向前邁進)**.**

- Be sure (務必)

- your ducks in a row (準備完善，安排妥當) (Casual Tone)
- done your homework (做好萬全準備) (Casual Tone)
- left no stone unturned (想盡辦法，不遺餘力) (Casual Tone)
- completed everything

- contacting them.

前一頁 小試身手 的解答 ❶ I tried to get a ticket, but they were all sold out.

我試著買到一張票，但是已經全部賣完了。

● 我們必須考慮到所有的事。

We need to take everything into consideration.（consideration：考慮）

- We need to → You should
- everything into consideration → a good look at the facts.（good look：仔細檢視；facts：事實）
- everything into consideration → some time to think about it.

● 與他們交易的時候，你應該要小心。

You should take caution when dealing with them.
小心，謹慎
交易
注意
be careful
謹慎處理
act with due diligence
談判
政體，政權
negotiating with that regime.
地區，地方
doing business in that region.

● 別忘了上次發生過的事。

Don't forget what happened last time.
Remember
what they tried
慘敗
the fiasco

● 拖晚一點再簽約或許對你最有利。

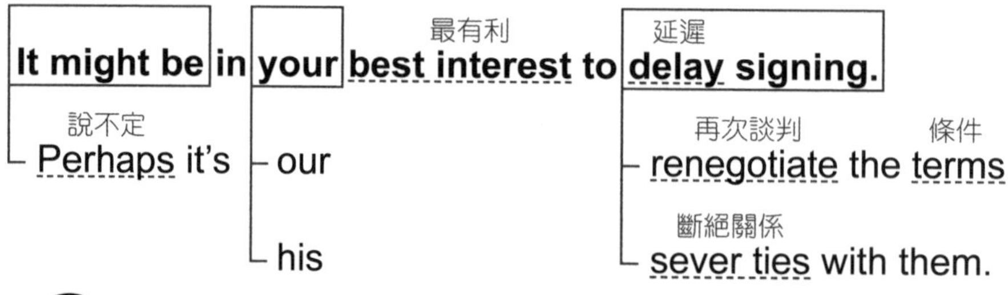

It might be in your best interest to delay signing.
最有利
延遲
說不定
Perhaps it's
our
his
再次談判
條件
renegotiate the terms.
斷絕關係
sever ties with them.

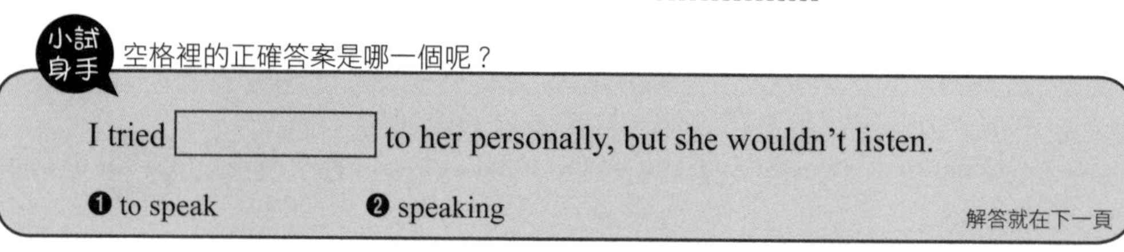

小試身手
空格裡的正確答案是哪一個呢？
I tried [ ] to her personally, but she wouldn't listen.
❶ to speak
❷ speaking
解答就在下一頁

06 提議讓步

● 也許我們應該讓步。

Perhaps(也許) **we should concede**(讓步)**.**

● 假如你現在保持冷靜，我們或許還可以繼續維持（買賣）關係。

If you stay calm now(保持冷靜)**, we can probably**(或許) **continue**(持續) **the relationship**(關係)**.**

- stay calm now → don't complain(抱怨)
- continue the relationship → reap(獲得) the benefits(利益) later.
- continue the relationship → work it to our advantage.(設法轉變成對我們有利的情勢)

● 只要同意他們的條件，我們總能達成共識。

We can always reach(達成，達到) **an agreement**(共識，協議) **by consenting**(同意) **to their terms**(條件)**.**

- reach an agreement → strike a bargain(買賣成交，達成協議)
- reach an agreement → make a deal(成交)
- consenting to their terms → agreeing(同意) to pay the shipping.
- consenting to their terms → cooperating(合作) with MJP Inc.
- consenting to their terms → lowering(降低) the price.

● 我們或許會考慮在價格上讓步，以獲取免費打廣告的機會。

We might think about giving in(讓步) **to the price to get the free advertising.**

- giving in → acquiescing(默許，默認)
- get the free advertising → secure the renewed(更新) contract(契約).
- get the free advertising → calm them down.(使他們冷靜下來)

前一頁 小試身手 的解答 ❷ I tried speaking to her personally, but she wouldn't listen.
我試過親自找她溝通，但是她根本不肯聽我說話。

01 社交辭令

● 感謝您長時間以來的惠顧。

持續的
Thank you for your continued business.
support.
興趣
interest.
迅速的
prompt response.

● 非常感謝您訂購我們的商品。

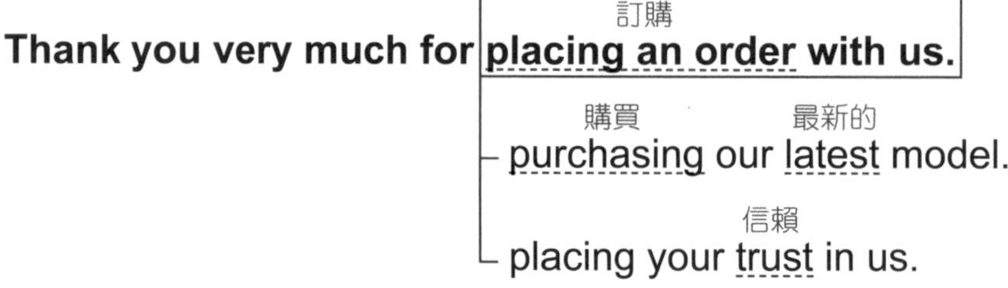
訂購
Thank you very much for placing an order with us.
購買
最新的
purchasing our latest model.
信賴
placing your trust in us.

● 我永遠不會忘記你為我所做的一切。

I'll never forget everything you've done for me.

● 能夠與貴公司合作，我們感到無比榮幸。

極大地，無限地
榮幸
合作，合夥
We're immensely proud to be associated with your company.
I'm
真誠地
truly
very
光榮的，榮耀的
honored
高興
delighted
感謝的
grateful
a part of
參與
involved with
this
group.
project.

02 感謝對方的理解與關懷

● 我們很感謝你的關心。

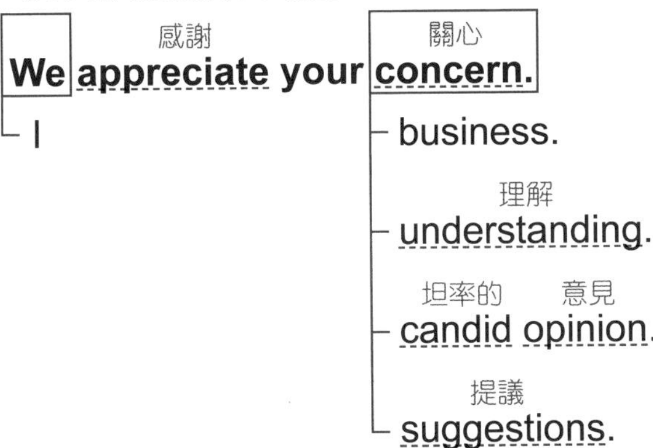

感謝
關心
We appreciate your concern.
I
business.
理解
understanding.
坦率的
意見
candid opinion.
提議
suggestions.

● 我很感謝你的支持。

感謝
I am grateful for your support.
We are
捐獻，捐助
contribution.
慷慨的
捐獻
generous donation.
承諾，約定
commitment.

● 我很感謝你的協助和諒解。

感謝　協助　理解

I appreciate your cooperation and understanding.

● 感謝你的諒解。弄錯商品確實沒有藉口可以開脫。

理解　藉口　弄錯，混淆

Thank you for your understanding. There really is no excuse for the mix-up.

- 感謝　I appreciate
- 感謝的　We are grateful for

- error.
- extra charge.
- 混亂　confusion.

● 我很感謝你所做的一切。

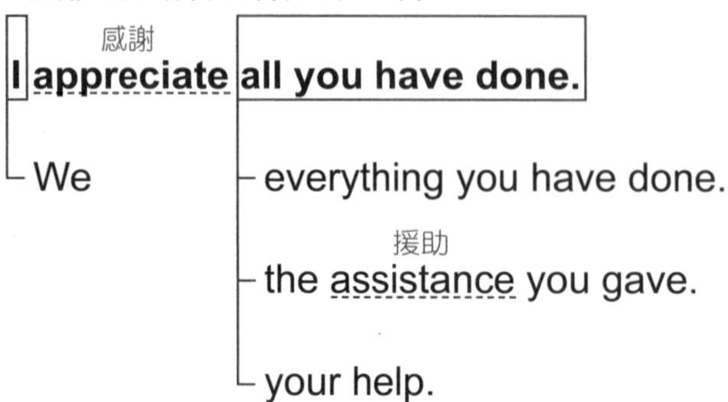

I appreciate（感謝） all you have done.

We

- everything you have done.
- the assistance（援助） you gave.
- your help.

● 我待在這裡的這段期間，謝謝你為我所做的一切。

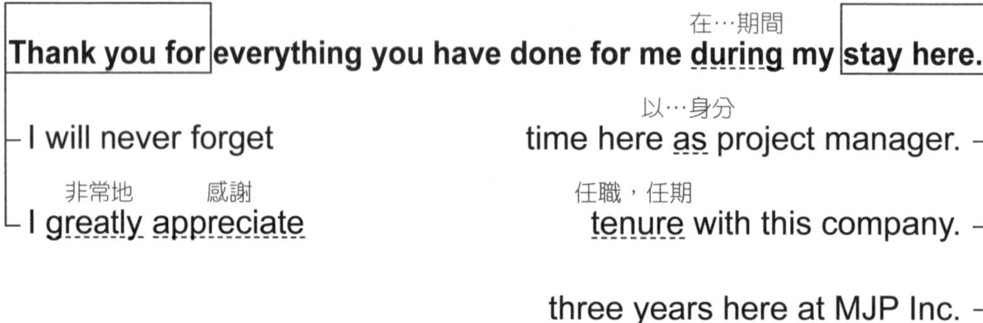

Thank you for everything you have done for me during（在…期間） my stay here.

- I will never forget
- I greatly（非常地） appreciate（感謝）

- time here as（以…身分） project manager.
- tenure（任職，任期） with this company.
- three years here at MJP Inc.

● 非常謝謝你提供如此絕妙的主意。

Thank you very much for your fantastic（絕妙的） ideas.

- as always（一如往常地）

- constructive（具建設性的） criticism（批判，批評）.
- unwavering（堅定的） support.
- understanding（理解） and cooperation（協助）.
- immediate（迅速的） response（因應）.

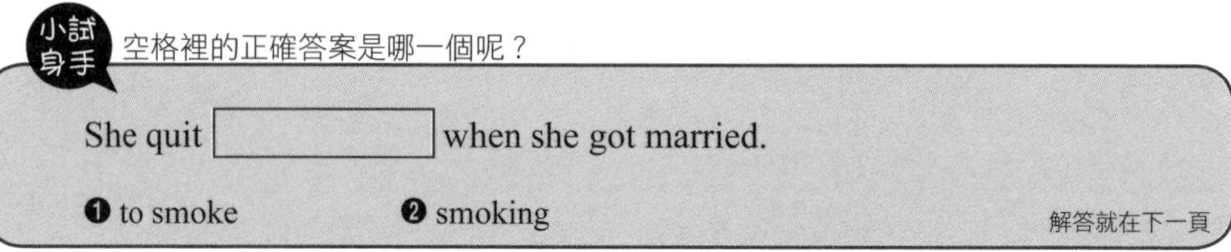

小試身手 空格裡的正確答案是哪一個呢？

She quit [ ] when she got married.

❶ to smoke ❷ smoking

解答就在下一頁

● 謝謝你的支持。

Thank you for **lending your support.** (lending：借出)

- choosing O Le Vai Resort.
- sending the documents. (sending：寄出)
- getting back to me so soon. (getting back to me：回應我；so soon：這麼迅速)

● 沒有你的協助，我絕對不可能成功。

協助，援助
Without your assistance I never could have succeeded.
成功
激勵
encouragement
help
love and support
減重
lost weight.
written the book.

03 感謝對方的付出

● 我非常感謝你把你的卡車借給我。

I'm much obliged to you for lending me your truck. (obliged：感謝；lending：借出)

● 謝謝你的迅速付款。

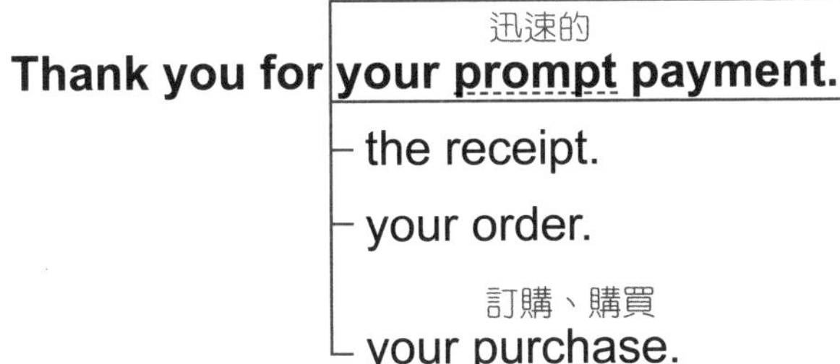

迅速的
Thank you for your prompt payment.
the receipt.
your order.
訂購、購買
your purchase.

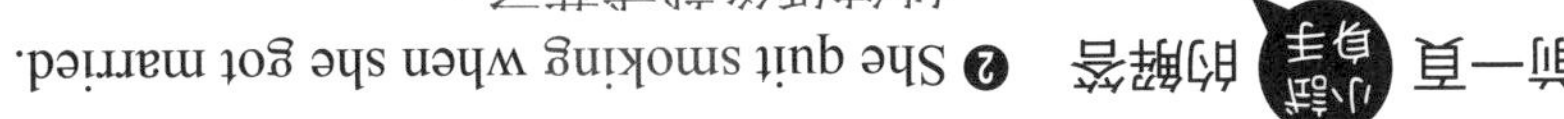

前一頁 小試身手 的解答
❷ She quit smoking when she got married.
她結婚後就戒菸了。

- 非常感謝你幫我餵狗。 Casual Tone

非常感謝 / 餵養

Thanks a million for feeding my dog!

謝謝

Cheers

- 謝謝你介紹露比給我認識。

介紹

Thank you for introducing Ruby to me.

coming to the party.

照顧

looking after the kids.

visiting me in (the) hospital.

- 我們要感謝你提醒我們注意這個疏失。

疏失，失誤 / 注意，留意

We'd like to thank you for bringing this oversight to our attention.

指出

pointing out the mistake.

告知

informing us of the changes.

04 感謝對方的用心

- 謝謝你的直言不諱。

正直，坦率

Thank you for your honesty.

深思熟慮

consideration.

耐心

patience.

幽默

humor.

●我寫信是要感謝你送我生日禮物。

I'm writing to thank you for the birthday gift.

●謝謝你在我身邊陪著我。

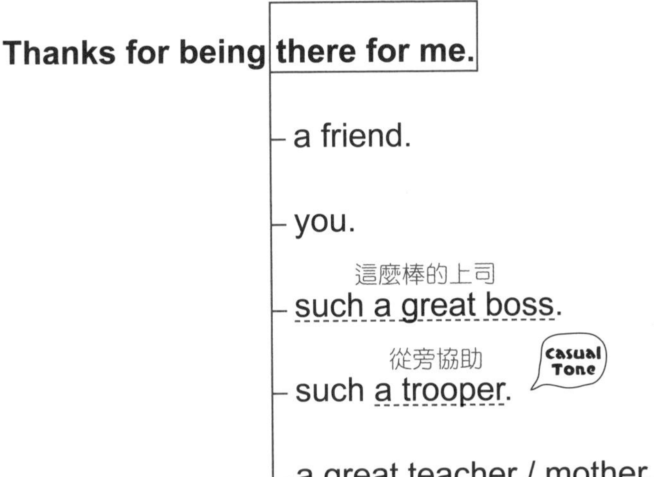
Thanks for being there for me.

- a friend.
- you.
- such a great boss.（這麼棒的上司）
- such a trooper.（從旁協助）Casual Tone
- a great teacher / mother.

●我想對你孜孜不倦的努力表達感謝。

I would like to express my gratitude for your tireless efforts.

express：傳達，表現　gratitude：感謝之意　tireless efforts：孜孜不倦的努力

- would like → want
- gratitude → thanks / appreciation（感謝之意）
- tireless efforts → selfless dedication.（無私無我的貢獻） / unwavering（堅定的） loyalty（忠誠）. / invaluable（無價的） input（貢獻）. / hard work.

05 應酬話

●託你的福，我才能如此迅速地適應這份工作。

It was thanks to you that I was able to settle in to this job so quickly.

thanks to you：託你的福　was able to：能夠　settle in：適應新環境

●我永遠不會忘記你強而有力的領導。

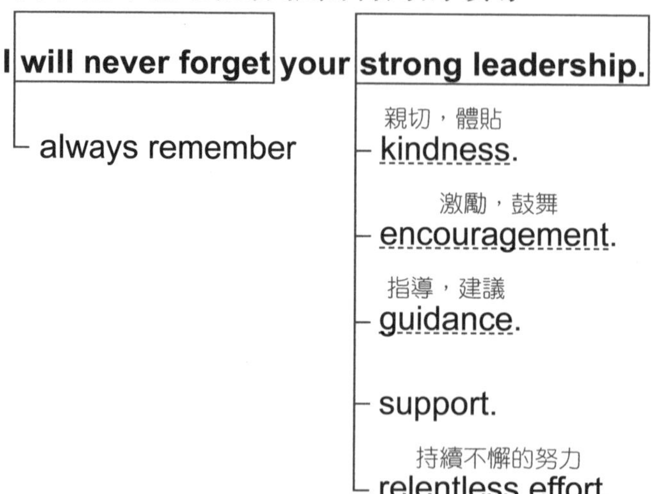

I will never forget your strong leadership.
always remember
親切，體貼
kindness.
激勵，鼓舞
encouragement.
指導，建議
guidance.
support.
持續不懈的努力
relentless effort.

18

致謝

應酬話

●我只想告訴大家，我很高興能和這麼優秀的團隊一起工作。

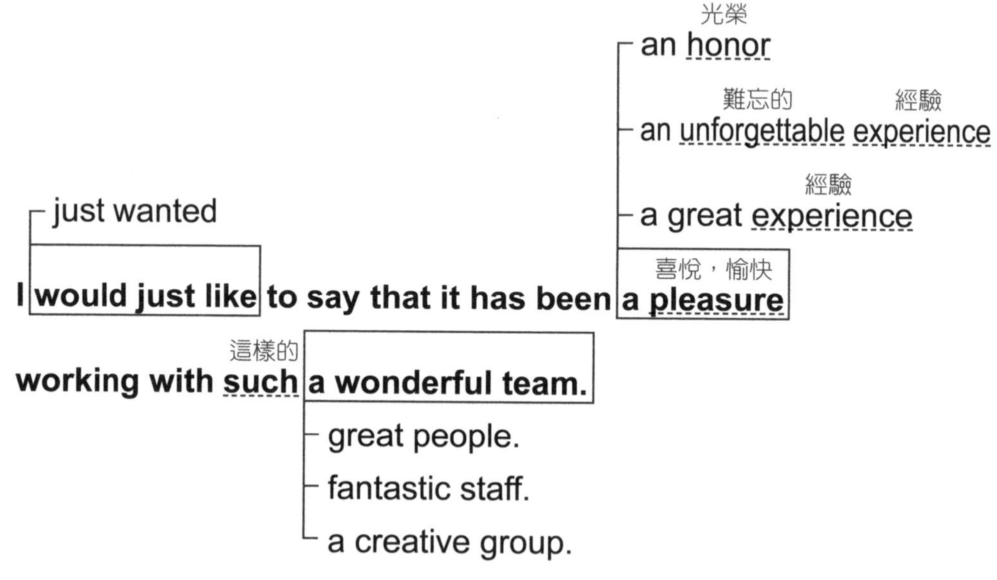

光榮
an honor
難忘的
經驗
an unforgettable experience
經驗
a great experience
just wanted
喜悅，愉快
I would just like to say that it has been a pleasure
這樣的
working with such a wonderful team.
great people.
fantastic staff.
a creative group.

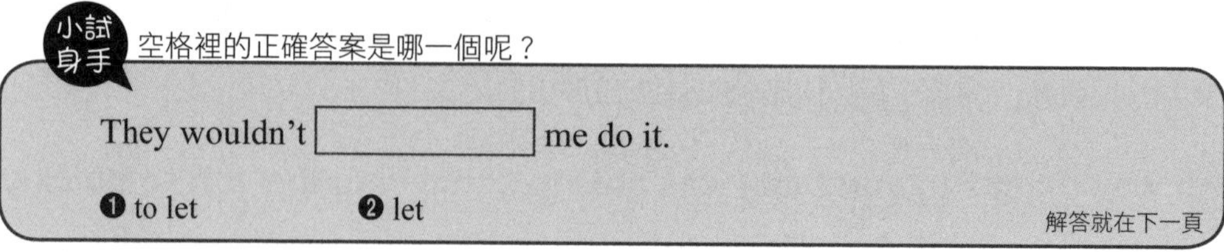

小試身手
空格裡的正確答案是哪一個呢？
They wouldn't ______ me do it.
❶ to let
❷ let
解答就在下一頁

● 因為有你絕佳的指導，我才能夠學到這麼多東西。

Thanks to your wonderful guidance, I was able to learn so much.

- wonderful guidance → kindness（親切）／ strong leadership（領導能力）／ constant encouragement（持續的／鼓勵）
- was able to（能夠）
- learn so much. → settle in（習慣，適應） with no problems. ／ get used to（習慣） the job.

● 我非常享受在這裡的時光，我會想念你們每一個人的。

I have thoroughly（非常，完全地） enjoyed my time here and will miss（想念） you all（大家）.

- have thoroughly enjoyed my time → had such a great learning experience（經驗）.
- you all. → the team. ／ each（每一個） and every one of you.

06 送禮

● 請收下這份代表我們謝意的禮物。

Please accept（接受） this gift as a token of our appreciation（感謝）.

- appreciation. → gratitude（感激之情）. ／ thanks.

前一頁  的解答 ❷ They wouldn't let me do it. 他們不會讓我做這件事的。

Dear Maggie,

This Saturday, for one day only, Crystal Sky is offering our entire line of needlepoint kits for 50% off!

Be sure to take advantage of this once-a-year opportunity! Simply place your order between 12am and 12pm EST. And that's not all. We are also offering free shipping on orders over US$75.

Click on the link below to start shopping now.

Crystal Sky

中譯

Crystal Sky本週六提供織錦畫工具組全系列產品五折優惠，僅此一天！

請務必把握這個一年只有一次的大好機會！只要在美東時間凌晨12點到中午12點之間下訂單即可。不僅如此，訂購金額超過75塊美金的話，我們還提供免運費的優惠。

現在就點選以下的連結開始訂購。

01 活動與促銷優惠

● 今年的烹飪博覽會時，務必到我們的攤位來看看。

Be sure to stop by our booth at this year's Culinary Expo.
（務必 = Be sure to；順路造訪 = stop by；烹飪的，廚房的 = Culinary）

- Don't miss（別錯過）
- Come and get your free gift at

● 本週六所有的露營用具都特價優惠，僅此一天。

This Saturday for one day only, all camping gear is priced to sell. ※1

- During our summer sale（在…期間 = During）
- Aug 20~28

※1 "priced to sell" 是指不管收益如何的情況下，把商品定在能夠全部賣完的價格。

- 我們要搬遷了，所有東西都必須出清！

搬家，搬遷 賣完

We're moving and everything must go!

- 本週末小野麗莎將在Jazz up Top現場演出；預購門票的價格是2,000元，現場購票的價格是2,500元。節目晚上7點開始。

Lisa Ono will be performing live this weekend at Jazz up Top; $2,000 in advance, $2,500 at the door. Show begins at 7:00pm.

- 讓你的生活增加一些趣味。下週六，七月二十八日，在湯淺海灘度假區將舉辦戶外爵士音樂節。

增加趣味，使有生氣

Jazz up your life a little. Next Saturday, July 28th, there's an outdoor jazz festival at the Yuasa Beachside Resort.

- 快找個朋友一起來公園裡的大型跳蚤市場逛逛。

抓住 來到 舊物的露天市集，跳蚤市場

Grab a friend and come on down to the big flea market in the park.

└ Bring the kids └ join us for a day of sun, song and barbecue.

歌曲 烤肉

- 還在尋覓你的真命天子（真命天女）嗎？邀請所有單身貴族共同參與快速約會之夜！

Still looking for that special someone?

Calling all singles to a night of speed dating!

Show Mom you care and treat her to a day off at the Via Paraiso Hotel and Spa!

We're having a special Mother's Day brunch that includes a one-day spa pass for moms.

Bring the whole family and enjoy a day in the sun on the terrace. Later, Mom can come back at her leisure for a day of pampering.

中譯

讓媽媽明白你有多在乎她，帶她到Via Paraiso度假飯店享受一天悠閒的假期！

我們將在早午餐時間提供母親節特餐，餐點附贈spa一日券一張，送給全天下的媽媽。

歡迎闔家光臨，全家人一起在露天陽台上享受陽光。以後，媽媽們可以在有空的時候，回到這裡來享受一天的尊寵。

02 公關

● 我們與自家的供應商之一協商後爭取到較低的價格，而我們會將節省下來的成本回饋給我們最忠實的顧客。

We have **negotiated** (交涉) a **lower price** (較低的價格) **with one of our suppliers**
- negotiated → worked out (制訂出)
- with one of our suppliers → with our shipping company (貨運業者) / on some key materials (主原料)

and we are passing that **savings** (節省下來的部分) on to **our most loyal customers.** (忠實的顧客)
- our most loyal customers. → you.

● 請看看第3頁到第7頁的各項新產品。

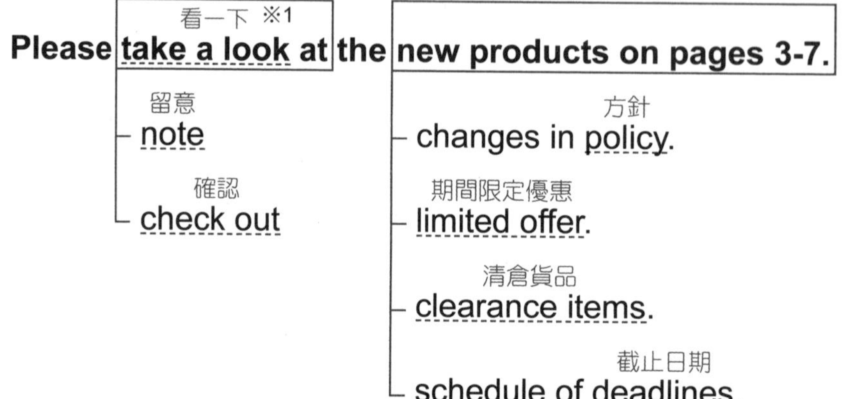
看一下 ※1
Please take a look at the new products on pages 3-7.
留意
note
確認
check out
方針
changes in policy.
期間限定優惠
limited offer.
清倉貨品
clearance items.
截止日期
schedule of deadlines.

※1 “take a look” 在商業書信裡也可以使用，是比 “look” 更口語的表達方式。它的意思是「看一看」、「看一下」或「瞄一眼」。更穩重的說法是 “have a look”。

03 客戶服務

● 我們已經按照你的要求，將箱子的內裡改成保麗龍。

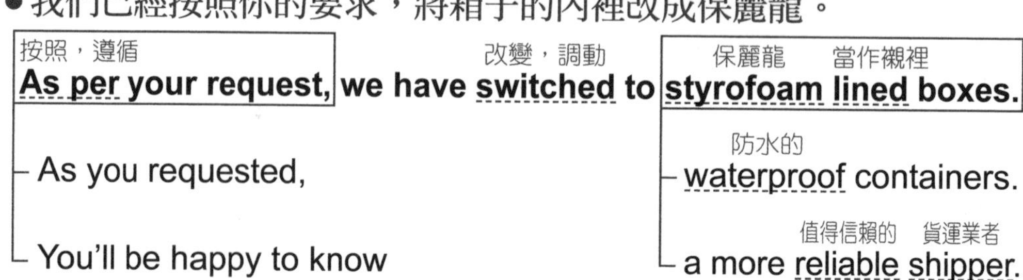
按照，遵循
As per your request,
改變，調動
we have switched to
保麗龍 當作襯裡
styrofoam lined boxes.
As you requested,
You'll be happy to know
防水的
waterproof containers.
值得信賴的 貨運業者
a more reliable shipper.

● 為了提供您更好的服務，我們已經重新檢討過自家的系統。

為了 / 提供您更好的服務 / 重新檢討

In order to serve you better we have reviewed our system.

- 提供 provide faster service
- 確保 順暢的服務 ensure hassle-free service

- 裝設 自動系統 installed an automated system.
- 增加 increased our service personnel.
- 停用 自動引導系統 done away with the automated guidance.

● 為了提供您更好的服務，我們計畫實施一套最新的系統。

為了 / 提供您更好的服務 / 應用，實行 / 最新的

In order to serve you better we are planning to implement a brand new system.

- 多樣的 貨運業者 use multiple shipping companies.
- 有效率的 流程 begin a stream-lined process.
- meet with you directly.

● 我們公司每個貨板的收費如下：

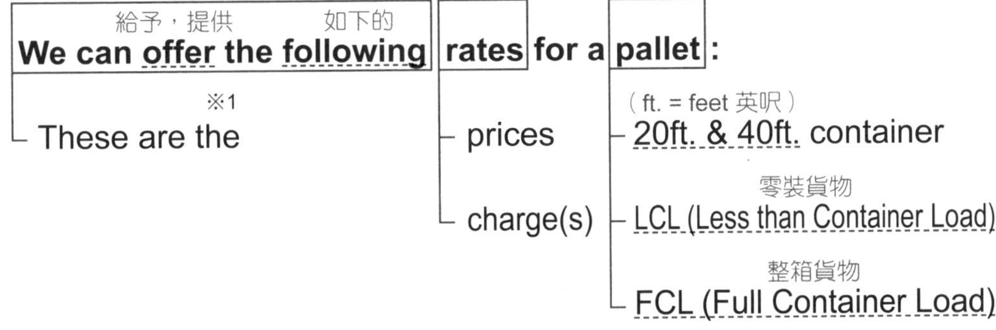
給予，提供 如下的
We can offer the following rates for a pallet :
※1
These are the
prices
charge(s)
(ft. = feet 英呎)
20ft. & 40ft. container
零裝貨物
LCL (Less than Container Load)
整箱貨物
FCL (Full Container Load)

※1 以 "These are the" 開頭的句子，之後如果使用 "charge" 要加 "s"。

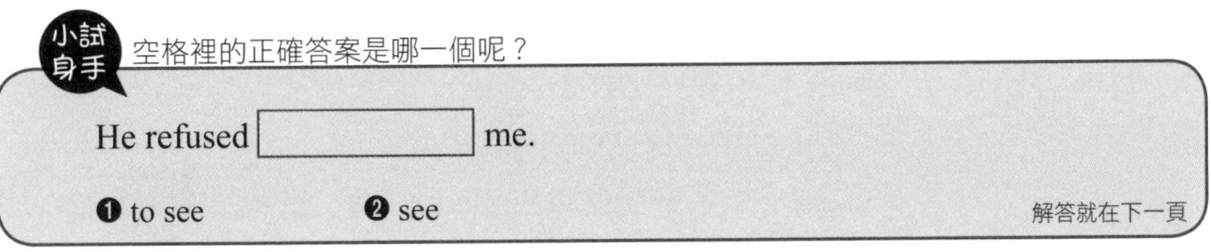
小試身手
空格裡的正確答案是哪一個呢？
He refused [　　] me.
❶ to see
❷ see
解答就在下一頁

19 活動・公關・告示 客戶服務

04 告知休假日

● 提醒您，本店將在聖誕節當天歇業。

This is just a reminder (提醒) **that we will be closed on Christmas Day.**

- Please be reminded (別忘記) [Formal Tone] — the contract (契約) expires (截止期限) on Jan 02, 2012. ※1
- I would like to remind you — we have a sales meeting (業務會議) this afternoon.
- Please remember — full payment (全額支付) is required (必要的) prior to (在…之前) loading (裝貨) on to the ship.

※1 寫日期時，如果該日期只有一個數字，最好在前面加上一個 "0"，這樣的表達會更明確。

● 很抱歉造成您的困擾。因為內部重新裝修，我們公司將歇業至七月一日。期待將來能以更完善的設施為您提供服務。

Sorry for the inconvenience. Our offices will be closed until July 1 for remodeling (重新裝修)**. We look forward to serving you** (為您服務) **in our improved facilities** (設施)**.**

- Our offices → This site (地點，場所) / The pool (游泳池) / This area
- remodeling → maintenance (維修，保養). / cleaning.

前一頁 小試身手 的解答 ❶ He refused to see me. 他拒絕和我見面。

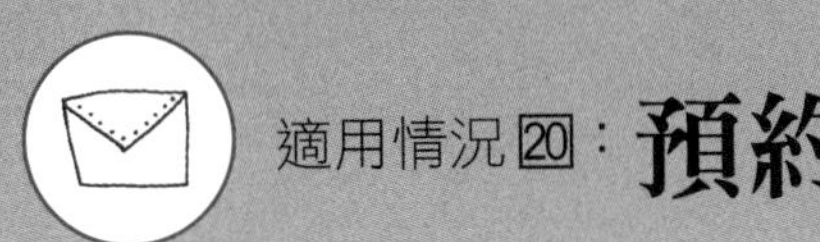

適用情況20：預約

01 住宿

● 我想要預訂三樓以下樓層的房間。

I would like a room no higher than the 3rd floor. ※1

- no lower than the 15th floor.
- near (靠近) the elevator.
- that is wheelchair (輪椅) accessible (可通行的).
- close to (靠近) an emergency exit (緊急出口).

※1「一樓」在英式英語中是 "ground floor"，美式英語則是 "first floor"。

● 我想預訂可以看到海景的房間。

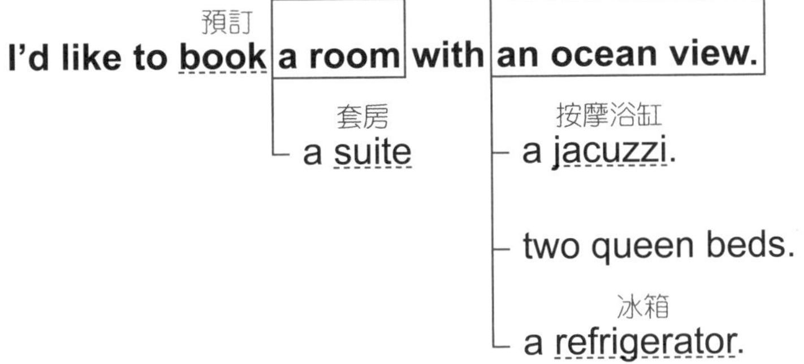

I'd like to book (預訂) a room with an ocean view.

- a room → a suite (套房)
- an ocean view → a jacuzzi (按摩浴缸). / two queen beds. / a refrigerator (冰箱).

● 我比較希望可以住在附有健身房的地方。

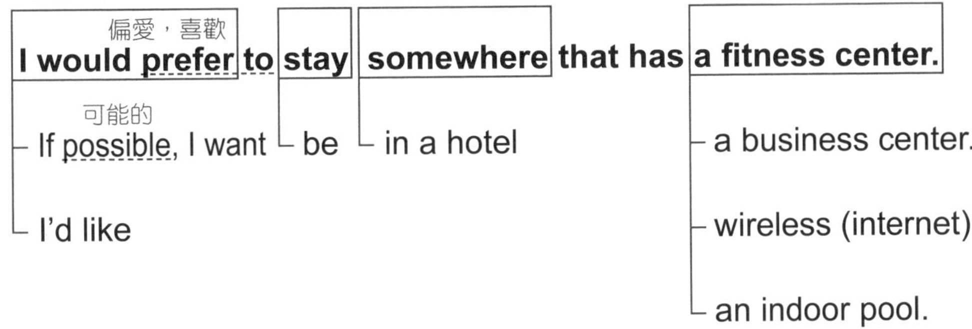

I would prefer (偏愛，喜歡) to stay somewhere that has a fitness center.

- I would prefer → If possible (可能的), I want / I'd like
- stay → be
- somewhere → in a hotel
- a fitness center. → a business center. / wireless (internet). / an indoor pool.

● 你會自己訂旅館，還是希望我們幫你安排？

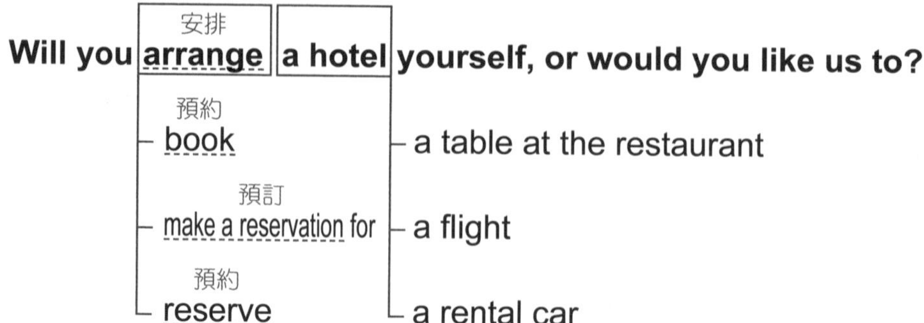
安排
Will you arrange a hotel yourself, or would you like us to?
預約
book
a table at the restaurant
預訂
make a reservation for
a flight
預約
reserve
a rental car

● 我還沒有訂旅館。

I haven't **booked a hotel** (預訂) **yet** (尚未).

- reserved (預訂) a room
- finished the itinerary (行程)
- decided (決定) my return date

Business E-mail Tips

告別中式英文

In the US, when you book a hotel room, regardless of whether there are one, two or three people staying, you are paying one set price for the room.

在美國，當你預訂飯店房間的時候，不論你有一個人、兩個人或是三個人住進這間房，你都只要付一間房間的費用。

以房間計價？以人數計價？

讀者們應該多多少少有到國外出差或旅遊的經驗吧？如果要自己透過網路預訂房間的話，請務必看清楚房價是以「房間」還是以「人數」計價。在日本，通常會以人數定價；但在歐美許多國家（尤其是美國），旅館房間的收費與住宿人數無關，是以房間的等級定價。

● 我們已經幫你在Xanadu Suites飯店預訂了房間。

預約
We have made reservations for you at the Xanadu Suites.
You will be staying
Your room is
提供你住宿
We will put you up
Casual Tone
不介意
I hope you don't mind staying
Vaitele Inn.
local backpackers.

● 我想確認我的旅館訂房。

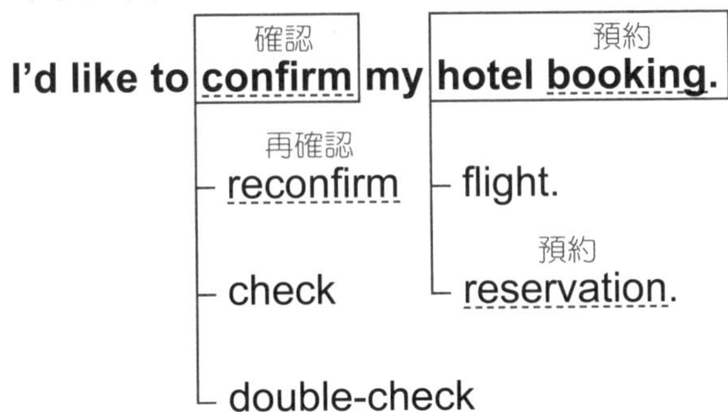

確認
預約
I'd like to confirm my hotel booking.
再確認
reconfirm
check
double-check
flight.
預約
reservation.

● 很抱歉，但是我們今晚無法接受任何預約。

接受
預約
I'm sorry, but we can't accept any bookings tonight.
很遺憾地
Unfortunately,
很遺憾地
Regrettably,
幫你安排
預約
can't fit you in for an appointment
可使用的
don't have any rooms available
完全地
客滿
are completely full
until Friday.
this week.

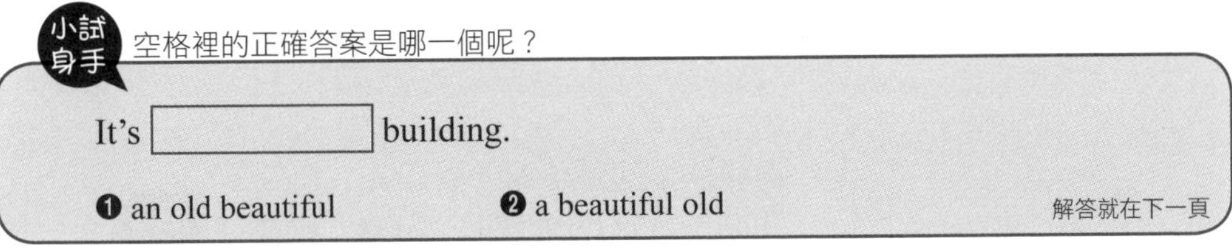

小試身手
空格裡的正確答案是哪一個呢？
It's [ ] building.
❶ an old beautiful
❷ a beautiful old
解答就在下一頁

20 預約 住宿

02 餐廳

●我想訂位，我們總共有五個人。

預約
總共有五個人
I'd like to make a reservation for a party of five.
是否有空位
check availability
the weekend.
March 19th.

03 金額

●這家飯店住宿要多少錢？

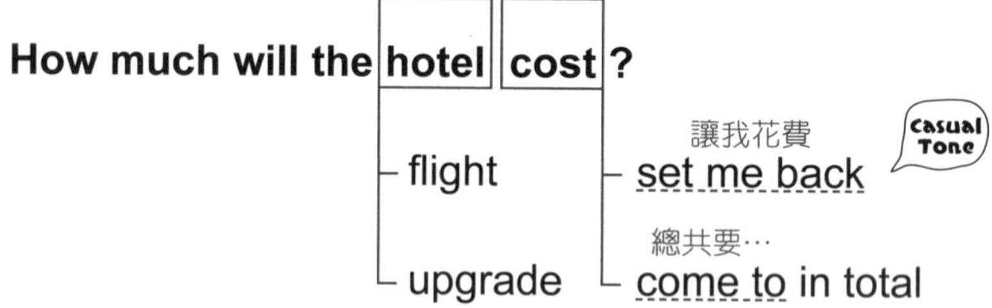

How much will the hotel cost?
flight
upgrade
讓我花費
set me back
Casual Tone
總共要…
come to in total

04 支付方式

●我想付現。

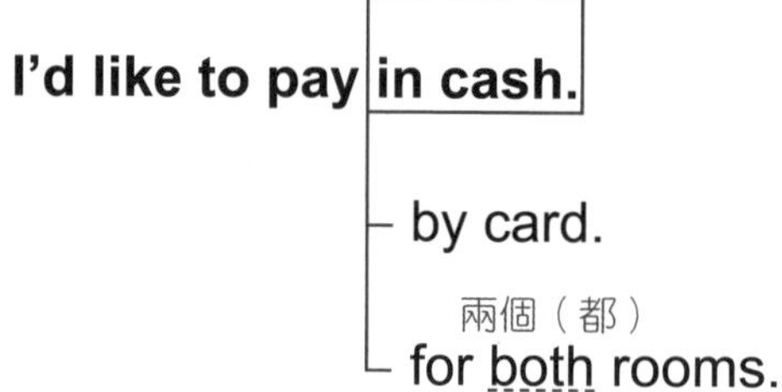

I'd like to pay in cash.
by card.
兩個（都）
for both rooms.

前一頁 

小試身手

的解答 ❷ It's a beautiful old building.

這是一棟美麗的古老建築。

05 預約優惠

● 上網預訂可以享受最優惠的價格。

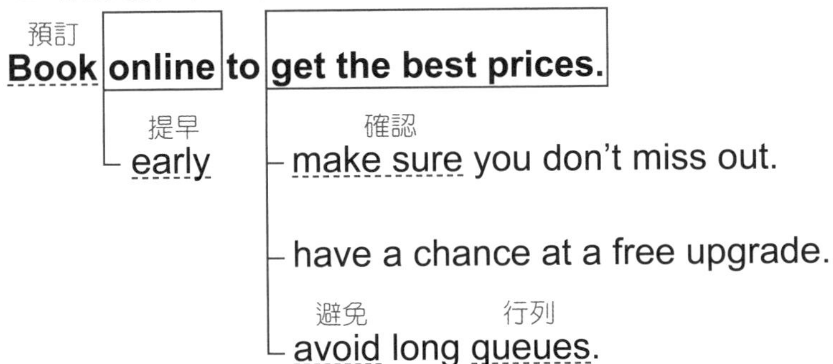
預訂
Book online to get the best prices.
提早
early
確認
make sure you don't miss out.
have a chance at a free upgrade.
避免
行列
avoid long queues.

● 現在就立刻撥電話，預訂假期套裝行程。

預約
Call now to reserve a holiday package.
Contact us
book
特殊優惠價格的
specially priced suite.
最前排的座位
front row seat.
seat on the Astroliner.
guided tour.

06 確認行程

● 我想確認你下個月來訪的行程細節。

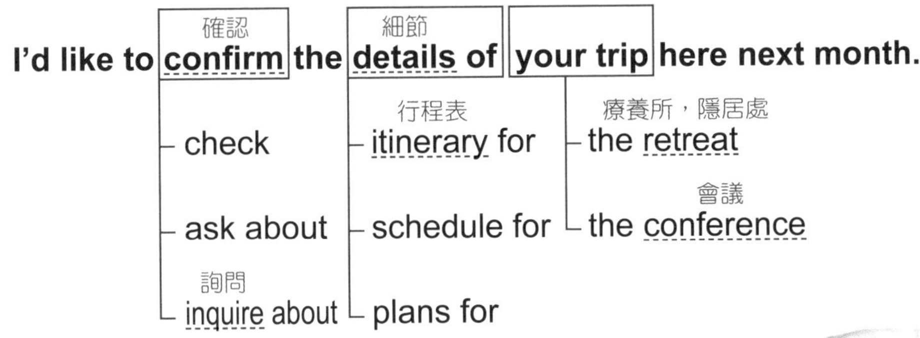
確認
細節
I'd like to confirm the details of your trip here next month.
check
ask about
詢問
inquire about
行程表
itinerary for
schedule for
plans for
療養所，隱居處
the retreat
會議
the conference

● 我到洛杉磯的日程已經確定。

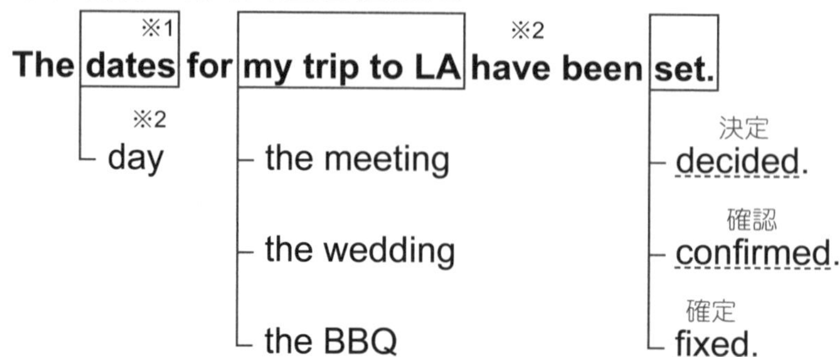

※1
※2
The dates for my trip to LA have been set.
※2
day
the meeting
the wedding
the BBQ
決定
decided.
確認
confirmed.
確定
fixed.

※ 1 "dates" 用於表示只有一天的時候，就要改為單數 "date"。
※ 2 在與 "day" 連用時，"have" 需改為以單數為主詞的 "has"。

● 按照我收到的時程表，你將搭乘華航0597號班機，在九月九日的下午三點抵達。

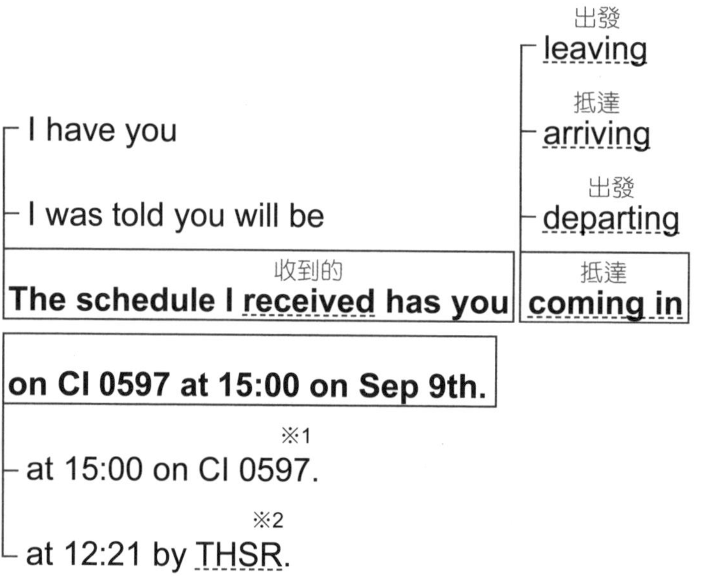

I have you
I was told you will be
收到的
The schedule I received has you
出發
leaving
抵達
arriving
出發
departing
抵達
coming in
on CI 0597 at 15:00 on Sep 9th.
※1
at 15:00 on CI 0597.
※2
at 12:21 by THSR.

※ 1 在這個句子裡，時間和班機號碼的順序互換也沒關係。
※ 2 THSR 是 "Taiwan High Speed Rail"（台灣高速鐵路）的縮寫。

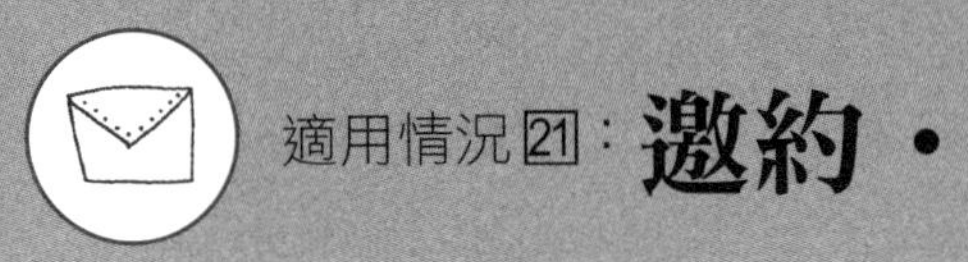
適用情況21：邀約・交流

01 相約見面

●我們下午兩點半左右在我們的東京辦公室見面好嗎？

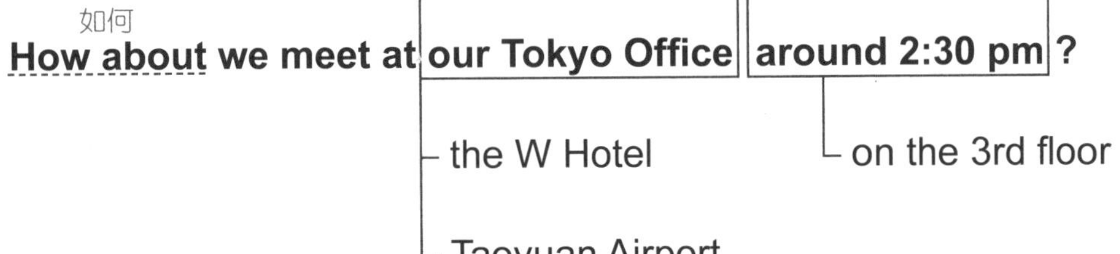
如何
How about we meet at our Tokyo Office around 2:30 pm?
the W Hotel
Taoyuan Airport
on the 3rd floor

●約在台北火車站的西出口如何？

如何
How about meeting at Taipei Railway Station at the west exit?
如何
What about
Casual Tone
…的前面 剪票口
in front of the ticket gate
on the platform near the front of the train
at the airport shuttle bus stop
on the 10th floor in front of the elevator
at Christine's Café next to Taipei Main Station

●約在淡水捷運站的2號出口如何？ Casual Tone

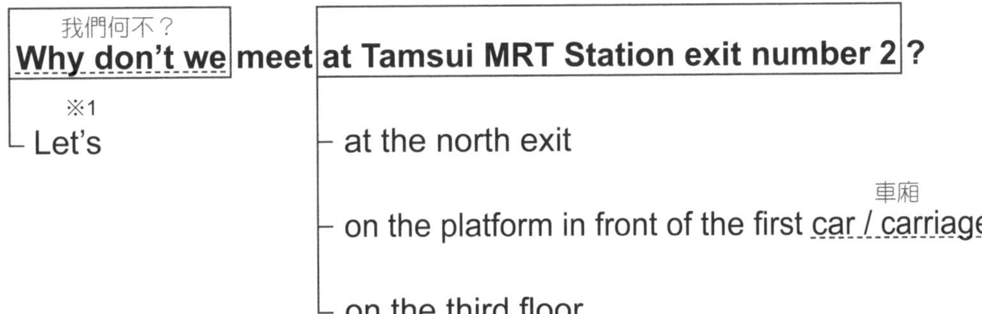
我們何不？
Why don't we meet at Tamsui MRT Station exit number 2?
※1
Let's
at the north exit
車廂
on the platform in front of the first car / carriage
on the third floor

※1 以 "Let's" 開頭時，句末使用的是句點而非問號。

Dear John,

I would like to confirm the details about your trip here next month.
Arriving 9 Sept. 15:00 on JPA 0597
Leaving 12 Sept. 17:30 on JPA 0596
We will pick you up and take you to the Xanadu Suites and get you checked in.
Afterwards, we can either go out for a nice dinner or just have a quick meeting in the lobby if you are tired.
The hotel has excellent room service if you would rather just eat in and make it an early night.
I have attached the itinerary.

Kenny

中譯

我想向你確認你下個月來訪的行程細節。
9月9日15:00，JPA0597抵達
9月12日17:30，JPA0596離開
我們當天會開車去接你，送你到Xanadu Suites飯店並協助你登記入住。
接下來，我們可以一起出去享受豐盛的晚餐，或者只在飯店大廳簡短地開個會，假如你覺得疲倦的話。
這家飯店的客房餐飲服務非常棒，如果你只想在房間裡吃些東西，然後早點休息也沒問題。
附件是行程表。

02 接送

● 我們開車去接你的時候，會在入境檢查站外面等你。

We will pick you up just outside the immigration area.

- pick you up：開車去接你
- immigration area：入境檢查站

We will
- pick you up
- meet you

- just outside the immigration area.
- at the station near the north exit.
- in the morning.
- before the conference.（conference：會議）
- in the hotel lobby.

● 我會順道去旅館去拜訪你。

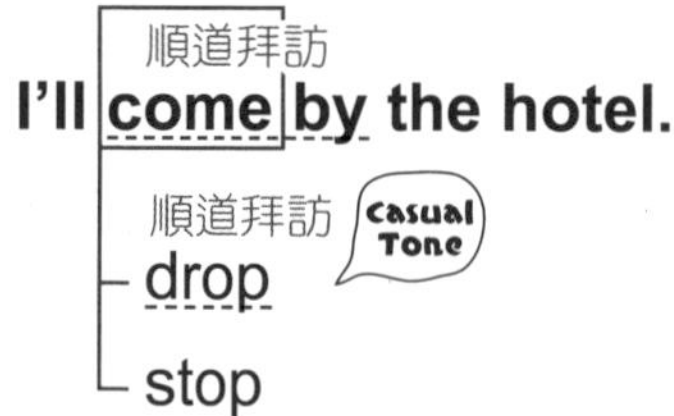

I'll come by the hotel.

- come by：順道拜訪
- drop：順道拜訪 (Casual Tone)
- stop

●我們將會帶你去旅館（並且協助你登記入住）。

we'll take you to the hotel (and get you checked in).

- drive
- accompany（陪同）
- show

●會有人開車到機場接我嗎？還是我得自己安排？

Will someone be able to pick me up（開車來接我） at the airport, or should I make arrangements（安排） myself?

●如果這個提議仍然有效，你能開車來機場接我的話，我會非常感謝。

If the offer（提議） still stands（有效）, it would be great if you could pick me up at the airport.

- meet me

03 活動安排提議

●我原本希望我們可以把歌劇表演排進行程裡。

I was hoping we could take in（排進行程） an opera.

- to check out the street music.
- you could introduce（介紹） me to your president（社長）.
- to catch a movie（看電影）.

● 如果你希望的話，我可以向餐廳預約晚上八點半（兩個人）的位子。

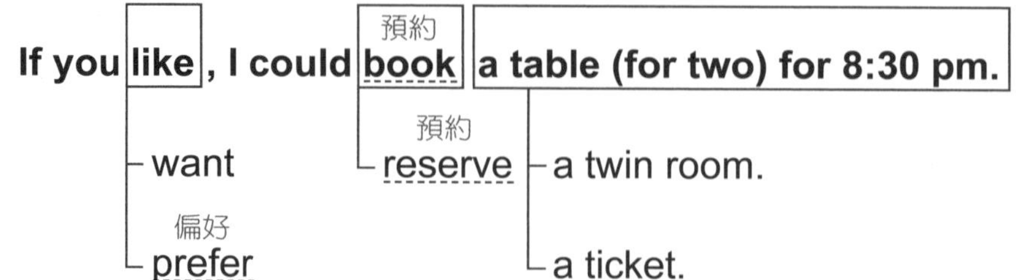
If you like, I could book a table (for two) for 8:30 pm.
預約
want
偏好
prefer
預約
reserve
a twin room.
a ticket.

● 我們可以先去吃晚餐，也可以先去飯店。

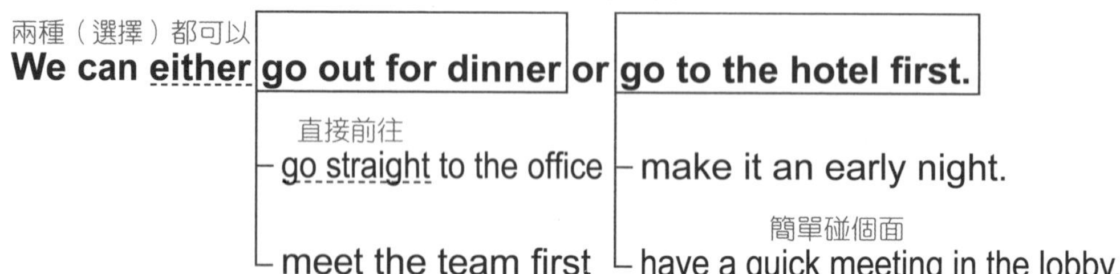
兩種（選擇）都可以
We can either go out for dinner or go to the hotel first.
直接前往
go straight to the office
meet the team first
make it an early night.
簡單碰個面
have a quick meeting in the lobby.

● 務必要帶著泳衣。他們的游泳池很漂亮。

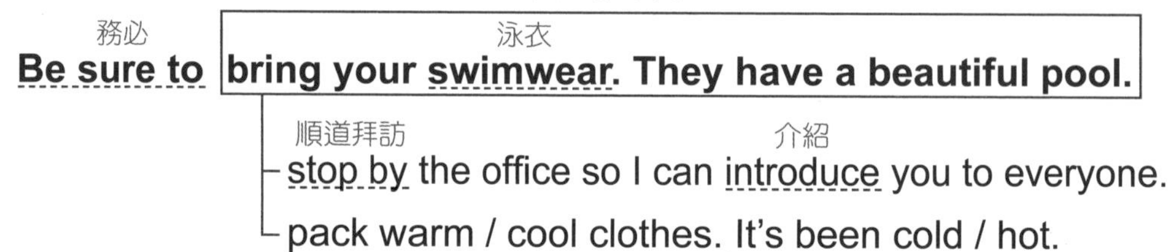
務必
Be sure to bring your swimwear. They have a beautiful pool.
泳衣
順道拜訪
介紹
stop by the office so I can introduce you to everyone.
pack warm / cool clothes. It's been cold / hot.

04 邀約

● 來市中心的時候，一定要來順道拜訪我們。

務必
Be sure to
順道拜訪
stop by
when you're in town.
Please
※1
Make sure you
順便拜訪
drop by
撥空
make time
順道來訪
come over
離開
before you leave.
for dinner sometime this week.
for a drink tonight.

※1 "Make sure you..." 比 "Be sure to..." 和 "Please" 的語氣更為強烈，有「絕對要…」的語感，所以使用時請特別注意。

Dear Giovanna,

It was so nice meeting you at the conference the other day. Thanks again for introducing me to your sales team. I'm sorry I couldn't join you all for a drink afterwards. I had to get back to my office and finish up a few things.

But actually, that is why I am writing. I wanted to see if you would like to come to a barbecue I'm having at Riverside Park this Saturday the 14th. You are welcome to bring some of the people from work or whomever. We'll probably start around noon and finish when the sun goes down. If you can make it, let me know and I will send you all the details and a map.

Hope to see you,

Angela

中譯

很高興那天在會議上有機會認識你。再次感謝你介紹我認識你的行銷團隊。很抱歉，當天會後我沒辦法和你們大家一起去喝一杯。我必須趕回辦公室完成一些事情。

不過，其實這也是我寫這封信給你的原因。我想知道你這個星期六，也就是十四號，有沒有興趣參加我在河濱公園舉辦的烤肉大會。歡迎你邀請你工作的同事或任何你想邀請的人一起來同樂。我們大概會在中午的時候開始烤肉，一直到太陽下山為止。假如你可以參加，告訴我一聲，我會寄出所有的詳細資料以及地圖給你。

希望可以見到你。

● 我們有機會去漁人碼頭嗎？

Is there any chance we could go to Fisherman's Wharf?

有機會嗎: Is there any chance

- chance → possibility（可能性）
- go to Fisherman's Wharf →
  - start one hour later
  - finish a little early（提早一點點）
  - have dinner together
  - meet first for breakfast（首先）

小試
身手

空格裡的正確答案是哪一個呢？

I loved the novel, but found the movie very ＿＿＿＿.

❶ disappointing　　❷ disappointed

解答就在下一頁

- 我想為恩佐安排一個驚喜派對。你覺得如何？

I'm thinking of organizing (舉辦，規劃) a surprise party for Enzo. What do you think?

└ having

- 噓，不要告訴別人！我們正在為史密斯夫婦策劃一個驚喜派對！

Sssssh, don't tell! We're throwing (舉行) the Smiths a surprise party!

- 跟我們一起來淺嚐海灘風情、烤肉和啤酒！

Come join us for a little beach, barbecue and beer!

- 所有美好的事物都有結束的時候。沒錯。傑夫就要結婚了，我們將為他安排一個告別單身派對，完美終結他所有的單身派對！

All good things must come to an end (結束，終止). That's right. Jeff is getting married (結婚) and we are planning the bachelor party (告別單身派對) to end all bachelor parties!

You're invited! We're having a party to celebrate Ariel's birthday!

Date: Feb 2, 2011
Place: The Old Cellar
Time: 8pm until they kick us out!
Cost: NT$1000 (includes two drinks and dinner buffet)
RSVP: satoh@coldmail.com

中譯

你被邀請了！我們即將為艾莉兒舉辦一個生日派對！
日期：2011年2月2日
地點：The Old Cellar
時間：晚上八點開始一直到被店家趕出去為止！
費用：台幣一千元（包含兩杯飲料和自助式吃到飽的晚餐）
出席與否請回覆到：
satoh@coldmail.com

前一頁  的解答 ❷ I loved the novel, but found the movie very disappointing.
我很喜歡這本小說，但是我覺得（改編自這本小說的）電影很令人失望。

- 歡迎！誠摯邀請你參加我在八月二十九日舉辦的國際友人餐會，分享大家自備的各式餐點。

Benvenuto! Willkommen! Mabuhay! Hyangyong-hamnida! Yokoso! Welcome!※1

You are cordially (誠摯地) invited (受邀) to my international pot-luck party (賓客自備餐點與大家分享的餐會) on August 29th!

※1 這是「歡迎」的各種語言說法，依序為義大利文、德文、菲律賓文、韓文、日文以及英文。

05 首次聯絡

- 約翰告訴我你的電話號碼。

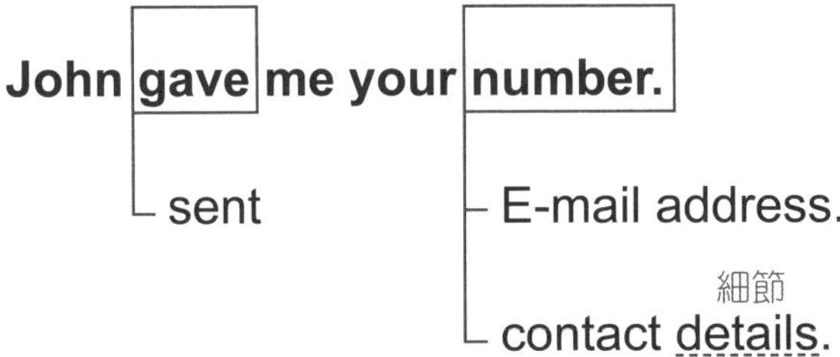
John gave me your number.
sent
E-mail address.
細節
contact details.

- 我是在臉書上的風帆衝浪社群裡找到你的。

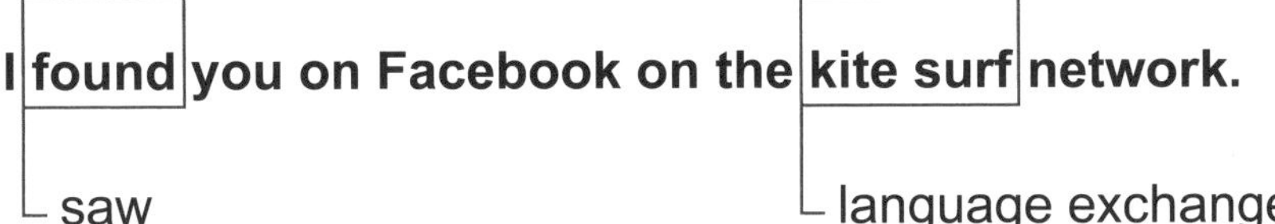
I found you on Facebook on the kite surf network.
saw
language exchange

06 接受款待

- 終於可以與你見面了，真是迫不及待。

急切的
最後，終於
I am eager to meet you at last.
I can't wait
終於
finally meet you.
與你面對面談話
speak with you in person.
hear more about the sales campaign.
當地料理
try the local cuisine.

● 我非常高興可以參加你的派對！

想要，樂意

I'd love to come to your party!

- join you for dinner.
- meet up with you for coffee.（見面）

● 在星期二早上共進早餐聽起來很棒。我很期待。

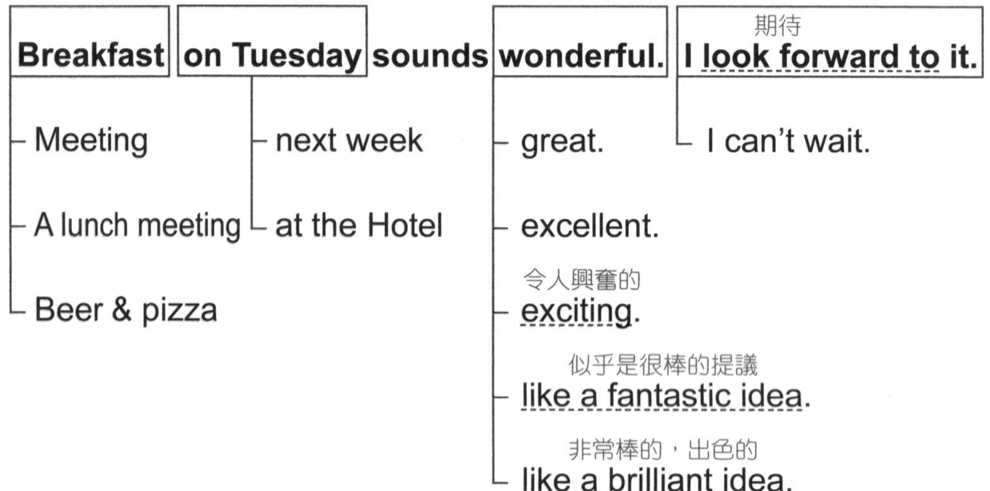
期待
Breakfast on Tuesday sounds wonderful. I look forward to it.
Meeting
A lunch meeting
Beer & pizza
next week
at the Hotel
great.
excellent.
令人興奮的
exciting.
似乎是很棒的提議
like a fantastic idea.
非常棒的，出色的
like a brilliant idea.
I can't wait.

● 關於你邀請我參加派對一事，我很高興能夠參加。

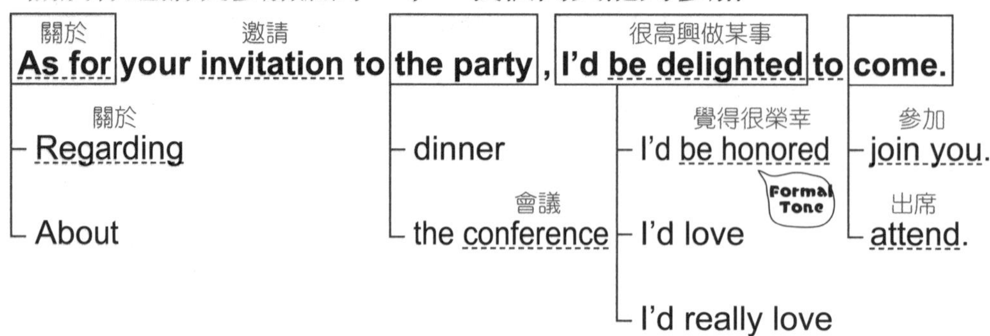
關於
邀請
很高興做某事
As for your invitation to the party, I'd be delighted to come.
關於
Regarding
About
dinner
會議
the conference
覺得很榮幸
I'd be honored
Formal Tone
I'd love
I'd really love
參加
join you.
出席
attend.

● 那個活動聽起來很有趣，我會先看看我的行程再跟你聯絡。

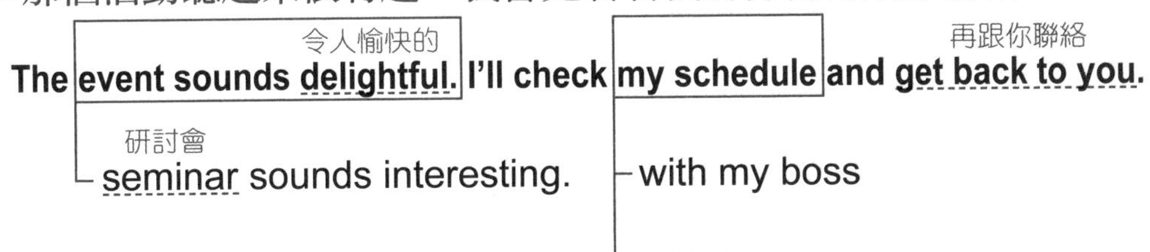
令人愉快的
The event sounds delightful. I'll check my schedule and get back to you.
再跟你聯絡
研討會
seminar sounds interesting.
with my boss
with Jack

07 參加活動的但書

● 如果你不介意我遲到的話，我可以出席這個派對。

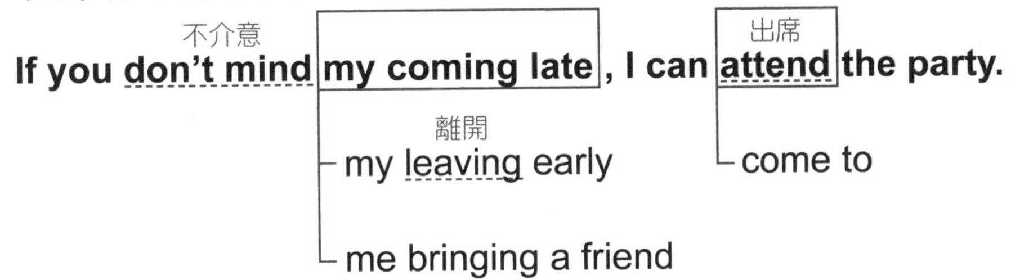
不介意
If you don't mind my coming late, I can attend the party.
出席
離開
my leaving early
me bringing a friend
come to

● 我可以帶朋友一起去嗎？

可以…嗎？
Is it all right if I bring someone?
閃人
duck out early
Casual Tone
come a little late

08 拒絕邀約

● 很遺憾，你的派對我沒辦法去。

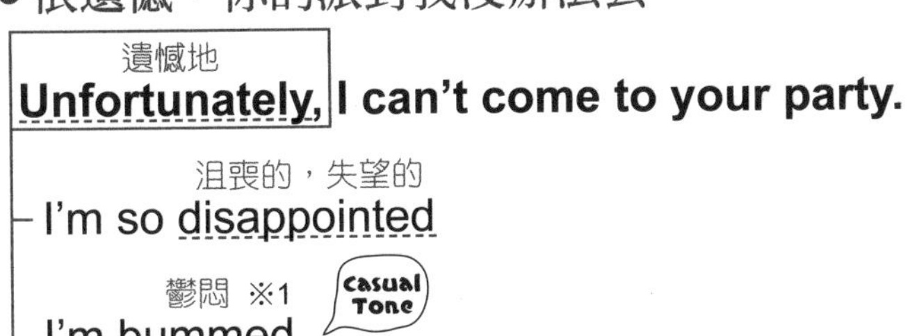
遺憾地
Unfortunately, I can't come to your party.
沮喪的，失望的
I'm so disappointed
鬱悶 ※1
I'm bummed
Casual Tone

※1 "I'm bummed" 是比 "I'm so disappointed" 更白話、更口語的說法。

Dear Ella,

Thank you so much for the invitation. Unfortunately, I have to decline because my brother is getting married this Sunday. I would love it if just you and I could get together for drinks next week, though. I am free on Wed. and Thurs. We could meet downtown at the new Goodfellas Grill.

Looking forward to hearing from you,

Stephanie

中譯

非常感謝你的邀請。

很遺憾，這次我沒辦法參加，因為我哥哥這個星期天就要結婚。不過，如果是下星期只有你和我兩人碰面一起喝點東西，我樂意之至。我星期三和星期四有空。我們可以約在市中心新開的Goodfellas Grill。

期待你的回音。

● 關於晚餐的事，很抱歉，但是我沒辦法參加。 Casual Tone

About dinner, I'm sorry, but I can't make it. （can't make it：無法辦到某事）

- dinner → golf / drinks this Friday
- I'm sorry, but → I'm afraid（很遺憾） / unfortunately,（很遺憾地，很不巧地）

● 至於晚餐的事，很遺憾的，我沒辦法參加。 Formal Tone

As for going to dinner, I regret to say that I can't make it. （As for：關於；regret：覺得很遺憾）

- As for → Regarding（關於）
- going to dinner → attending（出席） the convention（集會，大會）

09 告知拒絕的理由

● 我沒辦法參加，因為我這個週末要準備搬家。

I'm preparing to move this weekend so I can't make it.

- preparing to move → having lunch with my parents / meeting my boss for dinner

● 我必須和我未來的岳父母（公婆）見面。

I have to meet my future in-laws.（future：將來的；in-laws：岳父母或公婆）

- work overtime / late.（overtime：加班）
- prepare for a presentation.（prepare：準備；presentation：簡報）
- visit my brother in (the) hospital. ※1

※1 想表達「住院」之意而使用 "in hospital" 時，美式英語會加 "the"，英式英語則不加 "the"。

10 被拒絕時的回覆

● 好的。也許我們可以下次再約。

Okay. Maybe we can do it some other time.（some other time：改天，下次）

- No problem.
- That's alright.

- Maybe another time. Casual Tone
- Maybe next time. Casual Tone
- Let's do it another time.

● 聽說你沒辦法參加這次的商展，我感到很遺憾。

I'm sorry to hear that you can't make it to the trade show.

- What a shame（遺憾，懊惱）
- It's a pity（遺憾）

- the weather is still bad over there.（over there：在那裡）
- Michelle didn't get a raise.（raise：加薪）

小試身手 空格裡的正確答案是哪一個呢？

He's ______ lazy.

❶ extremely ❷ totally

解答就在下一頁

11 告知行程

● 我會把週六的時間空下來。

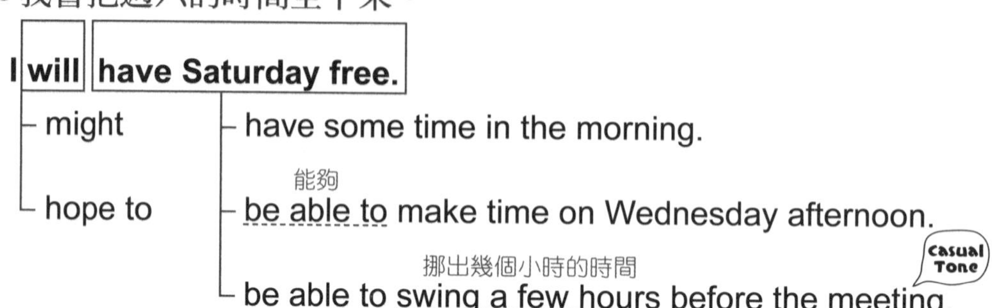
I will have Saturday free.
might
hope to
have some time in the morning.
能夠
be able to make time on Wednesday afternoon.
Casual Tone
挪出幾個小時的時間
be able to swing a few hours before the meeting.

● 我將會在九月二十一日抵達。

抵達
I'll be arriving on September 21st.
（搭飛機）前往
I'll be flying in
抵達
My flight arrives

● 今年夏天你還是會去義大利嗎？

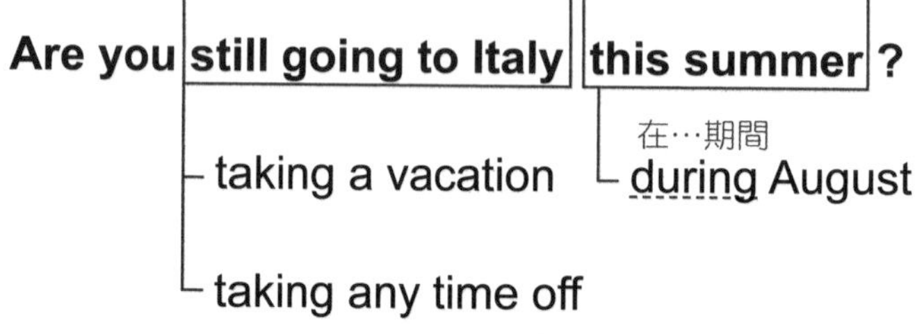
Are you still going to Italy this summer ?
taking a vacation
taking any time off
在…期間
during August

● 我六月二十一到二十八日休假。

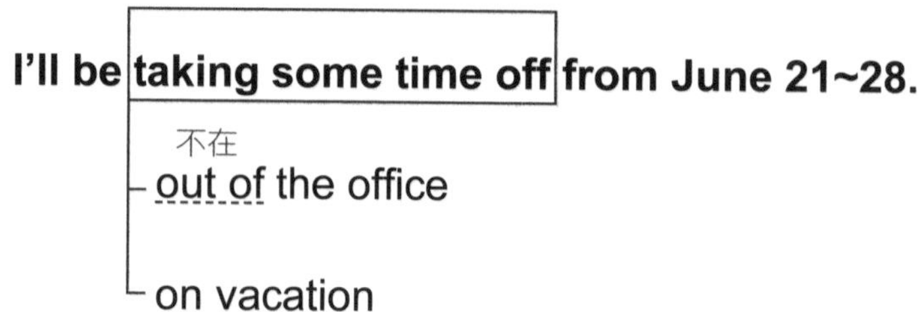
I'll be taking some time off from June 21~28.
不在
out of the office
on vacation

前一頁  的解答 ❶ He's extremely lazy. 他極為懶惰。

12 確認

● 我聽說你最近在日本開了一家分店。這是真的嗎？

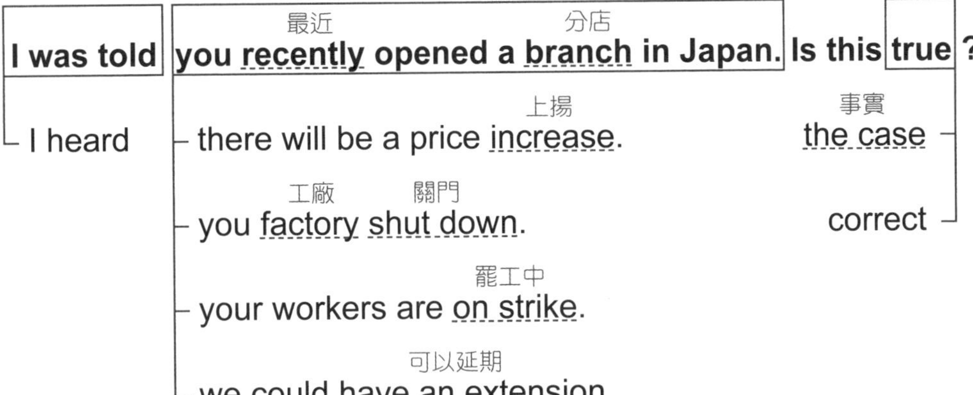
I was told
I heard
最近
分店
you recently opened a branch in Japan.
上揚
there will be a price increase.
工廠
關門
you factory shut down.
罷工中
your workers are on strike.
可以延期
we could have an extension.
Is this true ?
事實
the case
correct

● 不知道你是否已經收到邀請函。

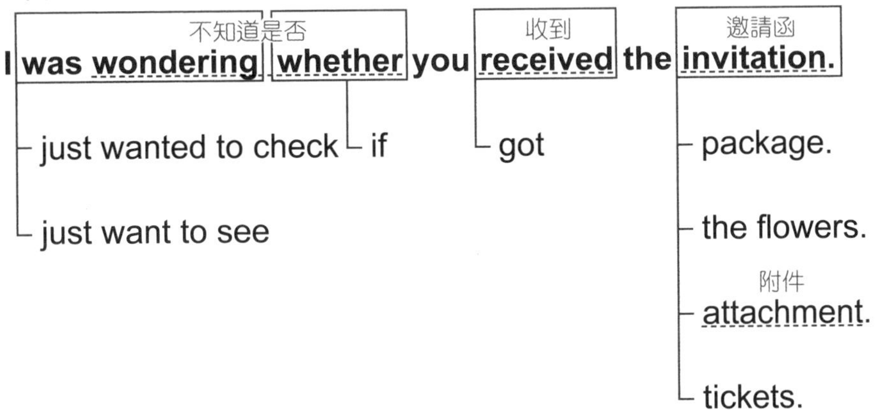
不知道是否
I was wondering whether you
收到
received the
邀請函
invitation.
just wanted to check
just want to see
if
got
package.
the flowers.
附件
attachment.
tickets.

13 日常會話

● 等我把一切安頓好就寫信給你。

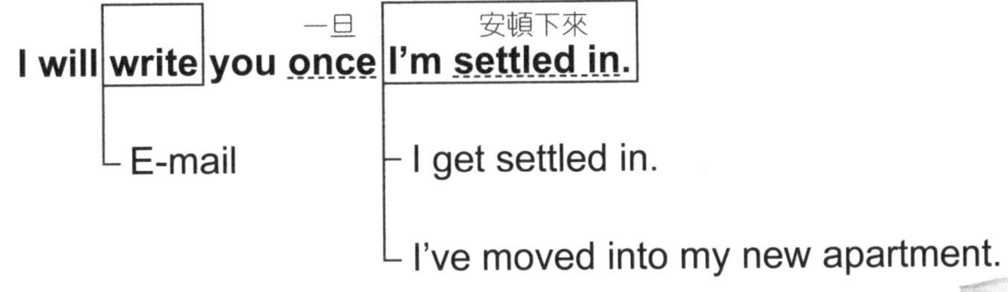
I will write you
一旦
once
安頓下來
I'm settled in.
E-mail
I get settled in.
I've moved into my new apartment.

● 請問你知道哪裡可以熨襯衫嗎？

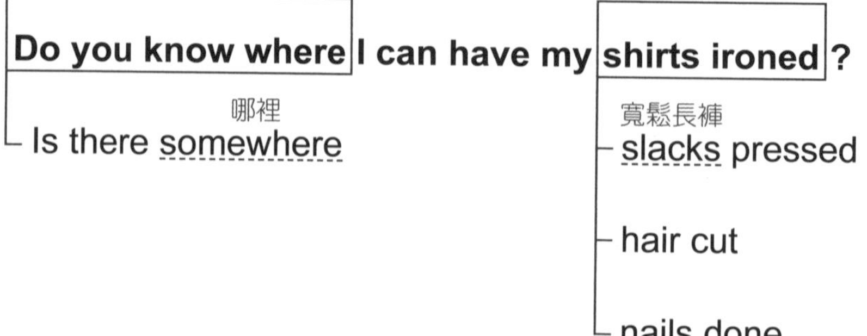
Do you know where I can have my shirts ironed ?
哪裡
Is there somewhere
寬鬆長褲
slacks pressed
hair cut
nails done

● 你能不能推薦一個靠近你辦公室的地方？

Could you recommend something near your office ?
推薦
Can
建議
suggest
Casual Tone
介紹
hook me up with
a nice restaurant
比較便宜的
a less expensive restaurant / hotel
a good tour company

● 待在那裡的那段日子，我可能需要買些補給品。

I might need to buy some supplies while I am there.
補給品
want to
access the internet
僱用
口譯員
have to
hire an interpreter
花粉症
藥品
buy some hayfever medication

● 我不吃生的魚。

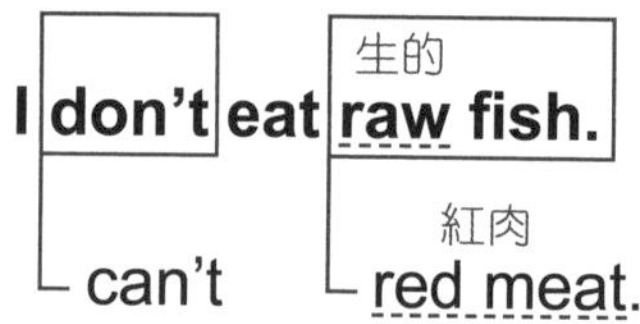
I don't eat raw fish.
生的
can't
紅肉
red meat.

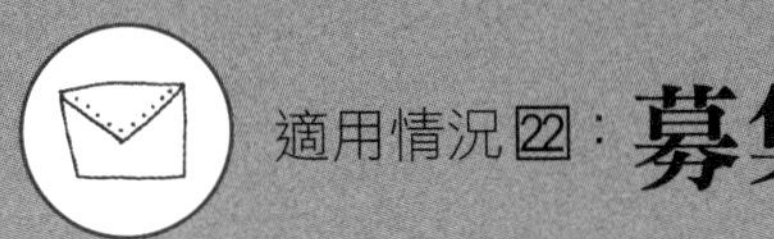

適用情況22：募集

Seeking English speaking staff to work at seaside cafe in Tamsui.

No experience necessary.

Hours: day shift 10am to 3pm, night shift 2pm to 9pm.
NT$150/hour.

Call 090-22XX for more information.

中譯

位於淡水的海濱咖啡館徵求會講英語的服務人員。

無經驗可。

工作時間：早班上午十點到下午三點，晚班下午兩點到晚上九點。

時薪台幣150元。

詳情請電洽：090-22XX。

01 徵才

● 我們目前正在徵求糕點師傅。

We are currently (現在，目前) **inviting applications** (徵求 申請，應徵) **for the position of pastry chef.** (糕點師傅)

- MJP Inc. is
- accepting candidates (接受 受試者，應徵者)
- holding interviews (舉辦)
- our summer internship program.

● 請到我們的官網查詢工作機會。

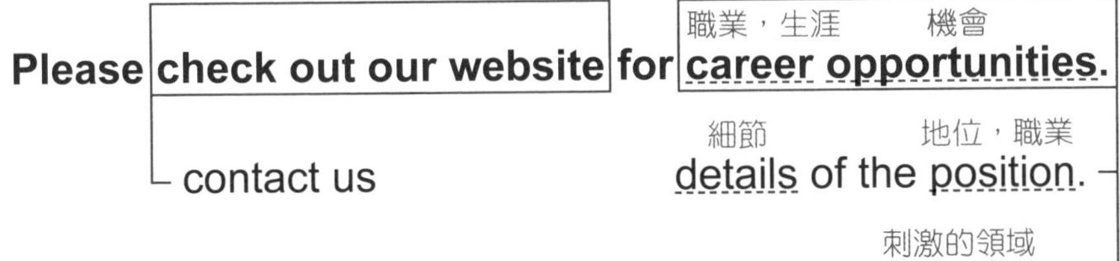

Please check out our website for career opportunities. (職業，生涯 機會)

- contact us
- details of the position. (細節 地位，職業)
- your chance to work in this exciting field. (刺激的領域)

● 徵求司機。

Drivers needed.

- Sales clerks (販售員)

● Crystal Sky洛杉磯辦公室徵求五名員工。

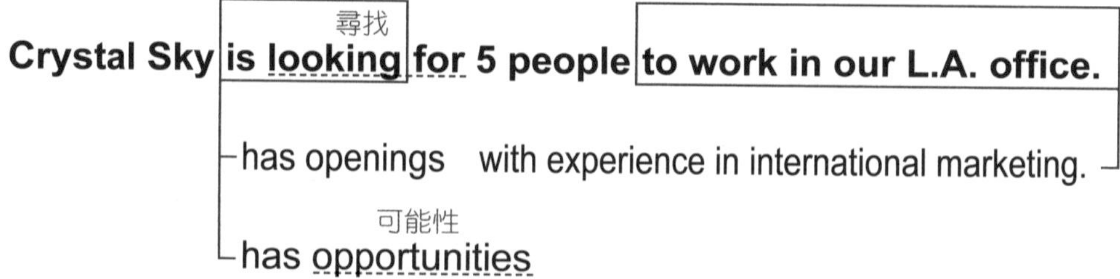
尋找
Crystal Sky is looking for 5 people to work in our L.A. office.
has openings
with experience in international marketing.
可能性
has opportunities

● MJP公司正在募集設計競稿。

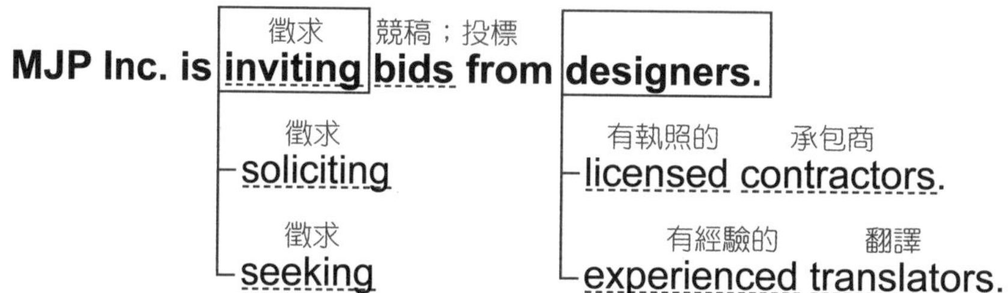
徵求
競稿；投標
MJP Inc. is inviting bids from designers.
徵求
soliciting
徵求
seeking
有執照的
承包商
licensed contractors.
有經驗的
翻譯
experienced translators.

● 我們希望得到你的回覆。

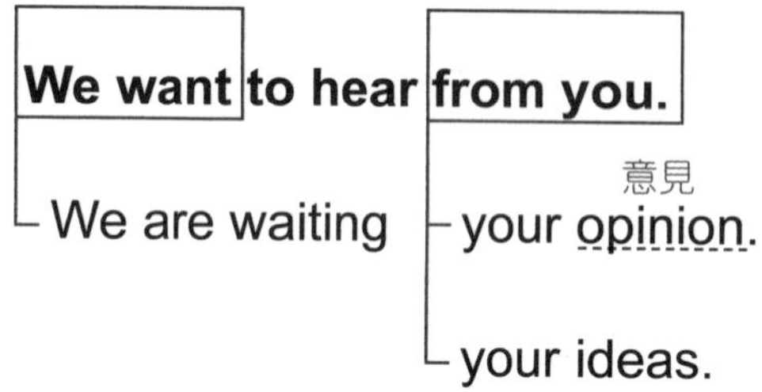
We want to hear from you.
We are waiting
意見
your opinion.
your ideas.

● 我們的客服中心正在徵求雙語服務人員。

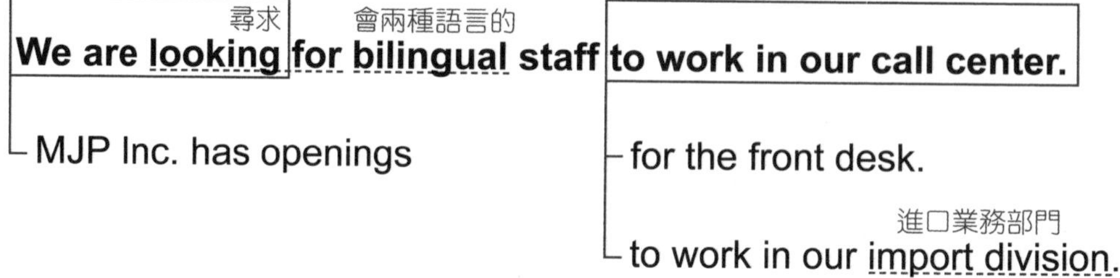
尋求
會兩種語言的
We are looking for bilingual staff to work in our call center.
MJP Inc. has openings
for the front desk.
進口業務部門
to work in our import division.

● 我們的台灣辦公室正在徵求有經驗的專案經理。

尋求　有經驗的

Looking for experienced project managers for our Taiwan office.

● 應徵者必須在服務業擁有五年以上的工作經驗。

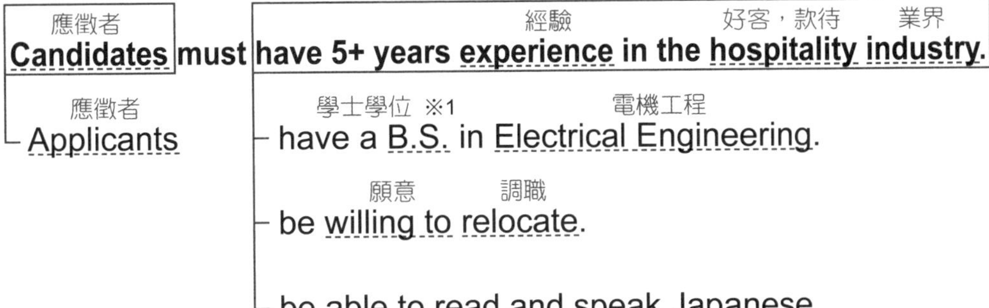

應徵者
Candidates must
經驗　好客，款待　業界
have 5+ years experience in the hospitality industry.
應徵者
Applicants
學士學位 ※1　電機工程
have a B.S. in Electrical Engineering.
願意　調職
be willing to relocate.
be able to read and speak Japanese.

※1 "B.S." 是「Bachelor of Science（理學士學位）」的簡稱。

02 募集資金・慈善捐款

● NCF正在為一年一度的「心連心趣味路跑」活動募集義工，這項活動的目的是為了幫助心臟病基金會。

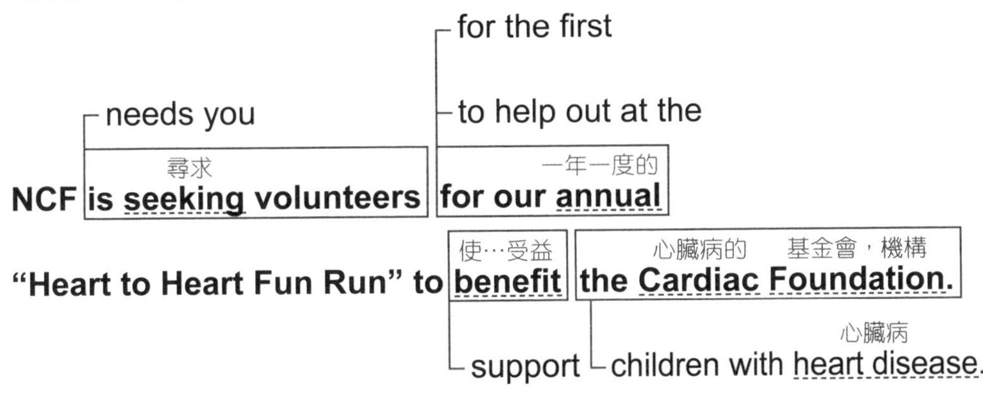

for the first
needs you
to help out at the
尋求
NCF is seeking volunteers
一年一度的
for our annual
使…受益
"Heart to Heart Fun Run" to benefit
心臟病的　基金會，機構
the Cardiac Foundation.
心臟病
support
children with heart disease.

● 發揮你的愛心，支持心臟病基金會吧。

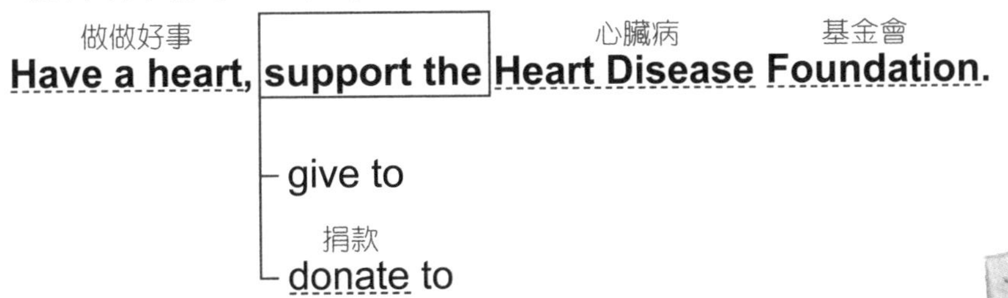

做做好事
Have a heart,
support the
心臟病　基金會
Heart Disease Foundation.
give to
捐款
donate to

Dear Friends and Associates,

We are looking for volunteers for our annual "Race for Life" event to benefit the local chapter of the Diabetes Charity. We need people to help man water stands and other activities. If you can spare an afternoon for this worthy cause, please contact May Chen at may@coldmail.com.

Thank you all,
Lindsay Leno

P.S. If you can't spare the time, please consider sponsoring one of our runners with a tax-deductible donation.

中譯

親愛的朋友和企業夥伴們：

我們正在為一年一度的「生活路跑」活動召募志工，本活動是為了支持糖尿病慈善協會的本地分會。我們需要志工幫忙照看飲水補給站以及協助其他雜務。假如你能夠抽出一個下午的時間支持這項義舉，請透過 may@coldmail.com 與陳梅聯絡。

感謝大家。

附註：假如你沒有時間，也請考慮贊助我們的任何一個跑者，本項捐款可列入納稅的扣除額。

● 請捐款給海嘯基金。

Please make a donation (捐款) to the Tsunami Fund (基金).

● 你的捐款將可救人一命。

Your donation (捐款) could save someone's life (生命).

- Just NT$10 per day (一天)
- Your support

- help find a home for an abandoned animal (被棄養的動物).
- send a child to school.
- help rebuild (重建，復原) lives.

● 我們需要五十名義工在十二月十六日協助處理慈善拍賣相關活動。

We need 50 volunteers to help out (幫忙，協助) at the charity auction on December 16th.

- We are seeking (尋求)

03 徵求創意

● MJP公司徵求所有的顧客一起來命名我們的新汽水。

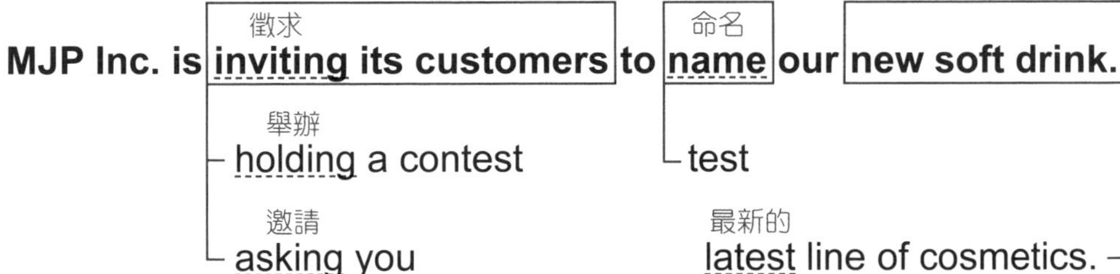
MJP Inc. is inviting its customers to name our new soft drink.
徵求
命名
舉辦
holding a contest
test
邀請
asking you
最新的
latest line of cosmetics.

● Crystal Sky徵求產品試用者。

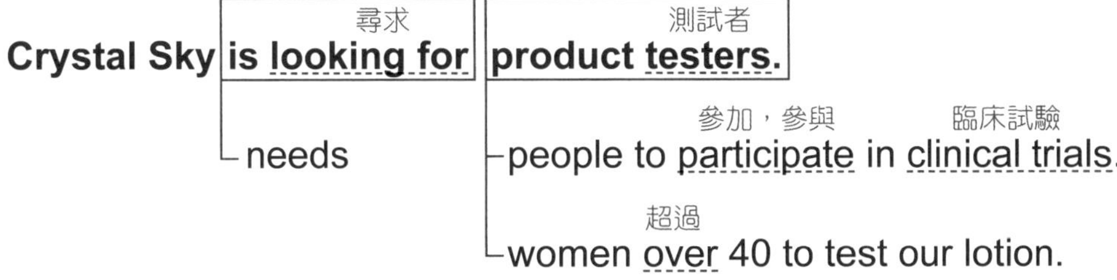
Crystal Sky is looking for product testers.
尋求
測試者
needs
參加，參與
臨床試驗
people to participate in clinical trials.
超過
women over 40 to test our lotion.

告別中式英文

Business E-mail Tips

Computer viruses are an unfortunate reality of cyber life.

電腦病毒是網路生活裡一個不幸的事實。

這是病毒信吧？

很遺憾地，電腦病毒是每個網路使用者都必須面對的產物。由於擔心來路不明的信件會讓電腦中毒，即使信件來自於我們認識的人，但許多人仍不願意貿然開啟電子郵件裡的附加檔案。這是因為有些病毒在進入你的電腦後，就會自動寄送附有病毒檔的電子郵件給通訊錄裡的每個聯絡人。

因此，為了避免收件人把你重要的電子郵件誤認為帶有病毒的信件，在寄出有附加檔案的E-mail時，務必說明這封信附加有什麼樣的檔案；如果分好幾封信寄出的話，則可以在第一封信件裡先做說明，你將會寄出附有檔案的信件。

Sherry,

Congratulations on your marriage!

I'm sure you made a very beautiful bride. I wish you and Paul all the best!

Sincerely,
Juanita

中譯

恭喜你結婚了！

我相信你一定是一個非常漂亮的新娘。祝福你與保羅幸福美滿！

01 祝賀

● 恭喜你（和喬伊思）訂婚！

Congratulations on your engagement (to Joyce)!
(engagement 訂婚)

- wedding! (結婚)
- firstborn! (第一個孩子的誕生)
- win against "The Demolishers" the other day! (against 與…對決；the other day 前一陣子)
- nomination for the Pulitzer Prize. (nomination 提名；Pulitzer Prize 普立茲獎)

● 祝福你的新生活一切順心如意。

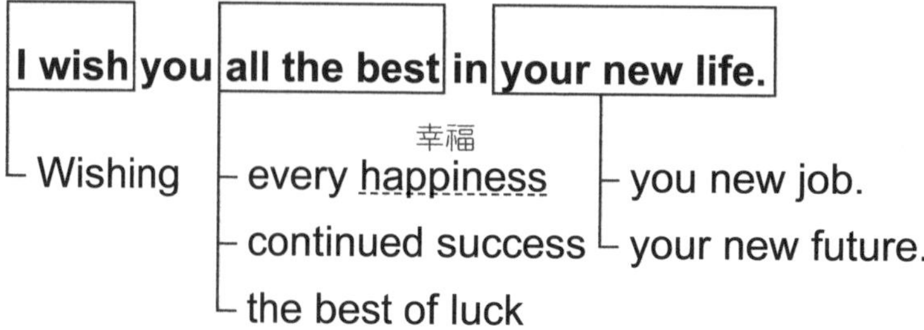

I wish you all the best in your new life.

- I wish → Wishing
- all the best → every happiness (happiness 幸福) / continued success / the best of luck
- your new life. → you new job. / your new future.

● 為你嶄新的未來獻上最美好的祝福！

Best wishes for your new future!

- All the best
- Best of luck

- many future successes.（successes：成功）

● 恭喜你榮升（為區域經理）！

Congratulations on your promotion (to district manager)!（promotion：升遷；district manager：※1區域經理，分店店長）

- new job
- transfer (to Tokyo)（transfer：轉職；※1）
- new position (as vice president)（※1；vice president：副總裁）

※1 如果要加上括號裡的詞彙，就必須搭配適當的介系詞。

● 真替你感到開心！ Casual Tone

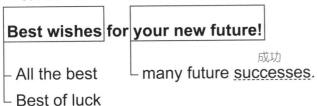

I'm so happy for you!

- Ayumi and I are
- thrilled for（非常興奮）
- proud of（感到驕傲）
- excited for（興奮）

Casual Tone

Mark,

Congrats on your latest venture!
You always talked about wanting to open a restaurant and now you have. I am very excited for you.
Marlene and I will definitely come by the next time we are in town.

Alex

中譯

恭喜你順利展開新事業！

你總說想開一家餐廳，現在你辦到了。我替你感到非常興奮。我和馬洛琳下次到市區時，一定會順道造訪你的新餐廳。

● 恭喜你獲頒「2010 年 WhoTube 年度最佳影片」大獎！

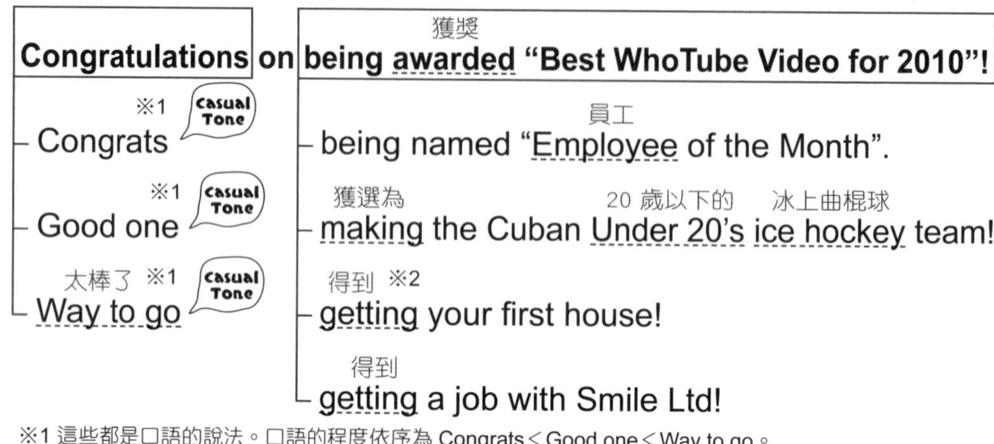
獲獎
Congratulations on being awarded "Best WhoTube Video for 2010"!
※1 Casual Tone
Congrats
※1 Casual Tone
Good one
太棒了 ※1 Casual Tone
Way to go
員工
being named "Employee of the Month".
獲選為 20 歲以下的 冰上曲棍球
making the Cuban Under 20's ice hockey team!
得到 ※2
getting your first house!
得到
getting a job with Smile Ltd!

※1 這些都是口語的說法。口語的程度依序為 Congrats < Good one < Way to go。
※2 這裡的 "getting" 還可以替換為 "buying" 或 "purchasing"。

02 送別

● Smile公司的全體員工都會非常想念你。

非常想念
You will be sorely missed by all here at Smile Ltd.

● 我希望我們能保持聯絡。

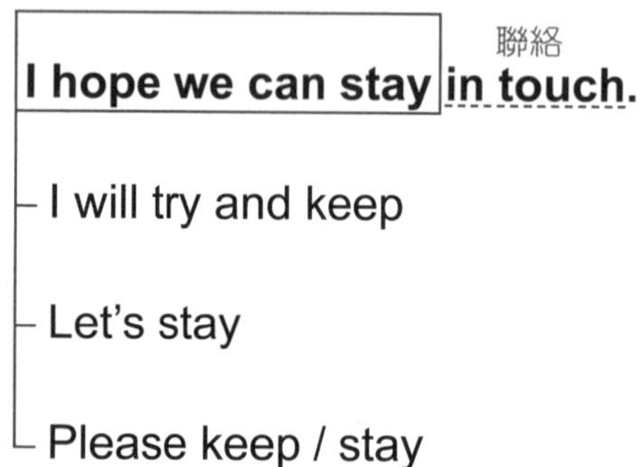
聯絡
I hope we can stay in touch.
I will try and keep
Let's stay
Please keep / stay

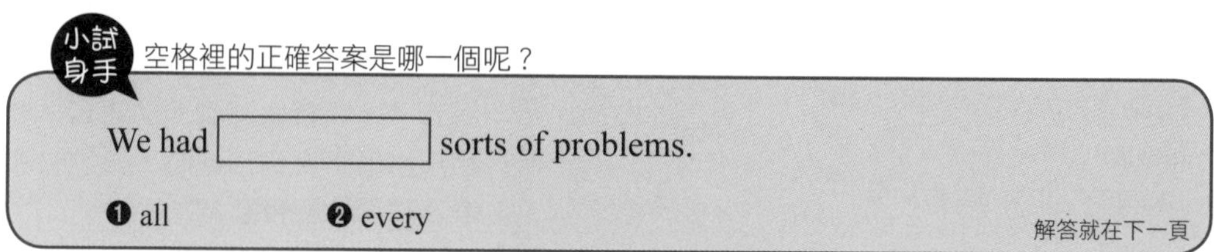
小試身手 空格裡的正確答案是哪一個呢？

We had [ ] sorts of problems.

❶ all ❷ every

解答就在下一頁

Dear George,

Please accept my condolences on the death of your wife, Leia. She was a dear friend to my family. I'll always remember her smile.

If there is anything I can do to help, please let me know.

Sincerely,
Lawrence

中譯

關於你已故的妻子蕾雅，在此謹向你獻上哀悼之意。我們家和她交情深厚。我永遠都會記住她的笑容。

如果有任何我可以幫得上忙的地方，請告訴我。

03 哀悼

Formal Tone

● 關於你兒子李的過世，謹向你和你的家人致上我最深的哀悼之意。

I would like to extend my deepest sympathies to you and your family on the death of your son, Lee.

- extend 致，給予 → express 表達
- deepest sympathies 最深的憐憫
- death 死亡 → loss 喪失

● 關於你妻子蕾雅的驟然離世，謹致上我的哀悼之意。

Formal Tone

Please accept our condolences on the untimely passing of your wife, Leia.

- Please accept 接受 → I would like to extend 傳達，表示
- our → my
- condolences on 弔唁 → sympathy for 同情，憐憫
- untimely 突然的 → sudden 突然的 / tragic 悲傷的，悲痛的
- passing 去世，死去 → death 死亡

● 聽到你父親過世的消息，我感到很震驚。

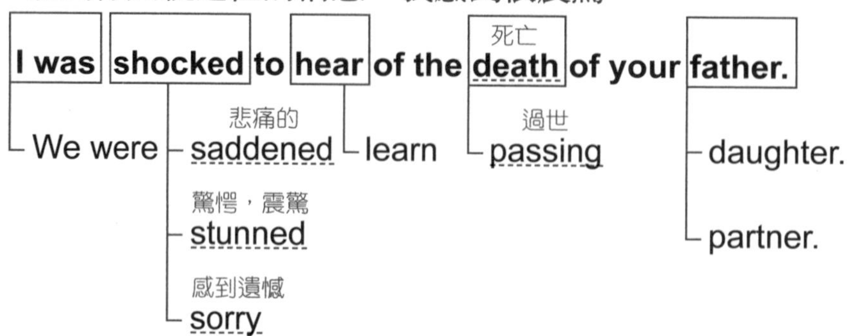
I was shocked to hear of the death (死亡) of your father.

- I was → We were
- shocked → saddened (悲痛的) / stunned (驚愕，震驚) / sorry (感到遺憾)
- hear → learn
- death → passing (過世)
- father → daughter. / partner.

● 我們難以理解為什麼會發生這樣的悲劇。

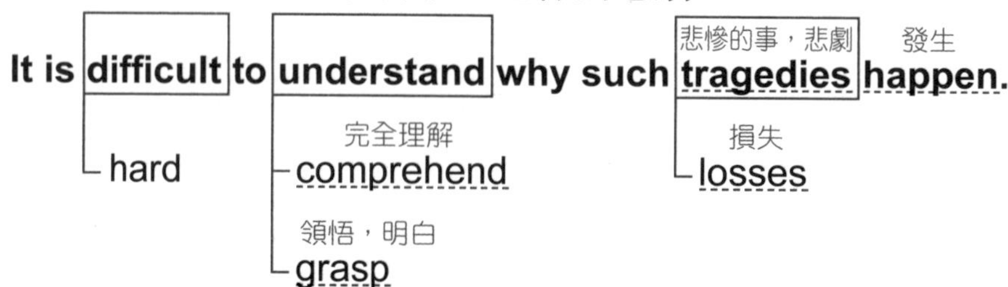
It is difficult to understand why such tragedies (悲慘的事，悲劇) happen (發生).

- difficult → hard
- understand → comprehend (完全理解) / grasp (領悟，明白)
- tragedies → losses (損失)

● 雖然我與令尊交情尚淺，但是我經常聽人提起他對生命的熱情。

Although (雖然) I didn't know your father very well,

- I didn't know your father very well → I only knew him a short time, / I only met Ken a few times (好幾次), / I never (從未) met him,

I often (經常) heard about his passion (熱情) for life.

- passion for life → warm (溫暖的) compassion (同情心) for his co-workers (同事) and friends. / enthusiasm (熱情，熱忱) for the outdoors. / love / fondness (愛好) of sailing. / countless (數不盡的) selfless (無私的) acts of kindness (善行).

● 我認識你父親很多年了，我會永遠記得他耀眼的笑容。

超過
over 20 years

I knew your father for **many years** and **I'll always remember** his beaming smile.

耀眼的笑容

I'll never forget

● 我和克利斯汀曾一起在Technical Recipes公司工作。

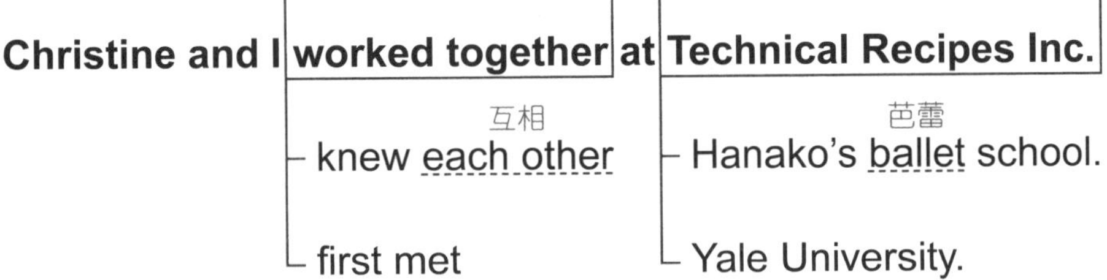

Christine and I worked together at Technical Recipes Inc.
互相
knew each other
first met
芭蕾
Hanako's ballet school.
Yale University.

04 生病・工作失敗・落選

● 聽到你父親生病的消息，我感到非常遺憾。

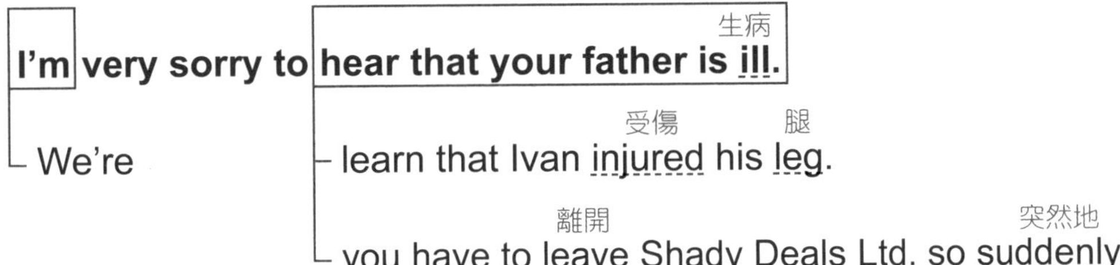

I'm very sorry to hear that your father is ill.
生病
We're
受傷
腿
learn that Ivan injured his leg.
離開
突然地
you have to leave Shady Deals Ltd. so suddenly.

● 我很遺憾你失去了你的工作。

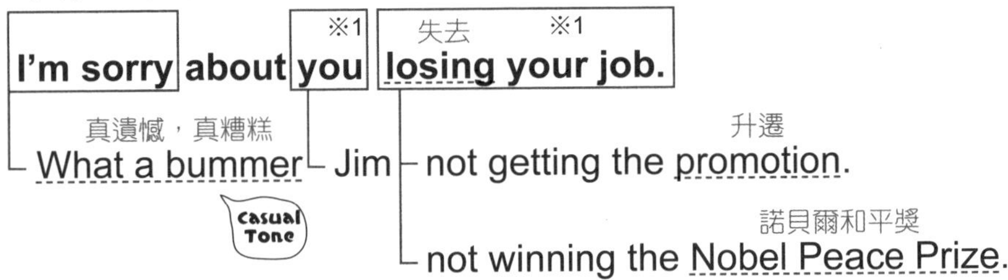

I'm sorry about you losing your job.
※1
失去
※1
真遺憾，真糟糕
What a bummer
Casual Tone
Jim
升遷
not getting the promotion.
諾貝爾和平獎
not winning the Nobel Peace Prize.

※1 要注意所有格的搭配，"you" 和 "your"，"Jim" 和 "his"。

● 聽說你的企畫案遭到否決，我感到很遺憾。別因此消沉氣餒！下次你會表現得更好的！

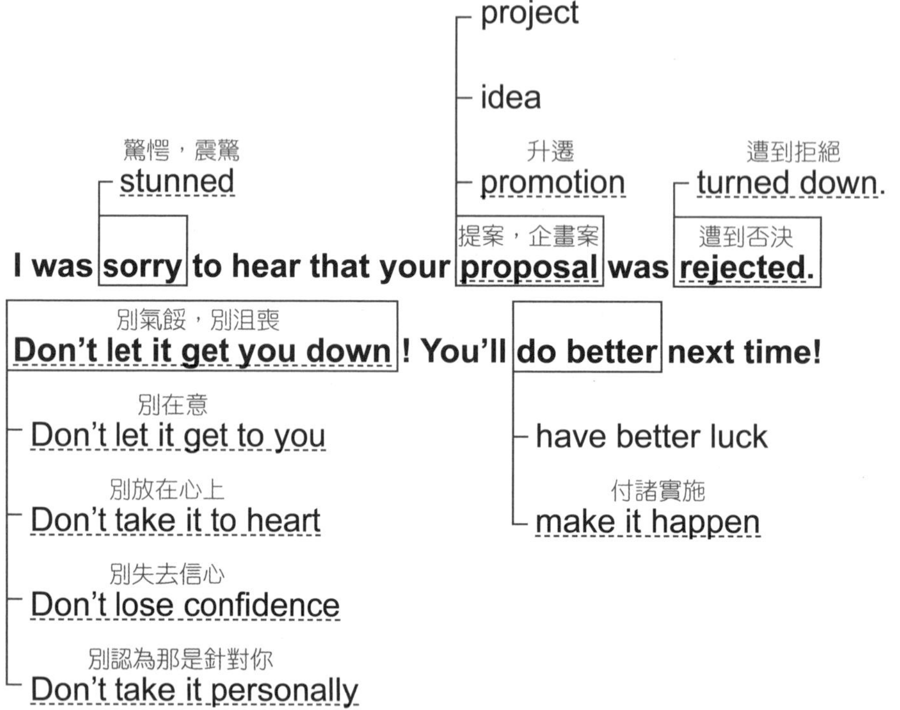

project
idea
驚愕，震驚
stunned
升遷
promotion
遭到拒絕
turned down.
提案，企畫案
遭到否決
I was sorry to hear that your proposal was rejected.
別氣餒，別沮喪
Don't let it get you down! You'll do better next time!
別在意
Don't let it get to you
別放在心上
Don't take it to heart
別失去信心
Don't lose confidence
別認為那是針對你
Don't take it personally
have better luck
付諸實施
make it happen

05 鼓勵

● 因為你全心全意地努力工作，如此的回報是實至名歸。

With all the hard work you've put in, you definitely deserve it.

肯定地 definitely；值得 deserve

- hard work
  - 長時間 long hours
  - 孜孜不倦 tireless effort
  - energy

● 無論你需要什麼，我都會在你身邊。

I am here for you, whatever you need.

無論如何，不管怎麼樣 whatever

● 假如你需要人幫忙帶孩子，就告訴我一聲。

If you need help with the children, let me know.

● 假如你需要找人聊聊，請不要客氣，儘管開口。

遲疑，猶豫
If you need someone to talk to , please don't hesitate to ask.
真的（強調語氣）
If you need anything at all
If there's anything I can do to help
I am here.
we are here for you.
please just ask.

● 如果有任何我能幫忙的地方，請不要客氣，儘管開口。

任何
協助，幫忙
遲疑，猶豫
If I can be of any assistance , please do not hesitate to ask.
提供
we
offer
help
安慰，慰藉
comfort
幫得上忙的地方
service

No Chinese English!

"Thank you very much for yesterday's dinner." 這句話是正確的嗎？字面上看起來，好像跟中文的「感謝您昨晚的招待」有點類似，但是一般說來，英語母語人士很少會這麼使用。從現在開始，請擺脫中文的思考，用更直接的方法使用英文吧！

Corporate Outline

Formal
Tone

Pathfinders Exports is Japan's leading exporter of glass and acrylic fixtures. Our exceptional quality and functional designs combined with competitive pricing make our glass and acrylic fixtures the best in the world.

Pathfinders Exports was started in 1890, by Taro Iwamoto as a one-man operation producing hand-blown glass bulbs for gaslights. In 1910, his son Kouji designed a method for mass-producing the bulbs, and within 10 years, Iwamoto Glass, as it was then called, was producing over 20,000 bulbs every month.

In 1952, the company was bought by Konomi Holdings and Pathfinders Exports was founded. The business was then expanded to produce acrylic fixtures. In 2009, under its current president, Miho Kanda, Pathfinders Exports had over 1.2 billion yen in sales. Pathfinders Exports currently ships worldwide to over 30 countries and employs 1,370 workers.

With our motto of "Unbeatable prices for unbeatable products", we are looking to make 2010 a year of continued growth. As part of our corporate philosophy of environmental sustainability, we have pledged 1% of our after-tax profits in 2010 to Cleanwater Charities.

中譯

Pathfinders出口公司是日本出口玻璃和壓克力設備首屈一指的出口商。我們公司的產品擁有卓越的品質和實用的設計，而且價格非常具有競爭力，因此我們的玻璃和壓克力設備堪稱世界一流。

Pathfinders出口公司由岩本太郎創立於1890年，最初是一人公司，只有岩本太郎一個人獨自以手工製作煤氣燈的玻璃燈泡。1910年，岩本先生的兒子浩司設計出量產燈泡的方法，不到十年，當時的岩本玻璃公司每月就能生產超過兩萬個燈泡。

1952年，Konomi控股公司買下岩本玻璃公司，Pathfinders出口公司正式成立。於是該公司開始投入壓克力設備市場。2009年在現任社長神田美穗的領導下，該公司的年營業額高達12億日圓。目前Pathfinders出口公司的客戶遍布全球30餘國，員工合計1,370人。

我們公司的格言是「無敵的產品，無敵的價格」，秉持著這樣的信念，我們期盼2010年公司業務能持續成長。而由於我們的企業理念重視環境的永續發展，因此我們承諾將2010年稅後純利的1%捐給慈善團體Cleanwater。

Company Name	MJP Inc.
Founded	December 12, 1970
Headquarters	8-5-26, Horifune, Minami-ku, Tokyo, Japan
Chairman & CEO	Yasushi Kawano
President & COO	Nobuo Kawano
Capital	10 million yen
Annual sales	1 billion yen (as at December 31, 2010)
Number of Employees	500 (as at December 31, 2010)

Formal Tone

中譯

公司名稱：MJP股份有限公司
設立：1970年12月12日
總公司：
日本國東京都南區堀船8-5-26
會長兼CEO：河野靖
社長兼COO：河野信夫
資本額：1,000萬日圓
年營業額：10億日圓
（2010年12月31日數據）
員工人數：500人
（2010年12月31日數據）

公司概要中常提到的項目

Services and Products 服務與產品
Shareholder Information 股東資訊
History of the Company 公司歷史
New Products 新產品
Motto / Mission Statement and Logo 企業理念與標誌
Headquarters 總公司，總部
Branch Locations 分公司，分部
Focus and Area of Expertise 專業領域
Certifications 資格，證明
Company Founder and Key Staff Members 創辦者與主要公司成員
Future Visions and Plans of the Company 未來願景與計畫
Contact Numbers, E-mail Addresses and Website 聯絡電話，E-mail與網站

01 公司概要

● Crystal Sky設立於1993年。

Crystal Sky was founded in 1993. （設立，創立）

- has been operating since （營運）
- began operations in （開始）
- opened its doors in （店舖開張 ※1）

※ 只適用於實體店面。

Casual Tone

Corporate Outline

Crystal Sky is Japan's leading retailer of specialty household items. We have been in business since 1993, when Marie Rossi and Geoff Case, two exchange students with a passion for food, decided to import kitchen gadgets that were not only functional but also stylish and affordable.

Originally formed with the ex-patriot community in mind, Crystal Sky soon found popularity with the Japanese community. In 1995, Marie and Geoff decided to expand into home furnishings, and the rest, as they say, is history.

In 2009, Crystal Sky proudly became the exclusive distributor of Jet natural cosmetics. We look forward to bringing this line of 100% natural aromatherapy oils and creams to the Japanese market.

Crystal Sky believes that the home should be an oasis from the hustle and bustle of life. To that end, we import only the highest quality specialty items for the home that offer true consumer value.

中譯

Crystal Sky是日本家用器具零售商的領導品牌。我們創立於1993年，創辦人瑪莉・羅西和傑夫・凱斯當初只是兩名交換學生，基於對食物的熱愛，決心將實用與時尚感兼具，而且價格大眾化的廚房用具引進日本。

最初，Crystal Sky的目標客群設定為住在日本但是愛用國貨的外國人社群，但是他們很快就發現自己的產品也深受日本人青睞。1995年，瑪莉和傑夫決定將事業版圖擴大到家用家具與室內陳設，此後的事就不必多說了，Crystal Sky就此成為眾所周知的知名品牌。

2009年，Crystal Sky很榮幸地成為Jet自然化妝品的獨家代理商。我們期待能將這一系列100%純天然的芳香精油和乳霜引進日本市場。

Crystal Sky相信家應該是讓人們遠離喧囂與煩擾生活的綠洲。因此，我們只引進品質最好的家用產品，讓消費者擁有真正令人滿意的家庭生活。

● MJP公司是日本第一的刀具製造商。

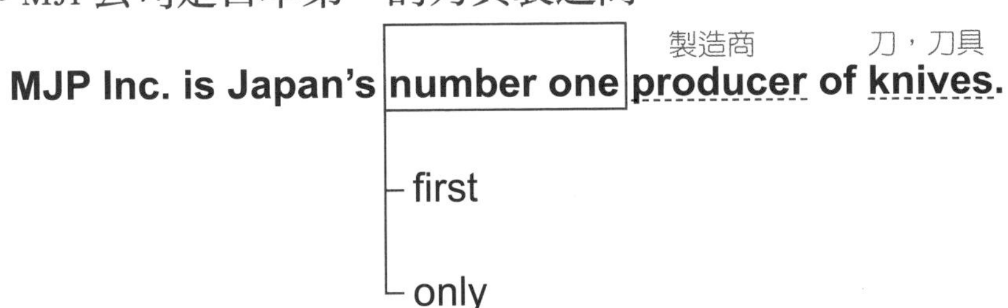

製造商
刀，刀具
MJP Inc. is Japan's number one producer of knives.
first
only

● 我們製造高品質的廚房用具。總公司位在東京，我們在全國各地僱用了100名員工。

進口
出口
import / export
銷售
market
design and produce
光學儀器
optical equipment.
批發，分銷
distribute
clothing.
製造
★
廚房用具
總公司
We manufacture quality kitchen gadgets. With our headquarters
僱用
在全國各地
in Tokyo, we employ 100 people nationwide.
出口
超過
export to over 20 countries.
進口
稀有金屬
全球
import rare metals from around the globe.

★標記的單字，可以用下一頁的部分形容詞替換。

● MJP公司自1984年以來，持續為全球的商務社群貢獻心力。

貢獻，有益於 / 自從

MJP has been serving the worldwide business community since 1984.

- 解決方案：is here to help you find solutions.
- 處理：will take care of your needs.

24 公司簡介 公司概要

適用於公司簡介的形容詞

high-quality 高品質的，優質的	state-of-the-art 最先進的（科學技術）
superior-quality 上等的，品質優異的	eco-sustainable 使環境得以永續的
inexpensive 不貴的，費用不高的	one-of-a-kind 特殊的，特別的
reasonably priced 價格合理的	disposable 拋棄式的
high-end 高級的	reusable 可回收再利用的
all-natural 純天然的	long-lasting 長效的／持久的
organic 有機的	comfortable 舒服的，舒適的
plastic/metal/cotton 塑膠的／金屬的／棉質的	lightweight 質地輕的
stylish 時髦的；流行的	heavy-duty 堅固的，強韌耐用的
functional 實用的，功能性強的	professional 專業的
unique 獨特的，特有的	traditional 舊式的，傳統的
cutting-edge 最尖端的	original 最初的，原創的

● MJP公司是高品質女鞋的製造商。

MJP Inc. is a manufacturer (製造商) of ★quality footwear for women.

- manufacturer (製造商) → retailer (零售商) / distributor (通路商) / producer (生產者)
- quality footwear for women → ★fine window coverings. / functional (實用的) ★ office furniture (家具).

★標記的單字，可以用上述的部分形容詞替換。

● 讓MJP公司為您處理所有的翻譯以及口譯需求。

Let MJP take care of (處理) all your translating (翻譯) and interpreting (口譯) needs.

- → find the right (正確的) solutions (解決方案) for your business.

1992	"Switchmode Technical Ltd." is founded by computer prodigy and entrepreneur, William Richards. Starts out selling and servicing computers. Annual sales for first fiscal year in business reach US$1,300,000.
1995	Invests heavily in software and propulsion research development.
1999	Develops and obtains patent for the "Electro-Gravitic Propulsion Device", which results in a sudden surge in sales. Year end revenue exceeds US$55 million.
2000	Founder William Richards steps down as CEO after merging with "Recipes Ltd." Company name changed to "Technical Recipes Inc.". Joe Nathan, founder and former CEO of "Recipes Ltd." takes over as CEO of the newly formed company.
2001	Sees remarkable progress in security software development, receiving a patent for its "All-seeing Wide-warning Surveillance Utility Matrix" spy software system, otherwise known as "AWSUM". Annual revenue for 2001 exceeds US$120 million.
2005	Invests in research and development of sustainable and environmentally friendly products.
2009	Begins development of DIY solar house made from sustainable materials.
2010	Awarded "Most Innovative Eco-house Design of the Year Award" for 2010.

中譯

1992年 電腦天才企業家威廉・李察斯創立了「Switchmode科技股份有限公司」。最初的業務為銷售電腦並提供相關服務。該公司第一年的年營收就高達130萬美金。

1995年 該公司在軟體與推進器的研究開發方面投入大量資金。

1999年 發展並取得「電動重力推進裝置」的專利，銷售成長因此突飛猛進。當年營收突破5500萬美金。

2000年 該公司與「Recipes股份有限公司」合併後，威廉・李察斯辭去CEO職務。該公司更名為"Technical Recipes"。由原Recipes公司創辦人兼CEO喬・納森接任新公司的CEO。

2001年 在保全軟體方面的發展呈現顯著的進步，取得間諜軟體「全知廣域警戒監視網」，又名"AWSUM"的專利權。2001年的營收超越一億兩千萬美金。

2005年 投資研究發展永續環保商品。

2009年 著手開發採用永續建材的DIY太陽能房屋。

2010年 獲頒2010年「年度最佳環保房屋設計創意獎」。

24 公司簡介 公司概要

● 2010年，MJP公司的年營收突破一千億日圓。

In 2010, MJP Inc. had annual (年度的) sales of over 100 billion yen.

- became the first company to produce (製造) acrylic glue (壓克力接著劑).
- expanded (擴張) into the European market (市場).
- spent (花費) over (超過) 50 million yen on research (研究) and development (開發).
- donated (捐出) 10 million yen to breast cancer (乳癌) research (研究).
- began (開始) with 2 employees (員工); we now employ (僱用) over (超過) 500 people.

- 從計畫到執行，MJP都能提供完整的服務。

From planning to implementation（實行，施工）, MJP is a complete（完整的，一貫的） service provider.

- marketing to sales
- start to finish
- conception（概念） to realization（實現）

- Pathfinders出口公司是日本住宅用玻璃與壓克力設備首屈一指的出口商。

製造業者
manufacturer
營銷商
marketer
改革者，創新者
innovator
生產者
producer

Pathfinders Exports Inc. is Japan's leading（主要的，頂尖的） exporter（出口商） of glass and acrylic fixtures（配件，設備） for residential（住宅用的） use.

- commercial（商用的）
- professional（專業的，職業的）
- educational（與教育相關的）
- research（研究的）

- 我們將協助你建立跨越文化隔閡的橋樑。

We'll help you build bridges（橋樑） across the cultural（文化的） divide（隔閡，差異）.

● 我們深感自豪的是以大眾化的價格銷售流行時髦的帽子。

對…感到自豪
提供
★
負擔得起的
We pride ourselves on offering stylish hats at affordable prices.
高品質的
quality
designer
discount
outlet
難以戰勝的
unbeatable

★標記的單字，可以用p224的部分形容詞替換。

● 從市場研究到尋找合適的地點，我們可以協助你在日本開創事業。

From market research to finding the right location, we can help you set up business in Japan.

- right（適當的）
- location → retail space（零售）
- set up business in Japan. → with all your relocating（遷徙） needs.

告別中式英文

Business E-mail Tips

The first thing to consider when writing your company profile is your audience.

當你在撰寫公司簡介時，首先要考慮你的讀者是誰。

公司簡介是寫給誰看的？

公司簡介聽起來好像不是非常必要，但是一開始和陌生的客戶談生意時，先將自己的公司做一番簡介卻是不可省略的。這時首先要思考的不是內容該怎麼鋪陳，而是這份簡介要以誰為對象來撰寫：是你們公司的一般客戶？求職者？企業客戶？還是投資者？先確定對象是誰，應該就能掌握書寫時遣詞用句的語氣。關於公司簡介的撰寫方式和項目，可參考本書p.220到p.225的幾個範例。

02 經營方針

● 我們決心發展對顧客有益但對地球無害的產品。

承諾，決心 / 開發

We're committed to developing products that

損害 / 地球

help our customers without harming the earth.

提高 / 生產力 / 增加 / 利益

- enhance productivity and increase profits.

提升，改善 / 營養

- improve health and support better nutrition.

適應 / 持續變化的需求

- can adapt with our customers' changing needs.
- save time and energy.

擴張

- help our customers to expand their businesses.

符合

- fit our customers' lifestyles.

符合需求 / 不必要的 / 煩擾，麻煩

- meet needs without unnecessary hassle.

提供 / 解決之道 / 提升，改善 / 效率

- provide solutions and improve efficiency.

促進 / 安全性 / 減少 / 受傷

- promote safety and reduce the risk of injury.

● 我們相信我們的產品應該創造信賴感，而不是擔憂。

相信 / 信賴 / 擔心

We believe our products should create trust, not worry.

- MJP Inc. believes

鎮靜 / 失序，混亂

- calm, not chaos.

解決之道

- solutions, not problems.

單純 / 複雜

- simplicity, not complexity.

● 我們的座右銘是「以簡單的解決方案帶來實質的經濟效益」。

解決方案 經濟的 效果、利益

Our motto is **"Simple solutions with economic benefits".**

只是更好

- "Not bigger, just better".
- "A happy life, a clean earth".
- "Life is better when life is simpler".

● 我們製造解決方案。

製造 解決方案

We manufacture solutions.

● 帶問題來給我們，帶著解答回家。

Bring us questions, take home answers.

● 你已經試過其他家的產品，現在來試試最好的產品。

其他的東西

You've tried the rest, now try the best.

● 當你的事業遇到難以跨越的障礙時，我們會教你如何飛越它。

感到困擾 障礙

When your business is plagued by hurdles, we'll teach you to fly.

● 當你的營收觸底，請致電MJP。我們將協助你讓業績觸底反彈。

損益表底線 底部

When your bottom line hits bottom, call MJP. We'll help give

提高，增加

you a boost.

● 我們的專業團隊隨時待命。

Our team of experts（專家） **is standing by.**（待命）
- has designed（設計，構思） a product with families in mind.

03 市場策略

● 我們在歐洲、亞洲和大洋洲都有分店。

We have stores in Europe, Asia and Oceania.
- operate（營運） in
- export（出口） to
- ship to（運送）

● 敝公司的鞋子在超過十個國家販售。

Our footwear is sold in over 10 countries.

- computers are
- office furniture（家具） is

- the best-selling（最暢銷的 ★） brand in Japan.
- made from the finest（品質最佳的★） materials（原料，素材）.
- produced（製造） from 100% recycled ★ materials（素料）.

★標記的單字，可以用p224的部分形容詞替換。

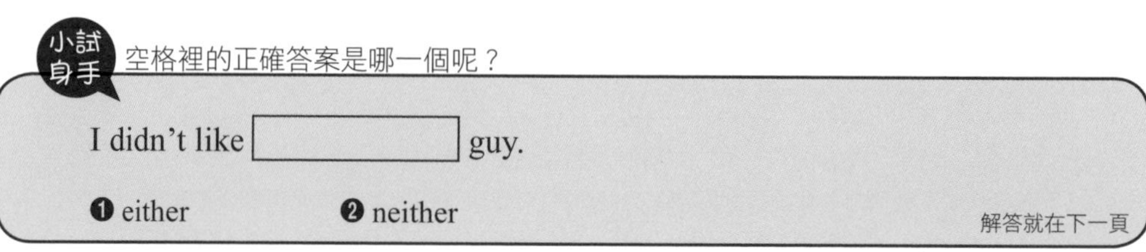

小試身手 空格裡的正確答案是哪一個呢？

I didn't like [ ] guy.

❶ either ❷ neither

解答就在下一頁

● 我們的商品可以在百貨公司買得到。

Our products [are available] through [department stores.]

- are available（可買到的）→ can be purchased（可以買到）
- through（透過）
- department stores. → mass-merchandisers.（量販店）/ wholesalers.（批發業者）/ retailers.（零售業者）/ home centers. / our catalogues. / the Internet.

04 商品介紹

● 我們的產品在業界是最受信賴的產品。

Our products are [the most trusted] in the [industry.]

- the most trusted（受到信賴）→ among the most trusted（在…之中最…）/ the strongest（最強的）/ the only all-natural ones（完全純天然的）
- industry.（業界）→ world.

● 我們最新的型號以最新的聲音辨識技術為主要特色。

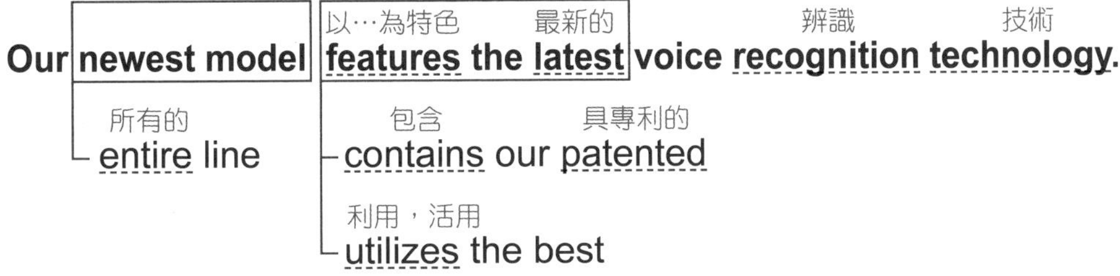
以…為特色
最新的
辨識
技術
Our newest model features the latest voice recognition technology.
所有的
entire line
包含
具專利的
contains our patented
利用，活用
utilizes the best

前一頁  的解答 ❶ I didn't like either guy.
那兩個男人我都不喜歡。

●我們公司的產品都採用環保素材製造而成。

Our products are made from environmentally friendly materials.

- environmentally friendly（對環境無害的）★ / real / genuine / natural（真材實料的） / synthetic（合成的） / quality（高品質的） / the finest（品質最優良的）
- materials.（素材） / ingredients.（成份，素材）

★標記的單字，可以用p224的部分形容詞替換。

●我們公司的產品不僅效率高，還具備時尚感，而且價格公道。

Our products are not only efficient（效率高的） but also stylish and affordable（負擔得起的）.

●了解到我們的產品能夠豐富生活，我們為此感到自豪。

We take pride（自豪） in knowing（了解） our products enrich（使豐富） lives.

- we offer（提供） the best products at the best prices.
- our customer service is unmatched（無與倫比的）.
- our products are enjoyed（受到愛用） the world over（在全世界）.
- we contribute（貢獻） to a sustainable（永續的） future.

●XYZ2012 是世界上第一個可攜式炸彈避難所。

The XYZ2012 is the world's first（最初的） portable（可攜的） bomb（炸彈） shelter（避難所）.

- is the only home sauna with Aroma technology（技術）.
- beats the competition（勝過競爭對手） in both（兩者都…） safety（安全性） and reliability（可信賴性）.

Dear Carol,

Here are the instructions for your new treadmill in English:

1. Place the magnetic key on the display board in the circle marked "key". Connect the other end of the key to your clothing. The treadmill will not operate without the key in place. This is to avoid injury. If you slip and fall, the treadmill will immediately stop.
2. Press the power button and select your desired course, speed and time.
3. Press the start button. The treadmill will automatically begin in 3 seconds.
4. Turn off the treadmill at any time by removing the key or pressing the power button.

CAUTION:
Do not operate while intoxicated.
Do not allow children to use unattended.

We hope you enjoying using your Runaway Treadmill.

中譯

關於你新買的跑步機，附上英文的說明如下：

1. 將磁卡置於螢幕上標示 "Key" 的圓圈裡。將磁卡的另一端繫在你的衣服上。磁卡沒有放在正確位置時，跑步機就無法運作。這是為了避免使用者受傷。假如你不小心滑倒，跑步機會立刻停下來。
2. 按下電源鍵並選擇你想要的跑步模式、速度和時間。
3. 按下啟動鍵。跑步機會在三秒內自動啟動。
4. 移開磁卡或再按一次電源鍵就能隨時關掉跑步機。

注意：

酒醉時請勿使用跑步機。

請勿讓孩童在無人看管的情況下使用跑步機。

希望你能好好享受你的Runaway跑步機。

01 貨物・使用說明書・包裝

● 內附出貨單

PACKING LIST ENCLOSED（附上）
IN THIS CONTAINER（在包裝的箱子裡）

● 此面朝上

THIS SIDE UP
WAY

● 禁止堆疊

堆積
DO NOT STACK
堆疊成兩層
DOUBLE STACK
堆疊超過三層
STACK MORE THAN 3 BOXES

● 使用前請詳閱說明書

READ INSTRUCTIONS BEFORE USE

02 開封方式

● 小心開封

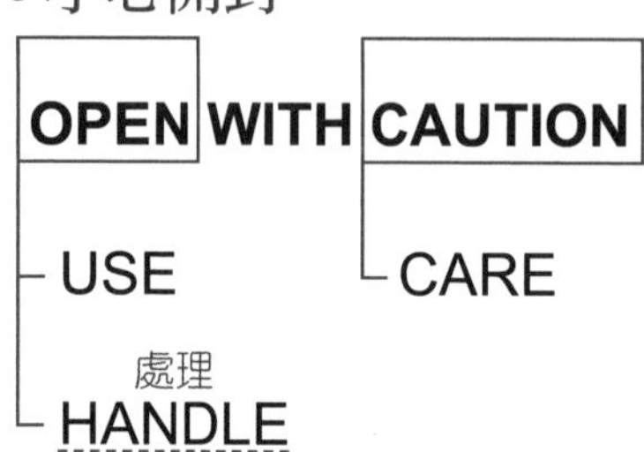
OPEN WITH CAUTION
USE
CARE
處理
HANDLE

● 禁止使用尖銳的物品開封

DO NOT OPEN WITH SHARP OBJECT

03 保存方法

● 請置於嬰幼兒拿不到的地方

KEEP **AWAY FROM BABIES AND CHILDREN**

- OUT OF CHILDREN'S REACH（避免孩童接觸）
- OUT OF DIRECT SUNLIGHT（避免陽光直接照射）
- DRY

● 請置於涼爽乾燥的地方

STORE **IN A COOL DRY PLACE**

- AT ROOM TEMPERATURE（室溫）
- BELOW 30°C（以下）
- IN REFRIGERATOR AFTER OPENING（冰箱）

04 對健康的影響

● 若皮膚出現紅疹，請停止使用

DISCONTINUE USE IF RASH DEVELOPS

● 若不慎誤食，請向醫師諮詢

SEEK **MEDICAL ATTENTION** IF **INGESTED**（嚥下，攝取）

- PROFESSIONAL HELP
- SWALLOWED（吞下，嚥下）
- EYE CONTACT OCCURS（發生）

25 標示說明的警語

保存方法／對健康的影響

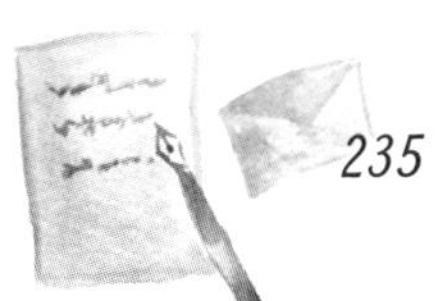

05 食物與飲品

● 若封蓋毀損請勿使用

DO NOT USE IF SEAL IS BROKEN

封蓋 (SEAL)

- USE IF PACKAGE IS DAMAGED　毀損，破損 (DAMAGED)
- PLACE ON HOT SURFACE　表面 (SURFACE)
- HEAT IN MICROWAVE　加熱 (HEAT)　微波爐 (MICROWAVE)
- FREEZE　冷凍 (FREEZE)

● 請在2012年4月8日前食用

USE BY: 4/8/12

- BEFORE: 13/8/12
- WITH CAUTION　謹慎 (CAUTION)

● 保存期限：2012年5月28日

BEST BY: 5/28/12

06 機械與裝置

● 戴上護目鏡

USE PROTECTIVE EYEWEAR

具保護性的 (PROTECTIVE)

- SAFETY GLASSES

● 必須有人看管

DO NOT LEAVE UNATTENDED

● 無人使用時，請關閉電源

TURN OFF WHEN NOT IN USE

拔掉插頭
UNPLUG

● 使用時打開窗戶

OPEN WINDOW WHEN IN USE

確認，確保安全　充分（適當）的通風
ENSURE ADEQUATE VENTILATION

● 在通風良好的環境中使用

充分（適當）的通風
USE WITH ADEQUATE VENTILATION

告別中式英文

Business E-mail Tips

It's a good idea to send a quick reply first if you are really busy.

假如你在忙的話，先寄一封簡短的回覆是個好主意。

就是因為忙，才要發個簡短的E-mail！

有時候工作太忙，你可能沒空立即回覆剛收到的E-mail。假如沒有時間回覆需要長篇大論仔細說明的E-mail，你也應該盡快寫封簡短的E-mail回應對方，讓寄信人知道你已經收到信件，同時也告訴他們你之後會再詳細回覆，請務必養成這個良好的習慣。例如，你可以只寫 "I got your message. I'll get back to you ASAP."

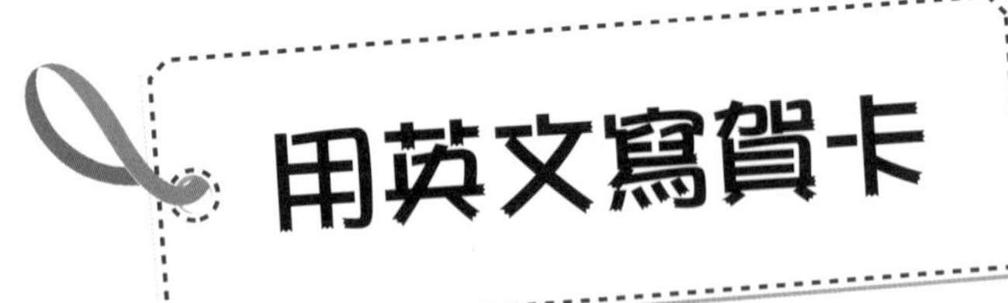
用英文寫賀卡

節慶假期

- Wishing you all a Merry Christmas and a Happy New Year!
  祝你們聖誕快樂，新年快樂！

- We sincerely hope the New Year is filled with peace, love and joy.
  我們衷心期盼新的一年充滿和平、愛與喜樂。

- Best wishes for a Happy Holiday and a magnificent New Year.
  祝福你們假期愉快，新年萬事如意。

- May the New Year bring you joy, abundance and happiness.
  願新的一年為你帶來喜樂、充實而幸福的人生。

- I hope you have a wonderful Christmas and a fantastic New Year!
  祝你有個精采的聖誕假期和美好的新年！

- To a joyful present, golden past and countless joyous years to come!
  向過去的黃金歲月與眼前的快意人生致敬，願未來的每一年都是美好歲月！

- May this season bring you success, health and happiness.
  但願這個季節為你帶來成功、健康和快樂。

- Wishing all the staff at MJP Happy Holidays and a wonderfully successful New Year!
  願所有MJP的同仁佳節愉快，新年萬事如意。

- Happy Hannukah!
  光明節快樂！（光明節是猶太教的慶典，從12月25日起為期八天。）

- Have a Merry Christmas and a Happy New Year!
  祝你聖誕快樂，新年快樂！

結婚・訂婚

- I would like to congratulate you on your engagement.
  I wish you all the happiness.
  恭喜你們訂婚。祝你們永遠幸福美滿。

- Congratulations! You and Matt are perfect for each other!
  恭喜！你和麥特是天造地設的一對！

- On behalf of everyone at Crystal Sky, I would like to extend our best wishes to you on your marriage.
  謹代表Crystal Sky的全體同仁，為你的婚姻獻上最誠摯的祝福。

- Congratulations on your wedding.
  May all your dreams come true and every day be a party!
  恭喜你結婚。祝福你夢想成真，天天都有派對般的好心情！

- I wish you a life full of joy. Happy wedding day.
  願你的人生充滿歡樂。結婚快樂！

紀念日

- Happy Anniversary!
  週年慶快樂！

- Happy 10th Anniversary! Wishing you many more years of happiness!
  十週年快樂！祝福你們未來年年都幸福！

- Happy Anniversary, Darling!
  I love you even more than the day we got married.
  結婚週年快樂，親愛的！跟結婚當天比起來，我變得更愛你了。

- To my loving husband, Happy Anniversary!
  You have made my life a joy.
  獻給我親愛的老公，結婚週年快樂！你讓我的人生充滿喜悅。

- To my darling wife, Happy 30th Anniversary!
  Each day has been better than the last.
  獻給我親愛的老婆，結婚30週年快樂！30年來，我一天比一天更幸福。

生日

- Happy Birthday!
  生日快樂！

- May you always remain beautiful / good-looking, healthy and young at heart!
  祝你永遠美麗、健康，常保赤子之心！

- Wishing you a heart-warming birthday filled with happiness and delightful surprises!
  祝你有一個充滿幸福與驚喜的溫馨生日！

- Wishing you a VERY HAPPY BIRTHDAY!!!
  Hope your day is filled with love and laughter!
  祝你生日大快樂！！！祝你的生日充滿愛與歡笑！

- Thinking of you on your birthday and wishing you many more to come!
  在你生日這天想起你，但願你年年都能快樂過生日！

- Best wishes and affectionate thoughts on this special day.
  Happy Birthday!
  在這個特別的日子裡，為你獻上最美好的祝福與誠摯的關懷。生日快樂！

- Happy Thirtieth! Welcome to my decade!
  30歲生日快樂！歡迎加入我的世代！

- Happy Birthday! Forty-three isn't old!
  It's just eighteen plus twenty-five years of experience!
  生日快樂！43歲一點都不老！只不過是18歲加上25年的人生經驗！

- I'm sorry I forgot your birthday!
  Can we reschedule it for another time this week?
  我很抱歉我忘了你的生日！我們能不能這週再重新安排一次時間（慶祝）？

- Happy Belated Birthday!
  慢半拍的生日快樂！

※ "Belated" 用來表達遲來的祝福，可以放在 "Happy" 之前或之後。

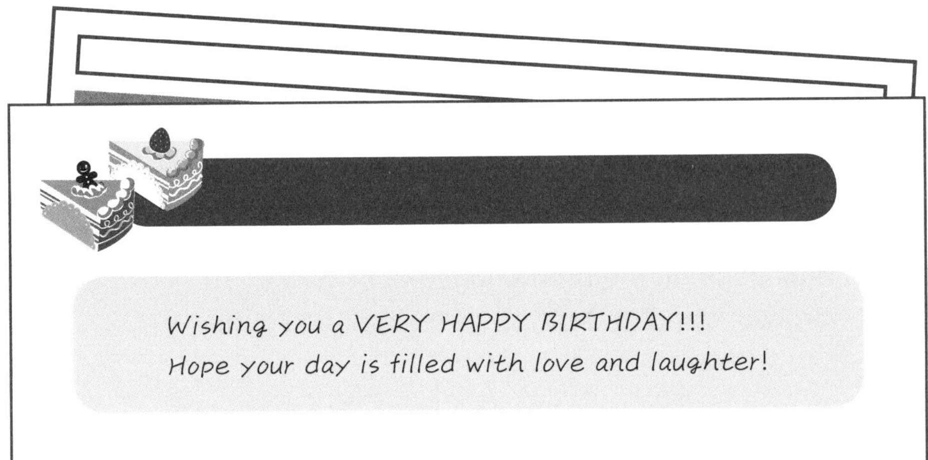
Wishing you a VERY HAPPY BIRTHDAY!!!
Hope your day is filled with love and laughter!

生產

- Congratulations on the birth of your baby boy!
  You and Jon must be so proud.
  恭喜你喜獲麟兒！你和瓊一定感到非常驕傲。

- Paul and Joanne Murphy are pleased to announce the birth of their son, Edward.
  保羅和喬安・墨菲很開心地宣布，他們的兒子艾德華已經誕生。

- Congratulations on the birth of your granddaughter.
  Wishing you joy with the newest member of your family!
  恭喜你的孫女順利誕生。祝你與加入新成員的全家人幸福愉快！

- Wishing you bundles of joy with your new little boy!
  願你剛誕生的寶貝兒子為你帶來無限的喜悅！

- Like a shimmering pearl, a new baby girl! Congratulations!
  你的寶貝女兒就像一顆耀眼的珍珠！恭喜你！

升遷・就職

- I heard you got a promotion. Congratulations!
  我聽說你升官了。恭喜恭喜！

- Congratulations on your new job! I know you'll be a big success!
  恭喜你找到新工作！我相信你一定會飛黃騰達！

- Congratulations on the promotion!
  Your hard work and dedication have finally paid off!
  恭喜你升官！你的努力和執著終於有所回報！

運動競賽

- Way to go on the win against Seaside! Congrats!
  能打敗Seaside真是太厲害了！恭喜啊！

- Bob told me you won the golf tournament! Awesome!
  You must be riding high!
  包柏告訴我你在這次高爾夫球聯賽中獲勝了！太棒了！你一定得意極了！

- Congratulations on winning the Tri-State Marathon!
  I knew you could do it!
  恭喜你在三州馬拉松中獲勝！我就知道你可以的！

生病

- Get Well Soon!

  趕快好起來！

- I wish you a full and speedy recovery.

  祝你早日完全康復。

感謝

- Thank you for the basket of bath salts.
  You always know exactly what I like.

  謝謝你送我那籃浴鹽。你總是剛好知道我想要的是什麼。

- Thank you for coming to the party. It was great to see you.

  謝謝你來參加這個派對。見到你真開心。

- Thank you for being there for me.
  You are a wonderful friend.

  謝謝你陪伴在我身邊。你是一個很棒的朋友。

- Thanks for your help with the move.
  I absolutely could not have done it without you.

  謝謝你幫我搬家。沒有你，我肯定無法做完。

- Thank you for your support. Because of people like you, we made over $100,000 for the Children's Foundation.

  謝謝你的支持。因為有許多像你一樣的人支持這個活動，我們為兒童基金會募集到超過10萬美元的資金。

Thank you for
coming to the party.
It was great to see you.

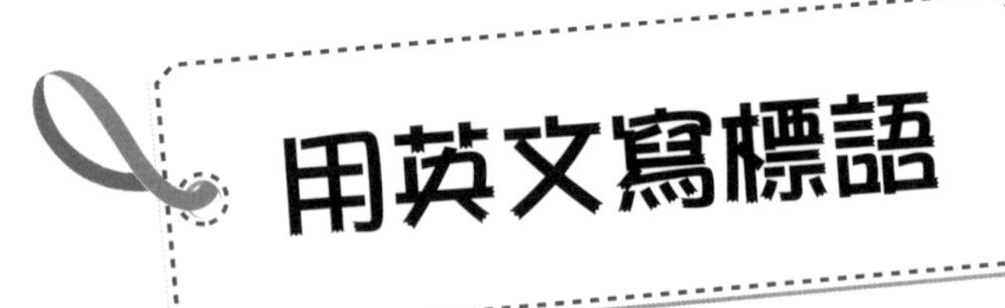
用英文寫標語

公司簡介

- MJP: making business for a sustainable earth.
  MJP以永續的地球為職志展開事業。

- Crystal Sky: better products for a better tomorrow.
  Crystal Sky提供更好的商品讓明天會更好。

- Our best strategy is satisfied customers.
  顧客的滿意就是我們最好的戰略。

- Making life simpler, one innovation at a time.
  每一次的革新，都在創造更簡單的生活。

- Your safety is our business.
  你的安全是我們的責任。

- Manufacturers of quality cutlery for over 50 years.
  跨越半世紀的高品質刀具製造商。

- At MJP, we create simple solutions for not-so-simple problems.
  在MJP，我們為複雜的難題創造簡單的答案。

- Making hand tailored suits since 1989.
  創始於1989年的手工訂製服。

※ 本書p220~232列有許多用於公司簡介的英文單字。

旅遊・飯店行銷廣告

- Experience the Japan of yesteryear.
  體驗日本的舊日風情。

- Your home away from home.
  出門在外就像回家一樣舒服。

- A culinary adventure, a relaxing oasis...
  一趟味蕾嚐鮮之旅，一塊讓身心放鬆的樂土⋯

- A delight in every season.
  一年四季皆享樂趣。

- Seasonal delicacies, local delights.
  當季佳餚，在地風情。

- Leave the city behind and stay a while.
  拋開城市喧囂，小歇片刻。

- Catering to business travelers since 1991.
  從1991至今，持續滿足商務旅客的需求。

- Conveniently located near Taipei Main Station.
  鄰近台北車站的便利地點。

- Affordable accommodations in the center of town.
  經濟實惠的市中心住宿設施。

餐廳宣傳

- We care about what goes into our food because we know you care about what goes into your family.
  我們關心料理的食材，因為我們知道你關心家人的健康。

- An oasis in the heart of Tokyo.
東京都心的世外桃源。

- Drop your stress off here.
把壓力留在這裡，把輕鬆帶回家。（例如按摩店的文宣）

- Personalized service for those who appreciate the finer things.
為堅持品質的顧客提供個人化的服務。

- Artisan bread and pastries.
大師級的糕點與麵包。

- Sweets for my Sweet.
最好的甜點獻給我的甜心。

- Hot food, cold drinks and cool jazz.
熱食、冷飲與酷炫爵士樂。

珍的有機素食餐廳&酒吧

在台北市中心淺嚐天堂滋味。

歡迎大家來享受阿嬤的家常菜。
保證滿足每個人的味蕾，
就連肉食主義者也不例外。
我們堅持使用最新鮮的有機食材，
為你們帶來「改變人生的美食體驗」。

更多詳情請上我們的網站查詢。

Jane's Vegetarian
Organic Restaurant & Bar
A slice of heaven
in the heart of Taipei.
Come and enjoy a taste of
Grandma's home-cooking.
Guaranteed to please all,
including carnivores.
We use only the freshest
organic ingredients to bring
you a "life-changing food
experience".
>>Check our website for more details.

- Gourmet style at family-friendly prices.

  行家的精緻美食，適合全家聚餐的經濟實惠價格。

- Cold drinks, warm hearts.

  透心涼的冷飲，暖呼呼的熱情。

- Where friends meet and love grows.

  讓朋友團聚、讓愛苗滋長的地方。

- A slice of heaven in the heart of Taipei.

  在台北市中心淺嚐天堂滋味。

時尚・美容

- Sensible style for the woman of today.

  適合現代女性的實穿風格。

- Find yourself in our fashion.

  在我們的設計中找到真正的自己。

- Fashion that won't break the bank.

  不會讓荷包大失血的流行時尚。

- Designer looks at discount prices.

  大師級的設計樣式，大拍賣的實惠價格。

- Hot Summer Fashion!

  火辣辣的夏季時尚！

- Great new looks for fall!

  迎接秋季的最佳新造型！

- Just arrived! The new winter line!

  新品上市！冬季新款！

- Latest Spring Dresses!

  最新的春季洋裝！

邁向

擺脫中式英文之路

1 「模仿」很重要！

請參考本書中的內容，從模仿錦言嘉句開始學習英文寫作吧！在寫出「好」的句子之前，先努力寫出「正確」的句子！

2 勤查字典

絕對禁止在單字的意義和文法方面自以為是！遇到一個不熟的單字時，不可以有「應該是這個意思沒錯吧？」的想法。雖然很麻煩，但還是要養成查字典的好習慣。

3 例句

別只是查單字的意義。請好好善用字典，仔細閱讀單字下方的例句，才能真正掌握每個單字的微妙意義。

4 善用Google

周遭如果有以英語為母語的人，盡量請他們幫忙審視你的遣詞用句。如果不認識任何以英語為母語的人，可以利用Google搜尋來檢視。使用方法是把自己寫的英文句子放到網路上搜尋，看看外國人是不是真的會這樣用，但記得要先切換到英文的頁面。

※使用Google搜尋時，不要用台灣版的http://www.google.com.tw/，請切換到美國版的http://www.google.com/或英國版的http://www.google.co.uk/，因為在台灣版頁面搜尋的結果，很可能會出現許多上述說的那種「自以為是」、可信度很低的用法。

後記

一邊撰寫這本書的時候，我們一邊想像著各種讀者的需求。「應該會有很多人想知道這方面的詞彙吧？」於是將各式各樣的詞彙集合起來，終於完成了本書。書中從非正式的日常生活用語，到非常正式的商業用語應有盡有。我們有自信，這是一本「讀起來絕對不會感到無聊，而且非常實用的英文書」。

最重要的是，書中所用到的單字100%源自以英語為母語的英語腦，保證原汁原味、是最道地的英語用法，絕對與市面上從中文直譯成英語的寫作書不同（使用這種書，就等於是在學習「中式英文」喔！）希望讀者務必將書中提供的詞彙，善加排列組合，靈活運用，好好享受英文寫作的樂趣！

In conclusion, we'd like to thank each and every one of you for purchasing this book.

▶▶ 此句中譯見P35

來自三位作者的感謝

Janet

I would like to thank Peter Chisler for his fantastic suggestions and lack of complaints despite the fact that I only gave him a few days to help with the editing. To my family: thank you for a lifetime of love and support. You mean the world to me. Lastly, thank you to my coauthors Mari and Patrick for inviting me to join the project. This is truly a dream come true. Love you both.

Janet Bunting

To my brother Lalogafau Andrew Kell: Thank you as always for your fantastic ideas, many long hours of editing, constructive criticism and unwavering support. To my dear Toshie Nishimura: Thank you for your help with editing, endless patience and support. To my mother in Samoa: Fa'afetai tele, tina (Thank you, Mum). Without all of your encouragement, love and support, we never could have finished writing this book. And finally, thank you to Mari and Janet for your endless positive energy.

Li'o Patrick Kell

Patrick

萬里

各位協力作者與編輯們，你們不僅在插畫和設計方面幫我很大的忙，還一直照顧支持忙碌的我，謝謝你們！也感謝在我執筆寫作此書時向我求婚，我最愛的Matthew。Matthew，託你的福，我才有機會撰寫這本書。此外，要是沒有Patrick和Janet兩個人跟我一起努力，我絕對無法完成此書。謝謝你們喔！下次再一起合作吧！最後，我要告訴在本書寫作過程中順利熬過大手術的媽媽，對不起，忙碌到不行時就沒能去探望你。我現在就帶著這本書回去看你！

中川萬里

國家圖書館出版品預行編目資料

英文E-mail複製、替換、零失誤 / 中川萬里, Patrick Kell, Janet Bunting著. -- 初版. -- 新北市：國際學村, 2016.04
面； 公分
ISBN 978-986-454-018-1(平裝)

1.英語 2.電子郵件 3.應用文

805.179 105004127

台灣廣廈國際出版集團 Taiwan Mansion International Group 國際學村

複製．替換．零失誤的英文E-mail

亞馬遜書店讀者評價第一名！實用性、正確度最高！

作者	中川萬里、 Patrick Kell、Janet Bunting
譯者	鄭佳珍
出版者	國際學村出版社 台灣廣廈有聲圖書有限公司
發行人／社長	江媛珍
地址	235新北市中和區中山路二段359巷7號2樓
電話	886-2-2225-5777
傳真	886-2-2225-8052
讀者服務信箱	cs@booknews.com.tw
總編輯	伍峻宏
執行編輯	徐淳輔
美術編輯	呂佳芳
製版／印刷／裝訂／排版	菩薩蠻／東豪／紘億／明和
代理印務及圖書總經銷	知遠文化事業有限公司
地址	222新北市深坑區北深路三段155巷25號5樓
訂書電話	886-2-2664-8800
訂書傳真	886-2-2664-0490
港澳地區經銷	和平圖書有限公司
地址	香港柴灣嘉業街12號百樂門大廈17樓
電話	852-2804-6687
傳真	852-2804-6409
出版日期	2016年4月 2023年6月14刷
郵撥帳號	18788328
郵撥戶名	台灣廣廈有聲圖書有限公司 （郵購4本以內外加50元郵資，5本以上外加100元）

「組み換え式」ビジネスメール作成術 英語フレーズ選ぶだけ!
"Kumikaeshiki" Business Mail Sakuseijutsu: Eigo Phrase Erabudake
Written by Mari Nakagawa, Patrick Kell and Janet Bunting

郵票黏貼處

台灣廣廈國際出版集團 Taiwan Mansion International Group
235 新北市中和區中山路二段359巷7號2樓
國際學村 編輯部 收
讀者服務專線：(02)2225-5777

複製・替換・零失誤的

英文E-mail

國際學村 讀者資料服務回函

感謝您購買這本書！

為使我們對讀者的服務能夠更加完善，

請您詳細填寫本卡各欄，

寄回本公司或傳真至（02）2225-8052，

我們將不定期寄給您我們的出版訊息。

- 您購買的書 複製、替換、零失誤的英文E-mail
- 您的大名 ______
- 購買書店 ______
- 您的性別 □男 □女
- 婚　　姻 □已婚 □單身
- 出生日期 ____年____月____日
- 您的職業 □製造業□銷售業□金融業□資訊業□學生□大眾傳播□自由業 □服務業□軍警□公□教□其他
- 職　　位 □負責人□高階主管□中級主管□一般職員□專業人員□其他
- 教育程度 □高中以下（含高中）□大專□研究所□其他
- 您通常以何種方式購書？
  □逛書店□劃撥郵購□電話訂購□傳真訂購□網路訂購□銷售人員推薦□其他
- 您從何得知本書消息？
  □逛書店□報紙廣告□親友介紹□廣告信函□廣播節目□網路□書評
  □銷售人員推薦□其他
- 您想增加哪方面的知識？或對哪種類別的書籍有興趣？
  ______
  ______
- 通訊地址 □□□ ______
  ______
- E-Mail ______
- 本公司恪守個資保護法，請問您給的 E-Mail帳號是否願意收到本集團出版物相關資料 □願意 □不願意
- 聯絡電話 ______
- 您對本書封面及內文設計的意見 ______
  ______
- 您是否有興趣接受敝社新書資訊？ □沒有□有
- 給我們的建議/請列出本書的錯別字 ______
  ______

請沿虛線剪下